S0-AJO-911

WITHDRAWN
Damaged, Obsolete, or Surplus
Jackson County Library Services

FOUNTAIN FOUND

LOCAL
AUTHOR

FOUNTAIN FOUND

A novel

Allen Broderick

JACKSON COUNTY LIBRARY SERVICES
MEDFORD OREGON 97501

© 2018 Allen Broderick
All rights reserved.

ISBN-13: 9781983552113
ISBN-10: 1983552119
Library of Congress Control Number: 2018900353
CreateSpace Independent Publishing Platform
North Charleston, South Carolina

Book summary

The single, most-disruptive technology ever to be introduced to the world is coming soon. A mixture of medical thriller and political intrigue with just a little plausible science fiction; *Fountain Found* explores current society's reaction to a technological leap that affects how long we live. A credulous cast of characters start a top-secret company that will eventually introduce their product and change the world as we know it. The author's insight into business, technology, economics, international relationships, and human behavior are important backdrops to a story that twists and turns and keeps the reader wanting more. If you are interested in a fresh perspective on a possible near future or if you are studying business, you must read *Fountain Found.*

To my lovely wife, Rhonda.

Rhonda is a great inspiration to me, and without her I would never have finished this book.

I would like to acknowledge Megan Reid through New York book editors and Emily Bestler Books for her incredible insight and guidance.

I would also like to recognize my late good friend Janet Hall who read my manuscript as it was being written. Her inspiration helped me continue writing. Wish she was still with us!

Preface

The year is 2018. The world population is 7.6 billion.

On December 26 1986 the world population reached 5 billion. Almost thirteen years later, on October 12, 1999, the world's population reached 6 billion. Ten and a half years later, on April 10, 2010, the population rose to 7 billion. It is projected that by July 2019, there will be 8 billion people living on our planet.

Every day 449,000 people are born and 132,000 people die. The world's population is currently increasing at an exponential rate of 317,000 per day.

Approximate population by continent:

Continent	Percentage of Population	Population Count
Asia	60%	4,520,000,000
Africa	15%	1,175,000,000
Europe	10%	750,000,000
South America	8%	645,000,000
North America	6%	460,000,000
Australia	<1%	37,000,000
Oceania	<1%	13,000,000
Total		**7,600,000,000**

The average life expectancy for a person is sixty-eight years; however, there are significant differences in life expectancy based on region. Here is how it breaks down:

Continent/Region	Average Life Expectancy (in Years)
Europe	80
North America	78
South America	71
Australia/Oceania	69
Asia	68
Africa	49

A poor economy, lack of resources and education, and AIDS are directly responsible for the low life expectancy in Africa.

On April 4, 2020, a cure for AIDS was announced.

By July 2021, 80 percent of the population in Africa is vaccinated, and AIDS is virtually eradicated.

On December 15, 2022, a medical breakthrough of historical magnitude was made public!

First Chapter

Karl loved math. Earning his postgraduate degree in statistical analysis was a significant milestone, yet the actual experience of graduating he found to be anticlimactic. It was the race, not the finish line, which inspired Karl. The discovery and comprehension of a new complex concept was more than an addiction; it was a necessary part of living for Karl. The more difficult the problem, the more Karl enjoyed the process of finding a solution. Math comforted him because there is usually a right answer, or at least there is proof of a right answer. He was frustrated with the study of philosophy because there is never a right answer or, in some cases, no answer at all. This frustration had matured into a love-hate relationship. His drive to be *certain* about his conclusions is what put him at the top of his mathematics and philosophy classes. As a result, he dual-majored in philosophy in his pregrad years.

Coming from moderate means, Karl enrolled in a local community college immediately after high school and, without any real direction, found himself taking all the courses offered in the mathematics department.

Though he enjoyed sports, an occasional beer with his friends, and other normal activities of a teenager growing up in southern California in the class of 2012, he always seemed to have a deeper and more analytical view of the world than his peers. This made him a bit of an outcast. His best friend, Jim Mankin, was every bit as bright as Karl was. Jim, unlike

Karl, placed a greater emphasis on being the center of attention, being the life of the party, and was very popular. Jim had great social graces and was immediately accepted by any group he encountered. He was a dogged competitor. Jim was not a clown; he just happened to be blessed with good breeding and a privileged upbringing.

Karl would spend his weekends hanging out with Jim. They would enjoy longboarding on the strand or bellyboarding when the waves were rolling just right. Being tan and fit was not a goal; it was a way of life. When they were not outside, they would match wits on a chessboard or engage in lively discussions of how someday they would become rich and powerful. Jim was a lot more serious about these fantasies than Karl; however, he enjoyed the discussions just the same.

Karl was deep in thought reading his graduate diploma the morning after ceremonies.

The trustees of
the California State University
on recommendation of the faculty of
University of California, Los Angeles
have conferred upon
Karl Louis Franklin
the degree of
Masters of Science
Mathematics (Applied Statistics)
With all the rights and privileges pertaining thereto
Given by the trustees of California State University at Long Beach
This day of May twenty-fifth, two thousand eighteen

His mind was racing through all the implications and ramifications of his accomplishment. What it meant to him on an emotional level; how his family felt such pride; the new career opportunities it presented; how his daily routine would be affected; and how it affected his identity and role in society. How did he get here? What did it all mean?

Next week he would start an actuarial internship program with a prominent insurance company based on the West Coast. He had been recruited by numerous firms and so had negotiated a starting salary of $75,000. He committed to a one-year contract. He maintained a strong desire to pursue his doctoral degree and a different career path but was firmly set on spending one year with gainful employment first. He owed $78,000 in student loans that had supplemented his living expenses while in school. He had always had a low-paying part-time job necessary to survive while enrolled in fifteen credits per term. He was excited about making the transition from a full-time student to having a real job and was not really all that enthusiastic about his new line of work. He thought about teaching, but the pay was not all that great, and he really wanted to apply his skills rather than pass them on. In the back of his mind, he knew this actuary thing was not what he really wanted. He needed money and was willing to do what was necessary. Like most people, he was settling. This bothered him, and he knew he would eventually have to change directions.

What Karl really wanted was to leave his mark! He wanted to make a difference; he knew his skills and intelligence provided the necessary tools to do so. He did not care much about money, but he needed it just the same.

"Welcome to the real world, buddy!" is what his friend Jim would say.

That was then; now eleven months later, he had saved enough money from his internship as an actuary to afford day-to-day living expenses for the next six months. Yet, subconsciously, the debts of his loans were constantly nagging him.

The daily grind as an actuary was not very exciting. Other than the nice salary, there was very little about the job that seemed fulfilling or purposeful; at least from Karl's perspective. He was doing a fine job and was in good graces with his superiors. Crunching the numbers, creating graphical representations of obscure vectors, sigma, and CPK analysis to ascertain risk by age, sex, marital status, zip code, financial history, health, and so forth...these complex matrix formats calculated risk and identified *overpriced* insurance-premium markets. In all reality his job was all about making money for the corporation. It paid the bills, and his internship was coming to a rapid close.

He had one month left on his employment contract, and he was counting the days. He would be free to choose a career path that not only used his education but also offered something meaningful to society—if that existed? As it turned out, Jim would be finishing his third year in law school a week before Karl's contract ended. Jim's father gifted Jim a dream vacation backpacking for six weeks in Australia as a graduation present. The trip included round-trip airfare and checkpoint accommodations for Jim and his guest of choice. Karl was the lucky recipient and probably more excited about the trip than Jim.

To counteract the negativity he felt in regard to his current employment, he focused on evaluating what he found stimulating in the work at the insurance company. Karl viewed himself as a "glass half full" kind of guy. The math was challenging. The demographic analysis, especially as it related to life-span, he found fascinating. Who lived longer and why? This seemed morbid, he thought, yet it was inevitable, and when faced with the data, it became very real.

He wondered, given the choice, whether he would choose to live an additional ten years if the quality of those ten years was dramatically affected by physical or mental detriments. Or, worse, whether he would be trapped into the lower quality of life based on false promises from medical professionals. Can a person really make a conscious choice when it comes to longevity and quality of life? Maybe in advance an answer could seem obvious, but when you are in the throes of the situation, it is easy to not see the forest through the trees.

Just the other day Karl was discussing this with Troy, one of his colleagues, during a lunch break.

Troy worked in the health-insurance department, and Karl worked in the life-insurance department. Because their tasks were closely related, they were encouraged to discuss their progress and findings with one another.

Life insurance concerns itself predominately with the *length* of life, whereas health insurance is focused solely on the *cost* to stay alive with the best possible *quality* of life.

The topic of discussion migrated to wealth and health correlations.

Troy told Karl, "I have recently provided the company with further evidence that wealthy people live healthier lives and that educated wealthy people live even healthier lives than the middle-class population. Further, it was proven statistically that the wealthy lived higher quality lives. This, of course, was no surprise to anyone, but the data was still pretty compelling."

Karl said, "Can I get a copy of your report? I am close to finishing up this quarter's review on life premiums, and one of the areas I am focusing on is the wealth component, as it relates to longevity. Your recent finding not only supports wealth-longevity ratios but also proves that the wealthier segment of the population affords the latest medical treatment that adds not only to longevity but also to quality of life."

Troy smiled and picked up his phone, pushed a few buttons, and said, "Done."

Karl went on to say with a shrug, "It really sucks to be middle class and bear the brunt of the stress that makes the world go round, which just results in a shorter life-span and a lower quality of life than those who live less-stressful lives. On top of that, we have to pay higher health and life premiums. The poor get subsidized by the government on health premiums, and because the wealthy live longer, healthier lives, they pay less for life insurance. We, the middle class, bear the brunt of the cost and live shorter lives to boot. I find it disturbing that we can reduce a specific individual to a number and have that number determine what they pay for insurance. Yes, statistically and for the sake of good business, it may be the right thing to do, but somehow it feels wrong morally." This was the root of Karl's discontent with his job.

Karl shared with Troy, "Did you know that our company has twenty-one prediction formulas for anticipated life-span based on demographics for each age group and sex? For example, married churchgoing males between forty and fifty, who are white, work in office jobs in the southern part of the United States, who weigh between two hundred twenty-five and two hundred fifty pounds, and who smoke are expected to live until they are sixty-seven. He had recently further defined and expanded the number of specific demographic segments from twenty-one to thirty-five. These additional factors provided more accurate estimates of life-span and, therefore, a strategic advantage in quoting premiums."

Troy piped in with a grin, "Bet your boss is happy with you!"

Karl replied, "Yes, she is, but I almost feel like I am doing more evil than good."

Troy nodded, indicating he fully understood what Karl was saying.

Karl was thinking that he did not yet consider his work to be of the highest calling he enjoyed the figuring. He enjoyed spending time imagining all the possible modeling deficiencies when one small change was made to the data in a profile.

Troy was reading something on his phone when Karl announced, "It is my human curiosity associated with these predictions that energizes me."

Troy looked up, saying, "What?"

Karl laughed and said, "Sorry, I was in my own world for a second there. I have to remind myself not to become obsessed with mortality. I have heard stories of colleagues who would obsessively monitor their own *mortality rating*. It would first start out with a natural desire to know how long they were expected to live. It seems like a simple and innocent process to put your basic profile information into the computer and have the program spit out a report and reveal your estimated life-span. What's the big deal, right?"

He went on, saying, "It is said that the addicted actuaries would start making small modifications to their profile to see if it had a positive or negative effect on their life-span. They might pretend to move to a different geography or quit smoking or lose weight or get divorced or plug the new info in and see what happens. Some of the actuaries would make these adjustments daily, but the actual stress they were causing themselves in fixating on death was negatively affecting their health and, hence, their life expectancy. Pretty ironic, isn't it?"

Troy's interest was obviously waning, and his phone was becoming more of an interest.

Karl said, "I am myself more interested in the macro and more curious about the human race as a whole than my own specific life expectancy."

Realizing he was losing his audience, Karl then said, "Well, nice seeing you, Troy. I am going back to my closet."

Troy mumbled something and wandered off.

Back in his cubicle, Karl started daydreaming about his upcoming trip to Australia. He looked at the clock; it was fifteen minutes past quitting time. He always stayed fifteen to twenty minutes past the time he could technically leave.

After dinner, he sat in his recliner, with his favorite brown ale in a frosty mug next to him, and went back to his thoughts of where he wanted to work or, more importantly, what he wanted to do for a living. He envied Jim, who was very clearly set on his path. Jim was finishing his third year in law school at Yale. He would graduate, take the bar exam, and work for his father's firm specializing in business law. Once he had earned the respect of his client base, he was set on starting a career in politics. His plan was to begin in state government and work his way into the state senate, where he hoped to make a name for himself and run for either governor or, even better, a federal house seat.

The helicopter buzzing over Karl's apartment complex startled him, and he immediately located his passport, hospice directory, and travel itinerary to put his reeling mind at ease.

Karl decided to give Jim a call and just see how he was doing. After leaving Jim multiple messages, he called one of Jim's roommates whom he had met during a recent visit. His roommate answered and gave the phone to Jim, who was busy packing.

"Hey, Jim, this is Karl. Your roommate said you were on your way to DC?"

"That's right, Mr. Franklin; I am meeting with one of my father's partners to discuss the opening of the DC office. They want me to...well...to..." Jim was silent for longer than a moment. He finally said, "Intern there this summer."

Jim's father's law firm operated offices in seven states and was in the process of opening an office in the nation's capital. The new office in DC would become the corporate headquarters for Mankin, Garrard, Williams, Beakon, and Associates. Jim sounded extremely embarrassed; he had been studying for finals, and now this thing with the DC office had just been sprung on him, but that was no excuse.

"Buddy, I just found out two days ago about the internship. I have been meaning to call you. As you can probably deduce, I won't be able to make the trip down under with you," he said sheepishly.

After a moment of silence, Karl said, "Crap, I was really looking forward to this trip."

"I know; so was I. But you know how father is when it comes to his number-one son. The truth is, I dreaded telling you; that's why I haven't called."

Karl paused for a moment and let the news digest and then almost like a flippant teenager with an attitude said, "You have one more month at Yale, then the bar exam and then a couple of grueling years at the office, then a fricking career in politics...the dream trip will probably just be a dream; whatever."

Jim grimaced and said, "I am going to have a week's grace between finals and the internship, and your contract should be up by then. Why not come out to DC and spend a week? Have you ever been...? Dad felt bad about the Australia trip and said he would spring for you and me to stay at a nice place and your airfare to DC, food, the whole nine yards. He knows it is not a replacement, but it is still a nice gesture. What do you say?"

"It's not Australia, but I could use the break. Your dad is really very gracious; I would never have been able to afford the trip without his generous gift. The monotony of my work is killing me. I cannot wait to finish this contract and do something else. The problem is, I don't know what I want to do. I envy you, man. Damn! Do you think we will ever get to take out trip down under?"

Karl was a bit shattered, and Jim felt bad. Before Jim could say anything, Karl said, "DC sounds like a plan; gotta go. I have another call coming in; talk soon."

The other call was from the US Census Bureau.

Karl had put out some feelers for employment during the last couple of weeks. The call from the Census Bureau caught him by surprise. He had been preoccupied with the planned trip to Australia, which was now quashed. Figuring he would get serious about employment when he returned, his search had been cursory at best.

Steve Ryan introduced himself as the Seattle, Washington, branch manager of the US Census Bureau. Steve explained that he would normally not handle such a call personally, but he had recently lost his top statistician to the Dallas, Texas, branch. He was browsing applicants through the Automated Commerce Employment System (ACES) and ran across Karl's résumé. Karl's education and background was a perfect match for the opening Steve had available.

Steve told Karl that if he could pass a background check, and assuming his references checked out, the job was his. Of course, Steve had already done a preliminary check on Karl Louis

Franklin. Karl was stunned. He said, "Don't you want to interview me or something first?"

Steve replied, "Let me be frank with you, Karl: not many individuals with your credentials apply to work at the Census Bureau. Most people here start straight out of undergraduate school. I can start you at sixty-nine thousand four hundred thirty-seven dollars per year plus benefits."

Karl, still reeling from Steve's direct recruiting method, said, "What would I be doing as your head math statistician?"

Steve said, "Well, I am glad you asked that question. Basically, you would be assisting me in writing some new and exciting software. Why don't you plan on coming up here and I will show you around. I have plane tickets reserved under your name at LAX with United for, not this, but next Friday evening. I will pick you up. We can have some dinner and get acquainted; I can run you over to your hotel. We will spend Saturday at the office, and you will be home Saturday night; what do ya say?"

Karl thought for a minute and said, "See ya next Friday!"

Karl felt impulsive, but he knew, in all reality, he was not making any commitment. This was just a little adventure. He would probably have a hundred reasons not to accept the position, the number-one reason being he had not explored his other options. He didn't even know what his other options were. He then stopped and contemplated, *When has that ever stopped me?* He didn't plan to get a BS degree in math, let alone a master's in statistics. He certainly didn't plan on spending a year working as an actuary for an insurance company.

He decided he better change his ways and get his act together. Within an hour, Karl had canceled his trip to Australia, made plans to spend a week in Washington, DC, and committed to exploring a job opportunity in Seattle with the US Census

Bureau. Being very cautious and methodical, Karl was not accustomed to this level of spontaneity. His mind spinning in a million directions, he decided to make a list of things to do:

- cancel airline tickets to down under
- make airline reservations for DC trip
- have suit cleaned and pressed
- review job description and application with the Census Bureau
- browse Internet for Seattle housing costs
- call Heather Beers

Heather was an old girlfriend. The relationship never got all that serious, and they parted good friends. He had dated her in his senior year at UCLA. Heather decided not to pursue a graduate degree and took a job with the US Department of Commerce that just happened to be located in Tacoma, Washington. Seattle and Tacoma have blended into one large metropolis; in fact, when you fly into Seattle, the airport is actually in Tacoma. The Census Bureau is a branch of the US Department of Commerce. Heather may have some insight that might be useful.

Heather received her BA in economics and minored in math. Now, three years into her career, she was part of a team that monitored and forecasted economic development for the West Coast. With five major ports and the fastest-growing population in North America, the work was interesting. Currently she was working on evaluating building starts for commercial real estate. The feds' persistence in raising the overnight interest rates in an effort to stay inflation had made short-term and commercial money 50 percent more expensive than one year ago. The manufacturing sector was booming due to the new solar, wind, and light aircraft technologies. Unemployment levels were near a record low. These were the major factors she was trying to get her arms around in an effort to post realistic forecasts for the upcoming year.

She was surprised to hear from Karl and even more surprised to hear that Karl was exploring a position with the Census Bureau right in her neighborhood. After Karl explained his bizarre conversation with Steve Ryan and his scheduled trip to Seattle the next week, Heather politely offered to meet him at the airport. Karl explained that Steve had a full itinerary planned and that he was mostly interested in knowing if she knew anything at all that may affect his decision to consider the position he was offered.

Heather was feeling slightly offended that Karl was being so business like. But she knew that when Karl was in uncharted waters he tended to be this way, so she decided to cut him some slack. "OK" she said, "What do I know about the Census Bureau here in Seattle?" leading Karl on a bit; she knew Karl well enough to know this would just drive him crazy.

Karl filled his chest with air and slowly exhaled. Heather could hear him on the other end and started to feel sorry for him. She finally said, "I really do not know much about the personnel or the work, but I can tell you that by government agency standards, Steve Ryan has a reputation of being a rogue manager."

Karl questioned, "What do you mean "rogue"? How so?"

Heather explained that his reputation was to overstaff in order to meet all the quota expectation and keep the Commerce Department off his back. This would allow him the available manpower to take the data to the next level. He was a brilliant mathematician and lived and breathed the data. Nobody was really sure what he was doing half the time, but everyone knew he was obsessed with forecasting.

2

Madelyn contracted with Anna in the fall of 2018 to patent her scientific discovery and assist her in gaining the financing to make it a reality. Prior to meeting Anna, she had approached two venture capital (VC) firms on her own and found both experiences very distressing. Money and finance were not her expertise. Talking with these sharks, she felt vulnerable and naïve. Fortunately, she never gave up too much of her research to cause her any long-term problems.

Anna worked for one of the largest legal firms in the United States (Mankin, Garrard, Williams, Beakon, and Associates). Anna had over twenty years' experience as a lawyer handling patents and general legal services for start-up and medium-sized companies. She came highly recommended from one of Madelyn's most respected graduate school professors at Stanford.

Anna only agreed to meet with Madelyn because of the referral. She was very busy but felt some obligation and thought she would spend thirty minutes with Madelyn and politely let her know she was too busy for new clients and refer her to one of the junior associates in the firm. It didn't quite work out that way.

Madelyn was a brilliant scientist and was confident in the way she moved in her world. She was a bit shy when meeting new people and downright uncomfortable if she was dealing with people who were not in her field of work. The experiences with the VCs were a perfect example of this. As a scientist, she needed to understand things. She needed to know things. She needed to be an expert. This driving aspect of her personality made it difficult for her when dealing with professionals outside of the scientific community. Her meeting with Anna was no exception.

Madelyn desperate to gain an ally to assist her in appropriating the necessary funds to continue her research and Anna already committed to pushing her off to a junior associate was not the makings for a successful meeting.

She was forty minutes early for their meeting at Anna's San Jose, California, office. Traffic was always heavy and fairly unpredictable from Berkeley, where Madelyn lived and worked, to San Jose south of the bay, so she intentionally gave herself plenty of cushion. Waiting in the understated lobby, she tried her best to occupy herself by reviewing her research synopsis. Madelyn had been working for the last year at Lawrence Berkeley Laboratories in their molecular foundry research center. After completing her doctoral program in physics at Stanford, she was recruited by seven of the country's top labs. She chose Lawrence Labs in Berkeley because of their leadership in the manufacturing of nano tubes.

She was involved in the development of mocin-mimic polymers that coat carbon-based nano tubes, making them nontoxic to human cells. She worked with Dr. Bryant to use this technology with the introduction of quantum stars. The tubes could be configured as machines or tools, where the quantum stars act as florescent probes activated by laser light. The quantum stars have two functions: they act as cameras at the cellular level and provide a means to communicate with the computer. Madelyn believed that nano technology was the key for not only the diagnosis of disease and sickness but also for actual repair or cure of cancers, spinal injuries, viral infections, and cellular degeneration (old age).

She believed she had broken through all the scientific barriers to make this a reality. All she needed was a pile of money to build the equipment and hire the team of people to perfect the process. The breakdown is as follows: $100,000,000 to develop and build the machines to generate the quantum stars, another $75,000,000 for the capital to build the nano machines, $25,000,000 to build the communication interface, $20,000,000 for facilities, and $30,000,000 for legal fees, operating costs and the assembly of fifteen to twenty top scientists who will need to work full time for an estimated three years.

She had been working on the presentation for over a year and was fairly confident in her ability to make the pitch. She was still nervous to meet with Anna because she was so highly recognized as one of the top professionals in her field, not to mention that she really needed her to make her dream become a reality.

When Anna popped in the lobby and greeted Madelyn, there was some immediate chemistry that happened. There was an unexplained connection that neither was necessarily cognizant of but both felt. Walking down the long hall to Anna's office, Madelyn felt adrift as if in a dream world. Once seated, Anna started with, "Kyle, your physics professor and my close friend, has told me a lot about you. He didn't say how young you were; how old are you?"

Madelyn was not used to this type of abrupt interface, especially with a question of a personal nature, and felt a little flush. She wiggled in her chair, straightening her spine and extending her hand out, and smiled and said, "Nice to finally meet you. I am twenty-six; how old are you?"

Anna laughed out loud and shook her hand while saying, "Forty-seven, but I will never admit that to anyone else."

The ice was broken, and they got down to business. Anna was startled at the level of detail and expert presentation of what could very likely be one of the most complex and profound scientific discoveries ever achieved. Madelyn was focused, and her work was meticulous. The science was not disputable. The total organization of process and the equipment design was genius. It was beyond compelling, and Anna was sold that someday this technology would be a reality.

A full hour had gone by, and the two women were immersed in the synopsis when the phone rang. Anna's secretary was reminding her that she had another appointment in thirty minutes, and she had not had lunch yet. Anna said, "Cancel all my appointments today." She politely asked her assistant to bring in some menus from a local deli. They ordered lunch and continued to review the work Madelyn had done.

A couple of hours later, they got up and stretched. Anna was beyond impressed with the work and even more impressed with Madelyn.

Madelyn excused herself to use the restroom, and Anna got on the phone with her secretary and started the difficult process of completely clearing her schedule for the next three months. She was hooked and committed to Madelyn and her discovery. She was being a bit presumptuous that Madelyn felt the same way, but the energy was so good she almost forgot that they needed to make financial agreements and set specific expectations from her office.

When Madelyn returned, Anna had the small conference table that they were working at cleared. The folders were in a neat pile on her desk just in front of where Madelyn had originally seated herself. Madelyn's heart sunk; she thought for sure that Anna was done, and she was going to need to look for another attorney. Anna asked her to sit down at the desk in front of her files. She seemed a little more formal.

When Anna sat down, she looked Madelyn directly in the eye and said, "I would love to represent you and become part of your team throughout the inevitable business start-up. You will need considerable legal assistance before you will be generating any profit. The first order of business is to write an ironclad patent; secondly, you will need a detailed confidentiality agreement so you can share your work with potential investors and contracted professionals. During the process you will need someone to provide financial forecasting for your investors. I estimate the start-up legal fees to be in the neighborhood of one hundred fifty thousand dollars."

You could hear a pin drop; the room was so quiet. Madelyn did not have that kind of money. She had some small student loans she took so she would not have to work for personal expenses. Her education and room and board during active semesters was paid for through numerous scholarships she had received. She had only been employed for one year after receiving her doctorate and pulled in a whopping $53,000 per year salary. She had saved $27,000. This was largely due to the fact she did not spend any money. She dressed very simply, in jeans and exercise wear. She opted for wet dry material over cotton because it never wrinkled, and it was more comfortable on her skin. She applied a small amount of mascara each morning in an effort to look civilized. She drove a 2005 Nissan Pathfinder she bought used when she turned sixteen. Her one-bedroom apartment was her only real expense that ran her $1,400 per month. Her apartment was so close to her work that she would ride her bike unless it was pouring rain, so she did not spend much on gas. Her mom poured wine at one of the popular wineries in Livermore, and her dad was a surgical tech for the hospital. Neither she nor her family could possibly afford this kind of expense.

Anna was aware that this was going to be a tough pill to swallow and let Madelyn take the time to digest the reality of the legal costs.

She was feeling despair but was not willing to let this become an obstacle. She had come this far, and Anna was a very important piece of the puzzle to make this technology a reality. Madelyn finally popped her head up and said, “I can give you twenty-five thousand dollars down, and one thousand dollars per month. I know this is not very much, but it is all I can do. Maybe we can work out a deal for the rest of the costs. I had some time to think about this before our meeting, and I am by no means a business person, so please forgive me if this proposal seems naïve or absurd. When we find an investor to fund the project, I am willing to take a reduced annual draw of only forty thousand dollars. I believe that eighty thousand dollars to one hundred thousand dollars customary. Once we have an investor on board, the one thousand dollars per month payment I make to you would go away and will be replaced with a lump-sum payment in full from the investor. An appropriate stipend would be built in for your services during the course of the R and D period.”

Anna was impressed again; she had not expected that Madelyn would have thought this through. She smiled and said, “There is quite a bit of risk in your proposal. Our company would be exposed to over six figures without any guarantee of payment inside of potentially years. The longer it takes to find an investor, if we can even find one willing to pony up a quarter of a billion dollars, the bigger our legal bill will get.”

Madelyn said, “That is why I am willing to offer your firm two percent of whatever share I receive in the company formed that takes the technology to the world. The better deal you make, the more you get paid. I have not run any estimates on what profit for something like this would be, but I know instinctually that any product or service that will be used by almost the entire world population will be huge! To say the least." She leaned toward the desk and raised an eyebrow.

Now the room was quiet again, but this time the ball was in Anna's court.

Anna picked up the phone and asked her secretary to set up an appointment with one of the senior partners, Hugh Mankin.

3

Karl's two-hour flight from LAX to Sea/Tac was smooth and on time. Outside the security terminal stood a tall, distinguished gray-haired man dressed in casual slacks and a sports coat with a sign saying, "Wanted - Statistician." That had to be Steve Ryan. Karl had not even thought about how he would know who Steve was until he was exiting the airplane. Steve put the sign down and held his hand out to Karl and said, "Welcome to Seattle, Mr. Franklin." Obviously Steve had seen photographs of Karl, perhaps student ID photos or maybe from the employee database where he worked but more than likely on Google or Facebook.

Maybe it was just good recruiting, but regardless of the motivation, Karl really enjoyed Steve. They went to a small bistro on the peer. Nothing fancy, but they served up some of the best fresh seafood he had ever tasted. Steve was different than most mathematicians or, for that matter, most government employees he had ever met. He had a real passion for life. There was a gleam in his eye that made you think that he knew something you didn't. Perhaps he did?

Though there was a considerable age difference between them, Steve treated Karl as an equal, and Karl couldn't help but feel that it was not a put-on. Steve seemed to genuinely disregard age. The information technology (IT) world changed so quickly, and either you were young and recently educated to today's techniques and practices or you were one of the rare experienced professionals that have kept up in the rapidly changing field. Steve worked with a lot of the former.

After just a few hours together, the two men had developed a true sense of mutual respect.

Settling in at his hotel with the TV on to keep him company, Karl thought, *Crap, I can't believe I am thinking of accepting this job.*

The next day at the office, Karl was overwhelmed. He thought the computer systems and software were state of the art at his insurance office; he was wrong. The sheer computing power here was beyond his wildest dreams. He began to understand why Steve had recruited him. It was crystal clear that Steve knew a lot more about Karl than Karl let on in his application.

When questioned about the hardware and software systems, Steve shrugged and made a half-ass comment about, "You mean my baby?" Obviously, all the Census Bureau branches didn't have the same technology.

After a three-and-a-half-hour tour of the facility, they sat down in the conference room and ordered in some lunch. Steve said, "Do you have any questions?"

Karl replied, "Other than a million questions about your systems and applications, just one—the same one I had on the phone: what will I be doing as your head math statistician?"

"Oh ya, that question." Steve had a smirk on his face and that little gleam in his eye that never seemed to go away.

Karl said sincerely, "There are three things that are important to me in determining where I will work, what I will be doing, who I will be working for, and what my compensation will be—in that order. The compensation is adequate after reviewing the cost of living in the Northwest; I don't mean to be a kiss ass, but I like you, so I guess I just need to understand what my energy will be spent on sixty plus hours per week." Karl thought about saying something about how important it was to him to be doing something to make a difference in the world, but after being in Steve's presence for a day, he realized how silly and canned that sounded. Steve acted like a teenager with a keen sense of humor but at the same time exuded extreme wisdom. This was really someone Karl could model himself after.

Steve responded, "Only sixty hours? Just kidding, not really; you may find yourself wanting to do nothing else. Like any other branch of the bureau, I have certain expectations, certain responsibilities that go along with what our main mission is, et cetera......but what I have in mind for you will have nothing to do with reporting the data the Census Bureau makes available to the government or the public. My passion is forecasting, so is yours, I understand. My superior in the Commerce Department recognizes the importance of my work and gives me some latitude and a little extra in the budget; hence the computer system you just witnessed, your position, and few other little perks. Do I have your interest yet?"

If there was doubt in Karl's mind, it was gone now. This was his new home, this was his new boss, and this was everything he had dreamed about in a job, but he wasn't ready to let the cat out of the bag yet. He really did want to better understand in more detail the purpose of the work!

"You have my interest," he said with his best poker face. "I know there must be some limitations to what you can tell me—after all, this is the government—but what exactly would be the purpose of my work?"

Steve thought carefully before answering, "Nice question; without getting you the appropriate clearance, all I can say is it is about forecasting. The purpose is to be able to forecast everything of importance based on a list of significant events......"

He paused for some time and then continued, saying, "I really am going out on a limb to say more, but based on what I know of you, I think you will be very happy with the work and with the application of the work. There is no subversive controversial dark side to our mission here, if that is what you are worried about. When I did my background check on you, I noted a number indicators that you have a high morale standard: Christian, churchgoing (so am I, by the way), volunteer at a number of organizations helping less-fortunate teens, mentor and tutor at the local high school et cetera……frankly, I am one of the good guys, and my organization and superiors are good guys as well. Hope that helps answer your question. Once you have formal clearance, I can show you in detail what we are up to here. If you hate it, you don't have to take the job. What do you say?"

Karl didn't hesitate. "I can start in six weeks!"

"Great!" Steve said and put out his hand and shook Karl's with uninhibited energy.

After Karl filled out what seemed to be an endless pile of paperwork, which included his formal application, some confidentiality agreements, and authorizations for comprehensive background checks, Steve escorted him out of the building, where a driver was waiting to take him to the airport. Once in the car, Karl was beating himself up for accepting so fast. At the same time, he was more excited about this job than he could remember being excited about anything else.

4

It had been almost a week, and Madelyn had not heard back from Anna. She thought for sure that she would have had a deal put together the day after they had met. After all, things had gone so well at their meeting! It went so well until the subject of money came up; Madelyn thought to herself. She was being hard on herself for not having some financing set up before approaching such a successful attorney.

Madelyn was not the type to have a pity party when things did not go her way in life. In fact, she was very upbeat and positive and looked at problems as obstacles she had to figure a way to overcome. She took these as challenges and took them in her stride where the people around her would give up, get grumpy, and have mini tantrums; she would be busy thinking and figuring. This time, though, she was feeling embarrassed. She was playing in the big leagues, and she felt young, immature, and naïve.

It was almost as if Anna had an alternative personality when it came to money and compensation. Madelyn was so not like that. Madelyn loved science; she loved to figure things out that no one before her figured out. Any scientist working in the forefront of their field felt the same as she did; she was certain. Madelyn thought it must be pretty boring and unsatisfying work to write legal contracts that protected people from other lawyers whose job was to find weaknesses to exploit in other lawyers' work. That must be why money was such a priority for Anna.

Madelyn was paralyzed. This was not like her. Still lying in bed, she decided to pray. She did her best praying in the morning even though she was brought up to pray before bed at night, which she rarely did. Her mom believed that you needed to be in God's good grace right before sleep in case you died in your sleep. Madelyn always thought that was silly. She knew God loved her every minute of every day. The morning was her time to reflect and give thanks to the Lord. She prayed hard to have the strength to find any alternative means to pursue her dreams. She didn't want it given to her on a silver platter, she did not want to win the lottery or any such thing, but when it ran across her mind, she thought why not. She then prayed to stay focused and not ramble on in her prayers the way she often did.

It was 7:00 a.m. on a Saturday when her phone rang. She was brushing her teeth and thought it must be a wrong number or one of those more common cell-phone solicitations and so disregarded it. She threw on a pair of shorts, a sweatshirt, running shoes, and ball cap and headed out the door for a quick run before her shower. The phone rang again, and she looked at it in a bit of shock. It was Anna.

She answered with, "This is Madelyn," knowing it was formal, but she didn't really know what was an appropriate greeting in this situation.

Anna replied, "This is Anna, dear Madelyn. I am truly sorry that it has taken so long to get back to you. I hope you can forgive me. I picked up the phone to call you a couple of times to update you on my progress, but without anything definitive to tell you, I thought better of it." She was speaking fairly fast and almost out of breath.

She took a deep breath and continued, "I have good news for you, so I hope it was worth the wait. As you know, I was in the process of getting an appointment with Hugh Mankin, our senior of all senior partners to discuss your proposal at the end of our meeting last week. We finally met last night for dinner. It turned out that he was going to be contacting me within the month to discuss a promotion opportunity for a director position in the new Washington, DC, branch. This is one step away from becoming a partner, so very exciting. Of course, I accepted. Oh, I am just blabbering on about my good fortune and completely ignoring yours. I apologize again; forgive me. Are you still there?"

"Yes, and congratulations, by the way."

"Oh, good. I received an e-mail correspondence thirty minutes ago from Hugh approving moving forward with the Madelyn Cooper business venture. He went on to say that he could really use a little rejuvenating, so he hoped you can get this off the ground sooner than later. He said there are a number of details that would need to be worked out and agreed on regarding compensation, but he was confident based on your initial proposal that something could be arranged to meet our individual requirements."

Madelyn actually jumped into the air and clapped her hands together, in the process dislodging the phone from her right hand. After picking it up from the floor, she said, "Oh my gosh, I am so excited, I can't even tell you. I just dropped my phone! Oh my God, I can't believe it!" She could hear Anna laughing on the other end of the phone.

Anna said, "So, do you want to hire me or what?"

Madelyn was smiling so big, she could barely talk but managed to get out a "Yes, absolutely, yes."

Anna then said, "I will get busy and get one of our junior associates started on the patent. Of course, I will write the final draft. My calendar has been completely cleared; I am yours. I will start on the confidentiality agreement today. We need both documents before we can approach the money!"

Madelyn let Anna know she was planning to go to a convention announcing the president's new plan for the National Nanotechnology Initiative. The now annual convention is scheduled in a few months in March and hosted by Sandia Laboratory in Albuquerque, New Mexico. The Albuquerque, New Mexico, lab is the largest of the multi-facility Sandia complex. A Livermore lab in California is the second largest laboratory operated in the Sandia group. The National Nanotechnology Initiative committee has endorsed the Sandia executive management with a leadership role for the upcoming event.

Nanotechnology deals with the little pieces. Once scientists succeeded in building microscopic machines at the molecular level, many of the top labs in the world and many of the wealthier governments in the world have started significant research projects surrounding the possible applications of such a technology. Sharing research on any new technology is always a bit of a challenge in itself.

These devices are smaller than cells and can be 80,000 times smaller than the width of a ridge on your fingertip. The applications can range anywhere from performing medical procedures (as Madelyn had designed) to enhancing energy or improving computing speed. Of course, there can be applications for modern-day defense weaponry as well. The US government has been at the forefront of nano technology research. Much of this research is kept under lock and key, whether it was derived from the government or the private sector.

It is widely anticipated that the president's initiative is intended to promote the sharing of technological innovations in the field between the private and public sectors. No small feat. A few years prior, the European Commission was invited into the fold. Perhaps we will be adding other nations to our combined efforts?

Anna discussed realistic time lines with Madelyn. She expressed, "I feel the government is not the place to seek funds unless it is in the form of some grants, but realistically the grant money available would not put a dent in the quarter of a billion they needed. I think I can have a working confidentiality agreement and a patent pending by the time of the convention. There might be some money there, since many large corporations are starting to allocate R and D funds toward the technology.

Madelyn said, "There might be some scientists there I can hire too!" She seriously was more interested in building her team than getting the money.

Madelyn could hear her fumbling around in the background before she said, "We need to set up an appointment as soon as possible so we can best describe the work you have done and so I can get a better idea of what parts of your work are not commonplace in the scientific community. We need to solely focus on the parts of your work that are unique and not already published somewhere. The patents on the machinery will be fairly straightforward, since there has not been machines made for this specific purpose to date. There are a million other tedious yet important things we will need to go over. Can you block out four or five hours on Tuesday midday? And, yes, I bet there are some potential staffing opportunities in Sandia. Did I get that right—Sandia?"

She said, "Sure thing, how about we start at eleven? You can have me for the rest of the day if need be. And, yes, Sandia is right."

Anna said in a genuinely excited voice, "I sure look forward to working with you! I am going to set your Nano Initiative Convention as our preliminary deadline for both the patent and confidentiality agreement. By the way, Hugh said he was going to poke around for some venture capital money. He is very well connected."

After saying their good-byes, Madelyn sat down and thought how lucky she was and how grateful she was to her professor for setting things up. She was about to call him and realized it was not even 8:00 a.m. on a Saturday and thought better of it. She looked up to her ceiling and said out loud, "That didn't take long!" Rather than call her professor, she went on her run and was consumed with thoughts about finally being able to start the work of proving her technology—a technology that will change the world as we know it.

The weekend flew by, and before she knew it, she was sitting in Anna's office. They spent the good part of the afternoon reviewing the specifics of the machinery she had designed to manufacture the nanobots and quantum stars.

Anna seemed to pick up on the mechanical portion of the technology with ease, which made the patent process more bulletproof. There were two separate pieces of equipment being patented. The first machine assembled the actual nanobot. This was called the nanobot generator. The second machine generated the quantum star and embedded it into each single nanobot. Once the quantum stars were successfully embedded into a batch of nanobots, they got coated with a carbon-based polymer.

The carbon-coating process enabled the machinery to be injected into the human biology without it being rejected or viewed as a threat. Human physiology is carbon based. Without the carbon coating, the molecular machinery would be targeted by white cells as part of our natural immune response.

The quantum star was integral to communication once injected into the subject's body.

It was the programming required to build the nanobots that was giving Anna headaches. Madelyn explained to Anna that she had only written three programs to date. She anticipated that there would be hundreds, maybe thousands of programs written by the time that the technology was released. Each nanobot was designed for a specific purpose, and the software is what gave it the instructions it needed to accomplish its task.

Anna was having difficulty staying focused on Madelyn's notes, so Madelyn decided to narrate. She explained, "The first program I wrote was used to interface with the nanobot generator. This program contains the code for the design and assembly of a nanobot exclusively for the purpose of destroying a cancerous cell in a lymph gland. The code is specific to the patient's DNA strand. Each patient's twenty-three chromosomes are analyzed, and the data is integral for the design process."

Anna glanced up and said, "So in order for you to design a nanobot, you have to first have the patient's DNA sequence?"

Madelyn said, "Yes and no; you can design the nanobot without DNA information, but in order for it to be useful for a particular person, his or her DNA must be evaluated and minor modifications made to the nanobot. You end up with a generic nanobot and finally an enhanced nanobot."

She went on to say, "The second program I designed was to assemble the nanobot responsible for gathering and evacuating the first nanobot and the destroyed cellular material from the body. I like to call this a *garbage bot*. Once a procedure is complete, it is necessary to remove all the destroyed cellular material and destroyer-bots, encapsulate that material, and haul it out to a predetermined location in the body via blood vessels."

Anna's head was swimming. All she could think was how in the world did such a young mind develop such a sophisticated and complex system. She just nodded and let Madelyn go on.

"The third program I wrote is probably the most complex code of the three. This code is responsible for instructing the nanobot. It tells the nanobot what to do. In order for this program to work, we need to not only integrate the patient's DNA strand but also incorporate data from CT-scan imaging. The code is designed to interact with the quantum stars via a remote transmission similar to Bluetooth and is used during the actual procedure. The quantum stars act as an array, and when signaled properly, they collectively interact in a desired behavior."

Anna was processing this and trying to put it into layman's terms. She took a breath and said, "So we assemble a nanobot that is designed to perform a specific task, and then we enhance it to perform that task on a specific patient. We then embed it with a quantum star and coat it with a carbon-based polymer to make it safe to put into the human body. After we program instructions for the task at hand, we inject it into the patient, run the program via Bluetooth-type technology, and then evacuate it with the help of some garbage bots once the task is complete."

"You got it!" Madelyn said with a big smile.

Anna said, "You really think this can work? Cancer would be cured?"

Madelyn enthusiastically said, "Yes, and many other things. In fact, everything! Everything can be cured—spinal injury, all cancers, digestive problems, vascular problems, everything you can imagine that goes wrong with a body. This technology is the key to fixing it all. My research also strongly indicates that the technology can be used to keep everyone young by repairing the actual gene sequences in your cellular make up. This, of course, is very complex and still needs a lot of research, but I believe it can be done. You know all this from the synopsis, but I just can't help but talk about it. It will change the world."

Anna was letting this sink in. She had been aware of Madelyn's discovery for a week, and she had done nothing but think about it since. In the back of her mind, she was being pessimistic about the actual fruition of the technology, but part of her was optimistic. When being optimistic, she became overwhelmed by the ramifications this would have. Just the political and economic impacts would be enough to shake up the world.

Anna said, "How much do you think a procedure will cost a patient?"

Madelyn said, "I don't really know for sure. There is virtually no material cost. There are no exotic molecules required, and the quantity of material is so small that I would say total material cost would be less than twenty-five cents. The cost to run the DNA sequencing and imaging with full utilization of capital is estimated at one thousand dollars. So my guess is one thousand dollars and twenty-five cents."

Anna almost dropped out of her chair. "Everyone could afford this!" she blurted.

Madelyn nodded. "Yes, getting excited yet?"

Anna's forehead was all scrunched up as she got back to the task at hand. She said, "How do you think we can patent the interface of the software with the delivery systems? We really want to avoid having to individually patent each program."

They spent the next four hours developing a strategy to patent protect any program used for the purpose of this technology.

5

Karl felt a huge weight lifted off him while sitting in the terminal at LAX, waiting for his delayed flight to Dallas, which would then connect his flight to Dulles in DC. He kept thinking he was going to Dallas to get to Dulles, going to Dallas to get to Dulles; this little jingle repeated itself in his head for at least ten minutes before he decided to stop it. Karl was on multiple highs, he no longer had to work as an actuary; he was going to go spend a week with his best friend in the world, and he was two weeks away from starting his dream job.

It took twelve hours from the time he entered the airport in LAX before he landed in Dulles. He was a little tired and a little buzzed from the cocktails he had had on the last leg. But as soon as he stepped onto the tarmac, he was immediately rejuvenated. Jim was waiting at the gate. They exchanged a hug and started the long walk to the baggage-claim area. Jim had only made a couple of plans: a day at the Smithsonian and dinner reservations on Friday night at one of his favorite spots. The rest of the week was wide open; no commitments, a real vacation!

Jim's dad had sprung for their hotel accommodations. He told Jim it was a token of his appreciation for canceling his trip to Australia. This was really a nice bonus. They had adjoining suites at the Hay-Franklin.

The hotel was located on 16th and H Streets, NW (One Lafayette Square), Washington, DC. It was only one block from the White House with 145 stately rooms, including twenty suites.

The lavish decor included ornamental fireplaces, balconies, and carved plaster ceilings. It's one of the more popular lunch hang-outs for journalists, politicians, and diplomats.

They both agreed that a drink and late dinner was in order. Jim called the hotel and made reservations for 9:30 p.m. Karl was three hours behind, so 9:30 was really 6:30.

After checking in and admiring their new digs for the upcoming week, they went downstairs to the bar. It was 8:30 p.m., perfect; an hour to relax with a couple of martinis before dinner. There were a few familiar faces, but neither Karl nor Jim could place them. Karl brought Jim up-to-date on the past few weeks' events, including his conversation with Heather and, of course, his meeting with Steve. Karl was very complimentary of Steve. He made comparisons with him and some of Jim's best traits. While explaining that he was grounded, knew what he wanted, successful and yet full of fun and energy, he could see Jim's attitude change.

Jim said in a rather dismissive manner, "Marry him, why don't you?"

Karl just went, "Wow, dude; chill out!"

Jim had spent the past few weeks cramming for finals and enduring hours of arduous tests. He was tired and a bit grumpy. He looked up and said, "Sorry, long day. I am exhausted. I am really super happy for you. Sounds like you will enjoy your new job. It is sure going to be better than that last job." He put his glass up and said, "Cheers!"

Before they knew it, they were ushered to their table for dinner. Jim ordered rack of lamb with blueberry demi-glace, and Karl went for the roasted duck breast on sliced pears in a creamy cucumber sauce. The food was excellent, and they were hungry and exhausted. Conversation was light, and when they finished dinner, they both went to their rooms and hit the sack.

The next morning they decided to go poolside and have some coffee and a Continental breakfast. It was a gorgeous day in mid-June, and the wisteria was just starting to bloom on the patio's canopy. They were dressed in shorts and polo shirts, typical of college-age kids, and feeling a little out of place among the professionals all wearing navy-and-gray tailored suits. At over $850 a night, this was not the typical place to stay if you were on vacation, especially if you were college age and on vacation.

Jim pointed and said, "Hey, there are Senator Marilyn Ryme of Connecticut and House Representative Dwaine Paxon of Rhode Island." Karl knew of neither, let alone recognize them in a crowd. He looked at Jim kind of quirkily. Jim said, "Oh, you must think I'm a freak, but at Yale you kind of just get to know who is who in DC."

Karl said, "Fair enough; I wouldn't expect you to recognize Pierre Milman."

"Who is Pierre Milman?"

"Exactly!"

"Oh, I get it. You're in one of those moods. I will remember that one," Jim said.

Sipping on their coffee, feeling rested and refreshed, they started to discuss what they were going to do over the next week. Even though they both would have liked to find some female companionship, neither of them enjoyed the bar scene. Karl was too serious and intellectual to fare well with women who would have sex with a stranger, and he was too moral to hire a hooker. Jim recently started dating Beverly, a political-science grad student at Yale. He thought that this might be the one. Chasing women was not going to be on the agenda this week.

Jim came up with a great idea to rent some longboards and hit the concrete at the Lincoln Memorial. There was a lot of open space there, and they were both craving some exercise.

After a few hours of skateboarding and taking in the sights, they stopped for a hot dog at one of the stands by the famous water feature in the center of the entrance to the memorial.

Plopping down on a bench and eating, they overheard what sounded like reporters having a dispute about the integrity of a source. One fellow, in a very animated way, was telling the other that he firmly believed that his source was the real deal. He had a slight Russian accent and was speaking very fast.

Quietly chewing on their hot dogs, both Karl and Jim found themselves engrossed in eavesdropping without the other even making mention of it.

The more cautious of the two was saying that this was a giant allegation. He said, "Vic, you just can't write that a senator is misappropriating tax dollars without having solid evidence; especially if that senator is the chairman of Commerce, Science, and Transportation Committee and has been in his elected office for over twenty years. He is a heavy weight here in DC, for God's sake."

"Yes, but if he is really diverting funds into coffers that are untraceable, he could use them for whatever end he chooses. I mean the kind of dollars we're talking about can't be for personal use. What does a guy do with two hundred fifty million dollars? You could start a small army with that kind of ruble."

Jim was searching his mind; who was the Chairman of Commerce, Science, and Transportation Committee? Was he the guy from Indiana? No, it was Mary Wright from Virginia. No, it wasn't Mary, he thought. Karl's interest was piqued as well; he was about to take a job with the Census Bureau, which is a branch under the Commerce Department.

The reporters got up and left, still debating.

Karl and Jim started talking at the same time. Jim finally said, "OK; you first."

"No, you first."

Jim said, "I can't remember which senator is over the Commerce, Science, and Transportation Committee. It is on the tip of my tongue."

Karl said, "They were talking about Arthur Birmingham, the senator in Washington state, Yale, boy."

Jim licked his finger and checked twice in the air, saying, "Two for Karl, zero for Jim."

Karl said, "It's really not fair; he is my new boss's boss." Steve had given Karl the chain of command in his interview.

For the remainder of the week, they periodically checked the local rags and the Internet to see if there were any stories written that could have been associated even remotely with what they overheard. The only story that could have possibly been related was written by Victor Rodchenko and ran in the Centennial two days later. It was a brief discussion about the finance committee's unwillingness to investigate all potential misappropriations of funds when the funds were within the agency's original budget. The tone of the article was bitter and led you to believe there was something more to the story than the journalist could write.

Other than the journalistic quarrel, the rest of the week was fairly uneventful.

A few days into the trip, the weather was unseasonably warm. After their breakfast on the patio, they decided to get their trunks on and make it a pool day. Jim was getting some serious attention from a few young women at the poolside. He liked the attention and flirted with them feverishly.

Karl thought Jim didn't have any intention to let it go anywhere, but some sparks were flying. One of the more demure girls in the group was subtly sending signals toward Karl. Karl was single, and she was beautiful and probably rich or at least from a rich family. He deduced this because she was staying at a swank place like the Franklin. After a few moments of contemplation, he decided she was out of his league, and he wasn't in the mood to put on false airs for a fling that would go nowhere.

Rather than get up and leave, which was his initial instinct, he decided to stay and be entertained by his friend who was now in rare form. Part of Jim's charm was his sense of humor. He had the girls laughing hysterically over nothing at all.

An hour went by, and a couple of cocktails were consumed when Jim turned to Karl and said, "Don't we have that dinner thing in an hour?"

Karl knew there was no dinner plans but immediately caught on and said, "Yes, we probably should get going if we don't want to be late."

Jim turned to the group of girls, who all had ridiculous pouts on their faces.

So obvious, Karl thought. He counted his blessings that he was not brought up in those social circles.

Jim got up and said, "Good-bye, it was a pleasure talking with you all."

Karl stood and said, "See ya," thinking *Wouldn't want to be ya*.

When they got into the elevator, Karl slapped Jim on the shoulder and said, "Nice talking with you all? Are you now from Mississippi or something? Where did that come from?"

Jim just laughed and said, "We better get away from here for dinner. My dad told me about this rib joint. Nothing fancy, ya know; picnic tables with red-and-white checkered-tablecloths-type of atmosphere. Want to slum it and get some ribs and have a few beers with your new southern friend?"

Karl said, "Sounds perfect."

They looked at each other. Both were wearing shorts and polos. When the elevator opened, they didn't move; Jim hit the lobby button, and they went back down. "No need to change," Jim said.

Karl could not get over how good the ribs were. He kept telling Jim that the chef must have some kind of magic dust he put on them. During Karl's third helping of the ribs, Jim's dad called. The screen on the phone said Hugh. Karl wondered what kind of kid would put his or her father's first name in his or her phone contacts.

Jim answered, "Hey, Dad, what's up? We are at that rib joint you told me about. Unbelievable; Karl is on his third plate. I'm resting."

Hugh said, "We picked up an unknown yet high-profile client last fall. Anna, you remember Anna."

"Yes, pretty Asian woman?"

Hugh laughed; his son liked beautiful women. "Yes, that would be the correct Anna. Well, anyway, she is going to head up the new DC office, and at the same time, she will need to dedicate herself close to full time to this client I mentioned. She needs help, and I am assigning you to her effective the minute you guys are done playing around this week. I hope you are having fun because the next three to six months are going to be brutal. I trust your new romantic interest—Beverly, is it?"

"Yes, we call her Bev or Bevy."

"Well, I hope Bev can handle your new schedule." Then in his signature way he said, "Love you," and hung up the phone. No time for Jim to say love you back or good-bye or anything; just love you click.

On the trip back to Los Angeles, Karl was the happiest he could ever remember. He had just had an awesome week with his best friend, who was doing quite well and was on a great career path. He was getting ready to start his dream job. Heather was on his mind.

6

It was Valentine's Day, and Anna had a working patent pending for both machines and the software interface. She also had a bulletproof confidentiality agreement satisfactory for approaching venture-capital investment firms. Madelyn had written a synopsis with limited but very compelling information on the technology. The full disclosure confidentiality agreement took a little longer to put together.

Both Anna and Madelyn being single without any romantic relationships decided to celebrate Valentine's together at Anna's house.

Anna lived in Los Gatos, an upscale suburb in the South Bay area. Her home was a restored Victorian cottage on a perfectly manicured one-acre lot located in a forested neighborhood. Madelyn fell in love with it; to her it was absolutely a dream. Anna loved it as well, but because she was moving to DC in two months, she was in the process of getting it ready to market, albeit reluctantly. She considered renting it and then renting in DC, but she hated being a renter. She wanted to fix this up or paint that. She was not cut out to be a renter. She was not even sure she would ever come back to the bay area; it had gotten so congested over the past twenty years that it just wasn't the same place it was when she moved there in the nineties.

Madelyn knew she had no business asking, but she was curious. "So what do you think you will be asking for this place?" She turned a slight shade of red immediately after asking the question.

Anna didn't think anything of it and replied, "Well, fortunately, we are in a seller's market right now, and the west side of the valley has little to no inventory. My realtor says that with a few small improvements and repairs, we can get two point seven."

Madelyn gasped. She knew real estate was expensive here, but she never realized how expensive. She said, "Good for you, selling at the right time! What does the DC market look like now?"

Anna smiled big and said, "I won't be spending all my money on a house; that is for certain. I am thinking of buying something metropolitan like a flat with a rooftop garden for about a third of what I get here. I have to admit this will be a major change in my life. I have been house poor since I moved to the bay area. I paid nine hundred thousand dollars for my house nineteen years ago. My payments are over six thousand dollars a month. When I got a substantial bonus in a good year, I would pay it all toward the principal. I only owe one hundred thousand dollars, and I have a countdown app on my phone for the payoff date. My plan was to paint the door red on that day no matter what else was happening. I guess it will never happen now. Why in the world am I telling you all this? Sorry, it is not like me to blurt out my personal stuff, especially my financials, to anyone. I must admit I am a little embarrassed."

Madelyn felt complimented Anna would be so open with her. She was intrigued to witness how a grown-up handled their money. She said, "No, not by any means should you be embarrassed. It is me who should be; I asked the questions. You just answered them."

Anna felt a little relieved. The last thing she wanted to do was alienate her new friend. Madelyn was beginning to be a surrogate daughter figure to her, and she was developing feelings of caring, admiration, and pride. She thought, *These are the things moms must feel.* This was natural and probably inevitable considering she never had children of her own. She thought about it for a minute and felt it was OK; it was not weird.

After pouring a couple of nice-size glasses of dry Riesling, they prepared a couple of lobsters for the broiler. The au gratin potatoes in the oven filled the room with the smell of cheesy goodness, making them both hungry.

Over dinner they discussed possible strategies for the two meetings Hugh had set up. The first investor they would be meeting was not likely to be fruitful but would give them a real audience to work out the kinks in their presentation. Hugh knew that the company did not have nearly the capital being requested, but there was always the slim chance they could contribute in a subordinate role or possibly provide a referral. This meeting was scheduled in five days. The second meeting was the big one and was scheduled a few days after their first meeting. Hugh knew two of the partners personally. They were not only friends at Yale but also had done some business over the years and had stayed in touch. They were more than business acquaintances. On more than one occasion, they had gotten together for backyard BBQs and even went on a few skiing vacations together in recent years.

Hugh had laid the groundwork. One of his friends revealed they had just executed a large sale of shares acquired from a start-up that they had invested in. He wouldn't give Hugh the details of whom or how much, but the way he was talking, it was hundreds of millions. That kind of liquidity needed a home, and Hugh had high hopes that Madelyn's project was a perfect fit.

Madelyn met Anna at her office an hour before their meeting with investor number one. They got into Anna's car and drove to Santa Clara for their meeting. What should have been a twenty-minute drive took forty because of some unscheduled work on a power line on Washington Boulevard.

Still ten minutes early, they were not frazzled. They were not nervous because they knew that this was really just a trial run. They sat in the lavish lobby, which had fountains and modern sculptures, for thirty minutes before someone came out to tell them it would be just a few more minutes. Anna whispered in Madelyn's ear, "They are posturing; this is typical and to be expected."

Once escorted into the large conference room that seated twenty, they were appointed seats at one end of the long table. Nobody else was in the room. They were offered coffee or something to snack on; they both accepted the coffee. Another twenty minutes passed before a group of five men dressed to the nines in very expensive suites entered the room and sat at the other end of the table. Introductions were made, and then two more entered, a man and a woman, both of whom were also dressed very professionally.

Anna was thinking seven to two. Hmm. She had received eleven copies of the signed confidentiality agreement a few days before. The seven in the room were all assigns.

Madelyn skipped any small talk and asked if she could hook up her laptop to the network. One of the men got up and assisted her. Madelyn made a motion to the TV on the wall and said, "The network is hooked up to that screen, right?"

The man nodded.

After a short boot up, Madelyn went right to work. The first seven slides on her presentation had to do with the sequence of the technology and a brief explanation of the type of equipment that would need to be developed to make the technology work. The audience was very receptive.

For dog-and-pony-show purposes, Anna would handle the next four slides, detailing just some of the specific procedures that could be performed starting with curing all cancers and ending with curing old age itself or at least slowing it down considerably. She, in very simple-to-understand terms, explained that at age twenty-eight (the age of physical maturity for the average person), a person could undergo a procedure that would bring their cellular structure to where it was five years previous. That person could undergo the same process every seven years.

She ended with, "So, every seven years you would only age two years. The average life-span would be increased to two hundred years. If further progress is made, who knows how long we could live? The best part is that the procedure is not expensive, and everyone in the world should be able to afford it. We estimate around one thousand dollars."

The room was very quiet. Madelyn knew they were sold, and she felt great about their presentation.

One of the men opened with, "Very compelling, but how do we know it will really work?"

Madelyn looked at Anna and said, "I will take this one. The probability is in the mid-ninety percentile. Math does not lie. All the underlying technology is proven. We just need to take it to the next level, and to answer your next question, we think it will take about three years."

Anna then jumped in and said, "Once we can refine the confidentiality agreement a bit more, we will be happy to have you put a team together to review our work before you spend a dime."

One of the men started laughing. "Refine the agreement; it was twenty-eight pages long, and I am not certain I even knew what I was signing. For all I know, you guys own our company," he said with another big laugh.

The woman interrupted and reiterated that her role with the company was evaluating the science and engineering of potential ventures and said, "We appreciate your offer to put together a team. Myself and two other trusted members of our company will be delighted to further review the proposal once you can have the legal stuff worked out." She was directing her entire being to Madelyn.

Madelyn nodded and said, "Look forward to working with you."

Another man, probably the oldest of the group and likely senior in the organization, said with a heavy southern drawl, "Well, that is all fine and dandy, but what kind of dough are you guys look'n' to git from us?"

Anna confidently said, "A quarter of a billion."

Those who were standing sat. All eyes were on the old Texan who simply walked out of the room. After just a minute, three of the other men in suites shrugged their shoulders and looked at Anna. One of them said, "I think our meeting is over; thank you for your time."

On the way home, Madelyn was going on about the gall of that guy to just walk out; the arrogance. How rude can someone be to do such a thing?

She was going on and on and getting more worked up when Anna shut her off with her hand up in the air and said, "I think we need to work on our introduction and engage in some small talk at our next meeting on Friday. Otherwise, I think we did great. Don't worry about the old guy. He was just pissed off because we wasted his and his team's valuable time; it is completely understandable. We were lucky we didn't get worse."

Their next meeting was with Matthews, Molly, Bernier & Young Investments Corp. located in Palo Alto, California. Peter

Matthews and Marcel Bernier were Hugh's friends from Yale and primarily involved in finance. Abraham Molly was a brilliant physical scientist born and educated in India, and Tonya Young was one of the top medical experts in the world, educated in Australia. The group had just cashed in on a fortune and needed a place for all that money to land.

Anna could not help herself counting her chickens before they hatched. She felt certain this was the right fit and that a deal was about to be made. Madelyn was floating on the same cloud.

The next few days flew by. Anna offered a spare room to Madelyn the night before the meeting to reduce the commute time. From Anna's home in Los Gatos, it was likely going to take forty-five minutes to get to the office in Palo Alto for the 10:00 a.m. meeting. From Berkley it would have taken Madelyn two or more hours to get there.

They ordered Pizza, prepped for the meeting, and hit the sack before 10:30 p.m.

Traffic was light, and they arrived twenty minutes early. Upon entering the building, they were immediately greeted and escorted into a separate waiting room from the main lobby. Before the receptionist left, a well-dressed woman in her fifties entered with copies of the signed confidentiality agreements. They all exchanged pleasantries, and the two women left the room. At five minutes to 10:00 a.m., Peter Matthews came in and introduced himself. He said, "Pleased to meet you both; glad to see you early and the traffic didn't cause you any trouble. We have a small team assembled in a room two levels up from here; please follow me."

On the elevator ride up, Peter smiled but did not talk. They walked down a wide corridor where the left side was completely glass, overlooking the Santa Cruz mountains. Close to the end of the corridor, they reached double doors that led into a large conference room. It was very high tech and reminded Madelyn of what she imagined a briefing room in the Pentagon would look like. There was seating for at least thirty with functional desktops equipped with power, Internet, and intranet inputs. The room was used to work in; it was practical, not opulent. The east side of the room was glass and overlooked the bay.

When they arrived, there were five or six people huddled in conversation and another seven or so people milling around. Anna instinctively was counting twelve to two and thinking, *Sounds about right*. Peter escorted them to a central seating position, and everyone else in the room immediately found a seat except for Peter, who remained standing.

Peter introduced Madelyn and Anna to the group. He referenced not only their individual accomplishments dating back to undergraduate work but also Anna's relationship with their good friend Hugh. The list of accolades for the two girls was long and detailed; Peter seemed to just rattle it all off, as if he was talking about his own child or a star employee. He hadn't even met them until five minutes ago, yet it appeared he had known them all his life? Anna thought what a valuable skill that must be to have.

He then pointed to the person nearest to his left and said, "Abraham, would you please start the introductions for our team. I will have to excuse myself, as I have another engagement. If I am done early enough, I may rejoin you." With that, he left.

Abraham introduced himself, and then in circular fashion everyone else did the same. Each person verbally acknowledged that they signed and agreed to the terms of the confidentiality agreement. All three of the remaining partners were present, plus one legal council, one IT staffer, and three team members who worked under Abraham and Tonya.

Marcel seemed to be the senior person in the room and the obvious person in charge. He was a very attractive Frenchman, with an ego as big as the whole country of France. This was accentuated by the way he carried himself and his personal body language. The way he paced himself when he spoke, when he walked, his general posture, his seemingly half-shut eyelids, the way he flipped his full head of hair around, and everything about him screamed narcissist.

After he had gone on about how great their company was and how successful they were, he finally got around to allowing Madelyn to begin her presentation.

Madelyn remembered Anna's suggestion to engage in a little small talk at first, so she opened with greeting each and everyone in the room personally. She had written their names down during their intros. This seemed to work beautifully. People felt more at ease and less formal by the time she was done. Once into her presentation, the science heads and their teams were firing question after question at her. She felt she was being interrogated, but in reality they were just extremely interested in her work. This was completely different from the previous meeting.

Anna was very pleased at how things were going, and through a few subtle gestures, she let Madelyn know.

Madelyn was definitely in her element. She was passionate about her work and proud of her accomplishments. She was responsible for a technology she knew would someday end human suffering. Unlike Marcel, Madelyn was not overly impressed with herself; she simply was grateful she had the opportunities, support, and God-given talents to put the technology together. The real turn-on for Madelyn was the figuring. The fact that her work was going to bring about a lot of good was the icing on the cake. She often wondered if she was working on a technology that could be used for bad things if she would still be so passionate. Good thing she was not facing that dilemma, she thought.

As her mind was spinning around with these thoughts, it dawned on her. She needed to be interviewing the people who would be providing the capital as much as they were interviewing her. Whoever provided the money for research and development would end up with a significant chunk of the company that would provide the technology to the world. Did she really want a "Marcel" type to have that much power and influence over such a technology? She put that aside and decided it would be a worthwhile discussion with Anna at a later date.

Anna was trying to read Marcel and his legal council. It was obvious that the science personnel were engaged. Undoubtedly there would be more meetings with Madelyn and the science teams. She had no read so far.

Madelyn, aware that her allotted time had expired forty-five minutes ago, said, "I would like to give the floor to Anna, who will talk briefly about the applications of the technology and some rudimentary financial forecasting."

Anna went through a long list of ailments that would be immediately remedied. Another list of injuries that could be repaired followed and another long list of diseases that could be cured. She went into great detail about how all cancers could be put into permanent remission. She talked about people getting out of their wheelchairs. It was quite impressive, and even Madelyn had some shivers at a few points in the presentation. She then turned the focus into cost of treatment, which was estimated at $1000. She then discussed slowing down the aging process, and this was where people in the room actually gasped. It all made so much sense. It was real. At the end of Anna's presentation, there was some gentle applause and a lot of smiling faces.

Madelyn asked if there were any other questions.

Marcel said, "I would like to meet with you separately regarding your estimates on R and D start-up costs."

Anna said, "We are prepared to provide that to you in detail today if you like."

He said with the slight bit of flirtatious innuendo, "Why don't you and I go to my office and review your proposal while Madelyn here spends a little time with Abraham and Tonya."

They separated, and Madelyn was immediately bombarded with more questions. She smiled and gladly answered as many as she could.

Anna felt a bit nervous when she got into the elevator with Marcel. She knew in her heart there was no real threat, but he still gave her the creeps. If he were not so good looking, she might have refused to be alone with him. He remained a complete gentleman but oozed sex appeal and was subtly directing it at Anna, and she was completely aware of it. By the time they got to the top floor, she was a bit flushed and fanned herself when exiting into the lobby. Just across from the elevator was a reception area staffed with a male receptionist. He looked up when the door opened and put his head right back down.

Marcel guided her to his office, which was absolutely not what she expected. For one thing it was only about three hundred square feet. It had an antique desk with a floor-to-ceiling bookshelf behind it, a small couch, and a wing chair, among a few pieces of antique furniture. Everything was wood: the floor, ceiling, walls, and furniture. The office was well appointed with decor but almost to the point of clutter. There were no windows in the office.

He offered her a glass of wine, which she politely refused but said a coffee would be great. He picked up the phone and said a few muffled words, and within a minute, a fresh cup of coffee was brought in by the receptionist. He had a small tray with condiments that Anna did not need.

Marcel sat down on the small couch and pointed to the chair across from it. Anna sat down while he was saying, "Nice presentation, and wow! If it could ever really work! Whew! We need the science people to do a much more thorough evaluation before we can commit to anything, you understand, don't you?" He then waved his hand and said, "Of course you do."

Anna nodded and smiled. She said, "I know you guys have deep pockets and are probably one of the largest venture-capital companies in the world." Marcel was nodding but squinting and slightly tipping his head in expectation for hearing a large number. She went on, "In this docket you will find a breakdown for the funds we are looking for and a corresponding cash-flow projection. I will warn you, the total number prior to the technology turning one penny of profit is very sizable. If you look past the initial investment and look at the potential return, it is a no-brainer."

She didn't want him to react the way the last investor did. Although fully realizing they were in completely different playing fields, she still wanted to be cautious.

She slowly started to hand the folder to Marcel when he backed up and said, "Hmmm, do I really want to open that?" He was kidding around and laughed. He held his hand out and received the folder; he then opened it, flipped through the four pages in it, and tried his very best to remain stone faced.

He simply said, "I will have to discuss with my other partners, of course. Is there anything else you would like to discuss while you are here?"

Anna, kind of taken aback that there was virtually no reaction, said, "Nothing I can think of. When do you think you will be getting back to us?"

He simply said, "There is a lot to consider here, so I can't really say. What I can promise is that we will not ignore your proposal. Fair?"

She said, "Fair," got up from her chair, and left.

7

It had been three weeks since their meeting with the investment group. Madelyn had had one half-day meeting subsequent with Tonya and one of her team members. The meeting consisted of a one-hour cursory overview of the process and then three hours of intense discussion regarding the quantum stars and their role in the communication process between procedure programming and the nanobot. They brought up a number of compelling arguments refuting the process, but Madelyn felt she did a good job in defending it.

Anna had not heard a peep from Marcel nor any of the other partners.

The National Nanotechnology Initiative convention was coming up in a week, and Madelyn was really hoping to have the funding approved prior to the convention. She was dreaming of meeting some of the top scientists in the field and making them offers to come to work for her. Without the funding, all she could really do was hobknob around and interview on the sly. Anna was knee-deep in reviewing the ever-expanding confidentiality agreement and decided that their energies would be better spent if she stayed back and had Madelyn go to the convention alone. The truth was, Anna was dreading the idea of hanging around a bunch of nerds for three days.

Madelyn was becoming inpatient with the investment group and had her reservations about Marcel. She called Anna for an update.

Anna answered the phone, knowing via caller ID that it was Madelyn, and said, "I haven't heard anything, and, yes, I am getting as frustrated about the lack of communication as you probably are."

This had a positive effect on Madelyn's mood. Knowing Anna was worried and frustrated somehow made it not her responsibility. She replied, "Glad to know I am not alone. I have been meaning to talk with you about Marcel. Peter seems like a nice enough guy, but there is something about Marcel, aside from his arrogance, that concerns me. I have not run all the numbers, but I believe the company that will form and successfully deliver this technology to the world will have a top line greater than our country's current GDP (*Gross Domestic Product*). This will undoubtedly be the largest, most powerful corporation in all of history."

She then went on to say, "I am a scientist and rarely concern myself with money, finance, and business, but recently my mind has been consumed with the business side of this technology. Frankly, some of what goes through my mind scares the heck out of me. One day I am working on solving some technical obstacle getting in the way of performing a procedure that will cure a person's cancer or let them walk again, feeling very altruistic, and the next day I am scared out of my mind how the technology will affect the world. I may have had some fleeting thoughts about notoriety in the scientific community and perhaps a dream or two about having enough money for me and my parents to never worry about having to have a paycheck to live week to week. What I have not thought about, until now, is how big this really is. The ramifications of this technology have tsunami-size ripples. With even the most integral and ethical people in charge, there will undoubtedly be issues overlooked that could have very negative impacts. With the wrong person in power, I can only imagine what could happen. If Marcel is the evil megalomaniac I fear he is, I am not sure we should proceed with their money or even if they gave it to us free of charge. There it is; I have formally spilled my guts."

Anna was impressed with Madelyn's integrity. She herself had similar thoughts. In fact, she had just discussed her concerns with Hugh. After all, Hugh knew Marcel fairly well. Hugh's take on Marcel was a little different. Probably in part due to coming from a male perspective but also from years of growing up with the man. Hugh did not defend Marcel's unscrupulous behavior toward women, but he did come to his defense on good and evil.

"The recent influx of money has probably gone to his head is all," Hugh had said.

Anna then explained, "It is really a moot point, if they do not offer us the capital. Maybe you will make a contact or two next week in Sandia that can lead to some funding prospects. Perhaps we are going about this all wrong?" Anna was now thinking out loud; something she did quite often. Some of her peers felt this was a weakness for an attorney, while others viewed it as outright assuredness and confidence. Anna called this the *loose lips verses baffle them with BS controversy*.

She went on, "Perhaps we should be asking for smaller chunks of money? Maybe we could separate the technology into multiple individual projects and sell them discretely? We could ask for slightly less than we actually will need in order to get the hook set? For example, if we prepared a presentation to build the machine to generate the nanobots and asked for sixty million dollars, it would be a lot more palatable to a lot more investors. We do not have to mention that we will need to build another more expensive machine to make them communicate with us. Once we have a working machine, then we go back to the well with the same or a different investor and ask for seventy-five million dollars to build the machine that generates and embeds the quantum stars. It's a little conniving and not completely above board, but it might just get us what we need. You see where I am going here?"

Although Madelyn desperately wanted the money and to move this project forward, she was not completely comfortable with where Anna was going. She said, "What if we instead brought four or five investment groups together and sold shares based on level of contribution? It might be easier to get to our number this way."

Anna liked the idea. They spent the next hour brainstorming their options. Getting multiple investors to cooperate was going to be complicated, to say the least. Selling it in pieces would be difficult because there was no realistic payback for the initial projects. One investor was the path of least resistance, but it also had its own set of complexities, one of which was the concentration of power issue. Finding one investor capable of funding or willing to fund such a large project was probably the biggest problem. They discussed pursuing foreign investors but decided against it for purely patriotic and political reasons. They might as well be pursuing money to build a hotel in space. Two hundred fifty million dollars before one penny of cash flow; neither of them could identify any previous endeavor that had that large of initial R and D requirement.

Most of their brainstorming was identifying the problems with getting multiple investors to work together. During the course of conversation, Madelyn said, "Too bad we don't know any rich philanthropists."

They were on the phone and could not see each other, but both knew that the other had the same expression of revelation.

Anna said, "That's exactly what we need to explore. Let's make a list of the richest people in America and see if there is anyone who might be worth approaching." They got off the phone and agreed to talk more tomorrow.

Madelyn called Anna in the morning with her list and notes ready. Anna was not as early a riser as Madelyn and was not as prepared but decided to let Madelyn take the wheel. Madelyn started off with, "My criteria was that each individual had to have at least twenty-five billion dollars in assets. That way the investment would only be one percent of their entire net worth. There are thirteen possible candidates. I grouped the family members with individual wealth together and only counted them as one possible candidate. We will need to evaluate the actual person before we make any decisions, but I felt it would help us if we categorized the list by the industry that created the wealth; so we have Microsoft (software and Internet interface designer), Berkshire Hathaway (investment firm), Oracle (database management systems), Amazon (online shopping), Koch (Industrial diversified), Facebook (social media), Bloomberg (financial news), Google (Internet browser), Walmart (one-stop discount shopping), Adelson (gaming casinos), FTLware (Internet infrastructure leader), Soros (hedge funds), Nike (shoe manufacturer), Mars (candy manufacturer)."

Anna piped in, "Nice way to break this down. Who do we want to be in business with, and who on that list could bring something to the table besides the money?"

After a lengthy discussion, they agreed that Microsoft and Google both had global ties that could prove very useful. Walmart, Nike, and Amazon understood consumers better than possibly anyone else in the world. Buffet was well diversified and well known for his philanthropic endeavors. Koch could bring some technical expertise to the table and be helpful in the equipment-manufacturing aspect of bringing the technology to the consumer. FTLware and Oracle could both provide technical and high-tech entrepreneurial management expertise. It was decided that Adelson, Soros, Bloomberg, Facebook, and Mars were just not good fits.

"Now let's evaluate the people behind the companies," said Anna.

Madelyn said, "I don't have much on that yet, but I do have a few insights that may help us refine our list. There are four different people who have over twenty-five billion dollars each associated with the Walmart money. It may be difficult to get them all to agree to a venture this risky and that is so outside of their wheelhouse. We really can't approach one without approaching them all unless we have very good reason. I think we will have some of the same problems we were concerned about when we discussed bringing multiple investors on board. Koch has a lot of practical industrial knowledge, but they have a reputation for being fairly involved in politics. Not sure who or what their ties are. That leaves us with Oracle, FTLware, Nike, Amazon, Google, and Microsoft or, more specifically, Larry Ellison, Dane Lindsey, Phil Knight, Jeff Bezos, Sergey Brin, Warren Buffet, and Bill Gates, respectively." Madelyn exhaled and then said, "Can you get us meetings with those seven gentlemen?"

Anna laughed. She felt like she was a little kid playing make-believe, but this was real. As absurd as it might seem, if Madelyn's science was what it appeared to be, anyone of these individuals would love to be at the helm of such an enterprise. Each of them can self-fund this project for less than 1 percent of their personal net worth. None would need to get board approval for funds; they could write a check.

More than a moment had passed, and Madelyn said, "Well, is that a maybe?"

Anna said, "Excuse me, my mind was drifting; this seems so surreal. I have no idea how, but I will work on getting these appointments. If you have any connections or ideas, let me know."

"You bet!" said Madelyn, and they hung up.

Madelyn was packing for her four-day trip to New Mexico the night before her flight when her phone rang. It was a 202 area code, which she was not familiar with but wondered whether it was East Coast. She picked up, and it was Hugh, which surprised her. They had never spoken before. Anna had supplied them both with enough information about the other that they both already felt they knew each other.

Hugh said, "Sorry to call so late; I know it must be after nine on the West Coast. I tried calling Anna, but she was not picking up, and I really wanted to relay this message personally, anyway. I got a call from Peter a few minutes ago, and they are going to pass on funding your project. He was aware that you are going to some important convention in which you wanted to start recruiting your team, and he did not want to leave you hanging. He apologized for the weeks of waiting without any communication. They were seriously considering your proposal and were not just sitting on their hands."

Madelyn said, "I really appreciate you calling and also for the definite answer before I go on this trip. I am not in the habit of asking, but may I speak freely, sir?"

"Of course…"

"I did not like Marcel, and I was uncomfortable with the idea of working with him, so I am very relieved that they will not be the financial partners for the project."

Hugh laughed. "Anna said you had integrity and that you would not sell your soul for this project no matter how much you wanted it to happen. I personally respect you for that."

Madelyn said, "Thank you. Has Anna filled you in on our newest idea for funding?"

"No, I haven't talked with her in over a week."

Madelyn thought for a second and decided that it would not be a betrayal or an inappropriate act to talk with Hugh directly regarding their progress. She said, "We have compiled a short list of six very wealthy Americans, who may fit the right profile to fund our R and D and assist in the management of taking this technology public."

Hugh was smiling. He was thinking how much he liked the tone of this half-full approach. "We were not on our knees begging for money. We were being selective in who we allowed to give us the money. It was refreshing," Madelyn said. Hugh pondered over this and realized he needed to take this approach more often in his own business dealings.

She went on, "Each of these individuals have a net worth of at least one hundred times what we need, so it would be less than one percent of their net worth at risk to fully fund it." She rattled off the list and asked him if he knew any of these individuals.

He said, "The closest I have got to knowing anyone on that list was when our firm bid and lost an opportunity to represent Larry Ellison for some patent work. I don't think I can help you, but I will ask around and see if someone I know can."

They said their good-byes, and Madelyn went back to her packing.

Madelyn's apartment was only three city blocks from the North Berkeley BART (Bay Area Rapid Transit) station. She briskly walked with her travel bag rolling behind her. The repetitive clicking on every one of the relief cuts in the sidewalk was annoying her. She thought about picking the bag up but decided she save her arms the agony would put up with the noise. Once in the station she was on a smooth tile floors and that made her very happy. She grabbed the first train to Balboa Park where she would then switch trains to get to San Francisco International Airport.

United had a good deal on a direct nonstop flight, so she would leave at 11:00 a.m. and be in Albuquerque at 1:30 p.m. The convention blocked rooms at three of the uptown major hotels. Madelyn was planning on staying at one of the nearby discount motels, but Anna convinced her otherwise. She explained that a big part of her trip was to make contacts and hopefully meet some people who would be able to eventually be part of her team; to do this she needed to be where they were. She was staying at the Marriott, which was only a ten-minute shuttle from the Phillips Technology Institute (PTi) collaboration center where the convention was being held. The PTi center was located on the Kirtland Air Force Base as was the Sandia Laboratory.

Madelyn was feeling great. She loved to travel and see things she had never seen. She really had not done much traveling since she left the house. Her family made a point of taking at least four mini vacations every year while she was growing up. She had never been to New Mexico and was interested to witness the desert landscape. She was going at the perfect time of year. Temperatures were forecasted to be in the mid-seventies during her stay.

Her flight was smooth and on time. She checked into her room and could not get over how comfortable her mattress was. She struggled to pull the bedding back to get a look at the label, which she then took a picture of with her phone. She vowed to herself that the first thing she was going to do when she received her funding was buy one of these mattresses. After a little frolicking, she decided to take a walk around the facility. There was a nice indoor and outdoor pool, a small bar, and a café with a decent menu. The hotel was in walking distance to a number of restaurants and bars. She was looking at some brochures at the desk, and the Sandia Peak Tramway ride caught her eye. She asked the concierge about it, and he said there was still time that day if she wanted to take the trip; she spontaneously agreed, and he put her in a shuttle, and off she went. Before she got off the shuttle, the driver handed her a Marriott sweatshirt and told her she might need this at the top. She was feeling very spoiled, and she liked it. She was wearing her signature 545 Levi jeans with a cotton blouse over a thin cotton tank top; perfect clothing for seventy-five degrees.

Once on the tram, she was in that perfect state of relaxation and excitement. There were a dozen other passengers on the tram when they started their fifteen-minute 2.7 mile ride up the mountain. The natural beauty that unfolded as they made their way up the mountain was more profound than she had expected. Once on top she was very happy she had the sweatshirt; it was forty-nine degrees, which made quite a blast when the doors opened. She shivered and immediately put the sweatshirt on. There were probably fifty people on the observation deck. They were above 10,000 feet in elevation, and the panoramic views were spectacular.

It was thirty minutes to sunset, and she thought it would be worth the wait. Meandering around on the deck, she noticed a number of other people with the same Marriott sweatshirts. After a relaxing trip around the platform, she decided she should secure a position on the rail overlooking the direction of the sunset.

The fresh air was thin but filled her lungs just the same. A man probably ten years older than her stepped up to her right side and leaned on the rail. He remained quiet and appeared deep in thought, so she did not say anything either. There were people lining up to view the sunset, so it did not feel awkward. After taking a dozen picture of the sun setting over the desert, she walked down to the tram gate and got on the first one available. She was one of only three people: herself and one older couple, on the tram. Most everyone was still enjoying the afterglow of the sunset, and because she had a big day the next day, she felt she should get back to the hotel, grab a bite, and hit the sack.

It took the shuttle ten minutes to get to Kirtland Air Force Base in the morning and an additional fifteen minutes at the gate to issue all forty passengers their badges. She thought there must be at least ten such busses for this event, thus a total of 150 minutes at the gates? At times she detested that she quantified everything into time, units, dollars, numbers, or some other measure. It was just the way her mind worked, and she had to accept it.

They arrived at the Phillips collaboration center an hour before the convention was to start. There was a buffet at the hotel and one at the convention center. She thought that getting to the center early and eating there made more sense than the alternative. Apparently over 150 others thought the same thing. The lobby was packed. After signing in at the registration table, she found her way to a banquet room, which was set up with an elegant full-course breakfast buffet. She served herself a healthy portion of food, poured herself a cup of fresh coffee, and sat down at one of the smaller tables set up against the wall out of the main traffic area.

About halfway through her breakfast, a familiar man asked if he could join her. She was usually nervous around men, but this man didn't seem to bring out that emotion in her. She knew she had met him somewhere; maybe in school? He looked at her with a second glance and said, "Were you at the top of Sandia Peak yesterday at sunset?"

She immediately remembered that he was the man standing next to her at the rail while she watched the sunset last night; that was probably why she did not feel nervous. He was so not threatening last night; in fact, he had never even said a word. She said, "Yes, and yes, please sit down. I knew you looked familiar."

He sat down and put his hand out. "I am Jake."

She shook his hand. "Madelyn; nice to meet you."

Jake asked, "Are you here with a team?"

Madelyn responded with a smidgen of a smile, thinking that Jake wanted to know if she was alone, "No, I work for Berkeley Labs, but I am really here on more of a personal quest."

Jake said, "Personal quest; sounds mysterious."

Madelyn could not quite determine if Jake was flirting with her or if he was just being friendly. She was used to men being attracted to her, so she always had a bit of a guard up. She was trying to decide how much, if any, information she wanted to divulge when he stood up and said, "I think I had better get into the conference room before all the good seats are taken. I have never been fond of being in the back of the room."

Madelyn found herself playing defense when she was in the middle of making an offensive strategy. She asked if she could join him. While walking into the mini amphitheater, Madelyn was telling Jake how she spent her college years sitting in the front row of every class she could.

Nodding, Jake said, "That was me too, but it has been a few years since I have seen the inside of a classroom." They were able to get a couple of seats in the third row near the center. The convention lasted four days, but only three were scheduled. The last day of the program was a free day where scientists from different disciplines could schedule independent meetings. Many of these informal meetings had been preset, and Jake was invited to one headed by Senator Arthur Birmingham from the state of Washington, who was also a member of the committee for the Nanotechnology Initiative. Senator Birmingham headed the Commerce, Science, and Transportation committee and had a special interest in any cutting-edge technology. He was educated and technical enough to know the right questions to ask and thus well respected in the scientific community.

The meeting the senator was heading dealt with the use of quantum stars for microscopic virtually undetectable beacons for GPS tracking of people, goods, and so forth.

Jake's postgraduate work was in genetics. He was fortunate to have been part of the team working on the final days of the human genome project starting in 2002 through its completion in April 2003. Though a brilliant geneticist, Jake's passion lay in mechanical engineering. His creativity and curiosity were his greatest gifts but also his greatest nemeses when working in pure research. He was driven to create!

The first speaker was a member of the European Union and was set to discuss applications for nanotechnology to exponentially increase computer-processing speeds. He was very dry and spoke with a heavy German accent.

Though he would normally never be rude enough to chitchat during someone's lecture, Jake decided this was an uncommonly hideous lecture, and he was more curious about the girl sitting next to him than he was in what Dr. Von Burg was rambling on about, so he leaned over and said, "Pretty interesting stuff, huh?"

Madelyn covered her mouth not to blurt out with a laugh and jabbed him with an elbow. She decided she felt comfortable with Jake and said, "Let's get out of here." It appeared that half of the once four hundred attendees, including physicists, chemical engineers, microbiologists, geneticists, and politicians, had also been bored with the keynote speaker and had left. They both got up and headed back to the café where they got a cup of coffee and sat down at the same table they had breakfast.

Madelyn asked Jake who he was affiliated with and what brought him to the convention. Jake had spent the past four years working in a top-secret government-funded program at the Los Alamos Laboratory in Texas. Jake's program was a spin-off from Bryant's quantum dot team at Berkeley. The government was interested in technology for tracking people, cargo, and electronic information. Jake was often concerned his energy was being spent in an effort to create some diabolical weapon that could be unleashed on an enemy nation. There was really no evidence suggesting that, but it isn't difficult to imagine such things when you are working on the front lines of scientific discovery. Recently his primary focus had been on the design engineering for the equipment required to manufacture quantum stars and the development of delivery techniques. A jack-of-all-trades—or, what he coined himself, a *Jake-of-all-trades*; he was a hands-on manager. His team included mechanical and chemical engineers, geneticists, software experts, and a promising young physicist specializing in quantum mechanics. This young man was Jake's best friend and confidant. Jake met Lou at a convention in New Orleans two years ago, and they hit it off. Jake hired him a week later.

He answered Madelyn's question the best he could by saying, "I have been working as a manager of a scientific team for the government at Los Alamos Labs in Texas for the past four years. I am educated in genetics but better skilled and more passionate about engineering."

Madelyn was intrigued. She said, "So I gather you can't tell me what you are working on. Are you here with your team?" She smiled that quarter smile again.

"No. In fact, I don't know anyone here at all except Senator Birmingham, who is, in a way, my boss, since he oversees Commerce, Science, and Transportation."

Madelyn jumped in and said, "I received an invitation from the senator to attend a two-hour meeting discussing quantum stars on day four; how funny. I am planning on being there unless I get a better offer."

Jake said, "So do quantum stars have something to do with your personal quest?"

Madelyn knew that was going to come back to bite her. She replied, "No," and left it at that.

Now Jake had a quarter of a smile. He was starting to like this girl. He remembered vaguely that he had heard of her. He asked, "Are you the same Madelyn from up north, who published some articles on coatings? Those were very impressive."

She smiled big and said, "Yes, me. Really? I didn't know anyone read those scientific rags. Thank you!"

Jake said, "That was some pretty ingenious work you did, but it must have been seven, eight years ago; you can't possibly be old enough to have written those articles."

That comment made Madelyn blush. She said, "Thank you again, but I assure you I am old enough to have written those articles. I do look younger than my age, and I suppose most women would be happy about that problem. For me it has always been a detriment. It is hard to get people to take me seriously."

Jake said, "I have the opposite problem; I have always looked much older than I am. I do have to admit, it has helped me in the workplace, but I would trade you for your problem in a flat second."

Madelyn did absolutely nothing to make herself attractive. At twenty-seven years old, she didn't wear makeup, she dressed in loose-fitting comfortable clothes, and her brown hair was straight and pulled back in a ponytail, yet she was extremely beautiful.

Jake, on the other hand, was not so good looking, and he accepted that fact fairly well. At thirty-nine he was still single, but with his work ethic, he had little time to feel lonely. The desk job didn't help his physique, and his super-high intellect made him feel different than most people when in a social environment. His hair was thin and a mess. He really did not do anything to help himself out in the appearance department. However, when in the right circles, he had the ability to be quite charming. Reared by two ex-FTLware execs who received stock options just two years after the hardware giant went public, he was accustomed to the social graces among the affluent.

From the time he laid eyes on her, Jake knew he had no chance of anything but a professional relationship with Madelyn. Madelyn was young but not as young as he had thought. She was beautiful and in good shape. He thought that her attractiveness could be described as *the girl next door with a milkmaid sex appeal.* There was no way she would ever want anything to do with an overweight, balding old man like himself. Oddly, this made him feel at ease.

Madelyn came from a typical middle-class home. Her dad being a hospital tech and her mom a part-time wine steward did not offer her the advantages Jake had in upbringing. She was a daddy's girl. She loved her mom, but they just did not relate to one another. Mom loved to dress fashionably and attend social gatherings. She tried to come off as sophisticated, but in reality she was just another snobby middle-class wannabe. Her dad had a passion for science, math, and astronomy and could care less what other people thought of him. He would spend hours with Madelyn working on home science projects in the basement or in the garage shop, while her mother was upstairs keeping a perfect home and cooking the latest recipes. It was a peaceful life, and everyone was happy.

For the past seven years, Madelyn's mother had been pressuring her to get herself a man. Though Madelyn liked men, she liked her work more. She had been in two serious relationships, but both ended within the first year due to her inability to give her partner enough of her time. It was not like she was unaware of her sexuality; she was reminded continuously by men in their forties and fifties, most of whom were married. Why married men in the prime of their life hit on young women was beyond her comprehension. She had more than once witnessed a middle-aged man have an affair with a girl twenty-five years his younger and watched it destroy his life. She had learned to never lead men on—even those of appropriate age.

She was not interested in the boring presentations that were to follow. She was here for one reason; she needed to make some professional contacts that could assist her in financing or scientific research. She was enjoying the coffee and small talk with Jake. They really seemed to hit it off, and she was surprisingly comfortable for just meeting someone. The connection reminded her of how she felt around Anna. Jake was genuinely interested in her work without the threat or innuendo of romantic intentions or other agendas. This was refreshing to her. Jake himself seemed well connected, and aside from taking pleasure in his company, she felt there may be some real business value in their meeting. He for one was obviously a brilliant scientist with a practical edge, which she really liked, and his parents were executives for the company owned by one of the seven possible financiers identified in her and Anna's research. The trip was starting to feel worthwhile. She silently thanked God for bringing her Jake.

After an hour of chitchat, Jake asked her if she was doing anything for dinner. She tensed up; Jake recognized this immediately and said, "Hey, don't get the wrong idea. I am having dinner with the senator, who is not only my boss but also a good friend of my father. When my dad found out I was attending and Art would also be here, we got roped into getting together."

Madelyn felt a little embarrassed and said, "I am sorry, Jake; you caught me a little off guard; I would love to join you and the senator for dinner. How could I possibly turn down an offer like that?"

They both laughed, and Jake said, "Good, I would love to have a fellow scientist at the table. Marcello's chop house at seven. I can meet you in the lobby at six forty-five, and we can walk over?"

She said, "I wouldn't miss it for the world."

Jake had some calls to make, and Madelyn decided on a run.

After her run and a quick shower, she called Anna.

Anna was very excited about the connection Madelyn had made. She brought her up-to-date with the research her junior associate had compiled on "the big seven" as they were now calling them. All seven seemed to indeed have the assets required, and so far there were no skeletons they had uncovered. Anna said, "We think we can cross Phil Knight off the list. We were able to make contact with the new CEO's secretary, who indicated she still handled some of Mr. Knight's affairs. She had made it clear that there would be no interest for Mr. Knight to get involved in another company; he was adamant that he remained retired for personal reasons."

Anna went on to say, "We did make contact with the CEO for the Gates Foundation, which also feels like a dead end. They are fully committed to Africa. Making direct contact with Bill or Melinda seems impossible. We will continue to try to make some headway with Warren Buffet, who would indeed create an inroad to Bill Gates. There is really nothing else to report at this time. Maybe Jake can somehow get us an appointment with Dane at FTLware."

Madelyn felt like she was really making a difference and was on top of the world. She was excited to meet the senator and had a fleeting thought about the government having a role in the financing but thought better of it. She and Anna had discussed this and decided that if the government was in charge of the project, there would be bias and endless red tape. Both were not something they were interested in dealing with.

Jake was standing in the lobby dressed in slacks and a nice wool silk-blend sports jacket. He wore a simple but expensive black T-shirt and had on a pair of comfortable slip-on patent leather shoes. He looked great. It was amazing how tailored clothes could make a man's extra thirty or forty pounds disappear.

Madelyn looked amazing. She wore a simple summer dress with some nice glittery sandals and had applied a small amount of mascara. She was transformed from beautiful to stunning.

They both noticed each other's appearance but said nothing. Jake escorted her out the door, and as they walked down the street, they started to say something at the same time. Jake prevailed and insisted she go first.

Madelyn humbly said, "I just want to say I am really happy you joined me for breakfast; it's a lot more fun to have someone to hang out with and sure beats sitting in my room."

Jake jumped in with a smirk, "Well, I am glad I could help you out."

Madelyn, embarrassed again, said, "I just can't help but put my foot in my mouth. I have done it all my life. Thank God my family and friends understand; I hope you do?"

Jake just laughed. He then said, "I was going to tell you a little about the senator before you meet him."

"Oh good, go on."

"Arthur Birmingham goes by Art. I call him senator out of respect. He is in his sixties, very handsome, and has been widowed for over ten years now. He has never dated since the passing of his wife and still loves her as if she were among the living. When she was diagnosed with cancer over fifteen years ago, he got very involved in cutting-edge science in an effort to save her life. He has not stopped his pursuit for even a moment since. Right after her death, he was engaged in this R and D effort or that funding committee et cetera…Art is a real down-to-earth nice guy, although he can be very intimidating just because of his position, power, and accomplishments. I believe he really does not see himself the way most of us mere mortals do. He is a scientist by education but has always made his living in politics. He has a bachelor's degree in engineering and a master's in physics. He is no slouch in the scientific community but has never really applied his knowledge in the field. He prefers to evaluate from the outside and keep things moving along if he believes in them."

Madelyn said, "Wow, I can't wait to meet him; he sounds wonderful."

Jake said, "He is. I know you guys will hit it off."

They got to the restaurant and were immediately seated at a nice table near a window.

Senator Birmingham arrived and was very pleased to see Jake. He poured on the charm when greeting Madelyn. She actually blushed. He was everything Jake described and more. His very presence was felt more than seen or heard. Conversation stayed light and revolved mostly around episodes of Jake's parents and the senator's annual vacations. Somehow a bottle of Oregon Pinot Noir landed on the table, and glasses were poured.

The food was outstanding, and Madelyn finished her entire plate. Listening to the stories of Jake's family, she started to believe they were millionaires many times over. Jake was embarrassed about his family's fortune and shifted the conversation over to Madelyn's recent accomplishment with polymer coatings.

The senator replied, "I didn't know you were on Bryant's team; congratulations! That is a key step in allowing the technology to develop into applications for health care and...hmmm." He then waived the waiter over and asked for another bottle of wine.

He went on, "So if you are on Bryant's team, I invited you to attend my day-four conference; is that right?"

Madelyn shook her head and said, "Yes, and I plan on attending."

He then asked the question she was most wishing he would not: "What were you hoping to get out of this conference? Do you have a particular mission? I know Jake is here because I insisted that his director make him come. His team hit an obstacle, and I thought Jake might find someone here to help out. How about you? Is there anything you specifically came for?"

"Well," she said, "I am working on a project, and I was hoping to make some contacts that could help it along."

This sparked the senator's interest, and he leaned in, indicating he wanted more.

Jake said while looking directly at Madelyn, "I have spent a good part of the day with you, and I have not asked her that question yet; I just assumed your boss made you come?"

Now feeling completely on the spot, she straightened her posture and said, "For me to give you much more than that, I would need you to sign a confidentiality agreement. I am afraid that at this early juncture in our undertaking, my attorney might insist on why the need to know before we could move forward."

Madelyn immediately felt ridiculous. Here she was, some twenty-seven-year-old kid who looked nineteen telling a senator of the United States that he would have to sign a confidentiality agreement for me to talk to him about her work.

If the senator and Jake were interested to know what she was up to before, they certainly were now.

Senator Birmingham was a little taken aback; not offended but caught off guard. He thought carefully and said, "I can appreciate that. We get together at these cutting-edge conventions and expect to be able to share. Unfortunately the world we live in does not allow that, does it?"

He looked at Madelyn and said, "Can you imagine a world where there were no secrets? We could all willingly and freely collaborate without there being fear of serious financial repercussions or credit being misappropriated or, worse yet, a technology being put in the wrong hands. I guess until we no longer need money, and we completely rid the world off evil, that world will never exist."

The curiosity was killing Jake. He decided he was going to ask her for one of those confidentiality agreements once they were alone.

Madelyn was impressed by the depth and insight of the senator. He truly was a classy guy. So many people in that situation would have either puffed up or made some lousy joke of it.

They parted, and the senator made a point of reminding them about the meeting on day four.

On their walk back to the hotel, Jake asked Madelyn if he really needed a confidentiality agreement or if that was a ploy to avoid telling the senator what she was working on.

She replied, "I wasn't kidding around about that. If I am going to tell anyone about my project, they will need to sign the agreement. I also was not kidding when I said the reason I am here is to meet people who can help me. To be blunt, I think you might actually be one of those people. Not only are you well educated and experienced in genetics and engineering but you also have some connections to a possible source of funding that we will need."

Jake was smiling. "*We*—I like the sound of that! Seriously, I am very interested, and if you have gone to the trouble of hiring an attorney, it must be big."

With a huge smile, she said, "Oh, it is big."

The next two days flew by. After long discussions with Anna, Madelyn had convinced her to allow Jake to sign the confidentiality agreement and get the preliminary overview of the project. Jake was the perfect complement to Madelyn. Her strengths in software and biology and his in engineering, physics, and understanding of genetics were the perfect combination to conquer the major scientific obstacles they were embarking on. She knew, and Anna reminded her over and over that she had just met him and didn't really know him. But Madelyn, like a girl with a major crush, couldn't see a future without Jake in it. She was not thinking about a romantic future but a professional one. It was destiny, and Madelyn truly believed God had sent her Jake. Anna agreed to do a quick background check before she would send over the agreement.

Late in the afternoon on day three of the convention, Jake signed the twenty-eight-page confidentiality agreement. It basically stated that if her technology, or any form of it, was ever to be developed as a result of the information provided, she would have all monetary rights and the ability to step in and have control of the entity or corporation pursuing the technology.

Once he signed the document in front of the hotel's notary, it was placed in Madelyn's safe, and a copy was sent via Fed Ex priority one overnight to Anna. They arranged for a small conference room with the hotel and ordered pizza delivery.

Madelyn had only known Jake for three days but felt a kinship for him in a way it takes years to develop in most cases. She trusted her gut. It had never let her down before.

Prior to the pizza arriving, Madelyn explained to Jake that she had developed a method to remotely program an array of cadmium-based quantum stars using microscopic laser pulses. She wanted that to sink in. In her own way, she was testing Jake to see if he could connect the dots.

Jake did not disappoint. He said, "Soooo, if you could find a way to stick one of those stars on a nano machine, you could basically tell it what to do?" As Jake was forming the sentence in his mind, he was starting to envision the possibilities of such a breakthrough. His mind was processing at abnormal speed. He was having a true revelation.

Madelyn recognized the state Jake was in. It is what scientists live for. It is more powerful than any drug and more addicting too. She let a few moments pass so as not to wreck the moment for him, and then impulsively in her excitement, she got up and hugged him. After the hug she grabbed him by the shoulders and said, "Pretty cool, huh!"

Jake was blown away. He said, "Think that might be the understatement of the year."

Madelyn sat back down and spread some papers out on the table. She was explaining she had a PowerPoint presentation for investors, but she wanted to just dive in to some of the technical stuff with Jake instead of the dog-and-pony show. He was in complete agreement with her.

She started with, "Let's start with the obvious. If we can talk to the nano world and give it directions, we can build molecular machines that can repair or rejuvenate human cells. Utilizing existing imaging techniques combined with nano imaging and nano programming, we can inject millions of molecular machines into the human body and put them to work!"

Jake's first verbal response was, "Why haven't you discussed this with the folks up at Berkeley?"

Madelyn's response was very decisive. "I do not trust them!"

Jake said, "OK, I get that."

Jakes mind was methodical and was in the process of digesting this breakthrough. He needed to evaluate this step by step. It was just the way his mind worked. He had no reason to disbelieve her. She was, in fact, a published and accomplished scientist. She was young and too naïve to have hidden agendas. There was one thing that he felt sure of and that was that the government was the wrong place to seek funding. He had firsthand experience with that environment.

Working for a government-funded program, he was well aware of what motivated the politicians in charge: power, money, and then power…in that order. Money by itself created a certain amount of power. Power, however, was predominately achieved by human relationships. Those who had an opportunity to gain from your success bestowed power on you. The United States was considered, hands down, the most powerful nation in the world. The measure: military force and economic strength, in that order. It all trickles down from there.

Jake could imagine Madelyn's dream turning into a nightmare. He could see the technology being used in a plethora of different avenues—avenues not the same as hers. The project would be classified at the highest security levels, and she would end up reporting to someone who reported to who knows who and what agency. He was relieved to find out that Madelyn had no intentions of approaching the government for funding.

Madelyn smiled and said, "I could probably leave the room, and you would not take notice." She said with some obvious sarcasm.

Jake laughed. "A lot to take in here. When you said it was big, you were not kidding. I am beside myself. I don't want to sound fatherly, but you need to be careful who you bring in on this." Why this was his first concern he didn't know.

The pizza arrived and was put on the table next to Madelyn's papers. Jake scooted over to look at Madelyn's work, which she spent the next hour skimming over the highlights. There was obviously years and years of work there.

She went through the process. The preliminary equipment designs were amazing. Jake was just beginning to get a glimpse of how brilliant Madelyn really was.

She explained that the first machine needed to assemble was the nanobot. Each nanobot was designed to do a specific task. Some were made to emulsify a targeted cell or cells. This type of nanobot could help eliminate cancer or vascular problems due to fat build-up. Some were designed to add cellular material to a damaged cell, which could be useful in repairing broken bones, spinal injuries, repairing DNA strands, and so forth. And then there was Madelyn's favorite, the *garbage-bot*, which was critical in removing unwanted material from the body at the end of the procedure.

Just when Jake was compiling his list of questions, she moved on to the second machine that generated the quantum star and embedded it into a nanobot. It then coated the entire microscopic machine in a carbon-based polymer. She then explained how the fully assembled nanobots would be used on a patient. The patient would undergo some imaging (CT or MRI) and have a DNA test performed to evaluate the specific gene sequences of the patient in order to generate a custom program to inculcate the nanobots. The program would identify the actual number of each type of nanobots needed for the procedure and interface with the two machines that would build them.

Jake quickly interrupted, "So if I get this right, a patient would get a CT or MRI, a swab in the cheek, maybe some blood drawn, and the data would be fed into the machines that would generate microscopic nanobots that would be injected into the patient and fix whatever is wrong with them?"

Madelyn said in a drawn-out voice, "Baaaasically, yes! What do you think?"

Jake said, "What do I think? What do I think? It is beyond brilliant. It is going to change the world." He leaned in to her and said, "This is probably the most profound scientific discovery in history."

Jake was just shaking his head and babbling about something. Madelyn laughed and punched him in the shoulder. She said, "There is one more thing."

Jake said, "More?"

She continued, "I think we can use the technology to extend life. Obviously if we cured most disease, cancer, and were able to repair damage from unhealthy living or physical injury, we will consequently extend the average life-span tables significantly. Beyond that, I think we can rejuvenate the cellular structure and substantially slow the aging process down. As you know every seven years all the cells in our body are replaced, except the cells in our nervous system. I believe that we can turn the clock back by about five of those seven years by repairing the genes responsible for cellular replication. If a patient were to undergo this process starting at full maturity, plus seven years (typically twenty-eight years of age), and were to repeat the process every seven years, they would only age two years every seven."

Jake was trying to do the math when Madelyn said, "Two hundred years, and if this works, it will only get further refined, and likely we may conquer aging altogether."

Jake was shaken. He said, "Oh boy, not sure I want to live forever."

Madelyn said with a soft smile, "Fortunately you won't have to make that choice. The only choice you will be making is whether to take a few years off your life with a simple inexpensive completely safe procedure." She handed him a cold piece of pizza, and they ate in silence.

8

Karl spent his first year at the Census Bureau engrossed in forecasting models that his boss, Steve Ryan, had spent the last fifteen years of his life developing. The intricacies and elegance of Steve's mind never ceased to marvel Karl. The pure amount of data, and the speed in which it could be manipulated, was astounding. The programs not only predicted future populations by region with precise measure but also extrapolated the microeconomic banking needs, natural resource requirements, energy consumption, food-supply requirements, transportation requirements, and so forth to support a region. Every factor that could have an impact was continuously being downloaded into the program, altering and fine-tuning possible outcomes. Human psychology and behavior were integral quantifications within the program. Forecasting human migratory patterns based on weather, natural resources, employment, political climate, recreational opportunities, education centers, and many other social and economic factors were just a few of the dynamics the software considered.

This data wasn't readily available to the state, let alone the public. The federal government knew that this information, if released, could actually change the natural course of events, which could then make the program incapable of maintaining its accuracy and ultimately make it useless. As an example, let's say that a new technology that required freshwater to generate hydrogen efficiently was the key to powering a future automobile factory; would it make sense to retool the Detroit factories for production? Likely not. Perhaps multiple smaller factories built near some of the United States 909 major freshwater lakes would be more cost-effective. This information, if spun by our media, could cause a chain of events that could create havoc and ultimately get the cart in front of the horse. If the horse is pushing the cart, the cart will inevitably go offtrack and crash.

The data and the programs were top secret. Very few government officials in the higher echelons even knew about the programs, and fewer had access to them. If our government is considering using military force, many scenarios can be downloaded into the program and then forecast the short- and long-term economic impact here and abroad. If our government was considering borrowing billions of dollars from China or Saudi Arabia, the program could be very useful in determining the long-term implications of such a debt. Karl found himself deeper and deeper into a world unfamiliar to any average citizen.

Though Karl never felt he was in the spotlight, he sometimes revered himself as one of the keepers of some great power like a character in one of the video games he had spent too many hours playing in his youth. He had let his hair grow and continued to work out regularly. He fantasized he was "Conan, the keeper of the future." He knew that the most powerful people on the planet would love to have access to this forecasting software. He feared he could be caught in some crossfire someday. When his mind went in that direction, he quickly changed his train of thought. Usually back to the math.

Despite all this hugger-mugger, Karl's life was normal as it could be for someone who spent most of his time deep in mathematical modeling. He and Steve had turned out be great friends, and Steve's love for life and passion for living brought the math and secretive nature of working for the government down to a level where Karl could function.

Karl and Heather had become an item again. The relationship had grown but not much past where it was back in undergrad school. This was not because there was a lack of potential but more because they could spend so little time together. They each worked eighty-hour weeks and were driven by their occupations. When they were together, all they talked about was work. Each was genuinely interested in what the other was doing. Karl, of course, had to be a bit more discreet with some of the details of his job, but nevertheless he was able to entertain Heather with a few nonconfidential details. In the back of their minds, they understood there would be time for a personal life later.

Steve, a self-proclaimed bachelor by choice, never felt he had time for any kind of serious relationship. Whenever he did share some chemistry with a woman, his work would eventually ruin anything good that once existed between them. He, Karl, and Heather would occasionally go fishing on Steve's boat or meet for dinner and drinks at a number of the great restaurants on the Sound. The three of them had a lot in common, and they always had a good time socializing together. Every once in a while, Karl and Heather would go on a date by themselves. They always felt like they were doing something wrong by not including Steve.

Karl and Heather were busy planning for a two-day social visit with Karl's friend Jim Mankin and his fiancée, Beverly Bransom. Jim had just finished his third year of law school at Yale. He had recently proposed marriage to Beverly and was taking a quick trip to the West Coast to introduce her to his family in California. The last two days of his trip was scheduled in Washington State to visit with Karl and Heather.

Karl couldn't remember the last time he had two days off from work. He and Heather planned to take Jim and Beverly to their favorite dinner house on the water and invited Steve to come along. The next day Karl and Jim had a tee-time at the West Seattle Golf Club, while the girls would spend some time shopping in Seattle. Karl planned to burn some steaks and eat in on Saturday night. Sunday was kept wide open.

Jim and Bev arrived a little early. Flights were on time, and traffic was surprisingly light. Fortunately Heather was already home doing some last-minute straightening up when they got there. This was a nice opportunity for Bev and Heather to get acquainted before they went to the restaurant.

Dinner was perfect; everyone unwound and relaxed. They had the ideal terrace table for five, overlooking the sound. It wasn't raining, but the night air in Seattle in June is a bit chilly. The waiter situated three gas patio heaters near their table, so it was very comfortable. Steve insisted on ordering and paying for the wine, which really was not such a bad thing. He must have spent over $500 on the four bottles ordered. They started with a wonderful California Chardonnay from Cuvison Winery in Sonoma County and finished with probably the best wine of the evening, a 2012 Leonette Reserve Cab from Walla Walla Washington.

Heather and Bev really hit it off. This put Karl and Jim at ease; their friendship was going to last a lifetime, and it would be a shame if their partners didn't get along. Heather, involved with monitoring economic growth on the West Coast for the Department of Commerce, and Bev, in her first year working as an activist for the Electronic Frontier Foundation (EFF), made for some interesting conversation.

The EFF works to insure that cutting-edge legal issues in the digital world maintained free speech, preserving the Internet's open architecture, innovation, intellectual property, international issues, privacy, and transparency. Because of this, Heather was given stern advice from both Steve and Karl not to discuss what Karl's work was really about. As far as Jim and Bev were concerned, Karl and Steve just maintained the huge databases managed by the Census Bureau—tedious boring work only math or IT geeks could possibly enjoy.

Bev was impressed by the detail, scrutiny, and resources dedicated by the agencies of both the Commerce Department and the Census Bureau to insure accurate and updated information. And, more importantly, this information was freely being disseminated to the public. Perfect examples of what the EFF was fighting for.

Jim explained how he was taking up residence in Arlington, Virginia. He would also have a small one-bedroom apartment in DC now that he was working full time for his father's DC branch office. The Arlington residence would serve two purposes; it would give him a nice place to spend his weekends away from the office and give him a Virginia address so he could eventually run for a seat in the House of Representatives. Karl was amazed at how Jim's boyhood life plan was so on track. Everything Jim set out for was coming together according to plan.

Karl paid for the dinner, and Steve picked up the tab for the wine. They were all a little buzzed, so Karl called a cab for a ride home. Steve passed on the cab ride, since he was close enough to walk.

The morning came fast. Karl and Jim had a 10:30 a.m. tee time, and the girls took forever getting ready. With clubs loaded, they dropped Heather and Bev off at the car they left at the dinner-house just in time to get to the course on time. Karl hated being rushed, especially rushed to get to a tee time. He was a little irritable on the highway and broke a few speed limits.

Once they pulled in, and they were not in fact late, he relaxed a bit. The weather was absolutely beautiful, one of those rare sunny days in June. The air was crisp, but it was warm enough to wear shorts. Karl was very excited to play this course. Neither he nor Jim were good golfers, but they had played enough to hold their own on most muni courses. It was the ad on the Internet that captivated Karl and made him choose West Seattle Golf Club. He had copied the ad, and he and Jim were reading it while waiting to tee off. The ad read thus:

> "*We'd all love to play empty golf courses with pristine greens and unblemished fairways, but not all of us are dot com millionaires. The Mizuno-blade and Pro-V1 crowd should look elsewhere for their highfalutin brethren—this is a course for the proletariat; for those happy to shoot in the nineties; for those craving tallboys and hotdogs at the turn. West Seattle is the best of the three Seattle municipals. Measuring in at 6,700 yards from the tips and boasting unparalleled views of the Seattle skyline, there's really no argument disputing its superiority. The signature #12 is case and point. An aspiring sports cameraman would do well to start here; the elevated tee-box looks across a sharp, lateral valley to the green looming precipitously atop the other side. The tranquil Sound and downtown cityscape provide backdrop, while large cranes in the foreground frame the southern edge of the picturesque mise en scène. A proper tee shot is to drive the ball just north of the Columbia Tower—how sweet is that?*
>
> *H. Chandler Egan designed the course, the acclaimed player and architect also responsible for the most recent Pebble Beach*

redesign. So you pick—Pebble for $550 or West Seattle for $55. Happily, the course isn't as prone to overcrowding as the more centrally located options, though a Saturday round on a nice day will still easily take five hours. Call the clubhouse, make a tee-time and show up ready for some public golf at its finest."

They were right on. It took exactly five hours and five minutes to get around the course. Both Jim and Karl enjoyed the round; they were paired with two college-age men, who were very polite and had great golf-course etiquette. Though there was a lot of waiting at the tee boxes, the time was useful. The college kids played the course regularly and were able to discuss each hole in detail before Jim and Karl played it.

It was 4:00 p.m. in the afternoon, and while having a draft beer in the clubhouse, Karl called Heather to see what the evening schedule looked like. Heather and Bev were driving back to Karl's apartment with a successful bounty from their shopping extravaganza. Heather told Karl that they had to make a quick stop at her office before heading home. Bev was interested in a tour.

After dinner, sipping some wine, Bev asked if she could take a tour of Karl's office the next day. Karl immediately felt uneasy. He could take guests into the main offices of the Census Bureau Branch, but he could not take guests into the area in which he worked. A person needed high-level government clearance to enter the area Karl worked. He knew Bev and Jim would want to see where he worked. Before he could say anything, Heather said she had never seen Karl's workplace; it was "top secret," and you needed special clearances to get within fifty yards of Karl's office. Karl was biting his lip. He did not want to arouse the curiosity of an EFF activist. Karl immediately downplayed the whole thing by saying that it wasn't high-level clearance but that it did take a background check, and things like that, to gain access. Heather started to blurt something out, but Karl put up his glass and gave her a quick stare; Heather got the message and, sobering up a bit, realized the position she had put Karl in.

Bev was already curious. She asked Karl why the Census Bureau offices would be classified; after all, the information gathered was accessible to the public, so why the strict privacy? Karl explained that the databases and computers used to manage the information were all offline 99.9 percent of the time to insure data integrity and reduce the chances of hackers infecting the data. He also explained that there was some proprietary hardware fail-safes that needed to be in place in order to reduce infiltration. Bev seemed to buy the explanation, but she was still slightly aroused.

Karl asked Bev a question to turn things around. He asked, "How can we fight for free open architecture and full access to all information when there are evil people out there who will either obliterate data for fun or manipulate data for misinformation or use the data for evil purposes?"

Jim piped with a wink in Karl's direction and said, "Hey, buddy, be easy on my soon-to-be wife." He knew this would score points with Bev and hopefully stop the train wreck that was inevitable. Bev was passionate about her new job, and she had already drunk the Kool-Aid.

Karl got the picture and looked at Bev and, with his best Clark Gable imitation, said, "I meant no harm, darling."

Everyone laughed.

9

After what ended up being a lively discussion on the possible uses of quantum stars during the two-hour meeting headed by Senator Birmingham on day four of the convention, Jake and Madelyn found themselves again alone with the senator. They chatted about the meeting for a bit and then Jake, out of courtesy, offered to take everyone to lunch. The senator gracefully declined due to a plane that was waiting for him. He was headed back to his home in Washington State for a three-day getaway before he went back to DC. The Senate was in session, and there were a number of bills he needed to vote on.

Madelyn said, “I will take you up on that offer; my plane doesn’t depart for six hours.”

Jake said, “Great, how does Mexican sound?”

“Perfect!” she replied.

During lunch Madelyn brought up their need for funding. She was nonchalant and posed the problem as though Jake was a partner in the project. She said, “Where do you think we can get the necessary funding for the project?”

Jake said, “I remember you saying that one of your reasons for coming to the convention was to make some connections for that purpose. After seeing what you showed me yesterday, I would think you would have people beating down the doors to be involved.”

She explained that they had already approached multiple reputable venture-capital firms, and they all turned her down.

The look of shock on Jake's face was genuine. He said, "You're kidding; really?"

"Yep, it's true. This may seem silly, but after being turned down by the VC, we made a list of the top twenty richest people in America and have narrowed it down to seven possible candidates to approach. Our thinking is that if someone could spend less than one percent or their net worth on a speculative venture with literally unlimited financial potential, they might actually choose to take the risk. The other thought regarding this approach is that these people already have the power money provides and a track record for us to evaluate them as possible partners. We know that if this technology works the way we anticipate it to, the top line will be greater than most countries' GDP, possibly greater than the United States' GDP. We want to know who we are getting into bed with. That kind of money and power in the wrong hands could be catastrophic. Your parents happen to have worked for one of our top seven possible investors."

Jake said, "You know my parents have a pretty good lump-sum stashed themselves. I love them, trust them, and would not have any reservation going into business with them. Dane and Solana over at FTL are also wonderful people. I have not seen them in years, but when I was a youngster, there were more than a few family vacations and get-togethers with the Lindseys. In fact, the senator and his wife were part of that group as well. Dane and the senator go way back. Do you want me to talk with my parents? Of course they would first sign that book of a document your attorney drafted up."

Madelyn was getting excited. How lucky was she to run into Jake and hit it off with him so quickly. She tipped her mind to the sky and thanked God. She said, "We need a lot of money if my calculations are right, which, by the way, they usually are."

Jake said, "Let me guess; we need to build proto-type equipment for nanobot assembly and quantum-star generation and embedding and coating." And then with his best sincere look, he said, "By the way, my engineering skills could be very useful for that." He went on, "We need at least one high-end piece of imaging equipment, a gene sequencer, a pile of computing equipment, a staff of technicians, and a lab. How am I doing so far?"

She said, "I think you have covered the basics."

He was doing some addition in his head and said, "Twenty to thirty million dollars should do it?"

Madelyn brought out her phone and pulled up a memo page with the breakdown and showed it to Jake.

He said, "I am off ten x? You really think we will need two hundred fifty million dollars? That's a quarter of a billion dollars."

She said, "I have been through it a hundred times. That is what we need." She was smiling inside because Jake was now saying *we* as well. She really liked him and had already decided he will be her right hand in the lab. He just didn't know it yet.

He said in slight disappointment, "Well, you can count my parents out; they don't have near that kind of jingle."

Madelyn with the most encouraging expression she could muster and said, "Maybe you can get us an appointment with Dane?"

He said light-heartedly, "It will cost you."

She said, "Oh really, Jake, and what might it cost me?"

He said squeamishly, "I want to be part of your…teeeam?" He bowed his head to portray he knew he was not worthy.

Madelyn put her index finger to her chin and said, "Hmmmm…maybe I can arrange that."

They hugged for the second time. Neither felt any sexual tension. The journey they were about to embark on was more stimulating and overshadowing than sex. They were scientists about to make history and change the world in a way unimaginable at this early stage.

That evening Jake went back to Texas, and Madelyn went back to California. It was probably one of the most incredible four days in Jake's life. Stepping on the plane for his return flight, he was already feeling separation anxiety from Madelyn.

The first thing Madelyn did when she got home was call Anna and fill her in on all the details of her trip, including everything about Jake and the senator and the possible meeting with Dane. Anna was so pleased that she had made some inroads. She brought Madelyn up to speed on her work to get meetings with the top seven, which was really now down to the top four.

Buffet and Gates have built what seem to be impermeable walls around themselves. Phil Knight of Nike is apparently not interested in taking on new projects at all right now; that leaves Dane of FTLware, Larry with Oracle, Sergey with Google, and Jeff with Amazon.

Anna had hired a top private investigator to do cursory checks on the top seven. Anna reported that all four of the remaining gentlemen and their wives and children passed Anna's ethics background check. They all had very high standards for their respective organizations, they were very generous in giving back to the community, none had been involved in anything scandalous, and they overall had no apparent skeletons in hiding. They were all cutting-edge technology firms in their own right. They would all be excellent fits.

Madelyn said, "Sounds like we are making some progress. I will let you know as soon as I hear from Jake."

When Jake got home, his first task was to call his dad.

Their relationship was good, though they had very little in common. They both respected the blood tie and had a true sense of family when it mattered most. Growing up, both Jake's parents were workaholics. FTLware was on the map, but it wasn't the giant it is today. Mom and Dad were both involved in the development and bundling of FTLware Internet Port that allowed data to move wirelessly, affordably and securely with speeds approaching the speed of light. This caused quite the hoopla among the competition, specifically the phone, cable companies, and switch/router hardware manufactures. Domestic and International lawsuits were pursuant. FTLware prevailed; how can you argue with giving the consumer what they want? Major technological leaps are always disruptive to industry. Jake was thinking how disruptive Madelyn's technology was going to be, and he shuddered.

Jake dialed the phone. His palms were sweating. "Hi, Dad, thanks for hooking me up with Art. We had a nice chat and a great dinner."

"Hi, son, glad to hear it. To what do I owe the pleasure? It can't just be about Art?"

"I need a favor."

"Ah; what can I do for you—anything reasonable, of course?"

"I need a two-hour meeting with Dane."

"You mean Dane Lindsey—founder of FTLware Dane?"

"Yes."

The phone remained silent for what seemed to be an eternity for Jake.

His dad then said, "It must be important. Can I tell him what it is about?"

"Just tell him if he thought the PC and the Internet changed the world; he might have the opportunity to help do something even bigger and more profound."

"Son, you know I love you, but Dane is a very difficult man to arrange a meeting with, let alone a two-hour meeting."

"Dad, this is really important; I would not dream of wasting his time. I have run across something truly extraordinary. Besides that, I am confident he will want to hear what I have to tell him. Oh, I almost forgot—he should have whoever is running the Dane and Solana Lindsey Foundation present as well."

"Can the order get any taller, son? Would you like our sitting president to be there as well?" He laughed. "This must be important. Let me see what I can do, but on one condition. If I get this meeting for you, you have to tell me what this all about afterward, OK?"

Jake got his curiosity from his dad. He replied, "I will be happy to do so after you a sign twenty-three page legal document," And then he laughed and said, "Let me know when and where the meeting will be and I will be there. Oh, I will be accompanied by a young scientist and her attorney. I really appreciate it dad. Neither you nor Dane will be sorry for the inconvenience; I promise."

After a week of long phone calls and massive data transfers, Jake began to understand how remarkable Madelyn's mind worked. Her formulas and biochemical constructs were brilliant. Where did she find the time at twenty-seven? Beyond the actual nanotechnology, she had roughed out ideas for the capital to produce the quantum stars, the nano machines, and the communication interface equipment. There were rough diagrams of complex components, software concepts, and the list goes on...... Jake was astounded at the level of detail Madelyn had achieved. It was an absolute wonder not one of the venture-capital firms didn't jump all over this.

Jake had enough information to feel justified in asking for a quarter of a billion dollars.

His phone chirped some hideous text-notification sound the cellular company had preprogramed into his new phone. He hated it and had been meaning to change it since he got the phone. He was startled as usual when receiving a text due the dreadful chirping sound. He was more startled when he saw it was from his dad. His dad had never texted him before. He thought the old man must be learning new tricks. He opened the message, and it simply said, "Next Tuesday May 21st Dane's home 10:30 a.m."

Jake immediately called Madelyn, who immediately called Anna.

Dane and his wife, Solana, lived in Washington State near Jake's old stomping grounds. Flights were scheduled, hotel rooms booked, and a dinner date was made for the Monday evening before the meeting. They were all very excited.

Jake and Anna hit it off very well. She was eight years older than Jake, and Madelyn was eleven years his junior, putting him in a unique position to relate to both women. They were beautiful, successful, and intelligent. He could hardly believe he was in such company. He thought to himself, *This sure beats having a hamburger with my buddy Lou back in Los Alamos.*

They all hit the sack early. Just because of really good marketing, they stayed at a Holiday Inn Express, each with their own room to make it more convenient in the morning for the girls. The plan was coffee in the lobby at 8:30 a.m. and then hit the road no later than 9:00 a.m. Dane's home was located about one hour northeast of Redmond in a rural area above Duvall on the Snoqualmie River.

The drive was gorgeous. They pulled up to the large gate in front of Dane and Solana Lindsey's home fifteen minutes early.

After a few minutes looking around for a buzzer or something to press to announce their arrival, the gates just opened. Jake thought they must have some pretty sophisticated surveillance equipment, but if it were there, it was not visible.

The winding black cobblestone drive through forested grounds was lined with rhododendrons and azaleas. Jake commented on how beautiful this must have been a month ago when they were all in bloom. There were some partially hidden clearings with large solar arrays and a smattering of satellite dishes all pointing south. Jake wondered if the residence was off grid. At the end of the drive, they arrived at the impressive red cobblestone landing. In European style, the landing met the structure of the old-world stone siding of the home. There were large pots with mature ornamental trees, Italian cypresses, and large shrubs adjacent to the home. The wide stone steps shaped in a half circle encircled a striking raised front entrance made of polished black stone leading to the twelve-foot-tall wooden arched doors.

Some large modern windmills could be seen from this vantage point further suggesting that they were off grid.

When they parked, they were met by two obviously fit men dressed in casual slacks and tight designer T-shirts. They opened the doors for Anna and Madelyn. Jake opened his own door fumbling around with his briefcase and laptop as he attempted to introduce himself. Madelyn was getting a kick out of Jake's nervousness. It reminded her of herself when she was about to meet Senator Birmingham. Now she was feeling quite calm and confident, and Jake was the one sweating. Madelyn had been working with Anna from the start, and she felt at ease whenever Anna was in her company. Perhaps having Anna at her side made her feel more organized and collected.

One of the men addressed the group stating that Dane and Solana were expecting them and asked them to please come in. They walked into the large starkly decorated foyer where they were then directed into a small but nicely appointed room open to the foyer where they were instructed to wait. All three remained standing.

Jake said to Madelyn, "Now remember, do not be shy. It's important you—"

Madelyn interrupted by raising her hand, smiling she said, "Jake, I know, I feel great, don't worry."

Dane had agreed to take the meeting with Jake as a favor to his old friend. When Jake's father called and asked to have the meeting set up with the foundation personnel present, he thought perhaps Jake was working on some charitable cause and wanted a donation. After thinking through this a little more, he remembered that Jake worked at the Los Alamos Government Lab. So he thought, *What would an accomplished physicist working in a government lab want with charitable funds?*

A couple of days before the meeting, his curiosity got the better of him, and he called his friend Senator Arthur Birmingham. The senator oversaw to the goings-on at the lab Jake worked in. He hated walking into a meeting without specific knowledge of what was going to be discussed. He knew that the senator was close to Jake's father and knew Jake personally. After typical pleasantries Dane dove right into the reason for his call.

"Hi, Art; Dane here. One of your science managers, Jake Dawson, at Alamos is asking me for an audience with the head of my charity foundation present. Thought you might have some insight on why or what this is all about?"

He was surprised by the senator's reply. "Is Madelyn Cooper going to be accompanying him?"

This brought a new level of inquisitiveness to the purpose of the meeting. He said, "As a matter of fact, yes, she is."

The senator said, "I am pressed for time right now, so I can't explain. Take the meeting, and if the price tag is too big, I will get you the funds you need." He then hung up. Dane was tempted to call Jake directly but decided to wait it out.

Now two days later, Solana walked into the foyer and immediately gave Jake a big hug, introduced herself to Madelyn and Anna, and escorted them into an elaborate living area with seating for at least twenty. Other than Dane there were five other individuals in attendance; three men and two women. They were all dressed casually. Dane introduced them to Victoria, the chief operating officer of the Lindsey Foundation.

Victoria then introduced the rest of the group. "These are my three top foundation managers, Dwaine, science advisor; Kathy, international lawyer; Ryan, lobbyist; and her personal assistant, administrative wizard and right hand, Drew."

After the appropriate pleasantries were exchanged, Solana brought order to the room by saying, "Well Jake and Madelyn.... how can we help the scientists of the world today?"

Madelyn addressed the group with exceptional poise, expressing her deepest gratitude for the foundation board taking the time to meet with them. She then turned to Anna and nodded. Anna, being the consummate professional she is, explained that before they could proceed, the group would need to individually sign the now ridiculously thick confidentiality agreement. They all agreed that Anna and Kathy should sidebar and while they were reviewing the document, lunch would be provided.

During the course of the next forty-five minutes, the group enjoyed an exquisite breast of duck sandwich and cucumber salad. The discussions mostly centered on Jake's parents and the rehashing of vacations they had gone on when Jake was still in high school.

Anna and Kathy emerged from the nearby library chatting with each other as they walked in. Kathy addressed the group and briefed them on the document she was requesting that they sign. In layman words any discussion of what was about to be presented was prohibited outside of the group in attendance. Any use of the information to pursue the technology was prohibited. Any attempt to sell the information presented was prohibited and so on. After the six foundation members signed the agreement, Madelyn asked Jake to give the group a summary of the technology and the cost to pursue it.

Jake, without hesitation, said, "No way; this is your baby, and I will not take the limelight away from you." He winked at her, and she smiled.

The next couple of hours seemed to pass in a flash. Dane had most of the questions. He was completely taken aback by the thoroughness of Madelyn's proposal. He was more taken aback by the implications that the technology would have on the world as a whole. Things would never be the same. He kept thinking that if it had not been for the insistence of the senator, he would not have taken this meeting seriously.

By the end of the meeting, he was convinced that the technology would work. Now the only real question was, what to name their new company?

Genanotech, a small start-up research laboratory in Vancouver, Washington, was founded in 2019 by Madelyn Cooper and Jake Dawson with funding from the Lindsey Foundation.

10

The year is 2020, and Dane Lindsey's personal assistant informed him that she had Senator Arthur Birmingham on the line. Dane took the call. The senator was calling to check on the progress in the Vancouver Washington Lab. What Jake and Madelyn didn't know was that the Lindsey Foundation was receiving the majority of their funding from the Commerce, Science, and Transportation Committee headed by Senator Birmingham. The Lindsey Foundation put up the first twenty-five million dollars, and the government had ponied up seventy-five million to date. It was informally agreed upon that the next one hundred million would come from the government, and the balance of fifty million would come from Dane. Though this arrangement was covert and less than half a dozen people on the planet even knew about it, it was not a dark scheme.

The deal the senator and Dane made was that the government would help foot the bill for the initial research to develop the technology, and once fully developed, the Lindsey Foundation would take the technology to the general public. The company would not owe the government anything. The money was now being used for its intended purpose: research and development. If the company was successful, the government would receive more than enough in corporate taxes to make their investment pay off.

The only ethic broken was Anna Kim's confidentiality agreement and more so being less than truthful with Madelyn and Jake.

Dane rationalized disregarding the fine print in the confidentiality agreement because he never even eluded to the senator any of the details of the technology. Arthur and Dane went way back, and there was almost a psychic bond between them. Dane knew that if he had asked Arthur for help for new technology research that Arthur would know it was for something big. Dane was a bit surprised at how easily it was to gain Arthur's support. He decided not to look a gift horse in the mouth. Because the Lindsey Foundation was so involved with helping third-world countries, the Federal infusion of cash could easily be explained in an audit.

What Dane didn't know was that the senator had personally met Madelyn. He knew the senator was aware Jake was one of the brightest and most capable "hands-on" scientific managers with exceptional mechanical skills. He knew the senator had done his research on Madelyn and knew that her focus and specialty was in quantum level coatings, the key to make nano machines capable of existing in the human body. Based on his insights, he believed the senator was aware of the main thrust of what the technology was but did not know the specifics.

Dane answered, "Hi, Arthur, good to hear from you."

"You too, Dane."

"How can I help you, Arthur? Do you need some more money for your reelection campaign?" He then chuckled a bit.

Arthur said, "No, Dane, but thank you anyway; I was just calling to see how things were shaping up down in Vancouver, Washington."

Dane said, "We are halfway there and slightly ahead of schedule."

Arthur responded, "I guess that is great news! I know you will let me know when there is something I need to know or if you need my help to move things along. I have been getting a little grief from some members of congress who are not on my committee. There have been a few inquiries regarding the allocation of unaccounted-for funds. There is a reporter who is poking around, and some congressmen are taking interest."

He took a breath and said, "I think I can keep a lid on things, and once we get through this election, it should be smooth sailing."

Dane assured Arthur that he was personally making monthly visits to the Vancouver facility to stay abreast of progress and budget. He also said in a very sincere tone, "I am absolutely overcome with pride in the work both Jake and Madelyn are doing down there; they are top-notch scientists and solid citizens."

11

Madelyn and Jake were taking a break and eating some take-out Chinese at 8:00 p.m.

They had set up living quarters at the lab, consisting of four small one-bedroom suites. Each of them occupied a suite, and Lou, the top young quantum mechanics physicist from Jake's old lab in Los Alamos, lived in the third suite. They decided to leave the fourth suite available to other staff members as needed or for Dane when he was down for periodic visits. They regularly gathered in the fourth suite dubbed, "The Presidential Suite," for meals. There was nothing presidential about the accommodations other than it was the only room in the 35,000-square-foot facility with a large table that could seat ten comfortably. It became a routine for Jake and Madelyn to eat dinner at the table between 8:00 p.m. and 9:00 p.m. The rest of the now eleven-person team ate their meals at their personal residences after they left work, usually much earlier than Jake and Madelyn. Lou was the exception, for he was a fitness junky and ate five small meals a day, usually at his desk. Lou had converted his living room into a gym. Madelyn and Jake would use it from time to time.

Today was a special day. Jake popped a bottle of champagne, poured each of them a glass, raised his, and said, "To milestone number four!"

Madelyn said, "To number four and two more to go!"

Jake had purchased six bottles of Dom Pérignon the day the Lindsey Foundation agreed to fund their undertaking; that was Milestone #1. Milestone #2 was moving into their lab once it was outfitted for work and the initial staffing was complete. Milestone #3 was completion of the polymer-coated quantum-star enerator.

Milestone #4 was probably the most challenging technical obstacle they faced. They had successfully built a machine capable of manufacturing design specific micro robots or nanobots.

The prototype was a work of genius. Madelyn was so happy with Jake's contribution. It was exactly what she had hoped for when she had first met him. His practical engineering knowledge and hands-on approach and creativity were exactly the skills she needed to help her get this far.

Dane was supposed to be here with Solana to celebrate, but there was some family emergency that required they were in Florida.

The new machine they built could manufacture tiny robots with as few as one thousand molecules; much smaller than a human cell. Each of these tiny robots incorporates a polymer coated quantum star for communication purposes and each robot is then coated in polymer, increasing the total molecules of the entire robot by about 50 percent. The final product was called a nanobot. The initial robot manufactured in inventory level quantities is designed to target and emit electrons to free radicals in human cells.

Free radicals are atoms in the human cell that have for one reason or another lost an electron. They damage the cell by moving around stealing electrons from other atoms and subsequently make slight changes to the cell configuration. When the cell reproduces, it reproduces an imperfect replication. This phenomenon is a primary contributor to illness and disease and something else we call "aging."

Lou loved telling a joke about free radicals; it went thus: "Two atoms were walking down the street. One bumped into a light pole and said to the other, 'I think I lost an electron.' The other atom said, 'Are you positive?'" Lou would laugh hysterically every time he would tell the joke, which was really funnier than the joke itself.

There are a dozen or so other nanobot designs ready for manufacture, ranging from complete cell destroyers to DNA strand viewers and DNA strand rebuilders. Destroyers would be useful in cancer treatments; DNA rebuilders/viewers could identify and repair, on the fly, flaws in cells caused by degenerative diseases or possibly even nerve damage or spinal injuries.

The nanobot generator can manufacture over one million nanobots per second. This is twice as fast as the polymer-coated quantum-star generator's capability. The beauty of this technology is that less than one million nanobots are required to perform most perceived procedures. One million nanobots cost less than ten cents in materials. This technology should be available to the consumer for less than the cost of a CT scan.

The R and D was complementary of the Lindsey Foundation; less than a dozen nanobot generators and two dozen quantum-star generators would supply most of a large city's requirements. Spread out over millions of patients, this would be just a few dollars per procedure. The majority of the cost associated with a real-life application is in the diagnosis, gene mapping, and case-specific procedural programming.

Once a program is generated and the combination of nanobot designs are assembled for a specified diagnosis, the procedure is simple. The nanobots are injected into the bloodstream in combination with plankton-infused plasma that has been saturated with high levels of white-spectrum laser light. Once in the body, the case program is run and transmitted wirelessly to the quantum stars. When the program is finished, it will send all the nanobots and much of the unwanted cellular material to a location in the vascular system, where a disposal valve will be inserted. End of procedure.

12

Karl and Steve were busy working on extrapolating data regarding worldwide land, sea, and air freight capacities. The ability to move goods is a key to any significant change in population demographics. Disruption in the economy caused by new technologies or inventions with wide spread demand can have dramatic short-term effects on the transportation of goods. Hot or cold job markets, seasonal crop variations, natural disasters, and even sometimes politics can create bottlenecks or overcapacity in providing movement of goods. Import-export regulations affect transportation providers, and the list goes on. The forecasting software Steve and Karl are in the final stages of development can accurately identify the tiniest ramifications caused by any transportation related event.

Karl was struggling with some of the permutations in the Asian model when Steve interrupted and said, "Stop whatever you are doing! Stop!"

Karl, unaccustomed to Steve having any kind of outburst, was taken aback. Karl, fumbling for words, said, "Am I…or what did I…did I do something wrong?"

Steve replied, "No, no, I am sorry, I just got off the phone with Senator Birmingham, and we have our first real-life world situation that will prove if this software is worth all the money and time dedicated to it."

Karl was stunned; what possibly did the senator tell Steve? His mind was racing; was there some major world catastrophe like an earthquake, nuclear explosion, or a meteor headed for earth?

Then Steve asked the question, "What would happen if we found a cure for AIDS? And what would happen if we could inexpensively and quickly vaccinate people and prevent HIV from infecting another single human being?"

Karl said, "You mean like we did with smallpox?"

"Yes!"

Steve went on to explain that a pharmaceutical company in Denmark announced today to a network of government-level personnel with international security clearance that they found a cure and that they were in the process of manufacturing large quantities of vaccine. The cost of making the medicine was just a few US cents. This was being kept very quiet until final testing was completed. The US FDA had been contacted for obvious reasons and had preliminarily concluded that the drug and vaccine would work, and work safely with no side effects.

Karl said, "Africa!"

Steve said, "Let's get to work."

The average life-span in Africa is only forty-seven years. HIV and the spread of AIDS are responsible for significant death tolls in Africa. In 2011, 4.8 million people were newly infected, and 3.2 million people died of AIDS. There are an estimated total of 38.2 million victims in Africa alone. Within five years it is expected that over six million Africans will die from AIDS per year. If HIV and AIDS were eradicated, the average life-span in Africa would increase from forty-seven years to sixty-six years.

Over one billion people living an additional nineteen years! With education and economic development still lagging behind the rest of the world, population will grow at a faster rate in Africa than any other continent. We will not see any significant increase in current population projections in the first few years, but when we hit year five, an estimated thirty-five million people will be on the planet than previously anticipated.

Without AIDS-related deaths five years from now, eight million people per year will live to see another year. In 2023, instead of our world population growing at a rate of 337,000 per day, it will be growing at a rate of 359,000 per day. That is a 6.5 percent increase over current growth rates; because the growth is exponential, the impact is phenomenal when you look out twenty-five or fifty years.

Though forecasting beyond ten years is interesting and does have some valuable long-range implications that should be planned for, the most valuable data is within the first decade of data. Karl and Steve were methodically entering the estimated changes to population based on the impact of this discovery.

AIDS-related death tolls by geography were isolated in the program and then with a flip of a switch replaced with zeroes. Once the change was made, new population growth by geography was calculated. This triggered the many subprograms to respond with updated information regarding natural resource consumption, food supplies, freshwater supplies, energy requirements, employment, housing requirements, transportation, retail distribution and more. These projections are vital to government planning of land use: farming; light and heavy industrial zoning; commercial zoning (retail and office); public lands for parks, government, police, and schools; and buildable land reserves with density zoning for residential use. They are also essential to predicting revenue generation from property and income taxes.

The program was running flawlessly. Within one day of Senator Birmingham's phone call, the Washington State Census Bureau had accurate forecasts for a post-AIDS epidemic world.

The senator would have this data at his fingertips when he would attend the medical technology symposium that would be held in Germany later that month.

13

It was April 4, 2020, and Madelyn was fixated while reading the research data and technical transcripts that Dane had e-mailed her early in the morning. The only comment written by Dane was, "Thought you might find this interesting." She had heard the news of the AIDS cure and HIV vaccine the previous day via worldwide news blitz. A world forum consisting of top scientists and government officials made the announcement live and in ceremonial fashion at 7:00 p.m. Pacific Coast Time, April 3, 2020. All broadcasts around the world were interrupted for the special announcement. Interviews with notable officials were aired throughout the night. Jake, Lou, and Madelyn stayed up till 2:30 a.m. watching the news.

There was an outpouring of financial and manpower commitments to execute the immediate inoculation of the most critically infected geographies. This was coordinated with the help of many governments in international community and charitable organizations worldwide. Dane was on television the previous night announcing a pledge of $100,000,000 from the Lindsey Foundation for drug manufacturing/packaging and mobilization of one hundred medical technicians to assist in disbursement. Jake thought this was odd considering he was under the impression their project was using most of the Foundation's resources. Where did an extra $100,000,000 come from? Was Dane planning on cutting their budget? Surely not; not when they were this close and had invested so much.

Jake knew Dane and Solana Lindsey had had a major interest in helping the underdeveloped nations in Africa with medicine and education. Maybe they just couldn't ignore such a calling as the eradication of AIDS in Africa. This news will save the lab from developing programs to search out the HIV virus; this was one of the priority programs they hadn't started work on. The teams were currently developing the programs for cell degeneration, which was not only needed for health maintenance but was also directly linked to nanobot design and instruction for cell removal and repair for the cure of cancer. Now without having to dedicate resources to virus detection, they will be able to focus on vascular problems to eliminate plaque and fat-cell accumulation in the bloodstream. Next will be neuron replication for the purpose of repairing spinal-cord damage and a number of other nerve-related injuries and illnesses.

The technology has applications for almost all known health issues. Once proven in human trials and made public to the scientific community, the technology will advance rapidly. Prior to releasing the technology to the public, it was Madelyn's, Jake's and the Lindsey Foundation's goal to prove that the technology can cure most cancer. Because curing cancer and reversing cellular degeneration are so closely linked with this new technology, a dual announcement is what they were thinking would be best. Basically, the technology will be announced as the proverbial "fountain of youth."

The basic concept for cellular repair and rejuvenation evaluates the gene strands in what would be considered a healthy cell and compares that to what the nanobots actually find when introduced into the body. The complexity of the human gene strand poses many problems for the nano-machines to completely identify flaws in the cells basic structure. In laymen's terms, the technology can only repair obvious flaws and cannot bring the cell back to a perfect state. Cells replicate one another and aging is a direct correlation between the gradual replication of imperfect cells.

Scientists believe that, on average, every seven years the human body replaces all of its cells. In other words, in seven years you will actually be a completely different person than you are today with the exception of the cells in the nervous system and brain cells, which last much longer. Utilizing the cellular repair and rejuvenation technology, a typical human physical chronology can be reversed four to five years. If a person underwent regular procedures every seven years, a human life could be extended an estimated 70 to 120 years. This technology cannot be deployed until full physiological maturity has occurred—typically at age twenty-three.

Conceptually, if a patient started regular cellular rejuvenation procedures at the age of twenty-eight, they would attain the optimum life-span. Animal trials have been successful without any negative side effects. The beauty of the technology is that it does not introduce any foreign materials into the system; it simply and effectively repairs what you already have.

In the beginning stages of development, Jake and Madelyn thought it may be possible to change the genetic structure from what nature gave us and allow us the ability to alter ourselves or, in an extreme application, create superhuman abilities. The idea was that if you wanted blond hair, change your genetic makeup instead of using dye. Other examples would include genetic alteration in lieu of plastic surgery or manipulate your genes to affect body height and/or shape. This would change professional sports forever. On the dark side, if one could undergo a procedure to replicate their appearance to match someone else's, the consequences could be horrific to society. Though there would be many positive uses for such a technology, there would be many harmful, damaging, and destructive applications as well.

Fortunately the technology does not work for the purpose of genetic alteration. All we can do is make what we have a bit more youthful. If we try to change the cellular DNA structure in a given cell, the cell breaks down and dies. Madelyn deduced from her experiments in cellular alteration that each cell has, for a lack of better terminology, a memory. When we reconstruct damaged portions of the DNA, the cell responds positively; it accepts the nanobots process like a form of nourishment.

Madelyn couldn't believe Dane had access to the technical journals she was now so engrossed in reading. How did he get this so quickly? Who was he not connected to? That was the real question. She was reading how AIDS was cured just hours after the news was made public. She thought about how absolutely amazing it was to move volumes of information around instantaneously. Born in 1992, Madelyn didn't really get to benefit from the Internet until she was in high school, and even that was fairly limited due to parental control. Today, grammar-school students all over the world do their homework online.

The world is changing at an incredible pace, and what Madelyn was working on will propel that change to a level of acceleration beyond what she could even fathom. She was so focused on the technology that all she could see was her own professional end game. *Recognition for perhaps the most profound scientific breakthrough in mankind's history.*

She knew that what she was working on would be for the betterment of humanity. Suffering people all over the world will not only get relief from their symptoms but also eliminate the cause altogether. People with a death sentence will have a second chance at life.

Neither Madelyn nor anyone at this point had completely thought through all the ramifications her technology was going to have. World population—for example, food, housing, energy, economics—were obviously all going to be affected, but no real analysis on the degree of change had been performed. Sociological ramifications will also permeate throughout human culture. What were people going to do with their time once they had earned enough money to comfortably live on the interest and investment income from their accumulation of wealth? How long would people really live? Could a person live indefinitely? There were some basic limits to the technology, and for now the best estimate is that the procedures could prolong a healthy life to 150 to 200 years before becoming ineffective. Madelyn was a scientist, and though she was brilliant, her mind worked black and white, true or false. She was not all that philosophical and, as a result, hadn't spent much time weighing in on the broader more ambiguous outcomes of her work.

Most people in developed countries work until they are between sixty and seventy years old. With an average life-span of sixty-eight to eighty years, retirement is a relatively small percentage of one's life. Most people never earned enough or, if they did, didn't invest their earnings wisely enough to really achieve financial freedom in retirement.

If people lived 150 years, they may choose to work until they were one hundred before retiring. By then they definitely could own their home outright and have enough saved to be financially secure. A population largely retired and financially secure would pose a profound change in the way people spent their time and how society functioned as a whole. If people lived indefinitely, what would happen?

These are the things Dane and Solana spent their time thinking about. They became so wealthy, so young, they had time to evaluate how they should spend their time with many years in front of them. Most of the people they knew who were even close in net worth were all in their sixties and seventies. Being in their forties, they had a different perspective. Helping their fellow man became their mission is life. What they were embarking on now would someday create a world where vast majorities of people could enjoy the freedom they have. How will people use that freedom is the question.

Dane often wondered if mankind was ready for the technology he was funding. He corrected himself: partially funding. In the front of his mind, he took credit for the funding, though in reality it was mostly money siphoned from the government through his "nonprofit" organization that, in turn, was funding a "for profit" company that would be incorporated once the R and D phase was complete. There was probably a number of 501(c) violations he was committing, yet he knew he would buy his way out of any tax infringement.

Dane trusted the senator but only so far. He believed the senator was working as a servant to the public. He was a man of country but also a man of humankind. In a world still threatened by terrorism and vicious economic cycles, Senator Birmingham seemed to be solely focused on science and technology. He had mentioned to Dane on more than one occasion that in a perfect world all youth would have access to quality education and, more importantly, be required to meet certain standards before being allowed to enter the workforce.

Knowledge for the many, not the few, is the key to a better world. The senator believed in all his heart that if all people had quality education and resources available to them to live respectable lives, the need or desire to harm one another would be diminished greatly. His vision was for a "wise society." He may get his wish if the average life-span would become 150 or 200 years.

Dane thought, *I wonder how far Art would go to bring this technology to fruition.*

Dane was sitting in his wingback chair in his home office thinking through all the things that needed to be considered if and when this technology would get released for general use.

Instead of citizens concerning themselves with leaving a better world for their grandchildren, they will be concerned about having a better world for themselves. This in itself is a dramatic departure from how human beings will make decisions about technology, lifestyle, environment, space exploration, and so forth.

Population control will become a hot topic with serious consideration by not only governments but also by individual citizens. Pro-life advocates and religious organizations around the world will be faced with a reality that inspires great controversy. Do we allow population to grow unregulated at the risk of facing depletion of natural recourses, food, waste management, environment, and so forth? Do we oppose the use of the new medical breakthrough that allows mankind to double or triple their life-span?

On the political front, will the world require a world government? Can hundreds of governments continue to collaborate peacefully? Will those in power have a new perspective if they realize they are just children with another 100 to 150 years of life? Our eldest and wisest will have half of a lifetime in front of them rather than ten to twenty years.

How will human behavior and the need for survival play into this new perspective? The psychological impact on the average person facing the reality, not some fictional fantasy, that their lives will last another hundred or more years will be dissected by all the great sociological and psychiatric professionals around the world. Government leaders will want to obtain the technology; if it is held back, even for a short time, war could emerge. Extremist factions will arise doing everything possible to stop the use of the technology. Governments will have to work together to fend off the new terrorist organizations that will undoubtedly form and rise from all corners of the world.

Dane was concerned that the senator may want to keep the technology a secret to avoid potential calamities; thus the reason for the financial involvement. Can a technological breakthrough, which will do so much good and change forever the social landscape of the human race, be kept a secret? In a way, Dane felt a sense of security in having the government's involvement. It could prove reckless in the short term if the private industry just made such an announcement without thinking it through.

He imagined waking up to headlines in the newspaper that read "Live to be 200 years old for less than $150 a year." If governments and their citizens were blindsided by this kind of news, who knows what could happen?

The technology was becoming a reality; with a lot of help from Lou, Madelyn and Jake were making excellent progress. It was getting close to the time he needed to consider getting a business team together to oversee taking this to the public.

Senator Birmingham just finished speaking at the World Technology Symposium in Germany. The spring of 2020 session was the second of a biannual event. Scientists and government officials from fifty-nine countries were in attendance. There were four keynote speakers, from Denmark, detailing the process of discovering the AIDS cure and HIV vaccine. Over 50 percent of the known infected people of Africa were cured. Thirty-five percent of the population in Africa had been vaccinated. That is, almost 400,000 people were cured or vaccinated in the world's most aggressive medical-related campaign since the eradication of smallpox. Most of the developed countries around the world had already completed attending to all known infected. Vaccinations were being voluntarily given to people between the ages of thirteen and fifty.

Originally the organizers of the symposium had slated time for the senator to discuss the latest updates on nanotechnology. Instead, he had requested that he speak on some forecasting techniques and data resulting from them that could prove useful to the continent of Africa. The major change in population growth will have extreme ramifications, and preparation for these changes will defer or eliminate many growing pains.

The senator knew that the forecasting software developed in the Washington State branch of the Census Bureau he directed would someday have to be used and made known to governments around the world. Having proven itself in the African circumstance will help the world to trust and embrace the data that can be supplied from Steve and Karl's work.

The level of detailed information regarding the forecast for population changes in Africa was digested by the audience at the symposium. Though probably the most crucial technological advancement presented, it was overshadowed by the media hype on the progress of eradication of AIDS and HIV. Arthur thought, *Perfect!*

14

The winter of 2021–2022 was the mildest winter ever on record for the northwest region of the United States; evidence for some, that global warming was a reality. It was January in Vancouver, Washington, and the highs were in the high seventies and the lows in the fifties. Jake had started a routine of jogging in the morning and was really enjoying the fact that he could exercise outdoors this winter. He had never been all that physically active during his life. He spent most of his time in front of a computer or in a lab. He wouldn't outright admit it to himself, but he had developed a serious crush on Madelyn. Though there was a significant age difference between them, intellectually and emotionally they were equals. As Jake started to accept that the technology they were working on was actually going to become a reality, he realized that if he and Madelyn both lived to be two hundred, their age difference was insignificant.

Jake was surprised how his body responded only after five months of regular fitness training. He was toned and lean, had more energy, and, probably most notably, had more self-confidence. He got indications that Madelyn had noticed, though she never said anything.

The work was consuming. They had successfully designed programs and the corresponding nanobots to destroy and evacuate cancerous cells from the body. They were very close to completing the program to regenerate cellular structure, the key to youthful health. They were not certain, but they believed that they could actually reverse aging beyond the seven-year mark. The initial technology was thought to be able to take five years off the aging process every seven years. There was no doubt in Madelyn's or Jake's mind that, in time, people of all ages will be able to reconfigure their body's building blocks to achieve an effective physical characteristic of a twenty-five-year-old via a sequence of procedures.

Animal trials starting with rats and then on to sheep, pigs, and monkeys have shown surprisingly perfect results. No negative side effects have been noted. A variety of cancers have been cured in all procedures. There is no evidence that human trials should be delayed any further.

Lou's mother had been recently diagnosed with breast cancer. Lou had been threatening to go all the way to Dane for approval to discuss the technology with his mother. Finally Madelyn and Jake agreed to take the discussion to Dane. They needed approval to include Lou's mother in the highly confidential research. Dane agreed reluctantly. He knew that someday human trials were necessary and dreaded the day in which he had to make the call to start them. He didn't know where the first candidate for human trials would come from. He anticipated it would be a terminally ill patient at a local hospital with no family. Even though legally the policy strictly prohibited it, he thought Jake or Madelyn might use the technology on themselves before subjecting anyone else to the procedure.

Lou's mom arrived with Lou the next day and was greeted by Madelyn, Jake, Dane, Solana, Anna, and her new assistant council, Jim Mankin. Anna, the attorney handling confidentiality and patent law for the project, was brought up to speed. Jim was a promising young attorney, son of partner James Mankin, who Anna brought into the fold of this project only two weeks ago. Everyone in the office knew that Jim had political ambitions and would likely not pursue a career in his father's firm. This made him approachable and less threatening to the other hopeful partners of one of the nation's largest legal firms.

It had been eight months since she last saw Madelyn. They had talked weekly in order to keep Anna current with the progress.

Anna could not believe the headway realized so soon after the research began. Frankly, all involved felt that not only they were ahead of schedule but also it looked like they would come in $50,000,000 under budget. Anna was trying to digest the reality of the technology. Aside from the insurmountable work ahead of her in securing the technology from a legal perspective, she let her mind wander toward the global ramifications of a life-span being extended by two or three times of today's life expectancy. The changes in the justice system alone would be phenomenal. Life sentences would take on a new meaning. Would criminals in prison be allowed access to the medical technology to continue life, or would they be sentenced to a natural death? It was mind-boggling.

After Dane made introductions, Anna took the floor. She had Lou's mother sign a pile of confidentiality paperwork. She explained that at this point she would turn the floor over to Madelyn, who would explain the technology, and at that point she would have the choice to consent or decline to the procedure. Lou had prepped her mother the best he could without breaking his own confidentiality. She understood Lou worked for a research lab that was working on advanced methods to cure cancer. After her diagnosis she had tried to get Lou to discuss his work. This was creating tension between mother and son. Lou was relieved to get his mom in front of the team. Not only because he believed she will be cured in a nonevasive way but also that he would no longer have to keep his work secret from her.

Madelyn explained in layman's terms to Lou's mother how the technology worked. She assured her that she felt it was safer than current radiation therapy and chemotherapy. She also made it very clear that the technology had never been performed on a human being. She would be the first.

Lou's mother, now in her early seventies, had lived an active and productive life. Lou was her only child, and since the loss of his father four years ago to cancer, Lou was the center of her life. She trusted him and felt a sense of pride only a mother could feel. She had made her mind up before arriving that she would take whatever experimental drug would be offered and/or agree to whatever new surgery they had come up with as long as her son was behind it. She looked at Lou; Lou nodded, and she said, "Yes, I guess I will be your guinea."

Thirty minutes later, after signing consent and authorization forms for electronic transfer of x-rays and CT scans from her physician, the team was preparing a custom program for the first human trial of the technology. She gave Jake a swab for genetic mapping. She was scheduled to come back in three days for the procedure.

Jake was overseeing the programming with Lou at his side. After receiving the genetic mapping and the imaging data of Lou's mom and downloading it into the procedure database program, the initial protocol for the program was automatically generated. From there, a meticulous process of reviewing the nature of the cellular configuration of cancerous cells versus normal cells was under way. This was the key to develop the exact molecular configuration of the nanobots required to successfully destroy all unwanted cells. Once fully understanding the quantity and composition of the destroyed cells, the appropriate "garbage bots" could be designed as well. "Garbage bots" coined by Madelyn were nanobots specifically designed to gather unwanted cellular material and herd it to a location in the vascular system, where a disposal outlet was secured. Kind of like drawing blood, the unwanted material would be sent into a vial inserted into the subject's arm. The trick was to gather the material in small enough sizes to permeate local blood vessels as to get the material into the bloodstream. In most cases the destroyed cells would need to be broken up into smaller pieces and then encapsulated by a 1,500 molecule-sized garbage bots and moved through the membrane of a capillary vessel.

The procedure is single phase; both the cellular destroyers and the garage bots would be injected into the patient simultaneously. They would work in harmony removing cancerous cells and then disposing them. The process was relatively simple, but the accuracy of the data and the sheer quantity of the data was phenomenally complex. If the destroyers misinterpreted healthy cells for unhealthy cells, they could remove cellular structure in the targeted area, basically eating away vital tissue. One of the basic precautions to avoid massive destruction is limiting the quantity of destroyers to only the estimated number of unhealthy cells. For the purposes of the first human trial, they are only going to inject Lou's mother with enough destroyers to remove 50 percent of her cancer. They will then perform multiple subsequent procedures to remove the balance. In-between procedures they will scan for progress and reprogram if necessary. If modifications are required, they can be made on the fly.

After two days of carefully evaluating the program for the first human trial, both Jake and Lou were comfortable in moving forward. Lou called his mother and let her know they were all ready for her. He again asked her, as he did at least three times a day for the past couple of days, if she still wanted to proceed. Each time she told Lou, "I trust you with my life, son; if you feel comfortable with the procedure, who am I to debate that?" She then added, "Besides that, the alternative today has no guarantees and is very evasive."

Lou felt a tremendous pressure, but every time he thought about it, he determined that the worse-case scenario with this technology was far less than the known damage his mom faced with radiation or chemotherapy, let alone the risk and brutality associated with a mastectomy.

Madelyn continued her work on cellular repair and rejuvenation. She felt she was close enough to develop a nanobot to repair any unforeseen damage the destroyers may do to Lou's mom. She was designing molecular machines to image, detect, and evaluate necessary repairs specifically for Lou's mom's cells in direct contact with the cancerous cells. She had a few members of her team working out the final details on nanobots designed to cauterize capillary vessels potentially damaged by the garbage bots. This was a precautionary measure in the event internal bleeding occurred after the procedure. She felt she was ready for the first human trial!

Early in the morning, Jake was busy preparing a sterile environment in the lab to perform the first nano procedure in history. He had multiple cameras positioned to record the entire event. Imagery data was being recorded at each step. They had planned for five total injections, each taking away a progressively smaller amount of cancer until ultimately it was completely removed. Precautionary repair injections were manufactured and ready for use if necessary. Each step would take approximately two and a half minutes from injection to removal of unwanted cells. Fifteen minutes for imaging and evaluation between steps if all went well as planned. The whole procedure should take less than ninety minutes and then the patient can walk out.

No pain should be experienced during the procedure, and the patient will remain fully conscious. There may be a tickle or tingling sensation while the nanobots are performing the cauterizing, but with only animal testing to date, it is not absolutely known.

Madelyn couldn't sleep; she was running on pure adrenalin. Jake had offered to sleep with her the previous night to get her mind off the big day. She didn't know whether he was joking or not, but she just smiled and shook her head. Being completely dedicated to her work for the past seven years and not dating at all in the last four years, she was accustomed to a nonsexual life. She did think about being with a man from time to time, and even in some of her fantasies, Jake was her partner—especially of late, since his physical conditioning was making him a lot more attractive. He had also become more confident, which was a turn-on. Jake being almost twelve years her elder was initially an issue with her. Now that she had spent the last two years working with him, she viewed him as someone her own age. She had thought if the cellular regeneration and rejuvenation process worked as she hoped, they could actually become the same age physiologically.

She joined Jake to help in the preparation of the operating room. When she arrived he said, "All finished and nothing left to do; would you like to join me for a light breakfast and a cup of coffee in the presidential suite?"

She said, "Sure, but I think I will pass on the coffee; I am amped out." They left the operating room after taking another quick look around.

At breakfast they discussed their excitement. Madelyn was still worrying about everything that could go wrong and was babbling on about the repair-bots' ability to accurately identify flaws and their feedback capabilities to the program...blah blah blah. Jake had heard it all a million times and was strained to go over it again, but he fully understood her behavior, so he forced himself to find a way to change the subject. He finally said, "Do you want shrimp or scallops with your Champagne tonight?"

Champagne? Then she remembered milestone number 5! She shyly responded, "Yes, if we are successful, I want Lobster!"

Jake said, "If?" He would take care of getting some fat Australian lobster tails delivered this afternoon. The last bottle of Dom Pérignon was being saved for the day in which their discovery was made public, and they were given public recognition for their scientific achievement.

15

Lou was in his room with his mother. She seemed very relaxed and confident. Lou, on the other hand, was a nervous wreck. His mother asked him if he had worked out this morning. He just looked at her weirdly and said, "Of course, I ran ten miles on the treadmill."

She said, "Well, good; it is important to stay on your routine; health is everything."

He thought about that. They were embarking on a historical ninety-minute procedure to cure her cancer. He said, "You're damn right, Mom; health is everything, and you are going to be a lot healthier than you are now, in a couple of hours."

She said, "Thank you, son."

Dane, Solana, Anna, and Jim arrived at the lab. Lou's mother was being prepped for the procedure. Anna had her sign a few more last-minute consent forms. Jake, Madelyn, and Lou were in the operating room joined by Lou's mom. The rest of the eleven-member team and visitors were just fifty feet away, watching via remote monitoring in the presidential suite.

Lou inserted the evacuation 10cc vial in his mother's arm. He asked her if she was ready. She just smiled. Jake prepared the 3cc injection of plasma, light-infused plankton, 627,000 nano destroyers with cadmium-based quantum stars, and 1,500,000 garbage bots. He looked into the camera and said, "Are we ready to make history?" And then he injected the shot into Lou's mom's armpit. They all immediately turned their attention to the array of computer terminals. The wireless communication was working perfectly, and the program was being executed exactly as planned.

Thirty seconds into the procedure, Lou asked his mother how she felt. She said, "Other than a slight tingle below my breast, I feel nothing unusual." The evacuation vial was already starting to fill.

About two minutes into the procedure, Lou's mom indicated she was feeling some dull pain to the right of her breast. The pain persisted and got worse but not to the point of being unbearable. The pain dissipated once the nanobots completed their mission and the evacuation vial was 90 percent full.

The evacuation vial was removed, and samples were immediately taken and put under the electron microscope. New images were taken of Lou's mom's breast and mammary glands. It was apparent that for the most part, the procedure was successful, but as the data came in, it showed that a significant percentage of the cells destroyed were healthy. Madelyn evaluated the data and started keying in relational commands connecting the data to the nanobot generator. After ten minutes of work, she left the room. Jake knew that the nano destroyers needed some refinement to avoid further damage of healthy cells.

Madelyn returned with two shots in her hand. One had been designed to repair some of the damage caused by the first injection and the second a 400,000 count revised nano-destroyer formula. She injected the cellular reader/repair formula directly under the breast of Lou's mom. Lou's mother indicated that she felt a warming sensation and that the residual pain was going away. There was no need for evacuation with nano-repair machines. Once complete with their task, the tiny molecular machines broke down into harmless molecular combinations that eventually passed through the body's own mechanisms.

The next scan made Madelyn's and Jake's day. The cells once destroyed and damaged by the first injection were now perfectly healthy. Rejuvenation of damaged human cells was now a reality! They injected the patient with the new revised nano destroyers and took more images. This time everything looked perfect. No pain was experienced, and no healthy cells were damaged in the subsequent treatments. They continued the process, and within ninety-eight minutes, Lou's mother was cancer-free! Of course, tests needed to be taken over the next few weeks and months to confirm that she was really cancer-free, but for now she had no signs of cancer whatsoever.

Lou's mom was in great spirits; she laughed, cried, and hugged everyone. She felt no different than when she walked in, in the morning. If this was true, it was too good to be true, she thought.

Dane and Solana were deep in thought; a combination of being stunned and anxious at the same time. They knew the process of implementing this technology, and the social obstacles ahead were larger than the human mind could grasp. They decided before the procedure that if it were successful, they would wait at least a week to inform the senator. They wanted to completely digest the breakthrough before bringing him into the loop. Solana looked at her husband, recognizing that they were acting strangely, and said, "Honey, we need to celebrate this momentous moment."

Dane said, "Absolutely!" and popped a few corks from some quality California sparkling wine.

Jake held up his glass and said, "Madelyn, this is your baby; you give the toast."

Madelyn, embarrassed but also grateful to Jake for giving her credit, raised her glass and simply said, "To the next one hundred fifty years! Hope to see you all in 2170." With a great sense of awe, the crowd was silent, and all took a drink.

After the celebrating was over, Dane and Solana left. Anna and Jim met with Lou's mother one more time and reiterated the need for secrecy. There were more documents she needed to sign regarding consent for periodic testing, termination of any relationship with her previous physician, and so forth. Then Anna and Jim left. The eleven-member team of technicians all went home early. Lou agreed to go home with his mom, who lived a short eight miles from the facility.

Madelyn went to her room and showered. She then went back into the lab to review the data from the procedure. Jake was busy preparing the lobsters and setting the table when Madelyn walked in. She was still running on adrenalin from the events of the day. She had brought printouts of the summarized data with her and was busy talking a mile a minute about each step of the process while Jake was putting the lobster tails in the broiler. Jake went to the refrigerator and retrieved the fifth bottle of Champagne he had purchased years ago for this very occasion.

Jake was barely listening to the words Madelyn was saying and would occasionally turn and smile at her. He popped the cork and served dinner. Madelyn relaxed a bit and enjoyed her food and drink, though she still continued to talk throughout dinner. Jake was so proud of her and felt so blessed to have had the chance to be a part of this discovery. He just listened and took it all in. By the time he had cleaned up the kitchen, Madelyn was starting to wind down. She had put on some music and was sitting on Jake's couch. She realized that she had been dominating all the conversation and had really not acknowledged Jake's part in all this. Jake sat down next to her with the last of his Champagne.

Sitting next to one another on the couch, she turned to Jake and looked him directly in the eyes and said, "I want to tell you something, and I want it to be meaningful; the words I have will not do justice to how I feel. I had the concept for this, but honestly I do not think any of it would have actually happened without your emotional support, financial connections, and not to mention your scientific pros." She went on kind of babbling when Jake put his finger to her lips and then kissed her like a man kisses a woman. It was quite a kiss, and there seemed to be nothing awkward about how either of them felt. They both just relaxed on the couch afterward not saying a word. Madelyn fell asleep in Jake's arms, and eventually Jake fell into a deep sleep as well.

16

Anna and Jim were now back in the Washington, DC, office, assembling Genanotech's corporate charter. The corporation itself was made up of four major shareholders and two appointed board members. These six individuals made up the board of directors. Dane (CEO) and Solana would each have 20 percent of the total shares, Madelyn (Chief Science Officer) was to receive 17 percent of the shares, Jake 12 percent, Lou 1 percent (non-board-member shareholder). The other 30 percent of the corporate stock would be held for future stock grants or options so deemed by the board of directors. The board could choose to sell some or all the shares privately or designate the shares for a public offering. The two appointed board members were Anna (legal council and treasure) and Victoria (CEO of the Lindsey Foundation and secretary of Genanotech).

In the event either Dane or Solana died, the Lindsey Foundation would receive their shares. If Dane and Solana both died, only 50 percent of their shares would go to the Foundation, and the other 50 percent would be split between Jake and Madelyn and any specified heirs outside of the Lindsey Foundation. Jake and Madelyn could only receive a maximum percentage so they would not breech the maximum 20 percent rule in the charter. The remainder of inherited shares would be distributed however Jake and Madelyn saw fit.

If Jake or Madelyn died, their shares would go into trust, with Anna named as trustee. The trustee would not have the associated voting rights of the shares controlled. Only the beneficiary or the beneficiary's legal guardian could exercise voting rights. If both Jake and Madelyn died, all their shares would go into trust for their heirs. The trustee would be Anna Kim, and she would only have limited authority. Anna will have full authority to disburse up to 25 percent of the stock in the trust immediately. The other 75 percent of the trust would require Genanotech's board of directors' approval for any disbursement but limited to whatever instructions Madelyn and Jake had set up in their individual trusts. These provisions were simply to preserve the balance sheet in the event the company was leveraged.

The prevailing concept was to never give one individual or one married couple more than 40 percent control. Anna had herself roughed out how the stocks would be split. She based her decision on what is customary in venture-capital deals. Typically, the investor or venture capitalist receives 40 percent of the company formed and the technologists 25 percent. In this case she increased the technologists' portion to accommodate having three separate scientists.

The magnitude of the demand for the company's technology was like no other product offering in the history of mankind. The corporate bylaws Anna and Jim were authoring were already hundreds of pages thick. These documents would inevitably be reviewed and scrutinized by thousands, if not tens of thousands, of attorneys in the years to come. It was critical that they addressed every possible scenario.

Public issues were not going to be made available initially, although if financing the anticipated growth became impossible from organic revenues, an IPO (initial public offering) would be executed. This was not expected to be necessary. Likely, 15 percent of the outstanding shares will be sold to other governments and possibly major vendors in the supply chain; the other 15 percent will eventually be granted to employees or be sold to the public. The idea behind making shares available to international powers is to allow the opportunity to reduce conflict and encourage cooperation between governments. Stock options could be issued at prevailing stock price to any employees the board felt deserving.

Lawyers see the world in a different light than other professionals. They are by nature cynical, skeptical, and always look at worse-case scenarios. This is especially true in business law. Business is now conducted on an international landscape. US law is only a piece of the puzzle. An in-depth understanding of international law is a basic requirement for any attorney working in business law today.

Because of the top-secret nature of this corporate charter, Anna and Jim were the only authors. They could use staff for some general research but had to be very careful how much involvement they gave anyone.

It had been three weeks since the first procedure. All the post-procedural tests on Lou's mom showed no negative side effects of significance. The only finding so far was that the quantum stars imbedded into the rejuvenation/repair nanobots had not completely evacuated her system. The nanobots themselves had dissolved and were no longer detectable in her body. Though the miniscule quantity of cadmium in her body was to likely never cause a long-term health concern, Jake and Madelyn believed they should develop a garbage bot specifically designed to evacuate the quantum stars. If they would still exist in Lou's mom for two more weeks, they would perform another procedure to evacuate them.

Jim Mankin ordered pizza for Anna and himself. They were about to pull another long night at the office. They had four more days before they would be back in Washington State to meet with the new board of directors and finalize the charter. They had been so busy that they hadn't really talked about what they had witnessed. The enormity of the discovery was hard to get your arms around.

Eating pizza and drinking a beer, Jim mentioned to Anna that it was killing him not to share the news with Beverly. Beverly, now a bigwig with the EFF (Electronic Frontier Foundation), hated secrets. Her beliefs were grounded in free speech, free intellectual property, open architecture, and so forth. The best way to keep a secret from Beverly was to not let her know you had one. The problem arises when you are working on a project as demanding and as enigmatic and guarded as the one he was; it is difficult to talk about work without lying. Jim decided that lying was best in this case. As far as Beverly knew, he was working for a new mega client the firms just acquired. The client was a venture capitalist, and they had gone through multiple firms. This new client was very demanding, and this was the firm's chance to impress them.

Jim explained to Anna that it was tough to look at his wife and know that they may be able to remain husband and wife for another hundred years and not be able to talk about it with her. Anna, being very intelligent and analytical, advised Jim, "In due time."

Jim said, "The ramifications of announcing this technology without thinking it all the way through could have many negative consequences. For this reason there has not been a timetable put together yet on how such an announcement will be made. It was agreed that more human trials were necessary to convince the scientific community before they should announce. I totally get it. We cannot for the sake of humanity recklessly let the news of this get out."

Anna was growing fond of Jim. She enjoyed his philosophical view of what Genanotech was working on. She was first a bit reserved because he was the boss's son. After weeks of working closely, she realized Jim was not relying on his pop or trying to ride his coattails. Rather, he was his own man, and working for his dad was not a privilege as much as it was an obligation. With his education, looks, and personality, he could work at any firm he wanted to. What impressed her most was his work ethic. He was determined to work as hard or harder than her. This made the monumental task in front of them a lot easier with each of them motivating the other to persevere.

Anna's cell phone rang. It was Dane; he said, "I need you in Washington State in my office tomorrow afternoon; oh, and I need Jim to be with you too. Jake and Madelyn will be here as well. We won't be discussing the corporate charter, so do not stay up all night working on it. I need you guys sharp tomorrow, and oh, I almost forgot—bring two more of your confidentiality agreements with you."

Anna said, "Of course, we will be there."

17

It had been two weeks since Dane and Solana discussed the successful procedure at the lab with Senator Birmingham. The meeting set up for the next day included the senator, and he would announce to Jake, Madelyn, and their attorneys his involvement with the senator. Dane was very nervous about how the news would be received. He had rehearsed numerous speeches, and none of them sat well with him. He had never broken a trust this great in his entire business career. It was not his style, and he was not in his comfort zone. He knew deep down inside his soul that his course of actions were honorable, but the idea he had not been up front with people he now considered friends and family haunted him. Tomorrow he would come clean.

Solana sat down next to Dane in front of the fireplace and rubbed his back. She said, "We always knew this day would come. Look at it as a beginning. Jake and Madelyn will eventually understand, and remember there was no other way to get them this far."

He explained to his wife that he had worked on multiple speeches and still didn't know how he was going to spill the beans. She continued to rub his back and said nothing. Dane's biggest concern was with the government being directly involved. He wasn't sure what power they might exercise and/or how it would affect the continued efforts of developing the technology.

His mind raced. Would it become top secret and never be made available to the public? Would hundreds of government scientists be given access to the technology in an effort to see if there were any military applications? His mind was spinning. He only hoped that the senator was the honorable man he thought he was and that his intentions were what he had stated them to be.

When Dane and Solana met with Arthur two weeks ago and reviewed the results of the first human trial, the senator was not taken aback. He was pleasantly surprised at the expediency of successful use of the technology. He reminded the Lindseys that he personally knew Jake and had done his research on Madelyn. He had actually had dinner with Madelyn three years ago. The senator knew precisely what the lab was working on. Though Dane thought he was keeping a lid on the details, the senator had known all along.

Dane was not afraid of Anna and her confidentiality agreement. They were too far along to try to compensate for any breach. After all, Dane was about to start spending some more of his own foundation's money on getting this corporation off the ground. He was also going to be instrumental in managing the extremely complex task of making the technology available to the world. At least he hoped that was the case.

Arthur made a comment to Dane that reaffirmed his suspicions.

In one of their affectionate man-teasing sessions, the senator let his chest puff out and made an inappropriate comment. He said, "Do you think Jake and Lou could have just left the Los Alamos project without us knowing where their energies were going to be spent?"

Dane had been bothered by this and felt he was just a pawn in all of it. He was not used to being *manipulated* or not being *in the know*. Today he felt both. This was the root of his worry. Tomorrow would provide some of the answers.

After a long day of administrative work, Jake and Madelyn were sharing some nachos and a coke and unwinding. They had spent the majority of the day summarizing, in writing, the lab's current status. This was part of an ongoing document detailing the completion of each milestone and current progress on work in process. They had recapped Lou's mother's current physical condition, which was quite excellent. There were no cancer markers in her blood work and no apparent damage to tissue in her breast.

The list of base-level programs for specific diagnosis was growing, and the technicians were busy knocking them out one by one. A base-level program saves time for the physician performing a tailored procedure to cure a patient's specific diagnosis. For instance, if the diagnosis is leukemia, a base program designed to address cancerous cells in the blood or bone marrow is downloaded. Coupled with the genetic map of the individual and any other patient-specific data, the program for the procedure is made complete. Each program designs the appropriate nanobot molecular machine specific for the mission at hand. This is then downloaded into the nano generator for construction of the nanobots.

Jake and Madelyn had amassed a total of 917 potential programs, of which only forty-two had been written. One of the main agenda points for tomorrow's meeting with Dane and Solana was the hiring of additional technicians. This is always a difficult topic; not because of budgetary reasons but for confidentiality concerns. The more people involved, the more difficult it is to keep a lid on the project.

Dane made it clear to Jake and Madelyn that there was much to consider before they made the technology public. They couldn't wait to have this out in the open. Not for the notoriety but for the freedom to expedite the development of the technology and ultimately start curing the human race of all known diseases. Normally they did not look forward to these business-related meetings, but Dane mentioned to Madelyn that in their upcoming meeting they would have a detailed discussion on when they would make a public announcement.

After they finished pigging out on the nachos and a whole tub of salsa, they moved into Madelyn's living room and relaxed in front of the news. They had become intimate over the past few weeks, and with Lou at his mother's, they had fallen into a routine of alternating which suite they slept in. They would eat in one of their suites and sleep in the other. They had talked about telling Lou, Dane, and Solana about their new relationship, but the timing never seemed right. Besides, there was something exciting about keeping their intimacy a secret. They would catch themselves flirting in the lab and wondered if people were beginning to talk.

They hit the sack early in order to get on the freeway at 5:30 a.m. to beat the traffic.

The only flight Jim and Anna could book was a red eye leaving Dulles just a few hours after Dane's call. Beverly packed a bag for Jim and met them at the airport. They had a four-hour layover in

Chicago. They planned to catch a little sleep in the terminal and then again on the early-morning flight to SeaTac.

While waiting to board in Dulles, Beverly was persistent in trying to get Jim to explain what was so important that they had to go to Washington State in such a rush. After listening to Jim trying to evade the subject, Anna interrupted and said, "I know how it is to be curious, but in this case, Jim simply cannot discuss the particulars of what we are working on."

It didn't help. It just made Beverly all that more intent on knowing what was going on. Because Anna was twenty-five years older than Jim, Beverly was not jealous or worried about an affair. She simply needed to know what he was doing. The trips were becoming more frequent and with less notice. Jim was off the hook for the affair concern, but that was about it.

Ever since Jim had heard of the Genanotech project, he knew the last person he could trust with the information was his wife. Beverly took the concept of open architecture to a new height. She believed that the world should have no secrets. No secrets at all. It would be an altruistic world where there was no need for military, and the government's sole purpose was to service local community's infrastructure. Jim would love to listen to Beverly ramble on how the Genanotech technology could be the catalyst toward a world with no secrets.

On more than one occasion, her obsession with total transparency at all levels professional, political, and personal had come close to destroying their marriage. The tension was mounting due to Jim's inability to share his work with her. Beverly had to remind herself that the world she wanted to live in was not real. She had committed herself to changing the world; she was a true activist!

They provided balance to one another, Jim always looking at everything that could possibly go wrong and Beverly always looking at what it will take to make things go right. The world will need both of these personalities in the upcoming era of Genanotech technology.

Jim and Anna were the only passengers in first class on the half-booked flight to Chicago. After settling in and ordering a cocktail, they speculated about the meeting they were summoned to. Why did they need additional confidentiality contracts? Who was going to be brought into the fold? Perhaps they were adding more technicians to work on programming? No, that's not it. Drew had a standard agreement for hiring lower-level employees and technicians. Certainly there must be some major player being introduced to the company they were not aware of. Speculation was futile; it could be anyone.

Jim had just touched on what the public's response to the announcement of the technology would be. In their field, the international legal consequences would be enormous. But beyond their field, how would the world receive such news? It would be one thing to be born in a society where the average life-span was expected to be 150 to 200 years. How would a society programmed from childhood to expect only seventy to eighty years react to a new era where they can extend their life an additional seventy to 120 years?

Beyond the doubling or tripling of life-span, there was included in this new era the ability to cure disease and repair damage to the body. How would this affect the behavior of athletes, thrill seekers, drug addicts, neighborhood gangs? The list goes on. If you knew your risk of permanent long-term damage was mitigated by the ability to make an appointment at your local nano repair lab and reverse the hurt you inflicted upon yourself, would you take the risk? Would mobsters be more willing to impose horrific torture techniques on their adversaries, knowing that the fingers they chopped off could be replaced later?

With that thought Jim looked at Anna and found her sleeping peacefully. He tried to get comfortable with a pillow, but his mind would not rest. Obviously the religious extremists will have a lot to say about the use of this technology. The controversy will be inevitable. Was it God's intention for mankind to extend his life with technology? Most people will argue that we have been doing that with current medical technology for the last half of the century or more. What if the technology matures to a level where life can be extended indefinitely? That would raise a few eyebrows in all religion!

Anna and Jim were awakened by the jarring of the less-than-smooth landing in Chicago. Both groggy, they gathered their baggage and headed for the terminal where they would try to go back to sleep. Jim set his alarm on his cell phone to wake them in time to catch their connecting flight to Seattle.

Steve and Karl were driving north on I-5 to meet with the senator. The subject of their meeting was not disclosed. The senator had asked them to meet at a residential address where he was supposedly staying for the weekend. The senator told Steve that they would be meeting with key personnel of the Lindsey Foundation. Without specifying the nature of the meeting, Steve had decided they better have with them the updated world-population forecasts resulting from the eradication of AIDS and the HIV virus. Steve and Karl both knew that the Lindsey Foundation was instrumental in funding the worldwide effort to inoculate the vast population of Africa with the HIV vaccine.

18

As requested, Steve and Karl arrived at the Lindseys' home at 11:30 a.m. on the dot.

The three-hour drive would have only taken two if they had not been stuck in traffic. The GPS navigator directed them flawlessly to the address, where they stopped in front of a stately gate surrounded by beautiful landscaping. In view was a long winding drive past the gate. There was no sight of the estate that unquestionably resided on the property. After being parked in front of the gate for fifteen seconds, the gate opened. The drive up to the estate was gorgeous.

Karl couldn't help himself from narrating the whole drive up to the house pointing out how the rhododendrons, camellias, and azaleas in full bloom were arranged perfectly to give the impression they were indigenous in the forested landscape. At one curve in the road, he said, "Look! Check that solar array out; there must be twenty—no—thirty thousand square feet of solar panels in that clearing."

Karl was like a kid on a trip. He continued to make comment. "See all those windmills. I bet this place is completely off grid. How cool is that?"

When they arrived at the home, they were met by two very muscular men in slacks and expensive golf shirts. After being politely scanned, they were escorted into the stark foyer, where they were asked to wait a moment.

Senator Birmingham entered the room with Dane and Solana at his side. He made introductions. Dane and Solana were very gracious and down to earth, which made both Steve and Karl feel at ease. They followed them through a number of corridors into a dining area where they all sat down. Dane asked everyone at the table if they had any dietary restrictions, which no one did.

He said, "Great. We have prepared some wild-turkey-salad sandwiches." He paused and exhaled. "We are in for a long day, so let's get you some food before we start."

Dane then explained he and Solana had some things that needed attending to and would not be able to join them. Three nicely presented lunches were served, and Steve and Karl were left alone with the senator.

Steve asked his boss what the meeting was about. The senator relaxed and looked at the two men, who were obviously curious, patted Steve on the shoulder, and said, "I will give you a small clue, but I cannot go into details until you are invited into the meeting. We will be starting the meeting without you, but you will be invited in once we have had a chance to discuss your participation."

Steve with his brazen personality said, "Well, now that we have the itinerary, can we have the clue?"

Karl was still not used to Steve's casual relationship with the senator. Not only did the senator deserve respect but also his whole demeanor almost demanded it.

Arthur laughed and said, "Of course; let's just say that what we are going to discuss today will require that you sign a confidentiality agreement and that it will put your software to use in a way you could not even begin to imagine."

Steve just looked at the senator and shook his head.

Lunch was delicious but for the most part went unnoticed by Karl and Steve. The senator finished up and on the way out of the room said, "I will see you in an hour; in the meantime why don't you gentlemen discuss some of the variables in which your software handles human psychology?" He then shut the door behind him.

This was the senator's hour; he had been looking forward to this day for years. Actually he had been looking forward to this day for his entire adult life. He was going to actively participate in mankind's greatest achievement ever. The senator's lifelong vision was becoming a reality, and he knew that he had a great deal to do with it. He also knew he would have a profound influence on how progress will be made from here on out. He was ready for the task. He had carefully organized an agenda to address the major obstacles that needed to be overcome prior to taking the technology public.

The senator was reviewing his notes in the garden room where a conference table was set up to comfortably seat fourteen. Victoria (COO of the Lindsey Foundation) and her staff Dwaine (science advisor), Kathy (international legal council), Ryan (lobbyist), and Drew, her personal assistant were also seated at the table.

Anna and Jim were in the foyer. Dane arrived and asked them to have a seat in the small nicely appointed room adjacent to the home's entrance. He apologized for the short notice and thanked them for getting here so quickly. He asked how their flight was. Anna said, "It was a bit grueling, but they did manage to get about five hours sleep"; she then asked if she could have a cup of coffee.

Dane quickly fetched two cups of coffee for Anna and Jim. He then shut the door. They all sat down, and after a moment of silence Dane said, "Well, I am sure you want to know what was so urgent. I am going to cut to the chase."

Dane explained that he had had to break the confidentiality agreement. Anna, who rarely showed any emotion, was obviously upset. She could feel her face flush. Dane went on to fill them in on what had transpired and explained in great detail how this technological achievement would never have been made possible without the senator's involvement. He explained that Jake and Lou would never have been allowed to leave their top-secret lab in Los Alamos without the senator pulling strings. That the Foundation would not have had the money required to develop the technology and get it off the ground without the influx of government funds. He went on to discuss his long-term relationship and friendship with the senator.

Anna was starting to relax but had enough adrenalin running through her veins that she had no need for the coffee she was clenching in her hand. She carefully set her cup down on the table in front of her and looked Dane directly in the eyes and asked, "Does Madelyn or Jake know about this?"

Dane said, "I thought I would leave that up to you; they will be here shortly."

Anna said, "Great, but you will be here with me when I explain, right?"

Dane said, "No, I will not, but I will be in shortly after you give them the news. I have thought this through; your professional relationship with Madelyn deserves the respect of a client attorney meeting. You need not have the traitor present."

Anna thought about it and realized Dane was right. She sipped her coffee, and Dane left.

She immediately got red in the face. She looked at Jim and said, "Can you believe this shit. You think that conniving piece of…could have given us this news a couple of weeks ago prior to us spending weeks on a charter that now will need a complete overhaul. I am not sure I am mad because we were deceived or because we will have to redo all that work. Aye, yi, yi!"

They could hear a car pull up outside. Jim looked out the window and saw Jake and Madelyn walking up to the front door. Of course, they were escorted by the same security personnel who had received them. The door swung open, and in came Madelyn. She greeted Anna and Jim and then plopped down. Madelyn explained that Jake was in the restroom and that the traffic was terrible on the way in. She then spaced out a bit and said, "Do you guys know what this meeting is all about?"

Anna said, "I have a good idea, but I can't say for certain."

Madelyn could sense that Anna was not happy.

Jake came in and sat next to Madelyn on the love seat. Madelyn adjusted herself, wiggling the way only a girl can do, and smiled.

Anna got up and shut the door. Standing next to the door, she paused and then deliberately disclosed to her clients the breach of contract that had taken place.

Jake immediately said, "Well, if it was going to be the government, I am glad it is Arthur."

Madelyn smacked him on the back of the head and said, "It was completely unacceptable behavior! I thought you said you could trust Dane and Solana?"

Jake, taken aback, fumbled around a bit, and finally gaining his composure managed, "I thought we could!" He then ducked to avoid another assault from Madelyn.

Madelyn was fuming; she slapped his head one more time for good measure. She was concerned. She wondered who else knew; she wondered if they would lose autonomy or, worse, be taken off the project altogether. Then a horrible thought crossed her mind. *What if the government would not allow the technology to be employed?*

Anna sensed what Madelyn was processing. Jake wanted desperately to say something, but he knew Anna was in charge of the situation, and his intervention would not be welcome. Besides, his head was hurting.

Jake stood up and paced the room. He was more upset about Madelyn being upset with him than he was about the senator being involved in the financing and operation of the technology. He walked over to her and knelt down and, placing his hand on her knee, asked her, "What can I do? I know both of these men, and there must be something I can do?"

Madelyn ignored him and looked at Anna and said, "Can Dane come in here…now?"

Anna started to say something, and Madelyn's expression changed her mind. She had never seen this sweet young girl look so serious.

Anna left the room and immediately returned with Dane.

Dane, in his own words, reiterated what Anna had already communicated. Dane's interjections of his friendship and long-term relationship with the senator started to soften the blow. Right or wrong, without Dane and the senator, she could not have proven her technology. She asked Dane if the senator had any plans that would alter their current course. Was he going to stop the technology from becoming public?

Dane said, "You can ask him yourself; he is in the garden room waiting for you." He then added, "I have been living with this secret for a long time. I wanted to tell you both on many occasions but never found the right time. Your progress was incredible, and the last thing I wanted to do was interrupt your work. I can tell you that the senator knew the basic work your lab was engaged in, but he never received one single update from me or anyone else on the details of the progress. Thinking this through I decided to come clean in an environment where you would not have to wait to get your questions answered, thus the purpose of our meeting today."

Madelyn took this all in and wanted to believe Dane at his word. She took a deep breath, took Jake's hand, and stood up. Jake was feeling a little awkward. This was their first public display of affection.

He thought, *What the hell*; their newfound intimacy was peanuts compared to what Dane just laid on them.

Anna noticed the two walking hand in hand down the corridor toward the garden room. She thought, *Good for them!* Anna genuinely liked Madelyn from the time they first met. She had been, or at least she had thought she had been, protecting Madelyn from the world that would love to exploit her invention. The more she got to know Madelyn, the more she realized how special she was. Not special because she was spearheading an extraordinary technology but special as a person in her life. They had created a bond similar to mother-daughter or big sister or little sister; probably something in-between. Anna's mother had died in an accident when she was young, and she had a brother but no sister. Madelyn was not close to her mother and also had no siblings.

When Anna first met Jake and was working on putting together the partnership Madelyn was agreeing to, she was very skeptical. After watching the two of them work over the past two and a half years, she had realized Madelyn's instincts were right on! Jake was a perfect complement to Madelyn's efforts. He brought so much to the table scientifically, and most importantly he had the connections for the mega-million-dollar financing to get the project on its feet. Beyond the scientific and business side of Jake's contribution, he was a great guy. He was courteous, humble, a team player, sophisticated, and had a good sense of humor. He placed Madelyn on a pedestal. He knew her brilliance, dedication, and drive were the real thing. His support and recognition of Madelyn's accomplishments throughout the development process had been unwavering. The fact that they were apparently involved romantically was just icing on the cake.

19

When they entered the garden room, they were greeted by Dane, Solana, Victoria, and her team. The room was absolutely beautiful surrounded by French paned windows on three sides, overlooking gardens in full bloom. The room was north facing, so there was not any direct sunlight entering the room. The east- and west-facing windows had canopies above them to maintain the saturation of only indirect light.

There was a small table against the only wall in the room with some food and drink. The large conference table was elegantly set for business and comfort. Fourteen large cushioned chairs with arms surrounded three sides of the table with a projector screen set up at the east end of the table. Of course, there was a secure high-speed wireless connection available for laptops and other portable electronic devices.

Jake immediately took note of the participants. He counted himself, Madelyn, Anna, Jim, Dane Solana, Victoria and her team of four, and the senator (not present yet). *What were the other two chairs for or, more specifically, who were they for?* He dismissed this bit of curiosity and shook hands with the rest of the group. There were name designation plates in front of each chair. The arrangement had been well thought out. The closest of the six chairs to the projector screen on the south side of the table was slated for the senator; Jake was sitting to his right and then Anna, Jim, Victoria, and Drew (her assistant). On the north side of the table, Dane was seated closest to the projector opposite of the senator. Then Madelyn, Dwaine, Kathy, Ryan, and Solana were seated in that order. This allowed for easy communication in four specific groups. Meeting leaders, scientists, the legal council, and business administration were clustered together. The two chairs at the end of the table had no name tags.

The only Genanotech senior participant and future stockholder who was not present was Lou. Obviously this meeting was not called to finalize corporate documents.

Jake made his way to the food table and assembled a couple of plates for himself and Madelyn. Victoria and her team were finishing up their lunch. The turkey-salad sandwiches were incredible. Everyone settled into their chairs and got their materials situated. No one mentioned the two undesignated chairs at the end of the table.

Solana dimmed the lights and took her seat. The projection screen read thus:

PUBLIC ANNOUNCEMT

How do we get there?

April 14th, 2021

The senator then walked into the room and addressed the group. The first thing he said was, "I cannot express in words the admiration and respect I personally feel for the work Madelyn and Jake have endeavored. The brilliance, scientific pros, dedication, and inventiveness of these two individuals will be imbedded in our history books for as long as mankind exists. We should all feel honored to be in their presence today!" There was applause from all at the table; Madelyn blushed, and Jake winked at her.

The senator went on to say, "I have envisioned the use of nano-technology for medical purposes for the last fifteen years. I had multiple top-secret labs working on components of the research scattered in nine separate locations. Madelyn and Jake have, on their own prowess, leapfrogged past any of the progress made in those nine collective efforts."

There was another round of applause from the table. "No other country on the planet is even close to developing such a practical and proven application utilizing this technology. Not one invention in man's history will have as profound an impact as this technology will!" Applause and more applause!

With that said, the senator pointed at the screen. He then dived into the discussion of making the technology public knowledge. "There are tens of millions of people who could immediately benefit from the technology. The longer we wait to implement the use, the more people will suffer or die unnecessarily."

Madelyn felt a bit relieved. Her work would continue, and it appeared that the senator would actually be a part of helping it get to the world—the whole world.

The senator reaffirmed the inability of the technology to restructure or alter genes. Jake, Madelyn, and Dwaine all engaged in a lively technical discussion that went over the heads of most in the room. They unanimously agreed that all the technology could do was fix physical problems within the context of the natural existing genetic map we all carry from birth. "All the technology could do." *What an understatement.*

The senator then reaffirmed that the technology could not promote life indefinitely.

He explained to the group that these two limitations in the technology would be the most important factors in our ability to take it public. Without apparent military application that genetic alteration technology would provide and without significant religious opposition that would undoubtedly manifest if we found a cure for death, we have a shot at getting this technology into the mainstream fairly quickly.

He said, "Of course, being a patriot, I did explore the idea that if we were the only ones with the technology, our soldiers could be healed and likely avoid death altogether in the battlefield, giving us significant advantage in direct engagements on the ground. Chemical weapons would become an obsolete threat. Well, you can imagine the benefits. After thorough thinking, I believe that in today's world we face less and less threat of conventional battle and more and more threat to terrorism. Since terrorism is typically aimed at the public sector having the technology available to all the citizens, all the public sector, all the military, basically all people in general, we have a better chance to stamp out violence worldwide than having a strategic advantage within just ours and our alley's military."

Madelyn had never thought of the limitations in the technology as a positive thing, but she could see where the senator was going with this line of thought. She was actually starting to believe it was a blessing that Dane included the senator.

Senator Arthur Birmingham was first and foremost a public servant. He had a passion for science and knew that any major scientific breakthrough required government involvement and in some cases approval. The Food and Drug Administration was evidence of this very fact. Senator Birmingham carefully positioned himself in government to oversee technological advancement in our modern society. He chaired the Commerce, Science, and Transportation committee and had a seat on the National Nanotechnology Initiative committee.

Nanotechnology had been a major interest of the senator for fifteen years. He had the same vision as Madelyn before Madelyn was even through puberty. He, of course, did not have the scientific expertise or patience to work on the development directly. He was a great manager and organizer with enough technical knowledge to communicate with the experts. He had dedicated his life to this very moment in history. He had found his calling, and his calling found him.

The senator called the meeting back to order and in his own eloquent manner asked Dane to say a few words.

Dane addressed the group and asked Anna to stand up. He asked Anna to update on the corporate charter and specifically the shareholders and their voting rights.

Anna, still reeling with anger toward Dane for deceiving her and Madelyn, bit her lip. She looked at Jim, who fully understood the situation. He felt somehow cheated as well but on a lesser degree due to the short-term relationship he had with Dane relative to Anna's longer and closer relationship with the man. He shrugged.

Anna finally said, "After some organizational changes I recently have been made aware of"—she hesitated while looking directly at Dane—"I believe we will be making some serious revisions to what we have put together so far. We will need a few more weeks to present our ideas."

Jim was taking notes out of nervous habit and thinking, *Good for you, Anna; he should not get off scot-free for what he has done here.*

Madelyn and Solana were well aware that Dane was squirming in his chair and using every bit of his self-restraint not to completely blow a lid. He was used to boardroom brawls, but he always had the upper hand. This time it was not the case.

He wanted the job as CEO of this company more than he ever wanted anything. He just didn't know it till that very moment.

The room remained quiet for a few minutes. Only half the room knew what was going on.

Weighing his options he decided it best to deal with this in a less-crowded venue. He said, "OK, we will discuss the charter at our next meeting. We have a lot to go over, so I think I should turn it over to the senator and get started."

Anna was staring at him from the time she finished till he turned the meeting over. He never looked her way once.

The senator looked at Madelyn and Jake and asked, "May I introduce two individuals to the group who I would like to bring into the fold. This was pure courtesy on the senator's part. He had no confidentiality agreement himself. Legally he could tell anyone he wanted to about the technology." Madelyn caught on to this right away but was impressed that he would go through the motions.

Madelyn looked at Anna, who shrugged. She didn't bother looking at Jake, who she was still a little pissed at for his nonchalant attitude toward Dane's misstep. She then nodded.

The senator then gave a brief overview of the forecasting software that was developed in the Washington State offices of the US Census Bureau. Providing samples of the detail the software provided for the African Continent post AIDS, he was selling most of the audience. He had timelines for infrastructure requirements for roadways, schools, transportation systems, government offices and so on…he also had slides depicting the residential, light industrial, and commercial land-use requirements; global energy requirements; natural resource requirements; agricultural requirements; and the list went on. All this was on a specific timeline based on new population projections.

He said, "I think this software could really help us take this technology to the public in the most responsible way."

Jim Mankin was in his own world now, not paying attention to anything the senator was saying. *Could it be possible that the senator was going to bring his best friend Karl into the mix?* This would be beyond awesome, Jim thought. They would actually be working together. He then thought, *No way!*

The senator paused and said with great preciseness, "If there are no objections, I would like to have Steve Ryan and his right-hand man Karl Franklin from the Census Bureau join us for the balance of the meeting. I would ask that Anna meet with them prior to joining us and have them sign her famous confidentiality agreement, and I would also like to sign one as well as a matter of good faith. Steve and Karl are in a room on the other side of the home." He then stood up and said, "Anna, Jim, do you want to walk with me?"

Madelyn was impressed.

Jake felt relieved. He knew that somehow his association with the senator would cause problems between Madelyn and himself if the senator became adversarial. So far his involvement appeared to be right in line with the direction Jake and Madelyn had hoped for. In fact, the expertise and knowledge that the senator brought to the party was not only welcome; it may turn out to be vital.

Madelyn thought, *Public announcement of the technology and making it available to the world in a conscientious manner is becoming as difficult an undertaking as the development of the technology itself.*

Jim stopped the group shortly after they had left the garden room. Before they met up, he wanted to let the senator and Anna know that he was close friends with Karl. This was a surprise to Anna. She had heard of his friend Karl and knew he worked for the Census but didn't make the connection.

The senator was already well aware of the relationship. Thorough background checks were routine in his line of work. He informed Jim that Karl and Steve did not know anything about the technology yet, but they did know that two representatives from Mankin, Garrard, Williams, Beakon and associates would be in to have them sign some confidentiality agreements. They both knew that a Jim Mankin will be one of them. He then smiled and said, "I feel it prudent to drip information rather than drop it like a bomb."

Jim was feeling as if this whole afternoon was one drip after another. The gravity of the day's events was difficult to digest. The senator was definitely a pro at the communication of complex subject matters. Jim was excited to see Karl.

Both Steve and Karl were happy to see Karl's friend Jim. Karl was charming in his introduction to Jim's boss, Anna. After a few minutes of pleasantries, the senator motioned everyone to sit at the table. He passed the chair to Anna and said, "Let's get this chapter finished so we can get to work."

Anna whipped out her briefcase and pulled three thick contracts out. Twenty minutes later they were finished, and Anna and the senator were headed back to the garden room. Jim remained with Steve and Karl in order to fill them in on the technology and some of the issues facing the team in taking it public and getting it employed. Steve had a million questions, most of which Jim could not answer. Jim did not mention the Dane situation.

Karl was in a state of shock. He could not believe the permeations of consequences for a scientific revelation of this magnitude. He went back to his days as an actuary calculating life-span. This would throw a huge wrench in those tables. For that matter he thought, *Life insurance would become so cheap that there would hardly be a commission for the agent selling it.*

Jim's cell phone rang; they were ready to get started as soon as the others were. They headed down the corridor leading to the garden room. When they arrived, there were two new nameplates at the end of the table, Steve Ryan and Karl Franklin. Solana introduced Steve and Karl to the group, and they all sat down.

Dane rolled his chair around the corner and faced the group from the end of the large table. He applauded the senator for his contribution and welcomed the newcomers. He went on to say, "We have a diverse and comprehensive collection of professionals gathered here today. We have science, business, government, legal council, and information technology represented. This is our core group for the undertaking we are about to embark on."

20

The meeting went on for hours; dinner was served in the garden room while work continued. They engaged in lively debates regarding potential problems that would inevitably arise after the public announcement. It was for the most part a brainstorming session—getting everyone's thoughts out on to the table. It also was an opportunity to get the main players in the newly formed company to get to know one another. This will be critical to team work in the future.

Dane was a brilliant CEO and leader/organizer. He knew he needed to prove himself now more than ever. His foundation had contributed twenty-five million and would likely need to contribute another twenty-five to fifty million dollars before the company received one penny from sales. He was feeling on edge due to Anna's reaction but knew deep down he was always working in the best interest of Genanotech and, for that matter, Madelyn and Jake.

He had divided their mission into five major focus groups and assigned personnel. They were as follows:

Science: Jake, Madelyn, Lou
Business: Dane, Victoria, Drew, Dwaine
Public Relations: Solana, Anna, Ryan
Government: Senator, Jim, Kathy
Forecasting: Steve, Karl

Special tasks were to be assigned with cross sections from the different focus groups.

For the purposes of today's meeting, Jake and Madelyn were to be teamed up with Steve and Karl. More human testing was required to solidify the technology. Drew had secured 220,000 square feet of commercial space adjacent to the lab in Vancouver. One hundred ten thousand square feet of the building was being retrofitted for pre- and postprocedure patient care and three state-of-the-art operating rooms. Ninety thousand square feet was being dedicated to Molecular Machine Generator and Quantum Star Replicator Capital Equipment manufacturing. The remaining 20,000 square feet was to include a couple of more suites and some dedicated space for administrative work.

The bulk of the existing lab would become procedure-programming headquarters. The two proto-type machines to generate nanobots and quantum stars would be moved to a mini lab located directly between the operating rooms in the new building.

The building was well under way and was to be ready for occupation in less than eight weeks or mid-June.

Victoria and Dwaine had been assigned the task to identify and obtain terminally ill patients for testing. It had been determined that all patients who willingly consented to the procedure would be sequestered after the procedure was complete. All outpatient sequestering would be for a period no longer than one year or when the technology would become public, whichever would occur first. The group had not yet come up with a practical explanation for family members or, for that matter, the patients on why sequestering was required. The fact of the matter was that they just could not risk success cases getting out to the public before they were ready.

It was agreed that solid forecasting via the Census Bureau programs should be made available prior to any public announcement.

Steve needed to understand how long life would be prolonged for a number of different scenarios.

First he asked what the estimated life expectation would be with repair technology only. In other words, if the fountain of youth, cellular-rejuvenation process ended up not working as planned and only curing cancer and disease were possible, how long would a person be able to extend his or her life? In this scenario he wanted to know if there would be any difference based on age group. For example, would a person in his or her twenties undergoing repair work for asthma and then again in their fifties for cholesterol and then again in their seventies for cancer have a better shot at extending their life further than someone who is already in their seventies and underwent the procedure to cure all known diagnoses?

Second, Steve wanted to understand in a scenario where cellular-rejuvenation technology was possible as prescribed by Jake and Madelyn, how long would life be extended by age group? Obviously, at age twenty-eight, a person undergoing the procedure would effectively become five years younger or twenty-three. If this patient repeated the process every eight years, they would only age three years for every eight years of life. If these were the facts, the math would look like this:

They based their analysis on an estimated life-span of seventy-five years without repair or rejuvenation technology. Estimated life-span with repair technology alone is equal to ninety years. Ninety minus twenty-eight is equal to sixty-two years. This is the number of years a person would have left without rejuvenation. If a person would only age three years for every eight years of actual life, you would need to divide life expectancy by three years and then multiply it by the eight years to determine actual life-span. So 62 years divided by 3 years is equal to 20.67 years, which, multiplied by 8 years, is equal to just over 165 years plus the original 28 years they already lived, which is equal to and the estimated life-span of 193 years.

> 90 – 28 = 62
> 62/3 = 20.67
> 20.67 × 8 = 165.36
> 165.36 + 28 = 193.36

A life-span of 193 years!

Now, on the other hand, if you had a seventy-year-old patient who was undergoing the same process for the first time, the numbers would look like this:

> 90 – 70 = 20
> 20/3 = 6.67
> 6.67 × 8 = 53.36
> 53.33 + 70 = 123.33

So a seventy-year-old person today, with a life expectancy of only five more years, with the advent of this new technology, can extend his or her life by an additional forty-eight years and live to be almost 125.

Jake and Madelyn, for the most part, agreed on the rough numbers for life extension for repair and rejuvenation. However, they are exactly that, just rough numbers. Madelyn felt that the number was really more like aging two years for every seven, but this was splitting hairs to her. To Steve, the slight differences in these numbers had exponential effects when calculating life expectancy and world-population-growth forecasts. Steve needed to refine the numbers and get best estimates. He decided to form two teams.

Karl and Jake were working independently of Steve and Madelyn to the same end. Each of them would, within a few weeks, produce their best estimates. Any differences would be discussed, and if there is not complete agreement, then the average would be used. This result will form the base matrix for which the forecasting program will operate from. As further testing would be completed, the matrix would be updated.

Dane (cofounder of the Lindsey Foundation), Victoria (president and COO of the Lindsey Foundation), Drew (Victoria's personal assistant), and Dwaine (Lindsey Foundation Science Advisor) were to handle business planning.

The priority task was to determine the ramp-up of capital production. The idea was to have a small inventory of nanobot and quantum-star manufacturing machines available for purchase and a production schedule available to the market at the time the technology is made public.

This technology will be hot! It will be highly sought after for immediate employment. Anything that can be done to expedite the ability to put the technology into use globally will reduce chaos and unavoidable unnecessary interruptions from powerful people and governments around the world. The wealthiest people in the world will want the technology at their disposal the day they learn of it. The rich are used to getting what they want when they want it. Genanotech had to be prepared.

The prevailing thought was that hospitals and clinics around the world would be retrofitted for Genanotech technology. Most surgery would become outdated and obsolete. The spaces for once-needed hospital beds dedicated to patients with extended stays would now be retrofitted to handle the requirements of diagnosis and nano procedures. Surgeons and surgical teams will need to be retrained to become expert technicians for the technology's many procedures.

Secondly, they will recruit and develop a small team of technicians who will have the sole responsibility to train other scientists and physicians around the world. Training would be specific to the use of the equipment and the procedure itself, which is fairly rudimentary. These technicians will need to be versed in training trainers. Multilingual candidates will be given preference. It will be critical that once the technology is public, it be made available to all corners of the world at once.

The third priority on the business side will be to beef up staff on the programming side of the technology. Lou was to be the point person for this. Other than the two main sites in Vancouver, there was discussion of setting up mini labs in multiple locations. Part of this discussion was to use these sites to sequester the outpatients of the planned trials. In fact, the significant increase in manpower required for trainers and programmers will make it difficult to keep a lid on the technology. The thought was to sequester all employees.

The eleven technicians on staff were heavily screened and trusted people. They had been able to live normal lives to date, if you call eighty- to ninety-hour work weeks normal. These individuals were likely to be given jobs at the off-site labs in managerial roles. They were to be sequestered with their employees. They decided to talk with the senator first, but the team was thinking that maybe the nine top-secret labs the senator had discussed earlier would be a natural fit for outpatient living during the sequestering period. They already had top scientific minds and technical personnel in place, not to mention the infrastructure was already there.

Anna, Jim, and Kathy were to complete the Corporate Charter in the upcoming weeks.

The timelines for all the above projects were critical to Steve and Karl.

Solana (cofounder of the Lindsey Foundation), Anna (senior of the legal council), and Ryan (lobbyist) were to spearhead public relations. They would canvas the scientific global community, familiarize themselves with domestic and foreign agencies that monitor medical practices and oversee controlled substances, take note of extreme religious factions that will undoubtedly make loud objection to the technology, study the economic disruption that will ensue, and formulate/execute the Genanotech public image.

Every agency like, and including, our FDA would want to bless this technology before they allowed the citizens they protect to use it. If left to each of them individually, it could take decades before the technology could be put to use. High-level officials in the Food and Drug Administration will need to be brought into the fold prior to public announcement. The initial buy-in of the FDA will be critical. In generations past, the Food and Drug Administration's public-health mission was limited to the confines of the US borders. It was a time when most FDA-regulated products were grown, produced, studied, and manufactured here at home. At that time, the FDA's international work focused primarily on protecting Americans from potentially risky products from abroad. The FDA's more formal involvement in international affairs began some fifty years ago, with one or two staff members who handled foreign inquiries and visitors to the FDA. Occasionally a representative of a foreign government would call the FDA to ask about a US regulatory requirement or to request a tour of an FDA facility.

In 1979 the International Affairs Staff was formed in the Office of the Commissioner as the first organized FDA effort to cooperate internationally with and reach out to foreign counterparts. A year later, the World Health Organization and the FDA played host for the first International Conference of Drug Regulatory Authorities.

Now, scarcely a day goes by without the FDA having intensive formal and informal interactions with our foreign counterparts. The FDA's international programs have grown in breadth and depth, and its experts are called on to direct, manage, and coordinate the growing body of international work across the agency.

The FDA and the People's Republic of China State Food and Drug Administration were the first to collaborate by setting up agencies in each other's country. The health minister in Beijing and the FDA has had, and to this day still has, a very close working relationship.

Codex Alimentarius Commission (*Codex*) is a United Nations–based organization that develops international food-safety standards and has close ties to the FDA, and recently India has engaged in joint working relationships with the FDA.

The bottom line is that if the FDA gets behind the technology, half the world will follow. With that kind of buy-in, there should be little or no resistance from most governments.

It will be necessary to identify the top religious leaders who could potentially make efforts to quash the technology. Understanding the impact the technology may have on the major religions, including Christianity, Islam, Buddhism, Hinduism and Judaism will need to be explored. Clearly there will be sects and extremist factions that will take opposition to a technology that will prolong life to this degree. Vatican City, the hub of the Catholic Church will create some unique challenges due the fact they are recognized as a sovereign nation and have significant moral influence in Europe, North America, South America and parts of Africa and Southeast Asia. More than a church, Vatican City is a government. The data on newly forecasted world population will provide fuel for the already controversial debate on birth control.

If mankind developed technology in small increments rather than in large leaps, the impact would be minor. If we increased the average life-span six or seven years every generation, it would take sixteen generations to get where we will be in this one leap. The gradual increase in life-span would not raise the eyebrows of any of the religious groups but all at once; that is another story. Genesis 6:3 of the Old Testament states that man's life-span will be limited to 120 years. Though this is left up to some interpretation, there are large numbers of believers that take this literally. A technology that clearly and immediately changes the expected life-span of man well beyond the 120-year mark will be a topic of controversy.

Probably one of the most difficult public-relations issues will be dealing with the prescription drug manufacturers. These powerful companies and their egotistical administrators will have a lot to lose when this technology hits the scene. We will still consume many commonly used drugs like pain relievers and antibiotics, but many of the cash cows will become obsolete. Male erectile enhancers, cholesterol-reducing statins, and cancer drugs will be first on the list of obsolescence. Research and development will come to a halt. This will be devastating to these empires. The lobbyists for these huge conglomerates will be on the streets in no time flat. It will be like a doctor telling a patient they only have six months to live. The irony is, they will be telling these executives they can live another fifty to one hundred years in the same breath.

There will also need to be preparation for the onslaught of justice-related dilemmas that will arise. Will prisoners be denied the benefits of the technology? Can rehabilitation occur after fifty years of therapy? Will the death penalty be perceived differently? Will the punishment for murder be perceived differently? Will life have more value from a societal perspective if it is extended seventy to one hundred years?

And then there is image. It is vitally important that Genanotech reflect its true reason for its existence. The world needs to see a company dedicated to humanity, not greed. It will need to become and, more importantly, be perceived as the largest philanthropic organization in the world. Genanotech will quickly control more of the world's money than any other single entity.

There will be those who portray the company as just another greed machine sucking the financial resources from the middle class. There will be accusations that the process is a fraud, that the elimination from symptoms is temporary, and that there will be horrible long-term side effects. Though completely unfounded, the stories are inevitable.

Inroads will need to be developed with all major news media. The major US networks will set the stage. FOX, NBC, CBS, ABC, and CNN will cover this story nonstop for months.

The news stations will create many new household names and celebrities. Individuals in the scientific community with a flair for the limelight will sit on panels debating the technical aspects of the procedures. There will be panels of sociologists and psychologists evaluating the world's response to the prospect of doubling or tripling the average life-span.

Future shock (man's ability to cope with change) will become a daily topic of discussion. Some believe that man has a biological limit in dealing with change. The stress human beings endure caused by change has a toll. When change becomes too rapid or frequent, the stress associated with it can have many ill effects. There have been comprehensive studies on this phenomenon.

Far right-wing conservatives and leftist liberals will have heated debates on man's venture toward immortality.

Top economists will discuss what will appear to be the beginning of an endless bull market. Economic growth is based on consumption, and consumption has a direct correlation to population. Population growth will be something very difficult to control.

The Los Angeles Times, *New York Times*, *Chicago Tribune*, *San Francisco Chronicle*, *USA Today*, and the *Wall Street Journal* will need access to press releases and exclusive interviews. Internet news, a growing mainstream source of news, will also need direct attention. MSN and Google are the predominate players.

Outpatients will be an excellent source of fodder in the initial year for all reporters looking for a story. Some outpatient coaching for media attention will need to be part of the routine until the media becomes exhausted with patient success stories.

The list goes on. Public relations is about anticipating what reactions will take place to an event and have plans to effectively dull or negate any unwanted repercussions. Steve and Karl will be able to provide massive amounts of detailed data that will give insight to humanity's reaction.

The idea is to trickle out in small pieces of the forecast at precise times. For example, if environmental debates heat up to a point where violence erupts, estimates on the length of time that fossil fuels will remain available for consumption can be introduced to the media based on the current population forecasts and known reserves. Many strides have been made for clean-energy technology in the last five years, but the world is still addicted to oil.

Media blitz on progress of hydrogen technology from freshwater reserves, solar-grid arrays, nuclear and wind technological updates will dampen the need for overreaction. When the forecast shows no immediate threat, human innovation and hope will prevail. This is particularly true if the time line faced is realistic. If we need to find a way, we will find a way.

Anna, Ryan, and Solana will build up an arsenal of offensive tactics to combat the over reactions of numerous segments of society. They agreed they would not be backed into a corner and have to defend themselves. They would remain in control.

The senator, Jim (junior domestic legal council), and Kathy (international legal council) would focus on government-related action items. The senator had to meet shortly with the Secretary of Commerce who directly oversaw the Census Bureau. The secretary was fully aware of the project Steve headed up on forecasting. The Secretary was a close colleague and friend, who understood the importance of keeping this software's capability undisclosed to the public and particularly the heads of other governments. Ultimately, the senator would call for a meeting with the president, the head of the FDA, secretary of commerce, and the secretary of state. In this meeting he would disclose the nature of the technology and pertinent forecasts associated with its deployment. He would ask the White House for support of a closed session of congress at a later date to brief them on the technology before making it public.

Before this can happen, he would bring his nine labs working on the technology up to speed and make the head of each of these labs report to Lou. Lou would be given complete and direct authority over the labs. The fact that he was a civilian and not on any known government payroll would make this arrangement a little outside normal protocols. His previous government background checks when he worked for Jake would help soften any hierarchal tensions. In all reality there was not much about this venture that fit into normal.

When ample data would be compiled on human testing, it will be necessary to involve some key officials in the FDA prior to any other government agency. The senator had been building a friendship with the director of the FDA for the past five years. He believed he could trust him to keep the technology quiet for a short period of time before they include the White House. FDA buy-in was absolutely critical prior to bringing the technology out into the open.

Kathy, who was fully versed in international law, and Jim, a prodigal expert in domestic business law, would team up to identify key individuals in other countries and non-US agencies around the world. Their mission would be to develop relationships with the individuals who will first be made aware of the technology. There will be specific protocols and cultural etiquette to consider. They will need to bring in some advisors to assist them in this undertaking. The advisors will not know what the technology is but will be able to provide much assistance in identifying the audience.

There are currently 192 members in the United Nations. There are two other independent countries, Kosovo and Vatican City, that are not members. Taiwan has a seat in the United Nations but is considered technically governed by the People's Republic of China. We currently recognize 195 independent countries in the world.

It is common to think of England, Scotland, Ireland, and Wales to be countries when, in fact, they are not recognized as countries because they are all part of the United Kingdom. Puerto Rico, Greenland, Palestine, and Bermuda also fall into similar categories and are not recognized as countries.

By definition, an independent country must—

- have a territory with internationally recognized boundaries (boundary disputes are OK)
- have people who live there on an ongoing basis
- have economic activity and an organized economy
- regulate foreign and domestic trade and issue money
- have power of social engineering, such as education
- have a transportation system to move goods and people
- have a government that provides public services and police power
- have sovereignty—no other state has power over the country's territory

There are a small number of countries that the United States is not friendly with. These countries we do not have a good working relationship with will have to gain access to the technology through other countries that are willing to trade with them unless they decide to cooperate with the White House. It would be unethical for the United States to impose global trade sanctions on a technology such as this. The royalty transfer will have to be dealt with where the United States has trade sanctions. The technology may, in fact, play a crucial part in giving our country's leaders the opening to start healthy diplomatic efforts in parts of the world we have historically been unable to see eye to eye with. Examples are Iran, North Korea, Afghanistan, Syria, Libya, and a few other rogue countries with anti-American sentiment.

The world is pretty much at peace at the present. There is terrorist activity from time to time, but these groups have no territory, no boundaries, and no government. They do require that our troops and allies' troops remain in hot spots around the world. Most of the leadership of the larger, more organized terrorist organizations have been captured or killed in the last seven years, yet these gangs still exist in force.

Once Jim and Kathy would compile a complete list of all countries and the associated agencies with current contact information, they would start working on developing a smaller list of countries and officials that the United States should have direct contact with. The senator had already identified twenty-seven countries he wanted on the list. Most of western Europe, a few countries in the Eastern bloc, Russia, China, Japan, Australia, India, Brazil, Argentina, Mexico, Canada, Israel, Saudi Arabia, Egypt, Nigeria, and South Africa will all be on the list for direct diplomatic interface.

The senator will also need to convene meetings with the heads of the FBI, CIA, and NSA.

Most of the activity the senator will be engaged in will be preparation for a flurry of meetings with our top government officials. He will also seek approval and advice from the United Nations Security Council.

The United Nations made up of 192 nations today appointed a Security Council at its inception in 1945 after the end of World War II. The Security Council is made up of fifteen members, five of which are permanent (China, Russia, France, the United Kingdom, and the United States). The other ten are elected for two-year nonconsecutive terms by the general assembly. Only the five permanent council members have veto authority.

The judicial arm of the United Nations is the International Court of Justice, which has jurisdiction only when nations agree it has. The US Senate must decide which issues are domestic and therefore beyond the court's authority. The United States has not accepted the 1998 international treaty establishing the international criminal court. The United States also decided to forgo UN Security Council approval for its invasion of Iraq in 2003. These moves have weakened the once dominate position the United States has in the United Nations general assembly. Although the United States no longer dominates the United Nations, the organization continues to be an important instrument of US foreign policy.

Kathy had a great deal of expertise working with many foreign countries. Heading international relations for the Lindsey Foundation was quite involved. The Lindsey Foundation had consistently worked with underdeveloped or poorly governed countries in order to bring basic medicine to their citizens. She was versed in dealing with foreign agencies and the corrupt, or not so corrupt, officials who worked in government or customs departments.

Genanotech will need to export equipment and materials to every country that uses the technology. All countries without open trade agreements with the United States will be jockeying for some arrangement to get the technology. The utopian view is that this may provide an opportunity to improve peaceful relations with all nations. Realistically it may cause additional tension. The United States will benefit economically in the short term with a significant increase in GDP. It is very important to underplay this; the technology needs to be provided from Genanotech, not the United States, in order to minimize political issues.

One of the larger and most difficult issues the teams will be facing is the initial implementation of the technology. There is no way to provide enough capital equipment and training to the entire world on day one. Every country will have the technology, but there will be a considerable shortfall of capacity to treat every person on their deathbed. There will be millions of people who will die before the technology can be deployed to all in need. With the current death toll of 145,000 people per day, Genanotech will be lucky to provide treatment to 10 percent or 15 percent in the initial days of deployment. The people who cannot be treated due to capital constraint will have the knowledge they can be saved but not get treatment in time. The family members left behind will undoubtedly suffer the most. The news will be overloaded with stories of individuals whose lives could have been spared but for one reason or another they were not able to get treatment in time. The company's goal was to minimize the trauma of the *those who could have lived*, by executing a rapid deployment of the technology worldwide.

It was after midnight when Dane gathered everyone together and suggested that they all hit the sack. Dane had prearranged sleeping accommodations for fourteen at the estate. It was a bit makeshift, utilizing the pool house and finished attic, but everyone would be comfortable. He suggested that they reconvene at 9:30 a.m.

21

It had been weeks since either Jake or Madelyn had slept in separate beds. They were both exhausted, and with their minds running a million miles a minute, another night in a shared room would have likely been spent hashing over the immensity of their undertaking.

Jake was wakened at 8:00 a.m. by his cell phone. It was Lou wanting to know where they were. He had arrived at the lab at 6:00 a.m. and was anxious to talk with them about the meeting. He also wanted to update them on the progress his mother was having with her rejuvenation regiment. Lou had successfully reviewed and approved of programs that were designed to rejuvenate bone, vascular-system degradation, digestive system, heart, exodermises, respiratory tract, and liver function. His mother had undergone treatment for each. She looked ten years younger and felt great.

Jake explained they would be tied up another day in the meeting. He tried his best to give Lou a briefing on what had transpired in the last twenty-four hours. Lou wasn't happy about the decision to sequester all the patients; he knew his mother was going to freak out. Jake said maybe they could make an exception. Lou was fine with that response but knew the importance of secrecy and the difficult time they were going to have with this once they started more human trials. He was excited about expanding personnel and resources. Surprisingly he was also feeling quite good about his new responsibilities and being placed in a position to manage the outpatient process. The space now dedicated to the capital equipment for nano-machine generation would be more than adequate to expand into.

Madelyn popped into Jake's room while he was still on the phone with Lou. At first she just posed in funny positions while Jake was talking, but then when she decided to physically maul him, he got off the phone.

Everyone but Dane and the senator were at the table enjoying a delicious breakfast at 9:30 a.m. Fifteen minutes went by, and Solana went to check on the two when they were just exiting Dane's study down the hall. She held the door open and waited until they were in before shutting it behind them.

Dane apologized for being late and elaborated on; the senator and he were trying to determine their next best course of action. He discussed the need for regular meetings and the logistic problem of having everyone spread out.

He then said, "We have been discussing our concerns over security. It is critical that the technology remain top secret and kept from the public at all costs. There are a number of concerns that have already been identified." He suggested that the group entertain the idea of everyone relocating to a centralized location and sequestering themselves and their families until the company went public. He raised his hand and said, "I know, I know this will be inconvenient, but it may be our best course of action. I urge you to consider it."

The group was taken aback. Even Solana seemed a bit shocked by the thought of it. He instructed Drew to locate and acquire suitable premises for the administrative function and living accommodations near the lab in Vancouver. Victoria hated it when Dane gave direct orders to her staff. This wasn't the first time, but it still didn't make it any easier. She thought, *I better get used to it.*

Steve raised his hand. Dane immediately went on to explain that Steve, Karl, and the forecasting computers and programs would be moved to the existing lab as soon as the adjacent building was ready and room could be made for them. Jake thought, *Well, there goes Lou's extra space.* He then went on to think about living quarters. If Steve and Karl each took a room, Lou would have to remain staying at his mom's? Maybe they could bunk together; *oh well, this will get figured out later*, he thought.

Karl was thinking that this was going to be too far to commute. What about his new wife? It did cross his mind that the senator was overseeing the commerce department where Heather worked. Maybe they could make arrangements for her to work up the road a few clicks. He also reminded himself that Dane said *you and your families.* He decided not to interrupt the whole group with his personal questions and figured he could talk with Steve later.

Dane clicked a few buttons on the laptop in front of him, and the lights dimmed, and the projector had a calendar on it. It was the kind you sometimes see on desktops—each day is a big square where you can write in your daily reminders. Two weeks from now would be the first annual board meeting; the location was Lindsey Foundation. Anna and Jim felt the pressure of time. They did agree to have the charter done in two weeks. The next day showed three separate meetings—Science/Forecasting, PR/Gov., and Business. The rest of the calendar was blank.

With that, Dane said he would like to conclude their first team meeting. He was getting back some of his fierce business style and enjoying it. Dane was a very fair manager/owner, but building a business as big as his, you had to know how to command respect.

Dane had nurtured respect from his newly formed team with the possible exception of Anna and maybe Jim. Everyone had plenty to do prior to their next scheduled get-together, so there were no questions. As they were getting their things together, the senator whispered in Anna's ear, "Can you and Jim stay back? Dane and I have something to discuss with you."

She stiffened up and said, "Of course."

Solana, a gracious host, was bidding farewell to their guests, while the senator and Dane escorted Anna and Jim into Dane's study. The fourteen-foot ceilings bordered in dark cherry wood crown molding, tall bookcases filled with hard-backed literature organized categorically, a small fireplace, huge mahogany desk, and ample seating area with ox-blood leather furniture created a relaxed, almost lodge-like environment where they could talk less formally.

After everyone was seated, Dane opened, "We have a few security-related concerns we need to discuss." He looked at Anna and asked, "Does Ben know the details of the work you are doing for Genanotech?" Anna knew they were talking about senior partner Ben Gerrard of her firm.

Anna answered, "Yes and no. He has known of Madelyn's work from the time she was first pursuing venture capital. Neither he nor Hugh (she looked at Jim for assurance) knows the progress made to date. I think they are under the impression that the original time line of the summer of 2023, over a year from now, would be the earliest we would have any preliminary results on the technology."

Dane said, "If we were to monopolize your time or hire you away from the firm, do you think they would put two and two together? The answer is yes, of course. I believe that both Ben and Hugh collaborated to assign Jim to work for you." Dane looked at Jim with a forced smile.

He then said, "I also believe that they would love to have their firm involved in a more substantial way on something this big." After a long pause, he added, "Jim, don't get me wrong; a little nepotism is completely expected. We don't hold that against you or your father at all, and we believe we are lucky to have you and Anna working on our team. Our concern is leaking the existence of the technology before we are ready. It would create chaos on a global level if the news of increasing life-span by eighty to one hundred years was revealed to the public without proper prior planning."

Anna interjected, "I completely understand your concerns and also understand the need for a strategy to communicate the need for mine and Jim's full-time attention to your company. I also trust that client-attorney privilege and the high level of ethics among the partners in Mankin, Garrard, Williams, Beakon and associates will prove to make this a nonissue. I really do not think I could have been assigned a better intern than Jim to assist me with this effort, regardless of bloodlines."Jim felt a bit flushed that Anna felt it important enough to have his back. He was starting to feel he was not among the deserving few who were engaged in this effort. He was only here because of his father. This reminded him of how he felt the first few months working at the firm. His wife, Beverly, would remind him that graduating first in his class at Yale Business School and then third in his class in law school at Yale had a lot more to do with his right to have a position in his father's firm than his connections. He was a hard worker and was only working for the firm to obtain some necessary experience and connections to pursue his political career. Now he found himself working on something much more important than his anticipated career as a public servant.

The senator said, "OK; client-attorney privilege, limited knowledge, and a good track record of high ethical behavior makes me feel better, but the real question is, how do we hire you and Jim away from the firm without some explanation? The other question is Beverly." Jim was now feeling piqued on; first his father, now his wife? He wondered if the rest of the team was undergoing this level of scrutiny. Paradoxically, he was flattered that they were interested in hiring him.

Jim's mind was trying to digest the information when Anna piped up and said, "It would be a lot easier to dedicate our time if we were employees of Genanotech. It would be much simpler to maintain secrecy without reporting to a boss who was not privy to the work. There is so much to do here."

After a big exhale, she said, "Senator, don't get me wrong here. After spending yesterday listening and working with you, I truly believe you are 100 percent behind this company's mission, and you will likely be instrumental in helping us break through some difficult bureaucratic layers of government necessary to get the technology into the mainstream. How do I say this? You were just sprung on us, and I am not sure I know what all that means."

She turned her steely eyes toward Dane and said, "I am still not sure how I feel about you being less than honest with Madelyn and Jake and myself for that matter. May I speak freely?"

He squirmed in his big leather chair and said, "Yes, of course."

"I need time to think about this. Madelyn and Jake are my clients, and that is where my fiduciary responsibility lies."

Looking at Dane again, she said, "You do have twenty-five million dollars invested and are committed to another fifty million dollars if need be; not chump change by any means. The US taxpayer has provided the lion share of the R and D costs, totaling one hundred seventy-five million dollars via a not-so-public pledge from the senator. We all know we would not be this far along without everyone's contribution. The questions remain as to how to form the corporation, who should be voting board members, who should receive stock and how many shares should be issued and to whom, what executive management positions needed to be created, and who should fill them. Jim and I had spent the last three weeks working on this exact set of questions. We had a proposed charter almost ready for review. Now, I don't know what is right? I can't speak for Jim. Jim, how do you feel?"

The senator appeared calm and collected, while Dane was clearly disheveled.

Jim said, "Me? I am going to go along with your lead on this, Anna. I don't have answers ready for you on how the charter should be modified. It should be modified." He said with some hesitation and nervousness in his voice. Here he was a kid fresh out of law school, debating the structure of what will likely be the largest corporation in the world with a senior elected US senator and one of the richest men in the country.

He caught his breath and continued, "I am also very interested in devoting my undivided attention to the successful launch and operation of this company. I must say, I feel like with my father and my wife being subjects of concern, I am possibly more of a risk to the operation than a benefit; if I were to leave the firm? I might be considered a bigger risk knowing what I know now. If I left the firm and moved to Washington State, I would undoubtedly have to either lie to Beverly or include her in our mission. Frankly, I am not one hundred percent certain Beverly would favor our need for secrecy, which I am sure is your concern as well."

The senator replied, "Exactly our concern, Jim. As far as the other, I will let you and Anna hash out whatever you need to with Dane. I have no interest in the business side of things here."

Jim thought for a minute and said, "What if you retain the services of my father's firm, as you are currently engaged and hire Anna as Genanotech's private council? This way I can continue working on our mission from DC at my firm's new corporate office. My proximity could be very useful in working with the government personnel in the White House and the Pentagon. When we are just a month or so away from making a public announcement, Anna can make me an offer I can't refuse to work directly for Genanotech."

Anna was nodding the entire time Jim was talking; she was really proud of Jim for being honest and forthright as well as creative. She interrupted Jim and said, "Yes! Then we could also hire Beverly as a consultant to assist taking the technology public; with only a month away from our announcement date, she would be inundated with hundreds of public-relations issues well into their development. She would not have the time or the motivation to leak the technology. In the meantime it would not be unusual for her husband to make weekly or biweekly business trips to Vancouver. He would be the new top council at his father's firm, representing a new start-up company that his former boss Anna was hired to work for full time."

Jim responded with great enthusiasm, "Exactly what I was thinking."

Both Dane and the senator relaxed in their chairs and took a moment to assess the strategy. Dane looked at the senator who was obviously deep in thought, his head tilted down and his index finger pointed into his right temple. Once the senator realized all eyes were on him, he sat up in his chair, firmly placed both hands on his knees, and with very a deliberate pace said, "I am impressed with the strategy. I believe it adequately addresses our concerns. I am particularly touched by the honesty and the loyalty to our mission exhibited by Jim here. I was initially concerned we would be offending Jim by expressing concerns about his wife's inability to maintain secrecy; the fact that Jim himself acknowledged the same concern without the words put into his mouth is reassuring." He then asked for a few moments alone with Dane and requested that Anna and Jim retreat to the garden room where they would join them in a moment.

After only ten minutes, they arrived, both smiling and laughing. Dane shut the door, though almost everyone had surely gone, as he didn't want to take any chances with privacy. He asked Anna if she could have a proposed corporate charter for himself, Madelyn, Jake, and the senator to review in one week.

The senator interrupted, "Dane, I said I am not interested in the business side." Then he looked at Anna and said, "I will be fine with anything the rest of the group wants to do here."

Anna looked at Dane and in a controlled, mechanical tone said, "We will have something for you and Madelyn to review in a week. It will not be polished, but the basics will be there."

Dane said, "Great. I know this has been a difficult past couple of days, and I know you will do the right thing. I would also hope that you would consider me the right choice to lead this company, but I understand that you may have some hesitations. I would like you to be head legal council and have a seat on the board. Once the corporation's charter is functional, we will arrange for yours and Jim's subsequent compensation packages to be put together. You are an expert in your field, so excuse me if I am preaching at the choir. I believe that fully functional boards of directors have at least seven members but not more than a dozen."

He then asked Jim if he would accept a position as legal liaison to the United States of America at a date to be determined.

Jim said yes.

22

It was about 2:00 p.m. when Karl and Steve arrived back at their lab. They were emotionally exhausted from the events of the past two days. During the three-hour drive back, they discussed some of the logistical issues in moving the lab to its new location.

They were wrestling with the news of the technology. This news created not only an enormous workload for them but was also causing them difficulties in dealing with the multifarious impacts it would have on them individually. Karl figured that if Jake and Madelyn's initial numbers were correct, he could live to be 189 years old, and Steve could live to be 163 years old. The thought of living another 150 years or more was a colossus mental adjustment. We are programmed from youth that life is short. It only lasts long enough to have children and grandchildren. By the time the grandchildren have their families, we are on our deathbed.

Steve decided that the next few days should be spent finalizing the HIV/AIDS cure data. This was a known reality not currently fully integrated into the software. Once completed, they will have a solid base to start from. They could then input some basic raw assumptions on the ramp-up of Genanotech technology, run the program, and evaluate some of the key predictions. By the end of the week, they will be ready to focus on developing a plan to move the lab.

The average life-span in the continent of Africa was going to jump from forty-nine years to sixty-four years. That is over a billion people extending their lives by fifteen years. The math showed a disproportional percentage of population increase in the first fifteen years.

The net effect is that for the next fifteen years, population will grow at a rate of 363,000 people per day verses the current 317,000. World population reached eight billion in November 2020. Nine billion people will inhabit the earth by 2034 rather than the previously predicted 2042, and there will be over 12 billion people on the planet by 2050.

Karl was thinking he would only be sixty-four years old in 2050, with 125 years left to live. When he was born in 1994, there were only 5.4 billion people inhabiting the earth, and in 2050 there will be over twelve billion.

Overpopulation has been a concern for the past forty years. With the HIV/AIDS cure and now Genanotech technology, the issue will be given serious attention. With the ability to increase life-span to 150 to 200 years, overpopulation will not be a distant problem our grandchildren will face. It will be a problem we all face in our own new lifetime.

In 1798 Thomas Malthus published an essay on the principal of population. The premise of his essay was that man would continue to reproduce beyond his ability to provide enough food to sustain the population. This later became known as a Malthusian Catastrophe. Modern agriculture and the industrial revolution have dampened immediate concerns, but the theory is still relegated as true in intellectual circles.

Population control has been mandated in some governments. China's "one child" per household policy is most notable. Other countries like India have limited rights for those households having more than two children. Iran is the only country in the world to require birth-control education prior to a couple's wedding.

It will be interesting to see how mankind will change their views regarding population control with a life expectancy of 175 years. The health of a man and woman's reproductive systems will be intact for the first 90 to 125 years of life. Perhaps it will become commonplace in the most modernized societies to start having children at age eighty-five. Of course, these kinds of changes in man's behavior will take some time.

It will be necessary to take into consideration the use of contraception when building the model for the forecasting of life after Genanotech. Currently, most of the population growth will occur in the less-developed regions of the world. In the most-developed regions, population is approaching stagnation. Post Genanotech, modernized society will grow at a moderate rate. Only one-third of the population resides in modernized society. Two-thirds of the population is living in underdeveloped nations and communities. The first order of business for mankind will be to develop these areas of the world. The founders of Genanotech were intent on providing the technology to all corners of the world. The modern industrialized nations and regions in the world will undoubtedly benefit initially. It was *not an option* for the founders of the technology to limit the availability of its use.

If the technology was employed without condition and injected into today's economy, only one-third of the population would get its advantage. This would create two very separate societies, an elite and a subsect. In a world society with two distinct classes, sectors of the elite class living in modernized cities with triple the life-span of the less-fortunate portion of the population would perpetuate a type of oppression not seen since the days of slavery.

Steve and Karl would endeavor to build a complex model detailing not only the ramp-up of the technology in the developed portions of the planet but also in the underdeveloped areas. The need to build infrastructure that includes modern roadways, availability of electricity, water and sewage systems, schools, hospitals, communication networks, grocery stores, and so on to support two-thirds of the population of the planet will be one of man's greatest undertakings in the next century. The economic benefit to the entrepreneurs that engage in this effort will be unlimited for centuries to come.

Steve stated, "As the senator brought up in discussion in the last meeting, many small countries will be forced to work with their neighboring nations to insure their citizens will have access to health and longevity. They will need to increase trade in order to build infrastructure. If the world were to stay fiercely independent with minor cultural differences creating the need for total sovereignty, many nations will find that they will be unable to administer the technology and educate their citizens to live in a rapidly changing world. The result may be a world with micro-geographic-based Malthusian Catastrophes."

Technology without modernization will perpetuate an increase in world hunger and famine. In the past three decades, the world has made very positive strides in reducing both hunger and the spread of disease around the world. The problem certainly still remains, but if underdeveloped nations were given access to the technology without a firm commitment to modernize their nation's infrastructures, the successes would be reversed.

Karl recalled Dane saying that this technology would become the world's largest bargaining chip. He was not in favor of bribery as a rule, but if it could bring governments together to create an environment where every corner of the world can provide the opportunity for its citizens to enjoy a middle-class lifestyle rather than living in squalor and poverty, the means justify the ends.

Of course westernization of the world as a whole will be scrutinized, criticized, and a topic of great debate for many years. Over time, this debate will have happened anyway, with many wars, civil unrest, and religious extremist uprisings along the way. With the advent of the technology, the debate will need to be accelerated.

Perhaps westernization can take place with some designed variation. A civilized modern society can be created where a family can survive on one income. Maybe only one car in every garage, maybe reading takes precedence over television and electronic games, and maybe spiritual life becomes a higher and more frequent focus in daily life? A simpler life, but a life with the benefits of waste management, sanitary living conditions, education for all, heated and cooled living quarters, and ample food for all. The poorest nations and regions of the world can modernize to the degree their culture believes acceptable, but they will have to modernize, not necessarily westernize.

Karl made a list of the key factors that needed addressing before they could start entering base data. Once basic entries were made, they will have a first swipe on the effect the new technology will have on population:

1) Identify the ramp-up of repair technology (curing the terminally ill)
2) Identify the start date and ramp-up of rejuvenation technology (extending life-spans of the population)
3) Determination of the effectiveness the rejuvenation technology will have on life-span
4) Time line for modernization of two-thirds of the world population centers

5) Contraception tendencies and population-control factors

Numbers one through four required crunching numbers in multiple databases premised by the known factors of today. Number five would be the wild card. To forecast the impact that any given event has on human psychology is very difficult. Karl thought about this as it related to himself. Just a few weeks ago, he felt the need to start a family within the next five years. Now he realized he could wait twenty, maybe forty, years to start his family. Perhaps if the numbers on population were run with only considering items one through four on the list, the data itself will reveal specific intervals where available resources to sustain the population are diminished to the point of inadequacy. In other words, if man knows when he is going to run out of food or energy far enough in advance to avert the problem, man will take steps to avoid the circumstance from happening.

Karl realized he was on to something. If, for instance, it was evident that the nation of India would have an inability to provide adequate food supplies to its citizens in the year 2049, they would have thirty years to take steps to fix or prolong the issue from being a problem. The first attempts would be to use advanced technologies to increase food supply. Secondly, business heads and government would evaluate ways to increase exports, which would, in turn, provide the economic capability to import the shortfall of food from other nations. Third, and finally, they would consider means to stop the growth of their population.

Karl determined if he ran the program without population control, he could divide the planet into a dozen or so geographic regions. Each region would have predictions for population limits with the anticipated food and energy available. Each region would then be evaluated for their natural resources, technological resources, economic resources, and any other resources available for export. Finally, each region would be evaluated for its infrastructure to educate and implement necessary population control. Taking this approach will provide a template where Steve and Karl can start to quantify human behavior, as it relates to controlling its population.

Some countries may determine that the only way to avoid poverty and famine is to make the Genanotech technology unavailable to its citizens. This would be a topic for the United Nations to address. The industrialized nations of the world will surely determine this is not the proper course of action and will likely create international law against such practice.

Then it dawned on Karl; the only way this technique would work was if it were kept a secret. The data showing the need for population control needs to be presented to the world in its raw form. If the information was released to the global community with the psychological factors of population control included, the data would not spawn the actions pertinent to its own assumptions. The data would then be wrong. The only way for the data to be right is for its results to be unknown. How can this world-class forecasting software be useful in planning infrastructures and setting up roadmaps to stable growing economies if it cannot be known?

Karl reviewed his plan to quantify human behavior with Steve. Steve broke the factors down to smaller pieces and through all his logic came full circle to Karl's original concept. Geography, existing food and energy resources, export capability, and population-control tendencies were agreed to be the basic building blocks of the analysis. Sometimes you need to keep it simple.

They identified thirteen specific geographic areas where models would be built. They broke the industrialized world into five regions: North America minus Mexico, Western Europe, Eastern Europe/ Russia, Eastern China/Japan, and Australia. The less-modernized regions of Mexico/Central America, South America, Middle Africa, Northern Africa/Middle East, South Western Asia, South Eastern Asia, the Caribbean Islands, and Antarctica rounded it out.

Steve was tired and wanted to call it a day when Karl said, "OK, but not before I plant this seed. I was going to take you through more of the process before I laid this on you, but I really need to have you start thinking about this." He explained his concern about the need for secrecy in order to have the model provide accurate data. He expressed his distress that the useful portions of the data would not be available for long-term infrastructure planning.

Steve said, "Thanks a lot; now how am I going to sleep?"

Karl said, "Well, at least I will be able to sleep, now that I know you are working on the solution."

They decided to stop at the bar and meet Heather for a drink before they retired. It had been prearranged between Karl and Steve that they would not discuss the technology with Heather before she was formally brought into the loop. This should be within the next week or two. In a way it was a godsend. When they were with Heather, they had to talk about something else. The diversion was refreshing and, probably more importantly, necessary to keep perspective.

What was life really all about? Regardless of how long you live, it matters much more how you love and embrace life while you are here. Quality of life verses quantity. Karl loved his wife, Heather, and he loved his friend Steve. Steve loved both Karl and Heather. When they were together having a few drinks, enjoying food, and harassing the local wait-staff, life was good!

23

Anna was particularly pleased with herself on the trip back to DC. She landed the job of a lifetime and was literally writing her own ticket to boot. She was to work with two scientists she had grown to love and respect. She was working on a project that would benefit the entire world. And regardless of what she had let on, she was going to be working for a man whom, despite his recent behavior, she truly respected and admired.

She and Jim spent the flight back having a few cocktails while they brainstormed some ideas on how to revise the charter.

They were wrestling with how to compensate the senator. Obviously he will have a role and probably a significant one at that. Anna brought up some interesting points. She said, "The senator has stipulated on more than one occasion he did not want anything to do with the business side of things, yet in a way this is really his business more than it is anyone's. He is responsible for funding seventy percent of the research-and-development costs. He has connections with my boss, Ben Gerrard. He knows Jake personally and has even had him working for him indirectly in the past. Lou has also worked indirectly for the senator. The senator has been a major liaison to the government for the Lindsey Foundation. He and Victoria have worked together more than half a dozen times in the last fifteen years. He is friends with Jake's dad. He is friends with Dane and Solana. Our new additions to the company are Census Bureau employees, who report directly to the senator. The only outsider in Genanotech is Madelyn, the inventor of the technology."

Jim had the look of revelation. He said, "Wow, when you put it all together like that, it is kind of creepy. I don't know much about the senator. Do you think we can ping Ben for an opinion without raising his eyebrows?"

Anna said, "We better not, but I think I will have our PI do some digging around and see what we can find out—that is, if there is anything to find out. My gut tells me that the senator is who he represents himself to be. I would also like to talk with Madelyn and Jake about him. Our reality is that the senator is part of our team and possibly is the only reason there is a team. We will need to work with what we have, and that includes Dane."

Jim smiled and said, "I think you are wise. Dane let us down, but he possibly also may have done us a favor in doing so. If we had known of the government's involvement during the proving-out stages, it may have interfered with the process. We will need Dane's expertise in leading the company forward. He has done an exemplary job so far; I think we can agree on that."

Anna was at peace for the first time since the incident with Dane.

After a few days of working on the revision, they were ready to call Madelyn and Jake for their input. They set up a mid-morning video conference call on a line Drew secured. Anna had e-mailed over the latest revision of the charter the night before for Madelyn and Jake to review. Neither Madelyn nor Jake really cared much for the corporate stuff, but they knew it was an important part of the process and would eventually be a critical component in deploying the technology. Madelyn showed her frustration each time her energy was diverted from the science, while Jake played peacemaker. The fact he was so easy-going and agreeable annoyed her, yet she loved him for it just the same.

Madelyn had had many thoughts about "patent and sell" verses "manufacture, employ, and control." Control was her main concern, not that she was a control person. Madelyn was not a person who felt she needed to control everything except perhaps her science-and-development methods. She fully understood that there were people who had specific talents and abilities she did not. The problem with this situation was her moral ground. She just wasn't OK with relinquishing her involvement with the technology; at least until it was made available to the entire world. Her biggest fear was that whether it was for fiscal or political reasons, with the wrong people in control, the technology be limited to only part of the population. Any percentage less than 100 percent of the population would not be considered acceptable to her. The thought of a two-class society where one class lives long, healthy lives and the other lives significantly shorter lives with less quality of life was just unacceptable to Madelyn. This was her invention, and she was dedicated to make sure it had an overall positive effect on the world.

They decided to review the document first thing in the morning rather than before bed. The last thing they needed was another sleepless night. Over coffee they started to look at the charter and put it down; way too many legaleses for them. Best if they just waited for the video conference call and let their trusted friends walk them through it.

After all the pleasantries, Anna said, "There are a few items we need to discuss while we have you guys on the net. The charter, of course, and the guiding principles behind it is just one. We also need to talk about the corporate structure and assign positions and areas of responsibility. Other than that we need to pick your brain on how you feel about the senator's involvement and Dane's recent indiscretion. So why don't we start with Madelyn and talk about the senator and Dane?"

Madelyn said, "At first I was nervous about the senator's involvement and really more so the government's involvement. I was also really..." She paused. "Pissed is the best way to describe the way I felt when we found out Dane didn't tell us what was going on from the beginning with the money and the senator. Since that meeting three days ago, I have had a couple of nice conversations with both the senator and Dane. I feel at ease with both men now. I truly believe they were doing what they thought was best, and I believe that we are all in line philosophically. The interesting thing about the senator is that he has connections, whether they are direct or indirect, with virtually everyone involved with Genanotech except for me. He has also shared with me something else I feel you should know about. I need to bring up client-attorney-privilege reminders here before I go forward."

Anna smiled and nodded her head in compliance.

Madelyn went on to say, "What I am about to tell you is the main reason I am comfortable with having the senator on board. He has authorized me to tell you this but no one else. The money that he has siphoned into our company's R and D accounts was not approved by the Senate or any other government agency. He has been rat-holing funds in unallocated, undisclosed accounts for ten years. He has basically embezzled this money for the very purpose it is being used. He shared with me that *if* this technology—no, he said *when* this technology—was close to full development, serious sums of money would be needed to get it off the ground. He knows better than any of us that if he were to try to get the money through normal channels, the technology would either never get developed or there would be so many strings attached to it that he would have preferred it had never been developed. He also reminded me that he had a complete above-board R and D effort in the nine labs around the country working toward the same goal as Genanotech. I just beat them to the punch. He remains convicted that he is a patriot and that he is working in the best interest of America. He also said that he has done an excellent job of covering his tracks. As far as any US official will ever know, the money all came from the Lindsey Foundation. That is why I am comfortable with the senator."

Both ends of the conference were quiet.

This changed the view Anna had for Dane. She put herself in his place and could now fully understand his actions or lack of actions. In essence, the government freed up the one hundred million dollars for Dane and Solana to send to Africa and saved their organization seventy-five million dollars to boot. The fact remained that Dane was not completely above board, so she still felt comfortable with revising charter.

Anna then looked at Jake and asked how he felt about Dane and the senator. Jake said, "I am in complete agreement with Madelyn on this, and personally I like both men."

Anna said, "Well, good, because I based our revised charter on you both feeling the way you do. We now need to discuss the organization chart."

Anna filled the screen with a chart showing Dane Lindsey, the chief executive officer, at the top. Directly below him was Madelyn Cooper, the chief operating officer. Next to Madelyn on her left, also reporting to Dane, was Victoria Tawfeek, the director of business administration. Next to Madelyn on her right, also reporting to Dane, was Anna, the chief financial officer. Drew Jackson had a position of executive assistant, reporting to

Dane, Victoria, and Anna. In Dane's absence Madelyn and Anna would have authority over Victoria.

Anna explained, "Jim and I really wrestled with the CFO position. This is a critical position that Dane originally wanted Solana to have. Dane has offered me the position of head the legal council, which I have neither accepted nor declined. I believe I can handle both the CFO and the legal-council hats as long as I get the right people working for me. By making this recommendation, I can act as a counterweight in the power structure. As you well know, my loyalties are to Madelyn, and I only assume Victoria's are with Dane. Victoria is the clear choice to oversee business administration. If Solana were to be CFO, three of the top four positions would be aligned with Dane, and that is not considering the senator's allegiances. Remember here, we are talking about a company that will quickly become the largest corporation ever to exist. Even with Dane's good track record of maintaining a balanced moral standing in the community with all the wealth he has accumulated, the kind of riches that will come with being at the top of Genanotech are almost unfathomable. We need to insure we have checks and balances. We do not want to create a megalomaniac and not be able to do anything about it. Again, I believe my being in the position of CFO will insure some stability and balance in the organization."

Madelyn looked at Jake and said, "I think we get it and agree…Jake?"

Jake said, "Yeah, absolutely. This is a lot to digest, but I can completely follow the logic. Please go on."

Anna continued her spiel and referenced another chart with some more detail, saying, "This chart has the same top organization as what you saw on the last one with some more detail. We show Jake Dawson, CSO (Chief Science Officer), working for Madelyn, and Lou Alexander in the position of science lab director. We also show part of Victoria's current team, Dwaine and Ryan reporting to Victoria. Kathy, whose current position with the Lindsey Foundation is international law, will move under my supervision. Jim will be taking a position as government liaison and continue to work for the law firm in DC. As far as his dad and his partners are concerned, Jim is replacing my role as legal council for the company once I formally leave. There is a key vacancy in Victoria's organization for a director of manufacturing to oversee the building of the nano and quantum-star machines. This leaves us with where to fit Steve Ryan and Karl Franklin (forecasting). We also need spots for the senator and Solana. We have a few different ideas here but would really like to do some brainstorming with you."

	Dane Lindsey: *CEO*	
Victoria Tawfeek: *Dir, Bus. Admin*	***Madelyn Cooper:*** *COO*	***Anna Kim:*** *CFO*
Dwaine: Science advisor	***Jake Dawson:*** *CSO*	*Jim Mankin: Legal*
Ryan: Lobbyist	*Lou Alexander: Lab director*	*Kathy: International law*
Vacant: Director of manufacturing		

Drew Jackson: Executive Assistant

Solana Lindsey: *?*
Senator Arthur Birmingham: *?*
Karl Franklin: *?*
Steve Ryan: *?*

Surprisingly, it was Jake who piped in first. He said, "Why are some of the names bolded and others not?"

Anna said, "Good question; the bolded names will also be members of the board of directors for the company. The board will be comprised of Genanotech employees and nonemployees. Any member of the board will be given voting rights weighted by the number of shares they hold or a number determined by the board for nonshareholders. Most board members, if not all, will have either actual shares or stock options. We will get deep into that in a few minutes."

Jake, now seeing where this was headed, said, "OK, I get it. So Steve and Karl both have jobs and, for that matter, so does the senator. Solana does not have a job, but she definitely could be useful to the company. Does anyone know what kind of ego she has?"

Everyone was shaking their head looking at Jake for that answer. After all, he was the one who hobknobbed around with them in his youth.

He said, "What! I really do not know these people the way you think I do. It has been fifteen years or more since I was in a social situation with them."

Anna said, "I think we should not consider her ego here. Let's decide how best to use her skill set. We know she has superb grace and social skills. She has been the thrust behind the Foundation and has broken down a lot of barriers with third-world-country bureaucracies. She needs to be involved in Victoria's business side when working with putting the deals together for use of the technology with the international community. She needs to be involved in my international legal efforts. Her role could be labeled public relations?"

Thinking out loud was one of Anna's greatest strengths and one of her biggest weaknesses. She decided a long time ago it was part of her makeup, and she just went with it and faced whatever the consequences. In this situation, she was among friends, and none of that really mattered.

She said, "I think she should be given a seat at the board and the title of Public Relations Officer. She could simply report to the board. What do you guys think?"

Everyone agreed and wanted to move on. They had only been meeting for a little less than an hour, but the information was so intense that it felt like two hours. Jake got up and stretched.

Madelyn said, "The senator has a huge job navigating all the facets of the government to fast-track this technology. Let alone the White House and, God forbid, the Congress, if they get involved, he will have to work with the FDA, FEMA, FTC, FBI, CIA, and probably a whole bunch of other alphabets. It makes total sense he remain in his elected position of senator to perform these duties. I don't know the legal side of it, but I think he, if anyone, deserves a position on the board of directors. I honestly believe that he does not have any interest in the money or business stuff unless it affects getting the technology out to the public. We could put him on the board with no compensation. Once the company is off the ground, we can make him rich enough to never worry about money again."

Madelyn felt awkward talking about money because it was not what drove her. She was now fully accepting how rich she will become, and it boggled her mind.

Everyone agreed that the senator be given a spot on the board. Now what do to with Steve and Karl?

They talked about them reporting to the senator, but a direct report into a person technically not an employee did not really make good sense. It was finally decided that it would be best for Steve to report to Dane directly and Karl to report to Steve. Anna said, "To summarize our changes, I will be given the position of CFO, overseeing both Finance and Legal; Solana will take the role of Public Relations Officer, reporting directly to the board; the senator will have a position on the Board of Directors and will not be directly employed by the company; Steve will take the position of Forecasting Director, reporting directly to Dane. Karl will report to Steve. Both Steve and Karl would be given positions on the board."

Anna then continued, "Good job, everyone; we now have our organizational chart ready to present to Dane for approval. Let's talk about share distribution, and then we will be done! We are forming a *C* corporation in the United States of America, issuing ten million shares of stock."

She took a quick glance at everyone to make sure there were no questions and continued, "Keep in mind that it is our strong recommendation we limit any one person to a maximum of twenty percent of the total outstanding shares and a married couple or family collective to a maximum of thirty-nine percent of the total shares. We also strongly encourage you to initially issue only seventy percent of the total shares. This can be done in three ways. You can assign shares to an individual giving them ownership and voting rights. These shares can be sold back to the corporation at the current stock valuation with whatever limits you so choose to impose as a board. For example, the board may choose to limit the number of shares the company will be willing to purchase to a maximum of one hundred shares in any given business quarter. Any transactions larger would take special board approval. Shares cannot be sold or transferred privately without board approval, and under no circumstances can they be sold or transferred to an existing shareholder. You can also allocate outstanding shares as options as an alternative to outright giving them to someone. An example would be you could give Drew one thousand options at one dollar per share. Any time Drew wanted, he could buy the option for one dollar and turn around and sell it for whatever the stock price is at that time. The third way to issue or allocate shares is to sell them. This can be done with an Initial Public Offering (IPO) or a private sale. An example of a private sale would be to allow all sovereign nations in good standing with Genanotech to have the right to purchase five hundred to five thousand shares based on the size of their country's population. If the average purchase was twenty-five hundred shares, and all one hundred ninety-two governments choose to buy, it would only equate to less than five percent of the total outstanding shares. Initially we need to allocate seventy percent, and we can use any of the above means to do so. The thirty percent balance can be sold outright, given away as options, or used to negotiate with other governments but should be under strict limits. An example of strict limits would include eighty percent or higher board approval and time-frame limitations. It might be prudent to split the thirty percent into ten groups of three percent and allow the issuance of group one in ten years, group two in twenty-five years, group four in fifty years, and so on..."

Everyone nodded indicating they understood.

She went on to say, "We all know how big this corporation will be, but Jim and I recently put some numbers down on paper, and it is actually scary big. We estimate a stream of earnings equaling forty-eight trillion dollars a year for the first ten years. It was complicated to make this estimate because there are a number of revenue sources. We have the capital-equipment sales, base-program sales, royalties on actual procedure revenue. We also will be charging a one-time technology transfer fee to be paid by every country in the world. The fee will be proportional to their population. The fee can be paid in a lump-sum or spread out over a few years. There will undoubtedly be other revenue streams to consider, but with just the mentioned, we will conservatively generate just under fifty trillion dollars annually."

Madelyn and Jake were in a minor state of shock. Jake said, "My God, we knew the numbers would be big, but forty-eight trillion! My God, that is almost three times our county's Gross Domestic Product! My God!" He was mumbling and shaking his head.

Madelyn said, "I am no economist, but if the company generates more revenue than our entire country, that would not only be historical but also could change the way governments actually work. To date, the major economies of the world are ranked in terms of countries, not companies."

Anna said teasingly, "Nice insight from a scientist. Right now the USA GDP is nineteen trillion dollars, and the largest company in the world ranked by revenue is Walmart. Walmart currently generates one half of one trillion dollars or five hundred billion dollars in top line per year. They are followed by the major oil companies, the largest being Sinopec, which is running around four hundred seventy-five billion dollars a year in revenue. The companies with the most assets are all big banks. The top three are Chinese."

Anna continued, but only to make a point. She said, "Initially Genanotech's profit margins will be enormous due to the influx of cash from selling the technology to each individual country. There will be no real cost to the company to do this. The quarter of a billion we spent in R and D will be covered in the first hour of operation. Genanotech will be over one hundred times bigger than Walmart in top line and will exceed the largest Chinese bank

(ICBC) within its first week's operation in assets. It will also be over double the size of the entire US GDP. In fact, the company's revenue will equal that of the combined GDP from the US, all of Europe, including the United Kingdom, China, and Japan."

Jake was still shaken up by the implications of what he had just heard. He looked at Madelyn and said, "Honey, I was freaked out by your scientific discovery and the actual concept of living a couple of hundred years or more. It is something I still have not completely come to terms with. The last two years has been a dream; in more ways than one."

He winked at her; she smacked him, and he turned his attention to Anna. "We know the technology is something the world is not quite prepared to accept without serious concerns. I am not sure the governments and corporations of the world have ever considered a company coming on to the scene that will reach the size of Genanotech. It sounds like the growth is going to be front-loaded, and the actual financials will be a reality before anyone ever figures out how big the company will be. It will just be. Not to mention the power that kind of money will have. I completely understand why the senator brought Steve and Karl into the fold."

Jim said, "I know. We have just touched the tip of the iceberg. There is so much to consider and to prepare for, but first things first. We need to get this corporate charter into effect so we can effectively manage the formidable challenge in front of us."

Anna said, "Nice prelude, Jim. We need to allocate approximately seventy percent of the shares. Our reasoning is that we want to insure that it will always take at least four board members' vote to pass any resolution or make any board-level decision. Remember we have a twenty-percent rule. No one individual can control more than twenty percent, and no married couple or family collective can control more than thirty-nine percent of the outstanding stock. Remember, options are part of the seventy percent. To make this easier, Jim and I have made some recommendations. We are certainly open to your opinions and comments, so please don't spare our feelings if you disagree with something. Think of this charter like our founders did when they came up with three branches of government. Not to be overdramatic, but think of this like we are writing the *Declaration of Independence* and the *Bill of Rights* all at once. The decisions we make here today will be reviewed for centuries to come."

Rather than set a heavy tone to the meeting, this analogy of our government seemed to lighten the energy in the group. It was perfect. In its own weird way, the analogy gave clarity to what they were doing.

Jim said, "We don't have a set way to do this, so I am going to just tell you what we think, and then you guys pipe in whenever you want to."

Madelyn interrupted before Jim could get another word out. "Excuse me, but before we get into any of the particulars, I want to express a few general items that are on my mind. I want to make sure that centuries from now, the control of this company is maintained with the highest possible integrity. I do not, and have never had, a vision of the company in itself having any political power. I have prayed hard about this, and I have developed some very strong opinions."

She took a very deep breath and continued, "My number-one guiding principle is that everyone in the world, regardless of what country they live in or how much money they have, have complete access to the technology. This is nonnegotiable and must be treated with the same spirit as perhaps the "Prime directive" on *Star Trek.* Not that I am necessarily in favor of a one-world government; I believe there has to be a short list of basic human rights, one of which is the right to have access to the technology. I think there needs to be some international consistency in our justice systems when it comes to the use of the technology. I don't have the answers, but let's hypothetically agree that our justice system entertains the idea that part of the punishment for a crime is to be rejuvenation therapy deprivation. We could assume that the severity of the crime would determine the number of seven-year cycles deprived. Let's just say for the sake of argument that assault carried a one-cycle deprivation sentence and murder a three-cycle sentence. I believe this law needs to be international. My personal preference is that deprivation cannot be imposed as a punishment by any country for any reason. We should be able to cure most mental-health issues with the technology. This should keep society safe from the true nut cases. Imprisonment can still be a viable means to protect society from violent people, and then there is the ever-controversial death penalty. Another likely controversial topic will be who pays for financial assistance for those who cannot afford necessary procedures and how do we determine who gets the financial assistance. Will some assistance be in the form of a grant and some a loan? If a loan, what interest, if any, is charged? Genanotech will have the power to impose such policies on its own accord. The question is, should they? The company could easily be the financial resource that backs grants and/or loans, but, again, should the company be involved at that level? The company may choose to delegate some decisions to an international board that would have power to make international law regarding such issues. How does the international community or the company deal with countries that are found out of compliance with international law or company policy? Can the company deprive individual leaders of the technology? It certainly would not be fair to the population under that leadership to suffer for their leader's indiscretions. I know this is a pretty big stick we are wielding, but as Roosevelt said, 'Walk softly, and carry a big stick, and you shall go far.' We must consider these and other profound concerns carefully when setting up our charter."

Jim said, "That is very interesting and philosophically pertinent, Madelyn, but how does that affect distribution of shares?"

She said, "It does in many ways. I agree completely with the seventy-percent issuance threshold. What I am having a problem with is the four-vote quorum. Two votes making a majority? If 70 percent of the shares are distributed, then thirty-five percent plus one is a majority. With our proposal, if the company does not distribute the balance of the shares, and one couple can control thirty-nine percent of the shares, can one married couple control the majority vote? Think about it; an economic power greater than the United States of America controlled by a man and his wife—people? If the company issues one hundred percent of its shares, then four people would make a quorum. I don't think it is enough. If four people can steer the direction of this company, that means two married couples or two families could have complete control. I think we need to spread this power out and create some checks and balances. I have some ideas, but we need to get our best minds on this. There is no need to give someone twenty percent of this business. Really, what could someone do with that kind of money? Let's figure this out. A company like this would be valued at?" She looked at Anna.

Anna said, "Conservatively one point five times of one year's annual revenue."

Madelyn jumped back in. "So, with ten million shares issued, that calculates to seven million two hundred thousand dollars per share. If someone was to receive just one percent of the shares, the value of those shares would be seven hundred twenty billion dollars."

Even Anna's jaw dropped. She had not thought it all the way through.

She said, "There is literally more money here than any of us could possibly ever need or want. The decision to allocate shares is more about principal, fairness to all those involved and long term protection of the corporation." Everyone let this sink in for a minute.

Madelyn went on to say, "I think we should cap one person at ten percent instead of twenty percent and a married couple or family collective at eighteen percent instead of thirty-nine percent. Everyone with a chief in their designation is issued eight percent. The CEO is given the full ten percent. I am kind of winging it here, but I think that Victoria should receive five percent and Lou two percent. That totals forty-one percent, if my math is correct; we will need to allocate at least ten percent more to insure our initial allocation comprises a majority 51fifty-one percent.

Anna and Jake both said in stereo, "I think you should get two percent more." They looked at each other and laughed.

Anna then said, "We have Steve, Karl, Solana, and the senator, who will undoubtedly become shareholders at some point. I suggest we give them options at one dollar per share." Everyone nodded. "I am thinking, based on pecking order and expectation of contribution, that the senator should get six percent, Steve five percent, Solana four percent, and Karl four percent of the outstanding shares in the form of options exercisable when they agree to become full-time employees of the company. I further recommend that their employment start one week prior to public announcement. I think they should all get a seat at the board of directors immediately with voting rights proportional to their option holdings. This leaves with sixty percent of the shares allocated. The new board can have access to up to an additional ten percent to distribute however they feel."

The elephant in the room nobody was talking about was Jim. He just witnessed ten people he worked with become Trillion-Aires.

Recognizing that this was becoming tense, she said, "Jim and I have not talked about what my plans are for him. I wanted to get things ironed out here first and then present an equitable offer to him as well, but I want to have the entire board agree to it first." She winked at Jim, who seemed to immediately relax. She said, "You didn't think we would leave you out!" She laughed.

Anna interjected, "I am a bit embarrassed by my complete lack of consideration to the voting weights. So, if we go back to the bolded individuals on the proposed org chart, we have nine voting members. I propose we include Lou, since he does manage the labs and will eventually oversee worldwide lab policy. I also recommend we add our vacant position of director of manufacturing to the board for obvious reasons and Jim since he will likely be heading up a massive legal department." She turned and smiled at Jim.

Jim, too embarrassed to talk, was saved by Jake who said, "So that makes twelve voting members but still potentially only four to make a quorum. What do we do about that?"

Anna, in an obvious state of overstimulation, said, "Madelyn brings up many great points here, the number on being that what we do here now will have enormous ramifications on the world. The sheer economic power this company will have must be backed by brilliant progressive policies that are administered with the same fervor and spirit as the best-run organizations and governments of the world. We are not starting a new typical for profit enterprise. We are selling quality of life and life itself. The control of this corporation must be structured in a way to insure to future generations that its technology and resources is not victim to corruption of any kind."

On a roll she continued, "Thinking out loud here, I believe we should include a number of 'heads of state' to sit on the board with voting rights. They would not be shareholders but would represent voting weights equal to one percent. We could have ten countries with permanent seats and fifteen countries with one-year terms on rotation. We could cap the total number of nonshareholder voting rights to no more than thirty percent of outstanding shares. The real value would be the input gained from the board members, not to mention the public perception that Genanotech is not an evil giant corporation bent on running the world."

Madelyn said, "I think you are on to something here. We could also include in our temporary rotation some heads of industry as nonshareholder voting members. Example might be CEO of Exxon and Walmart, one of the Chinese banks, and so forth."

Everyone was shaking their heads. Anna said, "Sounds like a topic for one of our upcoming board meetings. Thanks, everyone, for your time. If there are not any other pressing matters, we can turn these screens off and get back to our work." In a very genuine and warm tone, she thanked everyone again, and the meeting was adjourned.

24

Anna called Dane and asked if they could arrange a time to review the proposed charter. Everyone's schedules were crazy, and travel time was an issue with both of them, so they decided to have Drew set up a secure video conference where Dane, Solana, Anna, and Jim could meet virtually. Two hours later the four were looking at each other on seventy-two-inch plasma TV screens. Half the screen was split into four quadrants, with live feeds of each individual attending. The other half of the screen simply said "Welcome" and was where Anna would upload her PowerPoint presentation.

Anna was particularly concerned about presenting the newly revised organizational chart. Two weeks prior Dane had provided Anna an organizational chart and stock allocation plan. At that time he didn't expect any modifications on either and was mostly interested in the finer points in the charter. This was, of course, before Dane spilled the beans about the senator and his involvement.

Initially Solana was going to have the COO position with everyone but Science and Forecasting reporting to her. Rather than start with the org chart, Anna began with a slide that highlighted the expected share valuation at the public inception of the company. She explained that Madelyn and Jake had a similar meeting the day before and that surprisingly it was Madelyn who had the most input. She also made it crystal clear that Madelyn, Jake, Jim, and she were completely behind the proposal being provided today. Any modifications or suggestions would need to be run by Madelyn prior to taking this to the board; Jake was good with whatever they all decided. There was considerable pause while everyone took in the sheer immensity of the company.

Anna went on to slide two where some of Madelyn's major concerns and ideas were bulleted. The need to insure access to the technology for all mankind forever was number one. The size of the company relative to the GDP of the United States and largest companies in the world was second. The need for international enforcement for access-related issues, in the justice system particularly, was also outlined. Ramifications for countries who independently decide to deprive access and a few other insights were included on the slide. The need for checks and balances within the power structure of the company was the last item on the list.

If the utter expected economic power of the company didn't sober everyone up, the long-term ramifications of setting up the checks and balances to insure responsible and noble use of that power was a true wake-up call.

Dane finally broke the silence and said, "Wow, I knew this corporation would be huge and rival the largest in the world. I was accustomed to playing at that level and felt at ease having the responsibility of being at the helm. I underestimated the size, the power, the responsibility. The perspective and clarity your insights bring to light are difficult for me to digest. It is obvious that we need to treat this charter with extraordinary care and not treat it like forming just another mega corporation."

Anna said, "We came to the same conclusion and have made some significant changes to your original proposals."

Slide 3 was the organization chart.

Dane was privately relieved to see himself still in the CEO position. He knew there was a chance after revealing his collusion with the senator that he may have lost the trust required to remain in the top position.

Solana asked, "Who do I report to? I am just floating at the bottom of the chart."

Anna said, "We had long discussions about that and decided that you and Drew should report directly to the board rather than to any particular individual. Officers of the company who report directly to the board will have all the resources of the company at their disposal. The senator will also fall into this category when he formally becomes an employee. Steve and Karl will eventually report to Dane when they become employees. All three should be employed by Genanotech shortly before the company is announced to the public."

Solana nodded in agreement. Apparently being in the same company as the senator satisfied her ego.

Dane was studying the organization and said, "I really like what you guys have proposed here. I especially like the way you have the science section organized. I have no suggestions with the exception that Drew also become our secretary and be considered for some options."

Anna said, "I will take note of that, and I am sure Madelyn will not have any objections. Next we need to talk about stock allocation. Madelyn shot down the twenty percent individual, thirty-nine percent married or family collective maximums. She suggested ten percent individual and eighteen percent married or family collective maximums. This makes total sense considering the multimillion-dollar share price. We may, as a board, decide to reduce this allocation further. We can make mandatory limits on the percentages officers can sell or transfer to heirs within certain time frames. Heirs? That becomes a question in itself. What if this technology ends up extending life indefinitely? It could be possible we may want to transfer our wealth in the form of shares to thousands of offspring."

Anna put up slide 4, which bulleted some conceptual work on nonshareholder board members as a means to create the checks and balances to insure security of the integrity of the company's future.

Dane said, "I already have more money than I need or really want. It is going to be a large responsibility for all of us with shares to be good stewards with our newfound mega wealth. Solana and I have always looked toward our maker for guidance here, but what if this kind of money got in the wrong hands? We really do owe it to the world to get this right. What you have put together so far is a good start."

All of Anna's concerns were put to rest. There seemed to be no hard feelings, and all the major players were on the same page. She went through their thinking on the senator, Steve, and Karl, and everyone was in agreement. Anna could not help but think this was going a little smoother than it should. She ultimately decided not to concern herself with it and felt blessed that she was working with like-minded colleagues.

25

It was the end of February in the year 2022. The team had been very busy with weekly and sometimes biweekly strategy sessions. The main building adjacent to the original Genanotech lab designed for large-scale human testing and nano equipment manufacturing was ready for occupancy. Because of the short timeline for construction, the interior was fairly plain and lacked the ornament seen in most hi-tech companies' flagship operations. All the walls and ceilings were painted white. The floors were etched ultra-smooth sealed concrete with the exception of the five one-bedroom suites, which were carpeted and painted in contemporary colors.

The sign on the 220,000 square foot building next door to the Genanotech lab read, "Coming soon—Vancouver Offices for the Lindsey Foundation."

There was a need to get centralized and work in a sequestered environment. The senator was on the phone with Dane discussing some of the details. He asked Dane how his conference call with Anna went, and Dane replied, "Really good. I think we have some very smart people working on this project, and I can't blame her, but that Anna sure wrote herself a pretty nice ticket. I do not even want to get into the financial forecasts she brought up."

The senator said, "Excellent! You know how I feel about the business side of things; let's get to work on getting this company moving on a fast track. People are dying every minute we waste."

The senator knew Karl's newly wedded wife, Heather. She worked for a different branch of the commerce department than Karl. Karl was technically working for the Census Bureau; his actual job was to help Steve administrate one of the senator's pet projects. Heather worked as an economic advisor. Her position had grown into not only monitoring economic activity on the West Coast but also advising the White House on trends and significant impacts legislation may have on the localized economy. Not being educated in economics proper, other than the few requisite classes in her degree program, she had a real knack for the field. In a way, because she had not been exposed to formal study in economics, she tended to think "out of the box." This gave her an edge when debating with the "tried and true" colleagues in her arena.

The senator felt that Heather would be an asset to the work Steve and Karl would be undertaking. If Heather could spend a few months studying world economics, she may prove to have some valuable insights that can be incorporated into the forecasting software.

Jim's wife was another story. The senator said to Dane, "Before we offer Jim his place on the board and have him quit his job in DC, we will need to think through how Beverly fits in." Sequestering Beverly may not have the desired effect. She is an Internet junky, with radical views on privacy; she thinks there should be none. Keeping her locked up in a specific location does no good if she has Internet access. Taking Internet access away from her, or even restricting its use, would be like taking a bottle of booze away from an alcoholic."

He went on, "The mission to take the technology public will take all of five months and possibly up to a year. It would be difficult to have Jim stay focused if his wife lived three thousand miles away. This solidifies our plan to have Jim be an exception to our sequestering policy. He should be outside point man for direct contact with government officials."

If there was a threat of a possible breach exposing the existence of this technology, it was Beverly. Jim was already involved; this was Anna's doing, the senator thought, or was it? This may be Jim Mankin senior's doing. Anna worked for Ben Gerrard who the senator knew personally. Ben was one of Jim's father's partners. If Ben had been made aware of the details of Anna's work, it was entirely possible that Jim senior also knew about it. The question was, if so, how much did they know? How many other people had they talked to?

They decided to move forward without action per plan and keep a close eye on Mankin, Gerrard, and Beverly.

Drew secured a new hotel that was under construction and almost ready for occupancy. It was just a block away from the lab. The owners did not ask a lot of questions when Drew offered them sum equal to full annual occupancy, on a one-year lease. If that was not a good enough deal, the owners were not required to staff or manage the hotel for the entire lease. It had sixty-three rooms and eleven suites. There was an indoor swimming pool, small gym, and private restaurant/bar with a fully equipped kitchen.

To avoid unnecessary visitors, Drew had arranged for the fascia of the building to remain unfinished. The unpainted gray plaster and partially completed stonework gave the property a genuine appearance of being under construction. The sign on the building was temporary and said, "Opening in 2023." There were four or five large construction Dumpsters and three portable toilets in the parking lot. The entire property was bordered in temporary cyclone fencing customary with under-construction properties in the state of Washington. Drew had to have the senator pull a few strings with the local city government in order to gain an occupancy permit without completion of the exterior. The special request came straight from the governor's office. This was completely out of the norm, and it did raise a few eyebrows at City Hall. It was rumored that the governor was doing a favor for Dane Lindsey. Dane's foundation needed a temporary space for the employees and volunteers for its new foundation branch.

Victoria had a close friend, Franky, who at one time owned a five-star restaurant in Seattle. She coerced him into staffing and managing the restaurant/bar for the one-year gig. She told him she would pay top dollar, and at the end of one year, she would give him some stock options in a new start-up company she was working on. All he needed to do was provide excellent food and service to whoever happened to get seated in the restaurant. There would be no charge for whatever people ordered, and food costs should not be considered when preparing the week's menu. He was to have a small staff on hand to prepare a buffet-style breakfast every morning. Premade sandwiches and salads would be available, but lunch would not be served unless there was a special event. Dinner would be served from 5:00 p.m. to 11:00 p.m. seven days a week, and he would be provided living accommodations. She decided not to disclose the sequestering requirement until Franky was on board.

Drew made a few modifications to the building for security purposes. As most hotels, this one had a covered entrance to the lobby and reception area. He blocked the view of the entrance from the street, utilizing a combination of plywood and scaffolding. This allowed unobstructed pick-up and delivery of the scientists and technicians moving between facilities. He added security locks at the front and rear entrances. He reinforced the temporary cyclone fencing surrounding the building and parking lot and added two automatic gated entrances, one on the side and one in the back. It wasn't Fort Knox, but it would keep any uninvited guests out. There were also three active security personnel on the premises at all times. They did not wear uniforms, so they just blended in with the rest of the personnel.

All the suites were located on the third floor. Two of the eleven suites were retrofitted, one into a conference room and the other into additional space for workout equipment. Dane and Solana moved into the largest of the suites. After living in 14,700 square feet, this was going take some adjusting to. They would periodically make trips north to their estate, but for the next six to twelve months, this was going to be home. Victoria, Anna, the senator, Steve, Karl and Heather, Dwaine, Kathy, and Ryan each moved into a suite.

Drew took a room adjacent to the front office. He had a door installed from his room to a medium-sized office area that he converted into a full-blown security center complete with "common area" surveillance systems. Jim was offered a suite in the new building, but he opted for a room in the hotel, since he was primarily going to be working in Virginia. Besides, the hotel is where all the administrative action was going to be.

Victoria hired Carleton, a plant manager from a neighboring circuit-board-equipment manufacturer. Carleton had a combined twenty-two years' experience in managing the operations of three different companies that designed and manufactured automated optical inspection equipment for high-density inner-layer circuitry in printed circuit boards. The technology had some parallels to the equipment Jake and Madelyn designed to manufacture quantum stars. The equipment design and technology used to build nano machines was entirely foreign to Carleton.

The engineering and prototype phase was already completed by Jake. Carleton just needed to use his experience in design to build Jake's machines with end-user friendliness and material efficiency.

Carleton hired a materials manger and two manufacturing engineers. They had drafted designs for both the Quantum Star Generator (QSG) and the Molecular Machine Replicator (MMR). Jake was delighted with the result. Both machines were approximately seven feet square and six feet tall, a fourth the size of the machines he had built. They weighed 1,600 pounds each, well within the weight capacity to be used in existing multistory hospital buildings.

Carleton had designed these machines to include hardwired remote access and automated delivery systems. One set of machines could easily accommodate six operating rooms. The original thought was, only two operating rooms could be supported by a set of machines. Reconfigurations of the procedure rooms were under way. A trained technician could feed progress data into the machines directly from the procedure room. New mixtures could be ordered on the fly with modified molecular machines embedded with quantum stars and premixed in a specified plankton-rich solution. Delivery of labeled syringes was made via conveyor to secure compartments located in each procedure room.

Carleton and his team were working around the clock and took over four of the five suites on the old site. Prototypes of the new designs were in preassembly.

Madelyn, Lou, and Anna had collaborated in the hiring of Eric for the position of clinical operations director. Eric was the head of the Colorado Springs top-secret government nanotechnology research lab. The Colorado Springs lab was primarily working on genetic interpretation. They had successfully developed an observation technique to view and record defects in the DNA strands in human cells. The technology was obsolete in light of Madelyn's unique approach. Eric had an in-depth understanding of nano technology and human biology. There was really no better choice for the position.

Eric's replacement in Colorado Springs would monitor the outpatients from Vancouver, Washington. The need for sequestering the outpatients was causing some logistical problems as well as personnel challenges. The scientists in the nine government labs were complaining about converting their labs into hotels. They were not the most social of personality types to begin with, so the thought of sharing their space with civilian strangers was hard to digest. There were also some egos in need of care. These scientific teams had been dedicating years working on the forefront of a new technology. A technology that now had been fully developed by a complete unknown.

The senator had expected this. He had downsized all nine of the labs, eliminating over 70 percent of the personnel and leaving only those he felt were indispensable and could handle the transition.

Each of the nine labs was undergoing significant remodeling. Private outdoor courtyards complete with basketball courts, tennis courts, picnic tables, and garden areas were being installed. The sterile interiors were being retrofitted with small studio apartments with just the basics. Dining halls, exercise rooms, and a library/game room were being added to all the labs. The largest of the nine labs will accommodate 150 outpatients and the smallest, 90 outpatients, for a total of just over 1,100 outpatients combined.

Within his very first month, Eric had secured seventy-five candidates for human trials. He had lists of over two thousand potential candidates he was evaluating. To reduce the likelihood of family members taking offense to the sequestering, he had to think out of the box. With the help of Victoria and Kathy, he was able to obtain a number of candidates who were terminally ill residing in hospitals abroad. He was also able to tap into orphanages with terminally ill children.

A very small circle of officials at top echelons of the FDA were made aware of the technology in the last week. They were scheduled to visit the operation in three days. The hope was that with government backing and connections, additional candidates within their government rank and file may become available. The families of government employees have a much higher level of tolerance to secrecy, therefore making them ideal candidates for sequestering.

The first wave of patients were to arrive in two weeks. The operation would accommodate four new patients a day in the first week and then eight per day in the second week, and by the fifth week, Genanotech would be admitting twelve new patients per day. That was a comfortable two patients per procedure room per day.

The eleven hundred patient trials would take just under four months to complete. The technology would be used on a wide variety of health issues. Most known cancers would be represented in the testing. Patients with spinal injuries resulting in paralysis and muscular degradation would be rehabilitated. Heart disease, pulmonary disorders, vascular-system degradation, digestive-track conditions, erectile dysfunction, ligament repair, skin disorders, liver problems, and even depression would be represented in the trials.

Other than repair technology, a separate set of trials would be run with varying age groups to evaluate cellular rejuvenation technology. Both patients without any known medical problems and patients who had recently undergone repair procedures were to be evaluated. Eric and Lou had been burning the midnight oil developing the final clinical-trial road map. Lou's mom became cancer-free and underwent a complete rejuvenation process. She was very proud to be the first to undergo the procedures. Thankfully there had been no side effects. When the science would go public, she would have a permanent place in history books.

The public relations and government committees were working in concert now. Solana, Anna, and Ryan in combination with the senator, Jim, and Kathy were running into some major roadblocks on the public-relations front. The meeting with the Director of the Food and Drug Administration last week didn't go as well as expected.

The senator misread his relationship with the director. His initial response was insolent. He was offended by the lack of government involvement from the start. He was a man who was accustomed to being in control. When he was reporting to Congress, his word was revered. His ego was much larger than the senator had originally thought. He was infuriated that the technology had progressed through animal testing and human trials without FDA involvement. The fact that the scientists responsible for the development of the technology operated in total secrecy while utilizing taxpayers' money in the remote patient-sequestering centers put him over the top.

The senator was very concerned that the director's loyalties laid elsewhere.

26

Karl was feeling a bit disoriented working in the new digs. He, Steve, and Heather had moved into the new Vancouver, Washington, facility not too far from their old building in Seattle, 165 miles up the road. He and Heather were enjoying working together. Being sequestered in the hotel was making him feel claustrophobic. He hated the shuttling back and forth under constant surveillance. He had virtually no privacy. He longed for the old days of dining at the harbor and enjoying a round of golf from time to time. Even though his wife and friends were all around him, it just wasn't the same as being free.

The math wasn't the problem. The intricate software programming wasn't the problem. The model he and Steve built was directly aimed at addressing the task at hand. Karl's mind was wrestling with the necessity to keep predictive information from the nations in the world who were directly affected by the very predictions extrapolated from the software. The developed countries of the world could benefit greatly to have advanced warnings for potential economic, agricultural, or energy problems. The very knowledge of those problems could actually avert the appropriate psychological response of nations to take necessary steps to avoid a Malthusian event in many of the lesser-developed countries.

This was a dilemma for Karl. Other considerations included that many leaders and governments around the world who could benefit from the forecasting may not want the advice. Many nations' leaders are cynical when it comes to the United States or western ideology in general. If the United States were to provide the road map for each nation, to adequately address the infrastructure needs to incorporate the longer life-span of its citizens without potential of poverty and famine, it could be viewed as intervention rather than help. This is especially true for the developed nations with underdeveloped regions.

A worldview of one nation dictating the activities of another violates sovereignty. The world is not prepared to operate under one government, let alone to unequivocally cooperate with one government. Even in the best democracies in the world, some form of corruption is still present. A one-world government would surely allow for the possibility of massive-scale corruption.

The sheer economic power Genanotech would attain was going to be a supreme issue in itself. Steve was in the process of evaluating the projected Genanotech financials and the eventual effect the economic power will have on the world.

The United States of America would not be fond of the idea of relinquishing power to a one-world government. The United States has the most powerful military and largest economy in the world. To go from number one to anything else is just not thinkable. The United States was founded by rugged individualists pioneering freedom as the foundation for its existence. To relinquish power would be undermining the very principles of the Constitution.

The lack of willingness of the United States in 1998 to embrace the judicial oversight of the United Nations is a perfect example. It frustrates Karl to no end that humanity is so cynical. A helping hand is not always perceived as that. Human beings question the motives of charity and philanthropy. People are instinctually selfish, so when someone offers help, especially if there is not a clear-cut reason for the help offered, motives are questioned. And then there is pride. Some people just have too much pride to accept help; even when they desperately need it.

Karl turned to Maslow's Theory to gain additional insight into what makes man's mind tick.

Abraham Maslow wrote a paper on Human Motivation in 1943, which still, to this day, is considered a valid and relevant doctrine. Maslow blended philosophy and psychology in this work. He believed in studying psychologically healthy behaviors of exemplary individuals such as Albert Einstein and Eleanor Roosevelt rather than mentally ill or neurotic people, writing that "the study of crippled, stunted, immature and unhealthy specimens can yield only a crippled psychology and a crippled philosophy." *Need hierarchy* was the basis for his human motivation model.

Need hierarchy is broken down into five needs. The first being the most influential to our motivations and the last being realized only after the other four are satisfied. Here is how it breaks down.

According to Maslow our primary need or motivation is *physiological*, which includes breathing, food, water, sex, and sleep. The next is *safety*, which encompasses our need for security of body, property, and family. Thirdly we need what Maslow labels *love/belonging*, which is the need for friendship, family, and intimacy. The forth level is *esteem*, the need for self-esteem, achievement, and respect from others. Finally, if we have met all four of these needs, we will desire *self-actualization*, or morality, creativity, problem solving, spontaneity, and acceptance of facts.

Karl pondered that if their software could provide answers to problems associated with only the first two echelons of Maslow's *need hierarchy*, why would humanity be skeptical? Maybe it was because we would be messing with primal needs of man that brings out the fight-or-flight reaction and not our more esoteric ones.

It appeared that the only way to proceed was to provide the world with population projections that indicate when and where increased life-span would affect the ability of the geographic area to support itself. This in itself will trigger some proactive responses from nations. When they are pressed against the wall, they may be willing to receive help. *So that's that,* Karl thought; he would design the initial database to project the failures.

He had to repress the notions that governments will elect to limit the technology to only the privileged in society, which would then alter the outcomes of the data and thus remedy the problem by limiting the growth. Genanotech business agreements would have to be in place to eliminate this course of action.

Steve and Heather walked in with lunch to find Karl at his desk with his head down and the palms of his hands pressed against his temples. He immediately straightened up, and his face was a bit flushed. Heather said, "Did we wake you, darling?"

Karl smiled. "No, I was just thinking through the benchmark data and was reviewing the need to refrain from providing the world useful data to avoid a Malthusian catastrophe. I know we have been through it a hundred times, and I just cannot get my arms around it. I even revisited Maslow to see if it could stimulate another possible direction. It just reinforced what we have already decided."

Heather looked at him awkwardly as she often did when she knew she could not provide him with the answer he wanted or needed. She then relaxed and situated the conference table for lunch. As they were eating their cafeteria-style sandwiches and soup, they discussed Karl's thought processes on the subject of secrecy, keeping data from specific countries. He expressed he did not feel comfortable being involved in a deceptive tactic to achieve a calculated end. Even if that end were noble. The fact remained that there was a relatively good chance that 22 percent of the nations would limit the use of the technology rather than do what is necessary make it available to all their citizens. The consequences of that approach were unacceptable.

Steve had not said a word at lunch. Karl finally recognized this and asked Steve for his thoughts. He looked at Karl blankly and said, “What are we talking about? Oh, the Malthusian thing again. You know where I stand on this, Karl. Why keep on hashing it out?”

This kind of response was not like Steve at all. Karl and Heather both felt uncomfortable, as if they had done something wrong, as a child would feel when getting scolded for something they did not understand or realize they had done.

Steve sensed their discomfort and apologized. “I am sorry, guys. I understand your concern here, and I think they are justified. We just do not have a choice in the matter. It is clearly riskier to provide the world with a specific guideline to administer the technology than not to. I have something on my mind of far greater concern.”

Steve had just gotten back from the Seattle Census Bureau office. The decision was made to leave the original forecasting lab in place and simply build a second system in the Vancouver, Washington, lab. The transfer of data was relatively simple mostly due to FTLwares data transfer systems. Having two physical and separate systems created a level of additional backup.

The program itself and all the data associated with it was also backed up weekly and sent via courier on external memory chips to a government vault in Nebraska. There was one key module of the operating system that performed module combing that was intentionally not included in any of the backups. When analyzing Steve's complex creation, it would never be apparent that there was a missing module because it did not need to exist to perform any of the routines expected from the software. The missing module was designed to combine and encourage interaction between the worldwide political tendencies module, global economic forecasting module, and stock-market analyzer was stored safely in a safety deposit box in a small bank in Tuscaloosa, Alabama. Tuscaloosa is in the Central West region of Alabama with under 100,000 residences. It was also the hometown of Steve's late grandmother and cousin, DJ.

The *board of directors* were all aware that there was another copy residing in a place Steve had personally chosen. The board did not know where it was, but in the event something happened to Steve, they were instructed to seek out one of Steve's relatives named DJ after reviewing the contents of his safe and Karl's locker. This was not written down anywhere. The location of the Alabama safety deposit box could be ascertained by reviewing the contents of the safe, locker, and a quick conversation with DJ. DJ, Steve's cousin, was instructed that if for some reason Steve was to disappear, and someone from the board of directors of Genanotech contacted him, he was to give them a street name in Tuscaloosa. Karl had a piece of junk mail from a bank that was not local. In Steve's safe there was a single yellow sticky with a four-digit number on it, which was the safe-deposit-box number.

When Steve was updating the Seattle software system, he decided to play around with long-term forecasting based on the newly established population projections. Looking out long term was always fascinating, though the level of accuracy of the forecast was diminished the further out you went. The software achieves a respectable 97 percent accuracy ten years out and 91 percent at twenty years, 82 percent at thirty years, and so on.

Steve was looking one hundred years out. The best level of accuracy expected at this interval was 51 percent. The problem was, this was at least 50.9 percent more than the US government would feel comfortable with. The forecast revealed that a fully modernized and developed China with over two billion citizens (17 percent of the world population) would eventually govern the world. Steve changed the base data several times to see if the conclusions would be altered; each time the same conclusion was forecasted.

China being a relatively peaceful nation has a well-equipped army that has not engaged in combat in this generation. Their growing economy is intertwined with over 80 percent of the nations of the world. At present they are behind the United States in overall economic and military power but making great strides to catch up on both fronts. A fully modernized China would exceed our economic strength of the United States threefold. It is a proven fact that the strongest military is a direct result of the strongest economy.

The question we have to ask ourselves is what a kluge of communist or capitalist Chinese government of today will evolve into one hundred years from now. And once evolved, what will they do with their power? The forecasting software concludes globalized government. One police force, one currency, one tax authority, one government!

Steve had basically stumbled across this analysis. He was exploring the global economic forecasts and specifically the US stock market. He had started out with a search for top investments looking twenty years out. He knew he was going to come into some significant money via Genanotech options and was trying to figure out how to spread his investments out. This was a part of the program he had spent many hours developing technically off the clock. It was not part of his charter at the Census Bureau and nobody, including the senator, knew about this piece of code. He endeavored in this program writing to assist him in making some wise investments for retirement. It was purely for personal purposes. The database was already taking into consideration so many of the variables relevant to such analysis that it was not a huge undertaking to use the models to forecast industry growth patterns and then relate them to specific corporations' performance trends.

He had narrowed his investment opportunities to sixty-five companies at twenty years out. He then decided to look out fifty years. What the heck, he would likely live another 120 years to spend his money. This narrowed his top opportunities to thirty-seven companies. Then he thought maybe he would have some children along the way; it was doubtful, but you never know. He wondered what those investments would look like in one hundred years. That is when he noticed some anomalies in the results. Only twelve of his original investments were included, and they all had merger notifications. When reviewing the specifics on the mergers, he found that all were showing more than 90 percent lead indicators that these companies were now owned by the People's Republic of China.

This led him into combining the company specific database programming with the global economic forecasting module. He then melded the two modules and married them to the political tendencies module. The political tendencies module was newly revised to best indicate how nations would interact in the modernization efforts of the world. It was this combination of forecasting that projected that a world government was inevitable in eighty-eight years. It was then computed that without a doubt the ruling government would be China.

One of the key factors in leading to China's rule was the high likelihood that within forty years a Southern Asia Alliance would be necessary. India would become reliant on China economically. Then Japan and Korea would develop inseparable economic bonds. Once combined, their influence over the world was enormous. Western Europe and the United States and Canada would become polarized to the Southern Asia Alliance. They would become two great economic and military powers struggling for supremacy.

At this early stage of increasing life-span, death was uncommon. Only the very elderly who chose not to extend life when the technology was made available were dying. The baby boomers underwent the procedures for rejuvenation and still had fifty to sixty years of life in front of them. As a result the thought of dying was repulsive and considered unnatural. There had been decades of peace, and the thought of war was obsolete. The thought of ending another human being's life was unthinkable. Life seemed to be more precious because it was so lengthened.

Eventually, antipolarization sentiment became popular, and the two super-economic powers started working together rather than apart. With everything so intertwined, governing power shifted and finally matured into one single government.

The software could not with any accuracy determine the complexities of the form of government that would eventually blossom, but it could determine that it would blossom and would likely be empowered by a specific region, the People's Republic of China.

Steve wondered if right to private property would survive. In China, only the wealthiest and most influential were allowed to own real estate. The government owned the land and leased it to its citizens. The government owned the majority of the housing, which it leased to its citizens. Steve decided that he would not heavily invest in real estate for the long term. He would include it in his short-term portfolio. He laughed out loud when he realized he was considering his fifty-year investment strategy short term.

He extracted the code he had written to merge these modules that calculated the outcome of world government. He then decided to extract the stock-market analyzer he had written for himself and vowed to himself to extract it from the Vancouver, Washington, and the Nebraska databases as soon as possible. He would discuss his findings with only Karl and Heather; they would decide what to do next.

So there he was explaining the entire situation to his two most trusted friends in the world. It felt good to get this off his chest. The burden of knowledge is sometimes unsettling, and this was unsettling, to say the least. When Karl was talking about reviewing Maslow's *needs hierarchy*, Steve's thought was, this was one self-actualization he wished he had never encountered. The old sayings "curiosity killed the cat" and "be careful what you ask for" were taking on a new meaning to Steve.

After he finished, the three of them were sitting around the conference table with half-eaten sandwiches in front of them. Nobody was hungry, and everyone felt a little sick. Karl rubbed his head as he usually did when he was deep in thought. He finally said, "Thanks, Steve; I feel much better about the public release of Malthusian events now."

Steve said, "I knew you would; glad to be of service."

Heather had an affinity to bring things into perspective. She was not as overanalytical as her husband nor her boss. She interrupted Karl and Steve's little banter and said, "You know, if we were Brazilians or Mongolians or Turks, this news would be digested completely differently. We have been brought up as Americans with American ideals. The future you portray has many of the American ideals intact: peace, equality, freedom, and a modernized society where hunger and famine are eradicated. Does it really matter if the Chinese are in charge of this world, at least initially? If the government is peacefully achieved, which your software indicates it is, elections will take place; there will be a democracy. We as Americans are accustomed to being the most powerful nation on the planet. The thought of someone else having that role, even if that someone else has the identical ideology as we do, is somehow going to be construed as a failure to us. Those of us in power when this transition takes place will be anywhere from ninety to one hundred twenty years old. I hope by then we would have matured to the point where testosterone and competition are tamed. I hope we have the wisdom to do what is right for all of mankind."

Karl smiled and said, "Fascist!" and laughed.

Steve laughed as well. Heather had made them all feel much better. They immediately extracted the stock-market module from their system and sent off a new replacement file for Nebraska that was a few gigabytes smaller than the one currently on file.

They all agreed that this information was best kept secret. If the US government caught even the slightest wind of this prediction, they may stop the entire project in its tracks. It wouldn't be the first time attempts at self-preservation had the opposite response. Steve would ask for approval to visit his cousin in Tuscaloosa at the next board meeting for personal reasons. During his visit he would deposit the memory cartridge with the code merging the economic and political tendency modules with the stock analyzer into the local bank's safety-deposit box.

27

At 7:00 a.m. on July 30, 2022, without notice, Dane called an impromptu meeting of the board of directors. Drew had systematically knocked on the doors of all board members at 6:00 a.m. to announce the meeting. Jake, Madelyn, and Lou were being shuttled over to the hotel, and Jim Mankin was with them.

Jim had flown in the night before and stayed at the lab with Jake and Madelyn. He was briefed on the progress of human trials during dinner. He did not seem himself. Jim was usually happy-go-lucky and inspired a boyish zeal that was always refreshing during some of the most serious and complex meetings they had attended over the past three months. But now he seemed distant and extremely solemn.

Madelyn tried to break the ice after dinner. She offered Jim a second glass of wine, but he refused, saying he needed to hit the sack. Madelyn asked if everything was OK in Washington.

Jim replied, "We can go over that in the morning. I am exhausted and think I will hit the sack early."

On the shuttle ride over to the hotel, Jim was obviously tense. Jake asked how Beverly was doing, and Jim was nonchalant in saying, "Oh, she is doing well, driving me crazy trying to get information out of me. Otherwise, OK."

A miniature buffet table with breakfast and coffee was set up in the small suite converted into a conference room on the third floor of the hotel. The fifteen-member board of directors and Drew were all present. Everyone was situated at the table, and five or six separate conversations were under way when Dane addressed the group.

He opened by apologizing for the short notice. Everyone stopped talking, and all eyes were on Dane. He passed out an agenda, which had only two items on it: *Update from DC*, Jim, and *Update on human trials*, Lou. He turned the floor over to Jim and sat down.

Jim remained sitting as he brought the group up-to-date. There were many rumors floating around Washington, DC, regarding a secret operation in Vancouver. The FDA director and/or his officials had obviously leaked our operation. Two days ago a well-dressed CIA official visited his office making some inquiries about his involvement with the Lindsey Foundation. Jim explained his former boss was employed by the Foundation and that his father's firm was still on retainer. Jim had asked why the CIA was interested in this information. Of course, the official offered no reason and went on to ask about his relationship with Madelyn.

Madelyn cringed; she had not really thought about the government having a discreet interest in her; though it made perfect sense, it just never occurred to her.

Jim informed him that he and Anna had done some work for Madelyn regarding venture-capital agreements but could not discuss the contents of the work because of attorney-client privilege. To Jim's surprise the man said thank-you and left the office.

Jim immediately called the senator on his cell phone and explained what happened. The senator said he would make a few phone calls.

Senator Arthur Birmingham addressed the board. He said that he had made contact with some fellow senators and some friends in Congress. Only one of his colleagues, Allen Hughes, a senator from Nebraska, gave him any indication that there was something to a potential leak. Allen Hughes was newly elected and had a background in engineering. Arthur approached him about a possible seat on the Commerce, Science, and Transportation Committee. In general discussion, the senator from Nebraska let him know that there were some inquiries from the CIA regarding the nanotechnology lab located in his state. He had referred the gentleman to him and wanted to know if they had made contact. They had not.

The senator then turned the floor over to Lou. Lou was in charge of the nine remote labs being used for sequestering outpatients. Apparently there had been multiple breaches in the security of the lab in Nebraska. Only one was reported, but there must have been at least two. Lou explained to the group that for backup purposes, Steve and Karl's program was backed up onto external memory cartridges and shipped to the Nebraska facility. When they would receive new cartridges, they would send the old ones back. The problem was that when they received the last update two weeks ago, the old cartridges were gone. The backups were now missing as well.

Steve then explained that the backup data and programs were not usable. Key components of the operating system were being stored in another location. It still bothered him a great deal. There were over five million gigabytes of his life missing and in the hands of who knows who.

The senator then let the group in on the phone call he had received the previous night. The director of the CIA called him directly. He informed the senator that he knew what they were working on, and he congratulated them on their breakthrough.

He then went on to say, "A meeting at CIA headquarters was scheduled for—what is now tomorrow afternoon—and I needed to be there with Jim, Jake, Madelyn, and Dane. The director said he would make travel arrangements for us and have an itinerary by early afternoon today. Headquarters are located in McLean, Virginia." The senator had never actually visited the complex before. "We will be meeting with the director himself and the CIA's Directorate of Science and Technology." He was not certain who else may be attending.

Aside from the technology and the progress on human trials, they wanted to know what was on the memory cartridges.

The senator said, "They seem to know a lot about what we are doing, but they do not seem to know anything about Steve and Karl's direct involvement. This is really of no consequence to us because the program would eventually be made available to the government, anyway. They already know of its existence and its value from our recent data supplied to the African nations."

Steve and Karl turned a shade of pale, which was achieved only by an immediate evacuation of blood from the head. Steve wondered if they knew about Tuscaloosa. He wondered if they had followed him when he went there to store the extracted code merging the modules that forecasted the new world government. He thought this would not be such a concern if the people in the government were not going to live to see the day where the Chinese would be in control. Speculations one hundred years out were commonly dismissed by those in power. The normal conclusions were that the next generation would find a way to deal with any adversity. Now with a hundred or more years to live, the people in power will take these predictions more seriously.

The senator then asked Lou to update the board on the trials. Lou discussed the various statistical data routine to these updates: 301 repair procedures complete, 76 rejuvenation procedures complete, 213 separate diagnosis cured, 41 outpatients in Colorado, 18 outpatients in Texas, and so on. Karl and Steve were not listening; they were both in their own worlds.

Steve whispered into Karl's ear, "We need to talk with the senator before he goes to McLean."

Dane closed the meeting with, "I will send everyone here an e-mail when we get back detailing the events of our trip. Wish us luck, and continue the fine work you are doing."

As people were starting to exit, Steve tapped the senator on the shoulder, said a few words, and then came back to the table where Karl was still sitting. He told Karl discreetly to hang here for a few minutes and then meet him in his room. Karl pretended to be engrossed in his laptop, while everyone exited with the exception of Dane and the senator. They seemed to want some privacy, so Karl packed up his stuff and walked down the hall to his room, where he splashed some water on his face. He scrubbed his face briskly trying to bring some color back into his skin, which made his skin turn bright red. This was still better than the almost translucent color his complexion had turned in the last hour.

Karl entered Steve's room, and Heather was there pouring a cup of coffee at the counter. Steve was not in the room.

Karl asked where Steve was, and she said, "I don't know. I just got a call from him a few minutes ago, asking me to get up here ASAP. What's this all about?"

Karl fumbled around a bit and finally said, "I think I have a good idea, but I don't want to start without Steve here."

"What happened in the meeting? Am I not allowed to know that too?" she said with a little attitude.

Karl looked at her with a twinkle and said, "Have I ever treated you like Beverly?"

She laughed out loud. This was a standing joke between them. Information was "Beverly Approved" or it wasn't.

She said, "Poor Jim! It must be awful to be deeply involved with something as magnificent as what we are working on and not be able to include your own wife. Well, hopefully someday soon we will be public, and things will all get back to normal. The little time I spent with Bevy I really enjoyed. I am certain we will be great friends in time."

Karl was smiling and trying to think of a quick comeback when Steve entered the room carrying a globe of the earth.

He said he originally went downstairs to take the global map off the wall hanging in the library, but when he saw the globe on the table, he felt it would be easier to carry and get the job done just as well. He was talking a mile a minute pacing around the room so energetically that you would think the carpet would wear a path in it while getting Heather up to speed.

When he finished he looked at the clock and said, "The senator should be here in ten minutes. I need a cup of coffee." Karl and Heather both laughed.

Karl said, "I think you need a drink!" Steve looked at him for a minute and realized he had been maybe a little amped out and got the joke. He just shrugged his shoulders, took a deep breath, and plopped himself down on the couch.

Karl asked, "What do we do if the senator wants to involve other people?"

Heather piped up and said, "We need to tackle that when and if it comes, but I do not think we should disclose the whereabouts of the safety-deposit box."

Steve agreed and added, “I am comfortable telling the senator about the forecast, but giving him proof is another story. Besides, he has as much desire as anyone, if not more, to see this technology through.”

A couple of light wraps on the door and the senator walked in. Steve got up from the couch and seated everyone at the dining-room table, with the globe sitting as a centerpiece. He moved it to the right of him, so it didn’t obstruct the view of the four of them.

He started by saying, “We have something to confess. We thought it better not to say anything at this point, but in light of your recent request to visit the CIA, we have no choice but to bring you up to speed. We believe you will understand our initial reason for secrecy.”

The senator seemed unfazed. He was obviously preoccupied with tomorrow’s trip to CIA headquarters.

Steve humbly disclosed his work on the Stock Market Analysis module. The senator interrupted and said, “Steve, if that’s all this is about, don’t worry about it; you’re entitled to a little self-preservation. Besides, I may find that a useful tool myself in the future.”

Steve stopped him and said, “I wish that was all I had to report.” He went on to describe his twenty-year, fifty-year, one-hundred-year model and the merger notations when he hit one-hundred-year.”

The senator said, “Well, that would be expected in one hundred years. Heck, if a company can keep its name more than fifteen years today, they are doing well.” He chuckled.

Steve was starting to wonder if the senator was going to even care about his findings. Or maybe the weight of tomorrow’s meeting just made all this seem trivial.

Steve said, "Hmmm…I would have thought the same, but when I performed regression analysis, all twelve companies had merged with the People's Republic of China exactly on the same day eighty-eight years from now."

Steve grabbed the globe and ran the group through the Southern Asia Alliance in forty years and the progression toward a one-world government. The room went quiet. All you could hear was the hum of the HVAC system and the faint traffic of the freeway on the horizon.

The senator being a true patriot was bewildered. His typical expressionless demeanor was anything but straight-faced. His body was distorted, and his shoulders slumped as though someone punched him in the gut and took the wind out of him. After what seemed an eternity of dead silence, he straightened up and asked, "Are you certain the software is taking everything into consideration? What is the accuracy of the forecast?"

Steve answered, "Fifty-one percent, enough to be concerned."

The senator said, "I see and agree it is enough to be concerned. Does our system or the backup cartridges that were stored in Nebraska derive these conclusions?"

Steve then explained that the second set of backups with the missing gigabytes did not include the Stock Market Analysis Module that was integral in surmising the conclusions. Also not included in either of the backups stored in Nebraska was the code I wrote to merge the Stock Market Analyzer with Global Economic Forecasting and Political Tendencies Modules. He also brought the senator up-to-date on the fact that the key operating system code was not included on either of the backups that the CIA had in their possession.

The senator exhaled as though he had been holding his breath for minutes. "Ya know, Steve, the CIA is going to want that operating system code. They are also going to notice that your Stock Analysis Module had been deleted unless we can persuade them to only open up the more recent backup and disregard the other. Perhaps we can tell them that the first back up had redundant routines built in that were unnecessary and slowed the program down?" Steve nodded his head in agreement.

Though he did not say anything Steve was a bit relieved. Not the same relief he had when he told Karl and Heather. This was more than just getting something off his chest. He sensed the senator had the same concerns and same reactions that he, Karl, and Heather shared. He sensed that the senator's priority was to introduce the technology and that any negative by-products that may arise in doing so would have to be dealt with at a later time.

The senator was now feeling conflicted. Here he was making an effort to deceive the CIA. He was considering concealing evidence that was of importance to National Security. This went against every grain in his makeup. Was he simply willing to take the chance for his personal gain? Or was it his life's work just months away from culmination that was motivating him to knowingly endeavor in risking the United States of America's sovereignty?

Steve was reading the senator and sensed his conflict. "Senator, I know you must be conflicted as I was and as were Karl and Heather at first."

The senator relaxed again and said, "Thank you. I was starting to feel this whole burden was on my shoulders alone."

Heather decided to speak. She was going to be very careful. It was one thing to make light of the potential of a Chinese-headed world government to her friends, but to a senator of the United States of America, it was another story altogether. "Senator, we have all had time to process this, and this is what we have concluded so far: one, if we delay the release of the technology, many people will suffer and die unnecessarily; two, if we are forthright with the government about the forecast, they may decide to delay or limit the use of the technology; three, if we release the technology without promoting modernization, there will be Malthusian catastrophes or, worse, a Two Cultures society (one that lives three times longer than the other); and four, if we conceal the prediction of a Chinese-run world government and start reviewing the data supplied by the forecasting software after the first decade of curing the world of all known inflictions, we may be able to alter the course of events that put the Chinese in power. After all, there is a forty-nine percent chance they will not be in power."

Karl said, "I have nothing else to add." As if he was somehow responsible for the concise and well-thought-out analysis of the situation. Heather smacked him good on the shoulder. She hit the deltoid just right so she knew it would hurt.

Steve grinned and said, "See, Senator, it is not exactly treason to conceal this information. The world should not forego a benefit as great as this technology for political reasons, anyway."

The senator was proud of his team; they were not only intelligent and had perspective but also were honest and had integrity. Even if the CIA insisted on the operating system and noticed the Stock Market Analyzer, it was unlikely they would merge it with the Global Economic Forecasting and Political Tendencies Modules. With the code missing, it would have been at least a year before anyone in the CIA uncovered the program's ability to make such detailed forecasts as Steve or Karl could. They could have simply not told him and let nature take its course.

The senator asked Steve, "Do you still have the module-merging code, or did you destroy it?"

Steve just said, "It would be very difficult to replicate, and it is in a very safe place far from here. Only I, Karl, and Heather know where it is, and with all due respect, I would like to keep it that way." He then reminded the senator that the board had access to intentionally separate clues that would lead them to the location if something happened to him.

The senator replied in his most genuine tone, "I take no offense and am in agreement that this information discussed today remains between us. There is no sense in getting people concerned about what may or may not happen eighty-eight or one hundred years from now."

They all agreed and shook hands.

28

The small passenger jet chartered by the CIA director departed at 9:00 a.m. sharp from Seattle. Dane and the senator were seated opposite one another with a small table in front of them. Jim, Madelyn, and Jake were seated in swivel chairs located on both sides of the cabin. Conversation was light, and there was no discussion about business. The senator had cautioned the group that the CIA tended to record everything within earshot, so it would be better if they didn't discuss the technology or make mention of any of the other board members or Genanotech business in general while on the flight. They were not sure how much the CIA knew, and the less they knew, the better.

Lunch was served at 11:30 PST, and they landed at 12:30 PST on what appeared to be a private landing strip. All you could see during approach was a long narrow clearing in a maple forest with tan-colored pavement, three large hangers, and one small building at the end of the runway. The building looked like a mobile home. At lower altitude, there was nothing but forest as far as one could see. It was 3:30 p.m. on the East Coast.

Once they exited the jet, they were escorted around the corner of one of the large hangers where a helicopter was awaiting their boarding. After a ten-minute flight, they landed. CIA headquarters are located on 250-acre chattels just outside the city of McLean, Virginia. They loaded up into a large SUV and drove past several housing complexes, where a number of CIA personnel resided. They were well into an area of the compound where civilians were not allowed. There was very little activity outside, and the buildings lacked any architectural flair. They passed what must have been a shooting gallery based on the distinct sound of multiple rounds of ammunition being fired. Then they passed by a number of Quonset huts and a smattering of smaller plantation style buildings.

At 4:00 p.m. EST sharp, they arrived at a large but auspicious building, where they were escorted through multiple security checkpoints. Each was patted down and run through scanning devices. They had to provide special ID that the senator printed from a secure e-mail transmission the day before. The visitor ID was then compared to their photo ID and to what were apparently comprehensive profiles of them projected on a monitor facing the guards.

Once inside the building, they were ushered down numerous long corridors where they saw only a few passersby who were dressed in dark suites and walking with brisk, even strides. Jake and Madelyn felt way underdressed. Jake was wearing cotton slacks and a short-sleeve bright-blue golf shirt. Madelyn had on a pair of stretchy pants and simple white knit blouse. The senator, Dane, and Jim all had on suits. This was definitely not a casual environment. No one spoke to one another nor even hinted at acknowledging that another person was in their presence. Jake being the friendly guy was nodded at everyone he came into contact with and was completely ignored. Madelyn was extremely aware of her environment and noticed everything. She quickly emulated the CIA ways and walked with purpose and poise. She knew she could not change the way she was dressed, but she could control the way she behaved. She got a kick out of Jake being oblivious to environment.

After walking roughly two hundred yards through a maze of corridors, they reached a lobby with two elevators. Their escort put his eye up to a small screen, and the elevator opened. They entered it and immediately started to descend at an increasingly accelerated rate. Once they had reached the twenty-fourth subterranean floor, the elevator stopped and opened. They were taken into a brightly lit room with a large square table that would seat twenty comfortably. They were asked to sit, and their escort left the room.

The room was sterile like you may expect a hospital lab to be. There were white vinyl-coated tiles on the floor. The walls were painted white, and the ceiling was white hanging panels. The table itself was light gray laminate surrounded by office-style chairs with castors that were upholstered in battleship gray material. The room was too big for the table. Jake had visions of having races pushing each other in the chairs around the room.

Each placed their laptops in front of them and inserted the cards provided at the second security check. This would allow them secure access to the Genanotech intranet. By the time they had finished getting situated, the door opened, and four men and three women entered. One was obviously the director who had been blasted all over the news when he replaced his successor in 2020. Rich Humphreys, the director of the FDA, and one of his employees were also present; the rest of the group was unknown.

Another man carted in a refreshment table with coffee, water, and snacks.

Stan Braxton, director of the CIA, was a tall, slender man, with eyes the color of steel. He was specifically known for his high intellect and vast experience in the field. His appointment was a surprise to all the pundits. He had never even been on their radar. Rumor had it that he was very well respected internally as well as in the White House and Congress.

Everyone sat down, and the director positioned himself in the middle of one of the four sides of the table. There was one woman to his right and the director of the FDA to his left. He addressed the table by thanking everyone for attending. He gave special thanks to the visitors from the West Coast. He introduced himself and asked that everyone address him as Stan during the meeting.

Rather than having everyone introduce themselves, as it is popular to do these days, the director made all the introductions himself. Dane was impressed by the detail and eloquence of the director. He was very complimentary to all the Genanotech team, accurately describing each of their functions and how and when they got involved in the project. The senator was a bit unnerved. He wondered just how much they knew.

He then introduced the FDA director and his chief science advisor. Everyone suspected it was the director of the FDA who had leaked Genanotech to the CIA. Regardless, both gentlemen seemed quite normal and gave no indication of guilt or embarrassment.

The next introduction was Carla Sweeny, the directorate of science and technology for the CIA. Carla had impressive credentials, yet Madelyn and Jake had never heard of her or read anything she had ever published. Carla had brought Bret, genetics expert, and Nicole, who was the CIA's top physicist, with her. The final introductions were Max, the CIA's top information technologist, and his right hand, Viola.

The senator was relieved that only CIA and FDA personnel were in the meeting. He was especially thankful there were no public officials present.

Stan informed the group that Rich made him aware of the Genanotech technology after his visit in late June. He asked for understanding, as it was protocol for the head of the FDA to report to the CIA any new work being done with regard to genetics. He then went on to say that he appreciated the need for the science to be kept under wraps until which time an appropriate amount of data was compiled with regard to the safety of the procedures. He also needed some assurances that the technology did not lend itself to military application. We need to be certain that the rejuvenation technology is not a precursor to a technology that would allow genetic mutations. He then asked Madelyn to speak on the subject.

A little nervous at first, she addressed the table. Once she started talking about the science of extensive testing on altering the DNA sequences of cells, she was able to gain complete control of her own nervous system.

She explained in layman's terms that bringing a cell's DNA structure to the state—it was five to six years prior—by repairing the effects of aging in the DNA strands was not a dramatic alteration. The cell and body accepted the alteration or repair without notice. If they were to try and bring the DNA strand to where it was when the body's cells were seven or ten years ago, beyond the cell's memory for a lack of better words, the cell rejected the repair and became sick. If the DNA was altered in any other way, except as its prior state, the cells would become sick and die. The only use for the technology was to bring a person's cellular health to where it was five to six years earlier.

The mechanics of the procedure did allow for genetic alteration, but the feasibility of any such alteration providing a successful mutation enhancing human performance was nil. Obviously, with younger cells a person would be capable of physical attributes superior to what they have today but no more than what they had five or six years earlier.

She took a big breath and continued, "With that said, the only possible military application we have discussed is to keep the technology secret and use it only on the battlefield. We could treat our soldiers, significantly reducing casualties and allowing them to take greater risks to obtain their goal. We obviously feel that the military benefit does not come close to the humanitarian benefit; therefore, it is completely unacceptable to us."

Stan's straight face relaxed for just a minute as he nodded in agreement with what Madelyn was saying.

Carla was electrified. She asked if it would be possible for her to visit the lab and see firsthand how the procedure worked. Dane was impressed that she asked and didn't just announce she was going to make a visit.

Dane interjected, "You are more than welcome to visit our lab and bring your two advisors as well. We have nothing to hide from the CIA. Prior to the director's call the other night…"

"Please call me Stan."

"Excuse me; prior to Stan's call, we had on our agenda to meet with White House officials next month to let the government in on our little breakthrough."

Stan said, "Excellent. I think your meeting with the White House will be much better received in light that you have involved the FDA and, subsequently, the CIA."

Then the caveat, "Assuming our people confirm there is not a national threat to your taking the technology public, there should be no major obstacles for you to proceed. If that is the case, we will even assist you in getting a meeting with the president and the secretary of state. This technology is going to take congressional approval to fast-track, and from the sounds of it, it should be fast-tracked."

He went on to say, "Now we need to address the data on the memory cartridges we obtained. The senator has told us that they contain back-up files for the Census Bureau's forecasting program. Obviously the Genanotech technology will have a great impact on population growth and, consequently, resource allocation. We would like to take a peek at this forecasting software, but the files we have do not have the associated operating system included."

The senator was shocked at the absolute open and forthright approach of the director. He never envisioned a CIA director who was not somehow subversive. The direct and sensible approach he endeavored throughout the meeting was impressive. It is no wonder he so respected. He thanked the director for his candor and assured them they would have access to the operating system.

For the benefit of Max and Viola, he briefly exemplified the purpose and scope of the software. He started with the original purpose of its development, sighting the utilization of Census Bureau data banks to assist us in quickly working out strategies to effect appropriate action during catastrophes such as hurricanes, nuclear incidents, earthquakes and the like. Any significant changes in population, whether global or regional, could be evaluated with extreme detail. The software's value during the eradication of the AIDS epidemic was discussed in great detail.

In a matter of casual conversation, the senator made mention of the recent upgrades to the programming that eliminated redundancy and sped up the calculations significantly. He went on to say that the population migration module included some code that was a bit buggy and didn't interface well with the upgraded operating system. It would arbitrarily remap some of the executable files. He believed the repairs were successful. He all but directly stated that the first memory cartridge obtained in Nebraska was the old program and should be discarded.

He knew he had succeeded in his deceit when Max said, "That answers our question regarding the missing gigabytes of data on the second cartridge."

The senator went on to say, "The operating system and complex algorithms that connect the programs to the general Census Bureau database can be made available to the CIA, or Max and Viola are welcome to visit the Seattle branch of the bureau where there is already in place the infrastructure to readily use the program."

Max and Viola engaged in a sidebar conversation that was uninterruptable to anyone else in the room. When they finished, Max said, "We would like to take you up on your offer to come to Seattle; we can be there in two days. Will that work?"

The senator said, "Yes, of course."

He was very pleased with himself. Not only would the CIA be satisfied to have direct access but also having it on their own turf in a location that was not even the main hub of the program was perfect. We would know what they know.

Carla and her team paired off with Jake and Madelyn to discuss some of the intricacies of the technology and the equipment used to manufacture the molecular machines and quantum stars. The CIA personnel were capable. They followed Jake and Madelyn's science well until they got to the programming of the procedures. The complexities in developing a program for a specific diagnosis were immense and required a complete understanding of human physiology as well as doctorate level understanding of computer systems and programming skills. It was this, in addition to Madelyn's complete grasp of genetics and physics, that rounded out her brilliance and led to the development of the technology. Jake's grasp of genetics and physics was respectable, but his mechanical engineering skills were unparalleled. They were truly a forceful pair and had the complete respect of their audience.

The senator, Dane, Jim, and Stan had a short sidebar on the process of involving the government in their undertaking to take the technology public. It is not often that a technological breakthrough will gain such global attention, yet one that will literally have such a profound effect on mankind as the Genanotech technology is uncharted water. They agreed that there was nothing in our history to compare it to. It is this international dynamic that will require the attention of Congress.

The meeting was concluded, and everyone shook hands and exchanged personal contact information.

29

Jim was on the phone with the FDA's office sorting through some bureaucratic glitches in the paperwork recently filed when Beverly beeped in. Jim was working in his apartment in DC, and Beverly was at their home in Arlington. It was the first Saturday in September, and it was hot. The Labor Day holiday traffic was worse than Jim had expected, so he decided to stay in DC until Saturday afternoon to avoid the worst of it. Jim finished his call and called his wife back.

Beverly answered, "Hi, Jim." Jim immediately knew there was something amiss—Beverly rarely called him by his first name. She had several pet names for him, "bubba" being her favorite, although she used some of the more typical "honey" or "sweetie" from time to time but rarely ever Jim.

He was tentative, wondering if he had done something wrong. He hesitantly replied, "Yes, dear, what's with the Jim?"

"Honey, you know how I hate being kept out of the loop when it comes to your work." After a short pause, she asked, "Are you mixed up in something illegal? Are you in some sort of trouble?"

"No, absolutely not. Why would you ask such a thing?" he immediately replied.

"A reporter from the *Centennial* just visited and was asking a lot of questions. He was a little Russian guy…mmm…here is his card—Victor Rodchenko."

He said, "What kind of questions? You didn't let him in, did you? Did he hurt you or threaten you?"

"No, we talked on the front porch. The house was a mess, and I really didn't want anyone to see it, anyway. He wanted to know about your relationship with Genanotech, and he tried getting information out of me regarding what the company was working on. He knew an awful lot about us. He knew of my work with the Electronic Frontier Foundation and your position in your father's firm and that you represented Genanotech. Anyway, I obviously could not tell him anything he wanted to know, even if I wanted to, because I do not know anything!" she said with a huff.

Her voice was raised a bit, and that last comment made Jim cringe.

"Is the name of the company you are working for, Genanotech? What is going on? What does Genanotech do, anyway?" she asked.

Jim listened carefully to his wife, trying to take all this in. What did the media want or, a better question, why did the media have an interest in Genanotech? How did they even know about Genanotech? Who was this Victor guy really?

Jim took a deep breath; deep enough for Beverly to hear on the other end of the phone. He then explained, "I know the name Victor Rodchenko but can't talk about him on the phone. It will have to wait till I get home. I don't have a clue why he would be interested in Genanotech. It isn't a public company, and it doesn't have a product on the market. It is, for now, a research venture the Lindsey Foundation is involved with. Maybe he is doing an article on the Lindsey Foundation? That doesn't make sense; why would they come to see you, or me, for that matter? Did Victor ask for me, or was it you he wanted to talk with?"

"Well, now that you mention it, he did not seem to have any interest in talking with you. When I answered the door, he introduced himself and asked me if I had time for a few questions. In the course of our conversation, I told him you were in DC, working as usual." She paused, which irritated Jim. "He didn't seem to care one way or another where you were; he just continued with his questions. It is kind of odd, huh?"

"Yes, it is!" Jim thought why would a reporter investigating Genanotech make contact with his wife and not himself or, for that matter, attempt contact with any of the other board members? "I am just packing up my stuff and will be on the road shortly. Should see you in about ninety minutes, traffic allowing, and we can talk about this some more."

Beverly said, "OK, Jim," and laughed as she was hanging up the phone. This made Jim smile.

Jim got into his car and dialed Karl on his hands-free. "Hey, bud, you busy?"

"Hold on one second," Karl responded.

Jim could hear a group of people talking in the background and then a door shut. "Sorry about that; I am in Seattle at the Census Bureau. That damn Max from the CIA you unleashed on us is back and making a lot of work for me. Steve is still in Vancouver. He insisted I be the contact for Max and Viola. Anyway, enough of my whining. What's up?"

"Does a Victor Rodchenko ring a bell?" There was silence on the line. Jim was picturing Karl with his tongue stuck out of the corner of his mouth, which he did every time he was concentrating really hard. "Well, do you know who he is?"

"Man, I know, I know the name. I know, I—yes! Wasn't he the reporter who wrote that article in the *Centennial*? The one we thought was the same guy we overheard in DC when we were roller-blading. You remember, he had a Russian accent, we were eating hot dogs, he was telling some other guy he was going to find out what was happening with all that money some senator was rat-holing."

"Yes! You are right; that is the guy! Boy, a lot has happened since then, huh?"

Karl said, "No doubt; why do you ask?"

Jim explained, "Beverly was paid a visit by Victor today. He asked her questions about Genanotech."

It was all coming back. It was Senator Birmingham the reporter was talking about years ago when he and Karl were vacationing in DC. So Senator Birmingham was diverting taxpayers' money without full disclosure to the Lindsey Foundation that, in turn, was funding Genanotech research laboratories. It all made sense. Jim thought, *That is one persistent reporter and pretty impressive to tie the senator to Genanotech and to Beverly.* Jim wondered why he didn't try to make direct contact with him. Why his wife?

Karl said, "He has obviously made some pretty good deductions, but why approach Beverly? Why not you or Dane, for that matter?"

"My question exactly!" said Jim. "Hope those CIA folks get out of your hair shortly, buddy; talk soon, and say hi to Heather for me."

Karl hung up and went back into the lab where Max and Viola were busy hammering away at their keyboards.

On their first visit, they spent the better part of a week. He had hoped they would not come back, but here they were. Karl was given the privilege of being designated the guru of the software as far as the CIA was concerned. It was prudent to keep Steve off their radar, since Steve was the one who wrote the Stock Market Analyzer and the Module Merger programs. Karl had less overall knowledge of the module's actual framework than Steve. This made it less likely for him to inadvertently lead Max and Viola in the same direction Steve took when combining modules, leading to world government predictions. Keeping Karl as the front man was an added safety precaution in keeping the inevitable Chinese dominance in world government.

Max was paying special attention to the Political Tendencies module. Not surprising, since he belonged to the CIA. He wanted to find a way to take this program and meld it with the Military's War Games software. He could not bring the War Games Software to Seattle, and he was having a difficult time getting a fully operational forecasting system in place in McLean. The operating system Steve had developed was an open architecture and, therefore, as complex as or more than UNIX. Because it was homegrown, there were no real experts out there to assist. Karl did not have the clearance to participate directly in McLean. The CIA would not allow any civilian access to the War Games software. The code would have to be laid wide open for Karl to participate in introducing the code to marry the two operating systems. Max did not want to go through the red tape and the time to get Karl's clearance levels in place, so he decided he and Viola would just need to learn the operating system themselves.

They were making good progress but needed Karl's assistance every thirty to forty minutes when they would run into a stumbling block. They had been going at it for three days now. Karl would normally be frustrated, but he fully realized how fortunate this was for Genanotech. The CIA was focusing completely in the wrong place. It wasn't aggression or military might that would ultimately affect the position of the United States in the world. It was economics. It was money. They were on the wrong path, and Karl was happy to keep them on it, even if it meant sleeping alone for a few nights.

Jim arrived at his home in Arlington. To his surprise the house was in complete order. The dishwasher was running, and he could hear the shower running in the master bath. He unloaded his laptop and briefcase into his office and undressed on the way to the bedroom. The bathroom was full of steam. When he joined his wife in the shower unannounced, he startled her and caught a good one in the shoulder before she realized it was him. Once she did realize it was her husband, she hit him again for good measure. Then she let him wash her back.

After both were clean, they made their way to the bed.

Beverly preferred lovemaking in the afternoon. This was difficult for Jim during the first few years of their relationship. He preferred after dinner and drinks. When his mind was on work, it was hard to unwind and relax. There was never enough time during the morning or afternoon hours to allow for proper foreplay. Occasionally Beverly would show up at his work and take him to a storeroom and maul him. Jim never said no, even if it was the last thing he wanted to do. He was afraid if he rejected her too many times, she may find someone else to satisfy her or, worse, get her feelings hurt. Now, after almost five years, he was not only becoming accustomed to a little afternoon delight but also encouraged it. Their sex life was great!

"Good thing you came home. I was having thoughts of seducing that little Russian guy." She laughed.

Jim rebutted, "I have only been gone for a week. What would happen to us if I had to be gone for a month?" He smiled.

She hit him again on the same shoulder, and this time it hurt. He cringed and said, "Hey, not so rough; I am starving. Do we have anything in the fridge, or should I order some takeout?"

She was glowing. She grabbed him and pulled him close to her and whispered, "Order a pizza. I am not done with you." The pizza did get ordered but not for another forty-five minutes.

The doorbell rang, and Jim paid the pizza-delivery girl. It was twenty-one dollars, and Jim only had two twenties in his wallet. He was feeling pretty sure of his financial future, so he just told her to keep the change. He said, "Anyone willing to drive around in this heat deserves it." Jim thought maybe she wouldn't take notice of the sweat dripping down him and suspect he had just spent the last hour and a half wrestling with his wife. It was incredibly hot, though. The girl was thrilled and skipped all the way back to her car.

Jim took a pull off his cold beer and placed the pizza on the kitchen counter, took out two paper plates from the cabinet above him, and grabbed a couple of paper towels off the roll that he folded in half on the perforation line, design side out, just the way Beverly liked it. He placed a couple of pieces on each plate and brought them and a couple of cold beers back to the bedroom. Pizza and beer in bed with his wife was a true reminder of how happy the simple things in life made him.

Beverly obviously had an appetite; she gobbled down her two pieces of pizza and chugged down half of her beer before Jim finished his first piece. She started talking about the reporter again, but this time she was leading the conversation toward getting Jim to spill the beans. The fact that a news reporter had interest in Genanotech, an unpublicized research firm three thousand miles away, made her already curious mind even more curious.

She knew that Jim had client-attorney privilege and had signed confidentiality agreements, but she was his wife. *Why couldn't she know what her husband was working on?* Now, with the reporter thing and the recent flurry of unscheduled trips to Vancouver, she was not only curious but also was growing concerned. Her imagination was running wild. "The next thing you know, the CIA will be at the door." Her imagination was going wild.

He knew her well. She was beating around the bush, and if he let this go unattended for long, she would start to get upset with him. It drove Beverly crazy not to be in the know. This little visit today was going to put her over the edge unless he could somehow find a way to derail the train that was gaining speed and momentum and was directed right at him. He decided he would give her a taste or a tidbit of information and a date; a date in which she would be made aware of everything that was going on.

"I am not supposed to tell you this, but I am going to. I would prefer you don't tell your closest friend or, worse yet, your mother or your boss." He had her complete attention.

She was sitting Indian style in just her panties, nodding her head up and down in dramatic fashion. He went on to say that he knew she was an adult and that he could not control her, nor did he want to, but reiterated that he would prefer she keep the information he was going tell her a secret until which time it can become public knowledge.

She said, "Yes, yes, I will be cautious," and she started to pull her arm back as though she was going to throw another punch at his shoulder, when he raised his hand to fend it off.

Jim said, "Without going into any details, Genanotech is developing a medical technology that will obsolete most hospitals' current treatment and surgical procedures." He was proud of himself that he was telling the absolute truth. His watered-down version of the actual technology was significant enough for her to see the ramifications of such a discovery and why it would need to be kept quiet until which time they were ready to take it public. It was not detailed enough to be considered a breach of confidentiality because there was no discussion about the technology itself or what it was actually going to do. He simply speculated a by-product of the technology without giving anything up about it. In a random thought process, he fantasized his indiscretion would even hold up in court against the bulletproof confidentiality agreement his boss wrote.

"I can also tell you that I have received approval to bring you into the fold thirty days prior to public announcement. This is not only because you are my wife but also because the board of directors feel your expertise and involvement with the EFF could be useful to Genanotech when making the public announcement."

She was delighted that she was considered important on a professional level. "When is this public announcement scheduled, bubba?"

He knew he had successfully derailed the train when she called him bubba. He answered, "It looks like sometime in December, but nothing has been firmed up."

"I guess I can wait, and thank you for giving me this much; I know I have been sometimes difficult." Jim shrugged and leaned over and gave her a kiss on the mouth. Then they both sat up startled at a sound just outside their window.

Jim got up and looked out the window just in time to see a small man in his backyard running around the corner of the house. He ran to the front door, but it was too late; the man got away. They both were thinking it had to be Victor. "How long had he been there?" he asked Bev. "Was he listening to our conversation? How much did he hear?"

Jim went into the backyard to see if there was anything he could find. Beverly stayed in the house alone and nervous. It was one thing to be confronted with questions by a stranger, but to have him in your backyard without invitation was another thing completely.

Jim came back in and tried to comfort his wife, who was obviously shaken up. He called Karl again and explained what happened. Beverly called Heather. Karl's first response was to track the guy down and confront him. They discussed calling the police but decided the possibility of notoriety was not worth it and that they might just be falling into a trap laid by Victor. After going over things with Karl, Jim felt better. Karl had suggested he call Drew and have some surveillance and security equipment installed on the house for Beverly's protection. Jim thanked Karl and got off the phone and immediately dialed Drew. Drew agreed and said he would have a team there tomorrow.

Beverly decided she really liked Heather. They had not spent a lot of time together, but there was a true and undeniable friendship in the making. This was a good thing because their husbands were the very best of friends, and once this company would go public, they would undoubtedly be spending more time together.

Once they were off the phones, and Jim informed Bev they were getting some security equipment installed the next day, she felt better.

After the excitement was over, they returned to their bed/dinner table, and Jim kissed her passionately. She responded, and within seconds the beer bottles were secured on the nightstand, and the paper plates were flung across the room like Frisbees.

The rest of the holiday weekend would become some of the best memories Jim and Beverly would have; memories that they would have for another 150 years or so.

Though neither Jim nor Beverly ever discussed it, they both had a sinking feeling in their gut that Victor had overheard them talking about what Genanotech was and when the public announcement would be made.

30

The residents of the Vancouver bed-and-breakfast, as it was becoming commonly referred to, were beginning to get restless. After the incident at Jim and Beverly's home, a greater emphasis on security had been put in place. When the team was installing equipment in Arlington, they found a bug tied directly into the wiring of Jim's home. The assumption was that Victor had been in the process of installing the bug when Jim and Beverly heard him in their backyard. The one thing that disturbed Drew was the level of sophistication of the bug itself. The device found had micro amplifiers for audio reception capable of listening through block walls and electronic signal isolators and diverters that can capture keystrokes on a computer via the electrical outlet it is connected to. This type of equipment is way beyond what you would expect from a reporter. It is the type of equipment the CIA would have on hand, not what is available to the public at the local *Radio Shack* or *Best Buy*.

Security was getting tighter and tighter everywhere Genanotech personnel existed. All outside telephone communications were recorded as before, but now all personnel were limited to thirty minutes per week. The trials were well under way, and the work was becoming more routine and less interesting for the programmers and the technicians. The required workload was also reduced to about sixty hours per week, down from the ninety plus hours a week at the beginning of the trials. The extra time people had was not necessarily a good thing in sequestered life. Most personnel opted for the ninety-hour workweek after spending a couple of weeks with free time and no real freedom.

The warehouse was starting to get cramped. Drew was looking for a new secure location to store the NBGS (Nanobot Generation System) equipment that was starting to pile up. Each system included a molecular machine generator and a quantum-star generator/integrator with conveyorized automation to handle six procedure rooms. Each system was packaged in two crates, one for the generation equipment and one for the automation. Fourteen complete systems were built and three more were in work in progress (WIP).

Carleton felt he could lay out a manufacturing system that would allow for seven lines that will accommodate capacity for seven systems to be built simultaneously. Seven lines could produce an estimated five complete systems per day. With space and employees he would be ready to ramp to four per day in fifteen days and five per day in thirty days. He needed the finished product to be removed from the premises to accomplish this. There had been some nice design modifications made from the first model Carleton had produced. What were originally two machines (Molecular Machine Generator and Quantum Star Generator) that were integrated as two modules, there was now just one machine that accomplished both processes.

The footprint was now only eight by nine foot versus the previous two seven by seven foot modules. The entire unit now weighed less than one ton.

The labor was tedious, and he could only work his assembly crews nine hour days, six and half days a week. He would need some additional personnel to ramp up production. Another problem he was running into was that they didn't have accommodations to board the extra needed workers. Drew said there were only three rooms available, Carleton needed a minimum of twenty-four more workers. Even if they bunked three per room, he could only hire nine people. Getting the programmer and procedure technicians to adjust to bunking two per room was difficult during the procedure ramp-up. Drew refused to entertain stacking these individuals up any more. They had discussed having the two shifts share a bed, but there was overwhelming pushback to that idea, and it was tabled. There was a board meeting scheduled on September 9, two days away. Drew promised Carlton he would bring up the matter.

Security within the hotel was far superior to that of the NBGS manufacturing facility. The portion of the facility used for procedures was secure, but the manufacturing side was not. The problem was purchasing and receiving. There was no choice but to use outside vendors for the equipment housing, circuit boards, electronic components, wire harnesses, and numerous custom-machined parts. The individual Carleton hired, Lesa Jenny, to handle procurement was familiar with all the vendors from her previous career in Automated Inspection equipment. Because order volumes were low to medium size, there was no need to use an international vendor base. All materials were available through local distributers and fabricators.

It was Lesa's relationships with outside sales reps that kept Drew up at night. He did not allow sales reps into the facility. This put Lesa in a difficult position. Her vendors' reps always visited her and received plant tours and worked directly with the manufacturing engineers in an effort to provide superior customer service. On many occasions Lesa would have to accompany one of the Genanotech engineers for off-site visits to one of the vendors, but never could a vendor visit Genanotech.

This one-way relationship was not common in the capital-equipment manufacturing industry and raised a certain amount of curiosity and speculation among the sales and engineering departments of their fabrication vendor base. The distribution vendors supplying electronic components, nuts, bolts, harnesses, and so forth were not as affected by the unusual business relationship. It was the steel fabricator for the equipment housing, plastic injection molding, circuit board, and custom steel-milling vendor base that was having a hard time with the one-way street Lesa imposed.

On numerous occasions she would have to invite two or three vendors to a meeting at one of the vendors' facilities to work out design and manufacturability issues. It was awkward to operate this way.

She had worked with many of these people for ten years or more. They knew her; they had had dinner and drinks, exchanged gifts at the holidays, and so on. When one of these colleagues would ask her what her new company manufactured, all she could say was that it was confidential.

Carleton assured Drew that Lesa could be trusted, but one never knows. The other area where security may be a problem was in the nine outpatient facilities scattered across the country. Lou was conducting some investigations, making a whirlwind tour of the facilities. He would be back before the meeting in two days to report.

Drew's recent concern over security was prompted by the news of Victor's visit to Beverly and the bug that was installed on her and Jim's home. The senator had recently filled Drew in on some older news. Per the senator this same reporter (Victor) happened to overhear two congressmen discussing the nondisclosed appropriations of funds being used at the senator's discretion.

The amount of $250,000,000 was enough to pique the interest of the reporter. He dug around for more information and a way to confirm his findings but could never quite get enough to make any real news out of it.

He never directly approached the senator, but he had been watching the senator's every move since. It was not difficult for him to tie the senator to the Lindsey Foundation, but for him to tie the senator to Genanotech was a different story altogether. The only way Victor could do this was if he had informants or detectives watching the senator in Vancouver. The other big question was how Victor knew about Jim's relationship to the company and why he had not directly made contact with him. Obviously his plan was to make them aware of his awareness of Genanotech without confronting one of the board members directly. Why?

With less than four months before the technology would be made public, it was important to keep the media at bay. The first order of business was to reevaluate the security protocols and conduct one-on-one interviews with each and every employee. The purposes of the interviews were not intended to discover the leak but to reinforce the need for security. This would take some time considering there were now 156 personnel on board and over 450 outpatients sequestered. Carleton wanted to hire twenty-four more.

Drew recruited Anna, Solana, and Ryan to assist him in conducting the interviews. They happened to also be the group working on public relations.

31

Anna found it refreshing to participate in the one-on-one meetings; she enjoyed the confrontational aspect of the interviews. She had been buried in investigating the backgrounds of the major players in the world in order to identify potential moral or economic opposition to the use of the technology. She had less than four months to generate mini bios and planned responses for over one thousand leaders of government, industry, and church. Meeting the people working in multiple departments gave her a greater perspective on the challenges all aspects of the venture were undergoing.

She had drawn Lesa's interview.

Drew advised Anna to make Lesa one of the last people she spoke with. Lesa had more outside contacts than any other employee. The thought was that the more information they could gather prior to Lesa's inquisition, the better prepared they would be with questioning.

The first day of interviews went well, but by evening there were a lot of private discussions among the employee base. It was a distraction; morale and productivity were affected. In each interview the staff was told management understood the stress and inconvenience of sequestered life. They reminded each of them that there was now less than four months to go. Many of the employees had only been on board for two months, so four more seemed an eternity. Their compensation would eventually far exceed their wildest expectations, and when looking back, they would realize it was a very small price to pay.

With Lou traveling to the off-site outpatient centers, Solana spent the day interviewing Lou's programming staff. She had not spent much time with the employee base to date. She was extremely impressed with the quality of personnel in Lou's group. Their backgrounds were all in medicine. They all had graduated medical school, but instead of pursuing careers as doctors or surgeons, they had found various occupations utilizing their passion for information technology. Some were previously working for CT imaging-equipment manufacturers, some for Internet medical database software companies, and one individual was actually working as physiological expert for the NFL.

Morale was excellent among the programming staff. They were well ahead of the goal to complete the now 417 planned procedures. Three hundred and thirty-five, over 80 percent of the goal, had been completed. It was the consensus they would be finished before October 1. Lou was planning on finding them positions at the off-site outpatient centers to assist in monitoring the progress of the people who had undergone treatment. This would leave only three programmers in Vancouver to assist in fine-tuning programs during procedures.

Drew was tickled to find out about the accelerated schedule and specifically the new space that would become available. The programming staff was utilizing over 20,000 square feet of the original lab in Vancouver. He quickly calculated that if the finished NBGS systems were crated properly, they could be stacked too high, and the new square footage available would be enough to accommodate an estimated 280 systems—about 150 systems short of the four-month goal. Drew had recently met with the international committee and had long discussions on worldwide technology deployment strategies.

The issue was raised that it could take up to one month to ship the heavy equipment across seas. If the technology was introduced and only available locally, there would be a swarm of foreigners with severe terminal conditions pleading with the US government to allow them to come to America for treatment. This issue will exist even with treatment centers in place around the globe, but if only available in America… It was decided that they needed to start shipping the equipment now.

Each sovereign nation with the possible exception of Vatican City will want the technology.

Therefore, an estimated 194 treatment centers will be required initially to supply just one center per recognized government. The citizens of Vatican City could easily use an Italian treatment center. There was still the issue they had with unfriendly nations that they currently had trade restrictions with. Currently that number of nations was four, so there were 190 nations that would expect to have access to the technology as soon as humanly possible. The problem with this approach was that treatment centers would not necessarily be proportionate to population or need. If one sovereign nation was required to share equally with a neighboring sovereign nation, the potential for bias and political problems would increase substantially.

Training resources for treatment center start-up were also limited. A training center could be started up with an estimated two days' training, assuming there were appropriately qualified individuals available. Lou currently had thirty-three personnel identified and scheduled to be proficient in start-up training before announcement. At each two-day start-up, three to four technicians could be brought to a level to, in turn, become start-up trainers. Conceivably 130 to 165 treatment centers could be up and running in seven days. Inside of one month, the amount of treatment centers will be limited to the hardware on hand, which was anticipated to be just fewer than six hundred systems.

In order to create the space needed for the equipment and to supply the most expeditious deployment, they needed to start shipping the systems six to eight weeks prior to announcement. Drew was initially dead set against this idea for obvious security reasons. The systems would be shipped in large wooden crates. Medical and scientific point people had already been identified in most of the nations. Labeling the crates as MRIs or AOIs or any number of other large varieties of manufacturing equipment could keep things under wraps through the shipping and customs process. Even if someone opened up one of these crates, they would have no idea what it was. There was to be no instruction pamphlet with the equipment. The trick was to coordinate the expected date when the cargo would hit port with the announcement date. Systems could be shipped by air, but due to the weight, carriers would need to limit cargo to a handful of systems.

It was possible to let some of the shipped cargo sit on the docs for a few weeks. This would allow Drew to start shipping equipment almost immediately. The proverbial "slow boat to China" would be a blessing.

Most ports of call around the world are close enough to population centers to get a good start on deployment. There are some interior population concentrations where shipping air would have an initial benefit. However, with the two-day training phase already a limiter in the first seven days post announcement, units could be freighted via truck from ports of call and be in place prior to a realistic treatment center start-up.

A minimum of 280 systems was to be made available for shipment one month prior to announcement. With the assistance from Steve, a population proportionate array depicting the most equal distribution for 280 ports around the world was developed. Interestingly, there were only 19 out of the 190 sovereign nations who will have to share or wait, unless of course Carleton beats his projections.

Likely Carleton will have more systems available. He was notorious for underestimating production forecasts. A true cynic, Carlton honestly believed things would go wrong. He overfactored his negativity in his production estimates. Though very conservative, he was extremely hard driving and single-minded on task. His task was to build as many systems as possible prior to announcement. Hundreds of thousands of lives were at stake, and he took his responsibility seriously.

Carlton was not the easiest guy to work for. He worked harder than everyone else, and it was impossible to impress him with your work ethic. He simply just wanted more. If you increased efficiency by 12 percent, he would want 15 percent, and so on. He was difficult to communicate with because his mind was always elsewhere. Once you had his attention, he was very intense. If you tried to hide under the radar, he would seek you out. There was no escape or easy route to take working for Carlton. If you crossed him, he would make a scene, publicly humiliating you and himself in the process. In a sequestered environment combined with Anna's employment contract, running to HR was not really an option. Employees knew when they signed on that it was going to be very demanding and not your typical employee-slanted environment. For example, everyone was on salary, and there were no overtime rules. There was no HR director per se. There was really no chain of command. Carlton reported to the board of directors who were pretty insulated from any employee-complaint process. It wasn't a sweat shop because the compensation was tetra-quintuple of similar employment, and you were provided food and shelter to boot. If someone just couldn't hack it, Anna's contract allowed them to remove themselves from the workforce but remain sequestered without salary until announcement. Bottom line, everyone working here knew what they were getting into and just sucked it up.

The earlier than expected shipment of units resolved the problem for much-needed warehouse space. Genanotech will be running a rate of 150 systems a month at announcement and can be ready to ramp up from there, based on immediate worldwide needs.

The sheer management end of this deployment strategy was staggering when you considered human survival instincts as the prime motivator for people's behavior. It's not like limiting the number of new-version iPhones available before Christmas. The known ability to save lives was a different story altogether. There was discussion about introducing the technology as experimental and not proven, to slow the anticipated rush to get in line. It was later determined that the people in extreme need would still respond the same whether it was proven or experimental. The public-relations issue that Genanotech would face was an uphill battle from day one of announcing the technology until the vast majority of people in critical need of the treatment are treated. The world was just going to have to weather a very difficult and bittersweet year.

Carleton would be pleased. He would have not only the space in the main facility to expand to seven lines but also have the rooms available for his twenty-four additions to the workforce required to ramp up production.

32

Ryan spent the day interviewing Carleton's line workers. Ryan was a fairly down-to-earth guy who enjoyed sports, beer, and BBQ. He also happened to be brought up in an affluent family. His parents and grandparents owned and operated one of the largest steel mills in the North East. It was his family's connections and his Harvard University graduate degree that landed him a job as a lobbyist. If you didn't know about his background, you would think he graduated from a community college and coached football for a local high school. He was a natural choice to interview the assembly line personnel.

The receiving clerk was annoyed that he was stuck in the interview with Ryan for almost an hour. All the others seemed to be in and out in less than fifteen minutes. Ryan's persistence with the clerk was intentional. He had the closest relationship with Lesa and also worked in proximity to her. Anna was scheduled to meet with Lesa the next day, and Ryan needed to give her as much information as possible to prepare for the interview. He also wanted Lesa to be aware that the interview would likely be intensive and thorough.

The only information obtained that may be of use was that the clerk had first name relationships with the drivers from the printed circuit board shop and the steel housing manufacturer. He had known these guys for years, it seemed. He was also probably the most outspoken individual Ryan interviewed. He made it plain he did not like being sequestered. When Ryan asked why he took the job knowing the circumstances, the clerk replied because Lesa twisted his arm and the money was pretty ridiculous. This didn't stop him from complaining. He gave the impression he liked and respected Lesa; she was a good boss. Ryan thought, *I guess some people are never happy with a job, no matter how fair and reasonable their employer is.*

The nano surgeons, as they were now referred to, were a mixed bag for Anna to sort through. There were nine altogether, and it took the better part of the day to meet with them. This process gave Anna a completely new perspective on how challenging, from a PR standpoint, it was going to be converting to this technology in hospitals across the world. Trained surgeons were the most qualified people to perform the procedures. The problem was that the actual process of performing the procedure was fairly routine and mundane. The process lacked the need for physical skill and "on the spot" diagnosis and decision making. It also lacked the thrill that comes with the uncertainty of a successful operation. Whether doctors will admit it or not, they thrive on this uncertainty; when they save a life, it is a feeling of personal accomplishment.

To be competent in performing the procedure, you need a total understanding of human anatomy, a basic understanding of genetics, and, most importantly, be an excellent diagnostician. Today's surgeons meet the profile better than any other group of health-care professionals out there. The problem is converting them.

Some of the personnel Anna met with were having ego-related problems. They expressed that even though they knew that this technology was incredible, they were having trouble with the routine and the 100 percent success rate. The process was not challenging. It was humdrum. The repetitive nature of the procedure made them feel like they were working in a lab drawing blood or administering imaging procedures. All they could see was that they would spend the next twenty years of their lives processing thousands of patients a year. The key word here was processing.

Fortunately for Anna the first nano surgeon she spoke with mentioned that if it were not for the need to diagnose, they would bail on medicine altogether. She consoled each of her next eight surgeons by saying, "At least you will be able to use your diagnostic skills." This seemed to appease them, but it was still obvious that their future was going to change, and they may not like their new job.

A number of the surgeons were missing their freedom and getting tired of the seven-day workweeks. It was difficult for Anna to lift their spirits. She reminded each of them how critical their mission was, and within less than four months, they would be able to live normal lives. She did get a positive response from a number of them with regard to their next assignment, training the world's physicians to use the technology. This would be a refreshing change from the routine. Each of these nine professionals were slated for stock options that would set them up financially for life after just two years of training the next generation of nano surgeons. They really had no idea how wealthy they would become but knew that there would be some reward for being the pioneers of treatment processing.

Madelyn and Jake were genius-level scientists, to say the least, but managers they were not. Perhaps it would be a good idea to meet with each nano surgeon individually and give them their stock options now, rather than waiting until the public announcement was made. She would bring it up in the meeting in two days.

After spending almost eight hours with the surgical staff, Anna spent the rest of the day getting through half of the nursing staff. The nurse's main function was the administration of admitting and process of releasing patients to their respective outpatient facility. This required a compassionate and confident style that would reassure patients that they were in no danger. Interviewing the nursing staff was refreshing and uplifting for Anna. They did not have the ego problems the surgeons had. They were happy and warm by nature. The only real complaint they had was that their feet hurt by the end of the day. They were required to stand most of their fifteen-hour day on concrete. It did not matter what kind of shoes you had; the concrete would eventually win. Anna immediately ordered some rubber floor mats.

Solana and Anna both reported no security concerns after their first day of interviews. Drew was thrilled. Other than the receiving clerk, there were no potential concerns from Ryan's interviews. The assembly line workers seemed happy as clams. They were enthusiastic about the product and more than satisfied with their compensation. Many of them were planning vacations they could never have possibly afforded on their previous salaries when they were finished with the initial prepublic inventory. Not only were they making five times what they were accustomed to, they had no monthly expenses and nowhere or no time to spend money on discretionary items. They were banking good sums of money for the first time in their lives. There were high hopes for promotions once the operation was public and production was ramping up to accommodate the global requirements. Little did they know they would all be wealthier than their wildest dreams within a few years.

Drew spent the majority of his day reviewing the electronic security systems in place. He studied recent phone logs and conversations, Internet activity, and the entrance and exit activity for the past two weeks at the hotel and both labs. He interviewed his now seven security personnel and found everything to be in good order. Lou was scheduled to call and give him an update at 9:00 p.m.

Jake received a call from his father while he and Madelyn were preparing dinner in their suite. It was 7:30 p.m. on a Monday night. He had just spoken to his parents the day before. It had become customary for months now to have a little chat every Sunday evening. His father never faltered in reminding Jake each time they spoke as to how he was promised to be let in on what they were doing. Jake had made this promise as reciprocity for his father setting up the initial meeting with Dane. This had become an ongoing joke between them. Jake always told his parents that *if he told them, he would have to kill them.* It ended up being a good thing he never let them in on the technology.

Jake answered the phone. “Dad, is everything OK? Is Mom OK?”

“Not to worry, son; we are both fine. I know this call is not at our scheduled time to talk, but I did think I should inform you about a very odd visitor who just left our home.”

Jake’s mind was blank. “A Victor Rodchenko from the *Centennial* stopped by this evening asking a lot of questions about Genanotech. Do you know anything about a company by that name, son?”

“It happens to be the company I am working for.” He never told his parents the name of the company thinking it might somehow give away its purpose. “Dad, don’t worry about Victor. He has been digging around recently, trying to figure out what we are up to. We have our people on it. There is some concern of a possible leak. I can tell you that we will be making a public announcement at the end of December, and Genanotech will become a household word. That is all I can say."

"Thanks, glad to hear everything is good; just thought you should know. Talk with ya Sunday, and say hi to that lovely Madelyn of yours." He hung up.

Jake called Drew, who was starting to feel the pressure of being the head of security. Drew was surprised that Victor knew of Jake's involvement in Genanotech; first Jim and now Jake. Why wouldn't he attempt to make direct contact? Immediately after he hung up with Jake, Lou's mom called and reported that Victor had been at her house in the afternoon. She had been trying to reach Lou but couldn't make a connection. She made it clear to Drew that she had said nothing to compromise the secrecy of the technology. She just said that her son worked there and did some kind of computer programming. She wasn't a techie and couldn't give him any more information than that.

Obviously Victor was in the neighborhood and was intent on finding out what Genanotech was up to. It was only a matter of time before they would have to contact him directly. Maybe this was his plan, to make them aware he was on to them but not risk direct contact, which he knew would result in stonewalling. If he continued to work the periphery, he would eventually get others interested in knowing what the very secretive Genanotech was working on. Both the CIA and the FDA were in agreement with their timeline to bring the technology public. They don't need the press interfering with the plan. Drew was beginning to get perturbed with this Victor fella. "Maybe a visit from a CIA agent would get him to back off?" Drew said to himself.

Lou was not happy to hear that his mother was put in that situation. Drew consoled him and let him know she had handled herself admirably. He should be proud of her. He said to Lou, "I really think this was exciting and fun for your mom."

Lou settled down and gave Drew his update. He had visited five of the nine facilities, starting west and working his way east. The chartered jet was comfortable and made the whirlwind tour possible. Lou said he felt surprisingly energetic even though he had visited facilities in Idaho, California, Arizona, Nevada, and Colorado in a twelve-hour span. He was spending the night at the Colorado facility, which was the largest of the nine. He wouldn't perform his security review until morning.

The only possible security issue he felt needed some more attention was in Arizona. Apparently, one of the staff members was sneaking a group of outpatients off premises to play golf at a nearby resort. The group of seven retired men and the staffer made up two foursomes who were competing in some elaborate betting scheme. When he interviewed the seven, all they could talk about was how great they felt and how their golf game had improved since the procedure. One guy even said he hit his first three-hundred-yard drive in his life! This was likely harmless, but some further discussion with the golf-course personnel was in order. He needed to be assured that one of those happy-go-lucky golf fanatics didn't accidently mention the Genanotech procedure they had recently undergone.

Drew actually laughed. The vision of seven old men feeling better than they had in years, breaking the rules and escaping the compound to play golf! It was pretty funny. It reminded him of Ron Howard's movie, *Cocoon*.

Lou didn't see the humor in it; he was furious with his staff for not noticing what was going on or, worse, just turning a blind eye. He had already informed the head of the Arizona facility that he would be moving the seven outpatients and the manager of the Arizona facility to the facility in Maine. "Like to see them escape to play golf there this winter," Lou said with a huff.

Drew laughed again.

"It's not funny, Drew. How would you feel if one of your staff pulled a stunt like that, huh?"

Drew tried to gain control of himself without success. He was starting to crack up laughing when Lou was just getting more upset by the second and said, "I will talk with you tomorrow," and hung up.

Anna, Solana, Ryan, and Drew had breakfast together in the conference-room suite. They all got a good laugh over Lou's plight in Arizona. Solana added to the entertainment when she started to laugh uncontrollably with a full mouth of fruit, which she spit all over the table in an uncontrollable spasm. This was as embarrassing as it could possibly be for anyone. Solana was truly a gracious and elegant woman. To show this level of human weakness in front of her colleagues was almost more than she could handle. After what seemed to be an eternity of laughter from the table, she got herself together and saw the humor herself. They laughed some more and finally sucked it up and got back to normal.

After everyone was done eating, Drew laid out the agenda for the day. He was to review the transportation of personnel to and from the hotel and the transportation of outpatients to the off-site sequestering sites. Ryan was to handle the balance of the nursing staff and conduct interviews with the janitorial personnel. Solana would handle hotel restaurant and housekeeping staff. Anna would interview Carleton, his engineers, production control staff, and the purchasing manager, Lesa.

By 3:00 p.m. everyone was done with the interviews. They had successfully talked with everyone who worked for Genanotech, with the exception of the off-site managers Lou was handling. Drew had reviewed all communication and transportation security protocols. As expected, Lesa's interview was the most interesting. She was obviously a very intelligent woman, who was competent at her job. She had a broad understanding of manufacturing processes and possessed excellent people skills. She would be a tough opponent at a poker table. She truly engaged Anna and connected with her. Anna was well aware she was sizing her up the entire interview that lasted just over forty-five minutes. Lesa acknowledged that her receiving clerk had a less-than-desirable attitude. She assured Anna this was just his personality. He has been like that since the first day she had met him twenty years ago. She put up with him because he could do the work of three and was completely loyal and trustworthy. She appealed to his anal and detailed approach to verification of quantity and accuracy. No vendor would ever get away with a shortage or mis-issuance with him guarding the door.

Lesa herself was open and understanding to the company's concern over security. She said all the right things. Her mind was like a steel trap, clear, uncluttered, and sharp as a knife. Anna thought, *If she was our leak, we would never get it out of her. We would have to find the person she leaked the information to.* Anna went on to say, "We have a list of potentials, our primary being a guy who goes by the nick name Tombo, which is short for Thomas Bolingaski."

Tombo was an extremely handsome, well-built sales rep for the circuit-board manufacturer of Lesa's choice. There had been rumors of a love relationship between Tombo and Lesa. If there wasn't one, they certainly felt comfortable flirting with one another in plain sight of other office personnel.

Drew requested that Ryan give Tombo a call and see if he could uncover anything that would lead them to a breach.

Lou called Drew at 6:30 p.m. He said he was on the jet returning from Maine and would be back at the hotel before midnight. He spent most of his time in the Nebraska facility. The personnel there were very diligent and alert. They had actually put some new systems in as a result of the CIA's confiscation of the memory cartridges.

Lou was going to institute these systems nation-wide. They had identified how the CIA breached the security. It was during one of the first scheduled FDA visits. Three personnel showed up instead of the two who were planned. The manager thought nothing of it. Things got mixed up, and the three gentlemen introduced themselves as members of the FDA. The FDA was, in fact, scheduled to be there. One of these guys was actually from the CIA. On the rest of the tour of facilities, only two personnel were in attendance. This did not raise eyebrows because only two were scheduled for the tour, to begin with.

Even with a good explanation of what occurred, combined with the new systems in place and the heightened sense of security, Nebraska still had a black eye. The memory updates were now being stored in the Mississippi facility. Steve was personally delivering them every two weeks.

33

It was 10:00 a.m. on September 9, and the leaders of Genanotech were gathering in the conference-room suite on the third floor of the Vancouver bed-and-breakfast. The meeting was scheduled for 10:30, but the majority of the group was early, getting situated and having a snack or a cup of coffee. It had been a month since the whole group had sat down together, and a lot had happened. Everyone knew that the focus of the meeting would be security. News traveled fast about Victor and his visits to family members. Though the interviewing of the past two days did not disclose Victor's digging around, all the board members knew the reason.

Victoria and Dwaine were engaged in a sidebar about ramping up the NBGS equipment and trying to figure out a reasonable projection of inventory on hand by the 12-29-22 public announcement date. Lou was busy typing notes in his laptop. Anna, Solana, and Drew were busy compiling the results of their interviewing to share with the group.

Ryan walked in and sat next to Drew. He said he had just got off the video conference with Tombo. Ryan said he sure gave the impression he knew more than he should. Ryan explained that he had introduced himself as the Public Relations director for Genanotech. He said he was conducting a survey of the vendor base to better understand how the company could improve its image. Tombo had quite the personality and spent a lot of time talking about Tombo. He was extremely arrogant, very edgy, and competitive. Ryan was able to engage in some casual conversation on the subject of sports and fitness. He integrated his fitness discussions with the companies pro-health and fitness posture. This led to Tombo letting on that he knew the company was very involved in the health industry. The conversation became very pitted with Tombo on the defensive. Ryan, obviously fit and good looking, and intelligent as well, brought out the worst in Tombo. Without saying he knew what Genanotech was developing, he slipped and let on that he was aware of their December public-announcement date. That was too much information for anyone on the outside.

It seemed highly probable that Lesa was close enough to Tombo to let him in on a secret or two. When Ryan asked Tombo if a pesky little Russian reporter had contacted him recently, he became very scared and stuttered in his response. He stammered and hemmed and hawed. It was obvious Ryan hit a nerve. Ultimately, Tombo denied having any conversations with media personnel from any media. "I think we found our leak. Dane and Carleton will need to have a heart-to-heart with our little miss Lesa. She is going to need to plug this leak, or at a minimum stop it up well enough to keep things from getting out any further, in the next few months."

Everyone was present, and Dane opened with roll call. This was a recent thing they started at the last meeting. It was sobering and set the tone for the meeting. He then passed around an agenda.

Genanotech
Board Meeting
Vancouver WA
September 9, 2022

Meeting to Order

Roll call

Business update - Dane

Security update - Drew/Lou

Trials update - Madelyn

DC update - Jim

Public announcement planning - Anna

General discussion - all board members

Meeting adjourned

Dane went through the progress the programming department had made and his decision to move the majority of them to the nine off-site outpatient facilities to assist the staff with the growing numbers of sequestered patients. He went on to affirm that the evacuated space would be used for storage of finished NBGS equipment and the hotel space made available would accommodate Carleton's additional workforce requirements to ramp up NBGS production.

Victoria reports on the expansion plan, "Carleton can have over four hundred seventy-five units ready before we make our public announcement. This is fifty more than we originally forecasted. Anna will need to determine a proposed allocation for the first four hundred twenty-five systems. Fifty will be kept in reserve for whoever screams the loudest." Anna was busy typing this into her laptop's day planner.

"Based on new information provided from recent interviews, it appears we have a serious morale problem with the nano surgeons. Anna made a recommendation that we issue their stock options to them prior to public announcement. This may give them just the charge they need to finish the trials with enthusiasm. Let's vote: fourteen yes, zero no." Victoria motioned to issue options agreements to nano-surgical staff immediately. Dwaine seconded.

"Approved!" Dane motioned to Drew.

Drew stood up and walked to the head of the table and addressed the group standing up, "I know you have all heard by now that some of our family members have been visited by a n*ews reporter* from the *Centennial.* His name is Victor Rodchenko. He is a short man with a Russian accent. He appears harmless, but he seems to know more than we want anyone in the media to know at this stage of our development. Through some exhaustive detective work, we think we have identified the leak. To lower the risk in starting rumors, we have elected to deal with this through the chain of command. It will be better for everyone if the person is not singled out." He went on to provide a recap on the recent tightening of security, including the thirty-minute per week recorded outside communication limit. This was unpopular but necessary. He then looked at Dane and said, "Should I bring up the question now or during general discussion?"

Dane replied, "Now is better; go ahead."

"We believe that Victor is going to continue to raise awareness of Genanotech the more he pokes around. We want to stop this. We have less than four months now till public announcement." Everyone at the table was nodding their heads in agreement. He went on to say, "This is what I propose; have the CIA pay him a visit and tell him that it is a matter of national security, or something as ominous, and it is imperative he stop snooping around."

The senator's face was contorted; he was about to say something when Anna interjected, "I completely disagree."

Drew looked at her in total amazement; maybe he should have run this past her before he brought it up. It was unusual for any of the board members to speak out against another. To date there had been consensus on almost every detail brought up in the board meetings. Everyone was looking at Anna.

"I believe that any attention from the government will have the opposite affect and provide him with the silage no journalist can refuse to keep quiet. If he does not already know about the technology, he will be relentless in his pursuit of what the company is doing—if we make a big deal about it, that is. If he does know about the technology, taking it to press will be the only means he has for self-preservation. I was planning on bringing this up during my public-announcement update, but now seems as good a time as any. I think the only way we can get this guy to stop is to give him a nibble and promise him the whole piece of meat in exclusive fashion when it is the appropriate time for public announcement and not a day sooner."

There was spontaneous applause at the table. Anna felt a little embarrassed but also very proud.

Dane said, "That's why you are heading up PR!" He then looked at Drew to see if he had any concerns, which he did not.

Anna went on to discuss that the original plan to simultaneously broadcast the news to the top media sources was not really any better or worse than giving an exclusive to one source and letting everyone else quote the source. Either way the information was broadcasted almost instantaneously. The *Centennial* in this case will just get a little journalistic credit in the process.

Drew asked, "What do you propose we tell him in the meantime?"

Anna's response made Jim smile. It was exactly what he told his wife. "We tell him that at the end of December we will be making an announcement that will forever change the health-care industry. That should give him enough to know he has a story of a lifetime in the bag and should keep him off our backs." She went on to say, "The reality of this situation is that Victor is an annoyance more than a threat, but just the same, the last thing we need is distractions. The small effort we make now to subdue his activity will save us countless hours in the upcoming months."

The board agreed, and Dane instructed Anna to make contact with Victor immediately after the meeting.

Lou recapped his tour of the outpatient facilities and intentionally left out the Arizona golf outings. It took all of Drew's restraint to keep the information to himself. He met eyes with Solana for a brief moment, and they both almost started cracking up.

Madelyn updated the board on the trials. The procedures were being performed flawlessly. Almost five hundred procedures had been completed. The only issues to date revolved around the rejuvenation process for the youngest set. It was thought that at age twenty-eight, most human physiology had been at maturity for at least seven years. This was not the case. Most of the twenty-eight-year-old patients had some cells still present that were not of maturity. Slight modifications were made when running into this problem, and partial rejuvenations were performed without harm to the patient. Rejuvenation will not be performed on adults younger than thirty, going forward. The complete set of trials should be completed ahead of the scheduled date of December 15, 2022. Madelyn believed that all 1,100 patients would be processed by December 1. After consulting with Anna, she still believed they should keep their announcement date as December 29 as scheduled. There was no need to flood the media with news this disruptive just before Christmas.

Jim gave a brief update on the CIA's involvement with the forecasting software. "Our intended deception that Seattle housed the only lab with the forecasting system and that Karl is the inventor has been undisputed." He explained, "This was necessary for our own security as well as preserving our resources. Steve has been able to continue working here in Vancouver to insure we provide accurate and critical data to the world when we announce. Thanks to Karl for pulling this off! Max and Viola are true admirers of Karl and express their thanks to his accommodating them."

Karl piped up and said with his usual sarcasm, "They are nice people, but, man, can they suck up a lot of your time!"

Jim also cited, "The science directorate was absolutely blown away by the genius of the technology and wanted to have me express their gratitude for Madelyn and Jake's openness in providing them with data. They had done their own initial research and found no Genetic mutation capabilities with the technology—a good thing, of course. They confirmed there is no military application, as we concluded."

He continued, "The FDA director is taking his lead from the CIA director. It is an awkward position for the FDA, this Genanotech technology. The FDA is so entrenched with the health-care industry, they feel they have a role here. The fact that the procedure leaves no drug or material present in the body at the completion of the process makes it less than a perfect model for their involvement. It would be like trying to govern and control splints used for broken fingers. There have been discussions to bring the Surgeon General in on the technology, but because of his close ties with the president, we don't want to involve him until we are ready to talk to the White House. There is also the concern that the very people he supports are all going to lose their jobs, and his very appointment to the White House will become extinct. Perhaps he will be replaced with a Nano General?"

Jim went on to inform the group that they were scheduled to start talks with the White House in forty-five days, which should leave enough time for the Surgeon General to absorb the data from their trials and the CIA's independent analysis before the announcement date.

Anna concluded the agenda with a global update, saying, "We have identified the top twenty anticipated countries to reject the technology in the initial days post announcement. North Korea, Pakistan, Iran, Afghanistan, and Syria round out the five countries where our political relationships are stressed to the point of resistance to any US-backed policy, technology, or economic assistance. A number of smaller countries in middle Africa and the South Pacific are not developed enough to trust technology as a friend. And finally there may be a lack of cooperation in Cuba, mostly due to pride."

She identified eleven spiritual leaders who would likely campaign against the technology. She informed the board that she had recruited Kathy to assist in the development of a response for Middle Eastern religions and that Kathy's initial take was that mainstream Muslim and Islam leaders will support the technology. Anna said, "I have studied the current political climate in the Vatican and feel there will not be a negative response. Buddhist leaders should embrace the technology. Scientologists will be a walking billboard in support of the technology. The problems arise in the far-right factions of Christianity and extremist factions in the Muslim and Islam faiths."

Included in Anna's report were long lists of major corporations that would experience severe downturns in business. The recent boom in retirement homes, senior housing, and long-term care and elder-care facilities will be dramatically affected. Pharmaceutical companies will need to downsize an estimated 96 percent per Anna's figures. Medical supply companies focused on surgical tools, wheelchairs, power scooters, canes, walkers, and the like will virtually have no market. Hospitals, medical schools, and medical diagnostic equipment manufactures will need to be completely reinvented and revamped.

She went on to report on the industries that will prosper but will require new business models and infrastructure. The justice/rehabilitation system, construction-related industry, food, energy, emergency care, space exploration, banking, and real estate topped the list.

"Oh, there was another thing I thought I should mention," Anna said in her most empathetic tone. "There are a few of you, namely Madelyn, Jake, Lou and his mother, Dane, and Solana, who will become instantly famous around the world once we make our public announcement. I don't know if you have given this any thought, but I do not think it is too early to consider adding a few items to your wardrobe." Madelyn immediately felt a wave of nausea overcome her. In the back of her mind, she knew she would someday be in the spotlight, yet the reality of it had not hit her until that moment. Racing to the finish line was all that had been on her mind; what she would have to do after she crossed that line was the last thing she had been thinking about. "There will be television interviews, talk-show engagements, speaking engagements, consults, and so forth. You may want to prepare yourself for a busy January and February."

Dane asked the board if there was any other business. Zero yes, fourteen no. Meeting adjourned.

34

Anna was back in her room feeling pretty good about herself. She felt she was really making a contribution. She gathered her thoughts and called the *Centennial.* "Victor Rodchenko, please."

The high-pitched voice of the receptionist enthusiastically said, "Let me patch you through to the press room."

A man with a gruff voice answered, "Mac here."

"I am looking for one of your reporters, Victor Rodchenko."

"Vic's on assignment; I will try his cell," and he put her on hold.

A man with a light Russian accent answered. "This is Victor."

"My name is Anna Kim, special council for Genanotech." Anna could hear papers shuffling around in the background and a door shut.

"How can I help you?"

Anna was surprised at this response. Victor obviously was not going to let on what he knew. "I will cut to the chase; we are aware of your investigative interest in Genanotech and are willing to offer you a deal."

Victor simply said, "Yes."

Anna was expecting dialog from the man on the other end of the line. She was uncomfortable making an offer to him without any kind of a read. She needed to think quickly. Victor said again, "Yes."

"Are you staying in Vancouver?"

Victor replied, "Portland; no sales tax."

"Can you meet me at the coffee shop located at Holiday Inn across the river on Interstate Five in Vancouver in an hour?"

"Yes," and he hung up.

Anna said out loud, "That's odd." She called Jim and asked him to come to her room.

A few minutes went by, and she called Jim again, "Hey, where are you?"

"I didn't realize you needed me right now; I am with the senator."

"Can you break away?"

"Sure, we were just going over…" Anna had hung up.

Jim was at her door within a minute. "Is this an emergency? Are you OK?" said Jim.

"I am sorry, but yes it is, and I am OK." She explained her strange conversation with Victor and the appointment she made with him. She asked Jim if he would come along.

He said, "Of course, I will get Drew and have a transport arranged."

Anna relaxed and said, "Thank you, Jim; I was feeling slightly panicked. I don't know why, things like this usually do not bother me; I just have a bad feeling."

Jim said, "No problem; sometimes you need to trust your gut. We will handle this Victor fella. Everything will be fine."

Anna said, "I don't think we have a lot of alternatives; he is digging around, staying in Portland, and I think he knows more than we think he does."

Jim left, went to his room, grabbed his VR tablet, splashed some water on his face, straightened his tie, and proceeded to the lobby.

Drew had a driver waiting for them and asked how long they would be.

Jim said, "I don't think too long; maybe you should have the driver wait for us while we meet with Victor?"

Anna entered the lobby. She had changed into a navy-blue suit—her power suit as she called it. She had her laptop on wheels and was dragging it behind her when she walked right past Jim toward the door.

Jim looked at Drew, shrugged his shoulders, and said, "Guess I will see you in few hours" and followed Anna out the door.

They arrived at the Holiday Inn fifteen minutes early. Before they could talk with the hostess, a five-foot-tall stocky-built man with a pointed nose, high forehead, and thick dark hair approached them. He was wearing gray gabardine slacks and a light-pink men's dress shirt. "Greetings. I am Victor, you must be Anna, and this is Jim?"

The fact he knew who they were was impressive. Anna was always uncomfortable when her adversary knew more about her than she knew about them. Jim was starting to understand Anna's gut instincts about this reporter. At least it was two against one, Jim thought.

Jim and Anna just nodded, and before they could say anything, Victor was walking toward a table and waving them to come along. They sat down in a booth, with the little man on one side and Jim and Anna on the other. A waitress arrived, and they all ordered coffee. Jim asked for an English muffin with his. Victor just sat at the table quietly, occasionally looking up and smiling at them. Jim couldn't stand the silence but knew this was Anna's show, so he remained quiet as well.

The coffee and English muffin arrived, and Jim poured about five tablespoons of sugar in his and started to drink it.

Victor looked at him strangely. Anna was formulating what she would say when Victor broke the ice. "You said you had a deal for me?"

"Yes, we do. How much do you know about Genanotech?"

Victor puffed his chest out and considered the question. "I am not looking for money. I am looking for truth."

Jim thought, *At least he has integrity.*

Anna jostled in her seat. Her suit flattered her feminine figure. She said, "Excuse me, I need to use the restroom."

When she returned, neither Jim nor Victor had said a single word during her absence. Jim had his tablet propped up in front of him and was writing an attachment he planned to include in the standard confidentiality agreement stating that in favor of Victor stopping his investigation of Genanotech and any public or private statement concerning the company, he would have exclusivity in reporting the public announcement of the Genanotech technology.

Anna settled into the booth.

"So, what do you know about Genanotech?" Anna asked again. Jim was impressed; Anna obviously has had experience in negotiation.

Victor raised an eyebrow and slowly allowed a sideways grin to develop. "I know that taxpayers' dollars funded the company's research, and I know there are hundreds of employees working in a sequestered environment. I also know who the leaders are in the company. I am not willing to discuss my sources, so do not ask."

Anna thought, *Finally, at least we know he knows enough to cut him a deal.*

"Thank you for being forthright; here is our deal: you and your paper get exclusive rights to break the news to the world of our technology when we are ready to make the announcement, and not a minute before we are ready to make the announcement. In return, you will stop all investigations of Genanotech and its personnel. You will stop all contact with your sources. You will also stop all public or private conversation concerning the company."

"When do you plan on making this announcement?"

"When we are ready, the ramifications of premature announcement are significant. The sole reason we are making this offer to you is to get you off our backs and let us finish our work. We do not need the distraction. It is that simple."

Victor tipped his hand by asking, "The technology you speak of…has no military application?"

Jim and Anna were both stunned by the question; he either didn't know of the technology or maybe he knew everything but didn't know the technology's limitations?

Anna said, "Fortunately, no."

Victor was thoughtful; he said, "I will agree to your deal; where do I sign?"

Jim went through the attachment and the confidentiality agreement, obtained Victor's electronic signature, and posted it to Victor's private Google drive.

35

The Vancouver facility was a welcome relief for Karl after completing his fourth visit with Max and Viola in Seattle. This time he had spent almost two weeks with them. The CIA was relentless in its pursuit of forecasting political changes as a result of an increase in global industrialization. The software Steve and himself had written was like a new toy at Christmas for the CIA's IT department. For some reason they had not spent much time on economics but more on military capability and resource strengths and weaknesses. Who had oil reserves, what were nations' agricultural advantages or disadvantages, ore, precious gems, freshwater, popular exports such as coffee, sugar, rice, wheat, and spice?

It was almost November, and the CIA was not close to putting the economic and political modules together, let alone pursuing the development of a stock-market analysis interface that would assist them in predicting a world government. Steve, on the other hand, had been dedicating most of his time to this end. He had installed the stock market analyzer and the original program merging the global economic and political tendencies module to the system in Vancouver.

He and the senator were running numerous simulations based on political and economic alterations to the base assumptions in hopes to present a political agenda to the White House that would either stave or change the outcome currently forecasted. The problem was beginning to look larger than previously thought. The more sophisticated the programming and the higher quantity of variables introduced into the data the higher the probability became that China would someday rule the world.

The senator set the ground rules, only economic and diplomacy changes could be made in the base data. No military intervention that was not currently already deployed could be introduced to alter the outcome. It was critical to the senator that a peaceful means be achieved to reduce the likelihood of a global government ran by China. He would be satisfied if the forecast indicated that the changes to world government was slowed down and the inevitable was delayed for two hundred plus years.

Two hundred plus years, Steve thought. Just a few months ago that would have represented over three generations. Now, the babies born today could be alive in two hundred years!

Steve ran programs where dependence on oil was eliminated in fifteen years versus the current prediction of thirty-five years. This scenario actually expedited the global government and gave China a 67 percent likelihood of being the successor.

They ran a scenario where a disproportional economic-aid package was provided for India in hopes of reducing the forecasted Southern Asia alliance, which is a precursor to China's rise. Though the economic influx to India improved their relations and increased trade, it did not stop them from forming the alliance with China. China simply has the dirt and the proximity to grow the food that India will need within the next forty years.

They had run about fifty different scenarios and combinations thereof and none were giving them the results they wanted. The best forecast they could achieve gave China a 58 percent chance of running a world government in the year 2107, eighty-six years from now. Steve would be an old man but he would still be alive to see it happen. The original 51 percent projection eighty-eight years from now is null based on the increased data employed by the program.

Steve was working on a new simulation where early on, within twenty years, North America and parts of South America, Australia, and Western Europe formed an alliance that gave the United States special authorities. There would be a dominance so great worldwide at an early stage that it may set some precedence. It was worth a shot.

Ultimately, in an industrialized world where population was the main indicator of economic prosperity and power, an alliance such as Steve was simulating would only account for less than 25 percent of the world population. China alone will account for over 20 percent of the world population without engaging in an alliance with another country. If they were to just pair up with the neighbor India, they would account for 38 percent of the world population. An independent India or an India with an alliance with anyone but China is the key to staving off China as head of a world government.

The United States has the largest economy in the world. The country consumes more than any other country and exports more than it imports. This is not per-capita or population driven. These facts are just what they seem. The United States only has 4 percent of the world population and only a quarter of the population of China. When China starts to consume at the rate the United States does, which is just a matter of when not if, they will have an economy four times greater than ours.

The United States could count on Great Britain, Western Europe, Australia, and Canada to consider such a proposition; if given evidence, it would be necessary to avoid long-term rule from China. Mexico and South America are still ridden with corruption, and the individuals in power are not reliable and would compromise their own future for a small victory today. Steve was no political expert, but the senator and Kathy had extensive enough knowledge to set the stage. Karl and Heather were working with Steve, inputting all the necessary data into the system to run their simulation when the senator, Kathy, and Jim showed up unexpectedly. They were interested in the outcome of the simulation.

Steve informed them that they needed a few more hours. The original building where Jake and Madelyn set up shop was unrecognizable. More than half of it was converted into a warehouse for NBGS equipment. There were wooden crates containing completed NBGS machines filling almost half the warehouse. A significant portion of the space was dedicated to storing empty equipment housings in line for assembly. Steve was utilizing almost five thousand square feet, and Jake and Madelyn had set up a private lab in another five thousand square feet.

There were still four suites in the building. Jake and Madelyn occupied one, Steve and Karl and Heather the others. One of the suites remained a guest quarters with a large dining-room table where the residents often gathered for lunch or dinner rather than taking the bus over to the hotel. Carleton had moved into Steve's old digs and Lou into Karl and Heather's in the hotel.

The lab Steve created was impressive. The sheer computing power exceeded that of the Seattle lab. There were five large flat-screen panels on the main wall. They could be configured to run congruently for large displays of data.

Steve set this up so the world could be viewed left to right with a variety of formats. His favorite was a color depiction of population density. The red spectrum was used for the highest densities per square kilometer, deep red being the highest density. As densities were reduced, the spectrum moved to pink, purple and then blue, green, and finally yellow. Orange was not used at all because the spectrum included red and yellow, which were the highest and lowest densities. The far left was the Americas starting with the Hawaiian Islands, and the far right was Australia and the South Pacific Islands and a split screen with control legend info and statistics.

Karl found it fascinating to drag his cursor through the years of the future and watch the gradual change in colors. Five hundred years in the future the planet was red-purple-and-blue, with just a tinge of green and a bit of yellow on the polar caps.

Today Singapore was deep-blood-red with 6,489 people per square kilometer. Bangladesh was a large bright-red area with 150 million people squeezed into an average 1,045 people per square kilometer. South Korea averages over five hundred people per square kilometer, and Japan, India, and the majority of the eastern coast of China was a true red color representing around 350 people per square kilometer. The United States was mostly blue with an average of thirty-three people per square kilometer, and Greenland being the least populated place was pale yellow with less than .03 people per square kilometer.

Karl, Heather, and Steve each had sizable U-shaped workspaces with five to seven large-screen monitors and a maze of wires connecting to massive harnesses taken overhead and routed to a one-thousand-square-foot room, housing an impressive array of towers seven feet in height, each with 530 processors running in harmony. The server room was on four dedicated 400-amp services and kept at a cool 55 degrees. Steve had a nice stash of red wine in a locker, which was one of the only reasons anyone ever entered the room.

Though Steve could operate the wall panels from his workstation he had set up a special control area dedicated to the five panel screens. There were two rows of classroom style tables winging the control station for viewing. Sixteen people could be seated comfortably for a presentation. Steve had built this with the board in mind as well for what he hoped someday would be a venue for presentation to key US leaders. The room was dimly lit and kept at a constant sixty-seven degrees.

The senator told Steve they would stop over and see what Jake and Madelyn were up to and instructed him to give him a call as soon as they were ready to run the simulation.

Madelyn was working on a new project she wanted to keep from the rest of the group until she and Jake had worked out some of the glitches. The unscheduled visit from her colleagues was unwelcome, and she felt it as an intrusion. It took everything she had to remain polite, but once she accepted that they were not going to leave any time soon, she recalibrated her own internal work schedule and relaxed. In all reality she needed a break; she had been working nonstop for over nine hours.

Jake rolled up a number of large blueprint-size drawings and joined the group. The senator asked if it was OK to interrupt. Jake said, "Of course, for what do we owe the pleasure?" It was rare, if not unheard of, for any of the board members to visit Jake and Madelyn or, for that matter, the old lab building at all. This was a quiet place, a refuge from the hustle and bustle of the main building and the hotel. "Just killing some time. We are waiting for Steve to finish getting up a simulation he is going to run for us. Thought we would take a visit since we had the opportunity. Are you sure it is OK to barge in on you right now?"

Madelyn wanted to say, "No, leave," but she just sat there and let Jake handle the situation. Jake said, "No, you guys are fine. We could probably use a break, anyway; don't you agree, honey?" He was looking at Madelyn.

She said, "Yes, dear, we have been working straight through for most of the day." There was a slight tone in her voice, and her pupils were dilated in such a way to communicate to Jake that she was not happy. He shrugged and asked the group if they would like a beverage.

Kathy was walking around the lab and noticed a model of a piece of equipment. She asked, "Is this the original NBGS prototype?"

Jake said "No, just something I am playing around with." It looked like a long version of an MRI machine.

Kathy started to ask another question when Madelyn looked at Jake and said, "Maybe we should just tell them what we are working on."

She was an efficiency nut; she thought through the situation. They were going to have to kill an hour or two with these folks, so might as well make the time useful. "Sure, we are not ready to say it will work, but what is the harm in showing them the concept? Your show, Maddy—go ahead!"

She hated it when he called her Maddy. *Pet names were for pets; what was she—his dog? She reminded herself that she was just stressed out.* Ever since the meeting where Anna said she should prepare herself for TV and talk shows, she was not herself. She needed to talk privately with Jake and let him know how she was feeling and let him know it had nothing to do with him. She was in love with Jake, and she knew she had been difficult to be around this past month. He stayed chipper and his own man. Never argumentative, never cowered to her, yet was always patient and loving. She loved him more for that.

"We are working on a full-body diagnostic process utilizing nano machines designed to do nothing but read and evaluate a person's entire physiology. The idea is that we fill the body with the machines in precisely timed phases while the patient is sealed in a light-saturated chamber. Readings will be downloaded into a software program that will separate the data by physiological categories and evaluate the health of blocks of cells. This is similar to the rejuvenation process but not performing repairs. In fact, the first step of the process is to put the patient through a complete rejuvenation. At that point the data can separate healthy cells from the unhealthy cells more efficiently."

She went on to say, "We won't have to get sick and have symptoms to spawn diagnosis in order to complete repairs. We will rejuvenate, identify problems in one procedure, and then schedule a repair procedure if needed!"

Jake gave her a sideways hug and smiled really big. The group was amazed. Was there no end to the genius of these two? thought the senator. Kathy said, "I guess we can add diagnostic equipment manufacturers to the list of fatalities."

Kathy had a cynical view of the world. This was probably because she had spent so much time in recent months reviewing the political ties of all nations with the United States. We do not often think about the world as an accumulation of 192 independent countries. We in the United States tend to view the world as a combination of a handful of superpowers, friendly neighbors, and the rest. When you start digging into "the rest," you realize how backward our world really is. There are more dictatorships and corrupt political systems than there are true democracies or benevolent governments.

Madelyn, Kathy, and the senator were discussing the new use of the technology, while Jim and Jake were looking at the model of the machine and the blueprints Jake had just rolled up.

Jim said, "You look great, Jake; have you been working out?"

"Yes, for the past four months. I run five miles every morning and hit the weights twice or thrice a week."

"I wish I had the discipline; before Genanotech I used to roller-blade almost every day and occasionally played some hoops when I could find a game. I need to get into some routine again; I feel fat and lethargic."

"You don't look bad, but you are probably ten years younger. It really makes a difference, you will see. Well, maybe not for another fifty years or so, thanks to Madelyn!"

"You're forty! I would have put you at thirty five max."

"Forty-two, pushing forty-three."

"No way."

"Yep, but I will let you in a little secret. I was the second person to undergo a complete rejuvenation process; Madelyn doesn't even know. I don't know why I am telling you this," he said with another casual shrug. "It was right before we got together; you know what I mean by 'together.'"

"Yeah, got it," said Jim.

"She would have been furious with me, but when I saw how Lou's mom breezed right through it, I convinced Lou to put me through the procedure. When he was finished with me, I performed the procedure on Lou. Pretty irresponsible, huh?"

"Wow! No side effects?"

"Nothing but youth; I have never felt better. The procedure is what gave me the desire to start exercising. Madelyn probably attributes my youthfulness to the exercise. I don't think she has a clue, and I don't know how to tell her; I have tried many times, but the time never seemed right. I guess I am just chicken shit?"

"Your secret's safe with me. I just hit thirty, two weeks ago."

"Happy birthday."

"Thanks. As soon as these trials are over, and the board approves the technology's use for its members, I am going to get a rejuvenation right away; I can't wait! Looks like two of the board members already have undergone the procedure. Well, heck, hundreds of people have had the procedure, and I have not heard of one case that had any negative side effects."

Jake said, "Not one. This technology is the real deal; it is going to change the world as we know it, Jim. I just hope the world is ready."

"Amen."

Madelyn was making her way over to Jake. She asked him to join them. Kathy was asking her some questions she couldn't answer and wanted Jake to help out. The discussion was very technical. Madelyn was surprised at Kathy's grasp of the science; she thought, *This girl missed her calling.*

After almost an hour of question and answer, Karl popped in and said they were ready. After Jake and Madelyn were alone, Madelyn snuggled up to Jake and kissed him gently.

She said, "The last thing I wanted was company, but the diversion was invigorating. I think I gained some perspective bouncing the concept off some smooth brains; it got my head out of the sand."

She kissed him again and went back to her terminal where she started working again.

Jake said, "I am going to hit the gym and take a shower. Don't work too long." He wondered if she even heard a word he said.

Karl seated the group in front of the five wall panels. Steve was just converting the controls from his work monitors to the large screens. The world was viewed with outlines of every nation's borders. All landmass was a pale tan in color, and the oceans were a deep blue.

Steve remained in his work area, and Karl was providing the narrative. The simulation started, and the United States was colored green. The year in a large font on the far right screen read 2025. The simulation ran at three-second intervals for every year forward. In 2031, Canada was the same shade of green as the United States. In 2038, Great Britain was green, followed by Australia and then Brazil and a number of smaller countries in Central America. Karl explained that when a country changed to green, it indicated that they were part of the new United World Nations or the UWN.

The UWN was an alliance of nations, where the degree of sovereignty was somewhere in between an individual state in the United States of America and a nation that is currently a member of the United Nations. The main difference was military and currency. The United World Nations had one military and one currency. A base minimum amount or an agreed-upon percentage of a country's Gross Domestic Product was paid to the United States for military support and protection. All citizens in the UWN, as currently in the United States, were eligible to enlist in the armed forces. All other independence and government functions remained the same.

In 2039, Germany, Chili, Argentina, and Spain turned green. By 2043 most of Western, including Scandinavia, was part of the UWN. This continued until the program paused at 2048. Karl pointed out that based on input from the senator and Kathy, this was the best possible scenario of alliance the United States could expect inside of twenty-five years. It was optimistic yet possible.

In 2048, all of North America, Western Europe, Australia, Saudi Arabia, Egypt, Jordan, Israel, Poland, and every nation in South America with the exception of Venezuela was part of the UWN and colored green. This represented approximately 27 percent of the world population.

The screen then changed, and China was colored red.

Steve interjected from the back of the room. "Now we will run the simulation—green is good, red is bad."

The years continued to pass on their three second intervals. Nothing changed, until 2054 when Mongolia and Taiwan changed to red. In 2057, South Africa changed to green and so did a few Eastern bloc countries. In 2060, Pakistan, Iran, and Afghanistan changed to red. By 2067, most of the south Pacific was red, and there was no new green nations. Nothing changed until 2073, when Cuba turned red, and then the following couple of years the Dominican Republic and Jamaica and most of the Caribbean Nations were green.

In 2087, when India and then in 2088 South Korea turned red, there was a gasp in the audience.

When they hit the year 2092, most of the world was red or green. Only Russia, a few of its neighboring nations, and portions of Africa remained the pale brown originally represented at the beginning of the simulation. The legend on the right showed the following:

Red = 10.8 billion
Green = 5.6 billion
Brown = 1.5 billion

It was absolutely eerie to watch the years go by and see how the program predicted political evolution.

Steve let the program continue, although it was obvious the strategy failed to get the results desired. The world appeared to be headed toward a red world government. In 2133, all but Russia and a few former countries of the Soviet Union were all red or green. What was interesting was that none of the green nations turned red. If you stepped back, it looked like an elaborate Christmas decoration. The red and green landmass was not all that disproportional, but the population variance was lopsided as hell.

Steve stopped the program. He said, "Once we get out past a hundred years in the future, the reliability of the forecast starts to decline rapidly. It is really pointless to look at data with a 30 percent or less likelihood of occurrence. At eighty years out, the data is thought to be 70 percent accurate. At one hundred years, it is 50 percent accurate and at one hundred and ten years, it is only 35 percent accurate."

The senator said, "Damn, I really thought this might work; the geographic proximity plays a larger role than I anticipated. I do find it interesting that the program did not result in green nations turning red in the 2090s and turn of the century, or even into the early 2100s. Do we consider this a success?"

He looked at the group with wonder in his eyes. "We are not all red as previous simulations suggest. I just wonder if such an unbalanced tripod of governments could be sustained without all-out war!"

The thought sent chills down Karl's spine.

Steve got up from his chair and announced he would look at the base data one more time the next morning just to make sure there were no errors or omissions. And then with as much positive attitude he could muster, he said, "If anyone would like a change from the food at the hotel, I am cooking my famous rigatoni tonight, and you are all welcome. I will let Jake and Madelyn know as well. We can talk about what we just saw, have a few glasses of good wine, and relax. Why don't you all go and freshen up and meet back here in the guest suite in, let's say, one hour!"

Everyone seemed to perk up from the empty, fearful, and profound state they had drifted into in the matter of only fifty minutes while they watched the earth turn red.

The senator said, "Absolutely we would be delighted." This was one time Kathy and Jim didn't mind the senator speaking for them.

Steve asked Karl to go to the locker and pick a couple of good reds to go with dinner. Karl loved wine and was up to the challenge. Steve had all the wine cataloged on a spreadsheet. The approximate three hundred bottles he had collected were divided into three groupings: white, red, and dessert. The majority of wine was in the red category. Karl put on his coat vest and entered the server room where the wine locker resided spent thirty minutes reviewing his possible choices. Getting seriously chilled to the bone, he left with a selection of five different Italian reds dating back to 2005 vintages.

Steve was pleased with Karl's selection and was getting in the mood to cook. He had set the table for eight and had some contemporary blues music on. Karl opened the Barbaresco and poured himself and Steve a glass.

Heather, revitalized from her shower, arrived in time to help start chopping. She poured herself a glass of wine and immediately grabbed the yellow, red, and orange bell peppers, sliced them in half, and hollowed them. Meticulously, she sliced the halves into fireplace matchstick lengths, trimming the meaty parts in order for them to lay flat. Karl was cutting two pounds of lean bacon into one-inch squares, while Steve was washing and chopping two pounds of fresh spinach. Steve loved working in the kitchen with Karl and Heather managed teamwork without the necessity of verbal communication. The blues on the stereo was excellent and enveloped the kitchen with atmosphere.

Steve moved Heather out of the way to get a large pot and skillet from the cabinet beneath. He gave her a thumbs-up on the bell peppers. They were truly beautiful and added more to presentation than taste in the dish. She chopped up a medium-size onion, while Karl was frying the bacon pieces. Steve toasted some walnuts and in a separate dish crumbled what seemed to be a couple of pounds of Gorgonzola and Fontina cheese. After Karl removed the browned bacon from the pan, they all went into the living area and sat down.

Heather asked Steve if Jake and Madelyn knew about the forecasting software and the eminent threat their government may face. Steve smiled and said, "No, but they will tonight. The senator and I both agreed last week that we needed to bring them into the loop. This seems as good a time as any."

Karl interjected, "At least we do have one simulation where a developed world is not completely run by one government in a hundred years."

Heather stiffened a bit and said, "Yes, but I can't get the senator's words out of my mind."

They all sat in silence for a moment.

The senator's analysis of the last run was, "How can a lopsided tripod of world governments survive without war?"

Steve broke the silence by saying, "What's worse, a red China planet or a planet at war?" He then went on to add, "The variables are so many and so subject to change that even though the software points to strong probabilities of a one-government world dominated by the economic superior nation, it does not necessarily mean that that nation will have the same governmental structure or philosophies it has today. The issue is once you are on top it is not easy to relinquish power; even if it is in the best interest of all involved."

Karl and Heather started to speak at once. Karl being the gentlemen he was insisted Heather go first. She said, "What really bothers me is that a profound scientific breakthrough almost eliminating all human suffering and, not only, tripling life expectancy and greatly enhancing the quality of life, leaves us with political issues that can cause war. War is the polar opposite of what we are trying to do here. It goes against everything Madelyn and Jake set out to do." She pointed at Karl to let him know he could have his turn.

He said, "I agree with everything you have both said, but I think there is a variable we have overlooked. I am not sure how to quantify it or build it into the simulation, but here it is. We agree that we are in awe of the fact we will likely live another hundred and fifty years?"

Both Steve and Heather nodded.

"I for one have not quite got my arms around it, but I know one thing. I know I have a greater appreciation for human life than I did when we anticipated an eighty-year life-span. I look at someone who is sixty today. I used to see someone who had a few more years work and then, hopefully, a nice ten or fifteen years of retirement ahead of them. Now I see someone who has their whole life in front of them. The thought of putting young men in combat now is like throwing an infant overboard, as the life raft had too much weight in it. It is unthinkable. How do we, as a human race, cope with this change of view? Will empathy and respect for our neighbor become a natural evolution or at least an increased tendency among the general population? How wise will our elders be with three times the life experience of our elders today? Will goodness prevail in a world where everyone can live a healthy two hundred years? Will mankind assume that the technology will progress to the point where you can live indefinitely? How do we factor in this very real change in our humanity? Human beings all over the world will be undergoing physical and intellectual changes we have yet to thoroughly understand. When we model our forecast, how do we take this into account? I agree that a fully developed industrialized world will tip the economic scales in favor of the most populated nations. I also agree that the strongest economy will have the most power. The nation with the most power will likely want to rule the world or at least push its ideals around. That is the way we think today. But what if we develop into a wiser, deeper, more compassionate race? How will that play into what one does with power?"

Steve said, "Bravo! That is why I hired you. I also think we should keep Madelyn and Jake out of the loop on this thing until we can write some new software. No sense in screwing with their focus right now when we do not really know if we have a problem. Agreed?"

They gave each other high fives and took a big gulp from their wineglasses. Steve immediately called the senator and told him that this evening would be purely social; no forecasting software discussions regarding anything red. He insinuated that he had made a discovery that could put all this behind them. The senator was pleased. He said he could use a nice diversion from work; it could help his perspective.

Heather then interjected, "I know you guys have probably thought through this, but during the presentation, I never did see Genanotech itself show up on the screen as a significant economic power nor did I see anything to indicate it was taken into consideration in the GDP figures for the US. If by chance this was an oversight, I think you should consider it an independent entity; there will only be a few people in charge of it, and I believe that they will be fairly insulated from government influence. Heck, I know I will be." She smiled.

The room went quiet. Steve said, "Wow, that was a ridiculous oversight."

Karl was flushed with embarrassment. They had been working so hard that they literally did not see the forest through the trees.

Heather then said, "Guess you boys need to talk with Dane and get some company forecasts!" She laughed out loud, which was just another jab in her husband's already-bruised ego.

Everyone knew that Genanotech was going to be a corporate giant, the likes the world has never seen, but nobody had really stopped to figure out exactly how big, or if they had, they had not shared that information. What kind of influence would the company have in a world addicted to its technology?

The senator, Kathy, and Jim arrived. Karl was in the kitchen opening the rest of the wine, while Steve was filling a large pot with water to cook his rigatoni. The senator was dressed very casual in jeans and a sports shirt. He was almost unrecognizable from his normal formal dress. He grabbed three wineglasses from the table and entered the kitchen where Karl poured a generous glass of Barbara in each of them.

Jake showed up and said, "Madelyn will be right with us; she was just finishing up with her shower." Jake poured himself a glass of wine and sat at the table. The atmosphere was pleasant, and everyone seemed in a mood to enjoy a good meal.

When Madelyn arrived, she immediately sat down next to Kathy. She had really never spent any time with her since the inception of the board, but after her Q and A session earlier, she had developed an interest in her. She had a completely different background, but there seemed to be a previously unnoticed intellectual bond. It had been years since Madelyn had had any girlfriend relationships. Being consumed with science and her work, there was little time for friendships. Now she had science, success, a lover, and possibly a new friend.

The smells from the kitchen were delicious. Steve had the pasta cooked to tender yet firm. He removed it from the pot into a strainer and, after dumping all the water immediately, returned it to the pot where he poured the massive amount of cheese in and tossed it until it was evenly melted and then threw in some butter for good measure. He then added two pounds of freshly chopped spinach. The pot looked like a salad bowl with spinach mounded above the pot's rim. He poured a few generous splashes of brandy on the spinach while it was in the process of wilting. Heather was finishing up stir-frying the onions and peppers in the bacon drippings. When the spinach was completely wilted, she added the onion– bell pepper mixture, and Steve started stirring gently. The bacon was added, and dinner was finished.

Karl grabbed the plates, and Steve dished out a pile on to each one. Some freshly chopped green onions and the toasted walnuts were in bowls on the table to top the dish.

All were seated, and Brunello was poured. The senator raised his glass and toasted, "To the chefs and to our successful public announcement in—" he looked at his watch "in fifty-seven days!" Glasses clinked, Jake said a quick prayer blessing the food and the company, and everyone dug in.

Dinner was excellent, and conversation was light. The wine was enhancing the mood, and the music complimented the overall atmosphere. It was November 3, 2022. Jim was counting the days when his wife, Beverly, would be joining him. The board had agreed to bring her into the fold on Thanksgiving, which was on 24 this year. Twenty-one days to go! He was going to remain here until she arrived on the evening of 21. Jim figured as the days ticked away that Beverly would be in ever-increasing agony. Her curiosity was abnormally high as a general rule. She had been driving him crazy in the first few months of his participation with Genanotech. Beverly had surprised him in the past few weeks. She seemed to be looking forward to being brought up to speed on Jim's big secret, but she seemed to have an unusual calm about her; no anxiety, no prying, and no emotional escalations. It was almost as though she already knew what was going on. She couldn't, though; the only possible leak was from Victor and Lesa's friend Tombo. Neither Victor nor Tombo knew all that much yet. Perhaps she had just come to terms that there was a good reason for the secrecy and that she felt privileged to be one of a very few who would be informed prior to public announcement.

Still, this change in Beverly's behavior was nagging at Jim. He just couldn't wait until she was with him and part of this.

Madelyn and Kathy were engaged in heavy conversation about the new diagnosis application. Jim, Jake, and Karl were having a conversation about Beverly, while Steve and Heather were rinsing dishes. Everyone was satisfied and relaxed.

The senator was just contently observing the group. How proud he was of every one of them. How pleased he was with himself. His life's work and his life's dream were so close to culmination, he was having difficulty accepting it. The people in the room around him included what he considered the critical personnel responsible. First and foremost was Madelyn and then, in order of contribution, Jake and finally Steve. Without their individual genius and efforts, none of this would have been possible.

His phone rang. "Arthur here…yes, I understand…thank you; you too." He hung up the phone and stood up clanging a fork on the table. The room gave him their undivided attention.

"The president of the United States, the secretary of state, and the director of the CIA will be visiting us tomorrow morning at ten AM."

He looked at his colleagues. They were silent and sober.

Jake broke the silence. "Is there any preparation required—what can we expect?"

Steve said, "I need to reconfigure my lab to pose as a programming facility. Karl and Heather, we have some work to do." This had been done before for CIA personnel visits. The lab had been in a continual state of improvement since, and Steve needed to remember what it looked like a few months ago when he brought the director through. Not insurmountable, but it was not exactly what he had hoped he would be doing after dinner that night.

The senator informed the rest of the group, "Business as usual, and, oh, no mention of this visit to anyone outside of the facility."

Madelyn was in shock. She knew her invention would give her notoriety. She knew she would be on the cover of numerous scientific journals and likely major news magazines. But meeting the president—that was not something she had considered. Jake saw the distress on Madelyn's face and tried to comfort her by rubbing her shoulders gently.

She shrugged him off and stood up. "The president will be here tomorrow—the president?" The senator smiled and just nodded yes.

36

Drew was proud of the hotel cleaning crew's extraordinary work to prepare for the president's visit with the few hours allotted. At 6:00 a.m. he attended a conference call with the head of the secret service. His small security staff and the senator were also present. Because of the high security already in place, there was not much to do. Mostly it was a briefing to ensure that Genanotech personnel did not get in the way of the Secret Service detail.

Air Force One was landing in Portland International Airport at 9:15 a.m. The president, secretary of state, and the CIA director were to be transported via three separate government-issued SUVs. There would be two other SUVs in the concord. All of them would be of different colors and makes so as not to draw attention. They would arrive shortly before 10:00 a.m. at the hotel. A one-hour meeting and early lunch was to be held at the hotel, preceding a one-hour tour of the facilities. At completion of the facility's tour, they would be bussed back to the hotel and depart.

For the purposes of space, Madelyn, Jake, the senator, Dane, Solana, Jim, Steve, and Karl were invited to the meeting with the president. All other board members and Drew would be able to view the meeting live, via secure close-circuit monitors in the security room, and were invited to a private lunch in the hotel dining room. The rest of the Genanotech personnel would not even know the president was here until which time they may see him on the tour.

Carleton was making progress well beyond previous production goals. They had already built 225 Nanobot Generation Systems (NBGS) and were on schedule to have 490 units; hundreds more than originally scheduled would be completed by the 12-29-22 public-announcement date. The original Genanotech lab was now almost fully stacked with crated NBGSs.

Steve had his lab stripped. He had taken down the five large-screen monitors on the wall. He and Karl had removed two of the workstations, leaving dangling wires from the ceiling. He stacked some tables up against one of the walls. The room looked abandoned with the exception of three workstations for himself, Karl, and Heather. It looked like they had kicked out the programmers who originally used the space and had not done much with it except make it useful for their work. The room looked so innocuous that the members of the tour should not show any interest in seeing what was in the main server room. Forty linear feet of seven-foot-tall stacked state-of-the-art servers would be pretty hard to explain.

Stan did not know about the extent in which Steve had gone with his system in Vancouver.

As far as the government was concerned, the main hub of the forecasting effort was in Seattle. The CIA was aware that there was a satellite version of the system in Vancouver, Washington, but did not know the extent of it. It was vital they *not* find out about this system or the political evolution module Steve had been building for the past four months; at least not yet. After the public announcement and some further enhancements, they would share their work in entirety.

The senator had made it clear that if the CIA got their hands on the enhanced version of the software that the public announcement would be postponed and that the operation would likely be shut down until which time they could feel they have a solution to the "red/green" problem.

It was orchestrated that Karl would make mention in the morning meeting with the president that the forecasting infrastructure was safely hidden in the Census Bureau in Seattle. He would also casually mention that the CIA had their complete version of the operating system as well as total access to the system in Seattle.

It was decided that Jake and Madelyn would disclose the prototype diagnostic system.

The senator was meeting with Dane to prepare a concise presentation and tour. There was a lot to cover in only just three hours. They did not know what questions would be presented or for that matter what the purpose of the visit was. It was rumored that the White House was recently made aware of the technology and wanted to see it firsthand and meet the people involved. This made the most sense, and that was the model they were using for preparation.

The senator was informed that if things went on schedule, the president would like to stop by Colorado Springs and visit some outpatients. No notification was necessary until they were on their way. The secret service already had a detail waiting in Colorado in the event they had time.

Trial status agenda items:

- Nine hundred eighty-seven patients have completed procedures and have been transported to off-site secure facilities.

- Nine patients scheduled for procedure today.
- One hundred fourteen patients are in queue for procedure.
- Six hundred ninety-eight repair procedures complete.
- Five hundred seventy-seven rejuvenation procedures complete.
- Thirty-one varieties of cancer in one hundred eighty-two patients have been cured.
- Twenty-nine spinal and nervous-system injuries and disorders have been repaired.
- One hundred twelve heart- and vascular-system-related conditions have been reversed.
- Fifty-six digestive system and liver disorders repaired.
- Twenty-three pulmonary disease and disorders reversed.
- Sixteen endocrine imbalances modified.
- Nine MS patients cured.
- Seven kidney-related disorders repaired.
- Three patients have had blindness reversed.
- Two patients have had their hearing restored.
- Other repairs have been completed for eczema, baldness, tendinitis, torn tendons or ligaments, chronic migraines, and the list goes on. All with 100 percent success and no side effects.

Programming was still under way for brain-related illness. Tumors had been successfully treated in the brain. However, there had yet to be any trials on depression, schizophrenia, bipolar disease, or other more subtle psychiatric-related conditions. Next week the first of these procedures was scheduled for a patient with serious depression. If successful, the patient will have no withdrawal from cold-turkey elimination of SSRI medication.

Other agenda items:

- Forecasting software update
- Financial update, including royalty schedule and international subsidy—discussion of making technology available to all verses only to those who can afford it
- Estimated increase to US GDP over the next twenty years
- NBGS (nanobot generation systems) production status and initial delivery schedule; includes preliminary plans for start-up facilities strategically placed around the globe
- Review list of hostile nations and Genanotech's recommendations
- Review list of likely factions who will attempt to undermine the use of the technology
- Overview of the nine outpatient facilities
- Prototype diagnostic technology

Both Dane and the senator looked at the list and exhaled. They hoped they would be able to get through it without too many questions. The fact that Stan had been made fully aware of the program should help speed things along. The White House probably had most of this info already, and hopefully the president and secretary had been briefed.

They went up to the conference room on the third floor after carefully touring the downstairs dining room. The table had been set for eleven—eight Genanotech personnel and the three distinguished guests. Each had a blank pad of paper, pen, coffee cup, water glass, and a bound copy of the agenda with some additional detail in it. One end of the table was left without a seat where whoever was speaking could present via projector. There was the usual small table where fresh coffee, tea, juice, water, and some pastries were placed. The Secret Service requested no tablecloths be used in the dining room or the conference room. This was to reduce any concealed areas. The two rooms adjacent to and the room below the conference room in addition to the three rooms across from it were to remain vacant and available to the Secret Service.

All Genanotech personnel other than those directly involved in the visit were to be transported to one of the facilities. This was normal with the exception of the cleaning crew. Drew had told them that they were expecting some important guests, and they were to finish in the hotel and then assist the janitorial staff at the main building. All was going according to plan. It was 9:20 a.m.; he got word that the plane had landed and that they were on schedule. The last of the Genanotech personnel, including the cleaning crew, had been bussed to the two facilities.

Drew squeezed six chairs in the small security office to allow himself, Anna, Dwaine, Kathy, Heather, and Lou to observe the meeting via monitor. He had set up com link to allow the group to see them from the conference room and communicate if necessary. Drew's apartment behind the security room was wired for view of both areas. At least one Secret Service agent would be posted in Drew's apartment.

Franky was working furiously in the kitchen preparing lunch. When he had heard that cheeseburgers for the president and fish and chips for the secretary of state were what was requested, he almost tipped over. This was truly a challenge for an accomplished chef. At first he was disappointed he couldn't serve something like scallops in a champagne sauce or stuffed tenderloin of beef.

Now he was excited to make something traditional yet perfect and hopefully memorable. He had a wood-fired grill in the kitchen and seasoned hickory and fresh apple sprigs to complement the flavor of whatever was grilled. He chose an Extra Sharp Cheddar from the international award winning Rogue Creamery in Central Point, Oregon for the Presidents Hamburger.

He had on hand, some of the best pale reserve virgin olive oil from Corning California and some fresh pacific Halibut caught off the coast near the Oregon/Washington boarder. He was still deciding on whether to use a tempura batter or more traditional beer batter for the Secretary's fish. He finally decided that they were in the Northwest, home of many micro-breweries, so a beer batter using a good local oatmeal stout would be the way to go.

Franky thought, what a story to tell my friends and family. 'I made a hamburger for the president of the United States.' Who would believe me?

All the Genanotech board members participating in the meeting were now seated in the conference room. With ten minutes before arrival, the senator decided to go downstairs and greet their guests. When he exited the elevator, he noticed that the SUVs were already parked in front. Three men from each of the vehicles parked furthest forward and rear exited their vehicles from the back seats. Dressed in dark suits with electronic devises in their ears, they appeared as Secret Service just as one may see in a movie.

The six men entered the building just as the senator was entering the lobby. Drew greeted them and introduced them to the senator. There was a brief discussion, and they disbursed. One went to the elevator, three went up the flight of stairs, one to the dining room and kitchen, and the sixth followed Drew into the security room and then to his apartment. Within less than ten minutes, all the agents with the exception of the agent in Drew's apartment were back in the lobby. The senator could hear one of them saying "all clear." Four more Secret Service agents exited their vehicles and entered the lobby. Five of them disbursed—three went upstairs, one went into the kitchen, and one went out the back emergency exit.

The director of the CIA appeared from one of the vehicles, followed by the secretary of state and finally the president. They were escorted in by one of the agents while three remained positioned outside. Once in the lobby, the senator noticed two agents heading to the bus that was to transport the group to the two facilities a few blocks away.

The senator had met the president three times and had worked closely with the secretary of state on more than a dozen occasions when he was in the senate himself. He welcomed them and shook their hands. The four of them plus one agent entered the elevator, and the senator pushed 3.

When they entered the conference room, the room went immediately quiet. Once seated, the president gave his signature smile and in a very sincere tone thanked everyone for seeing him on such short notice. He asked for some water and requested that everyone relax and take just one minute before they got started. Karl provided water and coffee to their guests.

Before Karl could sit down, the president asked everyone to remain seated and stood up. He went around the table and shook everyone's hand and had them introduce themselves. He sat down. Then the secretary of state also thanked everyone for their time and acknowledged each of the board members present.

The president was thumbing through the agenda that was prepared and shaking his head slowly from side to side while reading. After just one moment of awkward silence, he smiled broadly and said, "This is the most amazing technological breakthrough in history. I am privileged to be among your company. I am further privileged to be the president in office when this historic American ingenuity—no, 'genius' is a better word for it—is bestowed on the world."

There was brief applause, and he held his hands up and went on to say, "Not only is the technology alone amazing and the amazing, profound effect it will have on billions of people, the entire human race itself, the work you have done to prepare the world for such a breakthrough, deserves recognition beyond which myself or our government can bestow on you."

He then raised his hand to suppress any applause and independently applauded the group, making eye contact with each member.

The other board members in the security room were amazed at how sincere and genuine the president seemed. They were all wishing they could have been in the room.

The president then said, "I understand there are some members of your board who could not join us for the meeting due to space constraints, but there is some kind of monitor system in place?"

Steve stood up and slightly turned the monitor and pushed a com button allowing two-way audio/video. The president had each of them introduce themselves and then personally thanked them for their contributions.

He then said, "We may call on you in the next hour, but if not, we will have a chance to chat during lunch." He smiled broadly again and relaxed in his chair and took a drink of water.

The president then sat up in his chair and took on a very serious look. The room was quiet; the president was obviously thinking. He said, "I and the secretary learned of your undertaking just two days ago. Stan here has had to endure our multitude of questioning over the past thirty-six hours. I believe we are thoroughly briefed on most of your agenda items, so if it is not too much to ask, I would like to spend the next forty-five minutes with an informal Q and A session and then proceed to lunch and just try to get to know this extraordinary team you have assembled. If lunch goes over a bit, that's OK—we want to take a quick tour of your facilities and head out to Colorado Springs, where I can meet some of the people you have put through the procedure and be back in Washington by ten p.m. EST. Sounds OK with everyone?"

The senator looked around the table quickly and responded with a nod.

Stan started the questioning by asking Karl if there had been any new updates or findings of interest with regard to the forecasting efforts.

Karl said, "No. However, we are still trying to get a handle on Central Asia and parts of the Middle East. It is difficult to predict the political climate there with such unstable governments and nonunified secular thinking. We would like to hand over a few parts of the world to the US government in order to negotiate deployment of the technology. We believe the private sector can handle all but about seven nations—you know which ones these are."

Steve was doing everything in his power not to smile too big. He was so proud of Karl and his ability to make the CIA believe he was the main brain thrust behind the forecasting software. This was necessary to allow Steve to work out of Vancouver and plow forward with the Political Evolution software.

The secretary looked at the president with a smile on his face. He then said to Karl, "We were just about to ask you to do exactly that!"

It was awkward to conduct an informal meeting with the president and the secretary. When do you participate? Do you need to be addressed first? The silence between what would normally be natural interaction was unsettling.

The senator was astute and recognized his colleagues did not know how to interact. He said, "Solana is in charge of public relations…Solana?"

"Oh yes, Mr. President, Secretary…Anna and Kathy have teamed up on this subject; perhaps we can get you together at lunch to discuss the best process for handoff?"

"That would be perfect; thank you," said the secretary.

Stan continued the questioning. He looked in Madelyn's direction and made a casual statement about something new on the horizon. Madelyn perked up and filled in the group on the work she and Jake were doing on utilizing the technology for diagnostics. She went on to say that she understood the dramatic impact this would have on medical-equipment manufacturers. She made a suggestion that perhaps with some royalties to Genanotech, the main players in the industry could manufacture and support the new equipment.

Her comments and sincerity were applauded. The president just kept shaking his head. The secretary stood up and clapped. Madelyn was embarrassed, and it was obvious by her flushed face.

The secretary made a comment about her reaction to praise. He said, "Well, it is evident that you are not accustomed to the limelight. All I have to say is, you better get used to it!" He smiled big and congratulated her and Jake for their genius.

The senator took the opportunity to discuss post-announcement security. He said, "None of these people have any experience being public figures. I believe we are going to need some help from the FBI in the first three to six months after making our announcement to provide security to the company and the team members."

Stan agreed, saying, "I think we can arrange that."

He looked at the president, who then said, "I think that is the minimum our government could do. Consider it done!"

Madelyn and Jake seemed to physically show some relief and relaxed. They had been so caught up in the science that they had had little time to consider the way their lives would be changed becoming worldwide dignitaries. The idea that there would be some federal security made them feel more at ease in one sense, but at the same time, it just solidified the reality of what life will be like in the months after announcement. Jake was braced for the celebrity, while Madelyn remained in denial.

When the group went downstairs for lunch, the president spent the first thirty minutes giving his complete attention to the group that was watching the meeting via electronic feed. Drew, Anna, Dwaine, Kathy, Heather, and Lou were overcome with gratitude to get this level of attention. Food was served, and everyone seemed to loosen up a bit. The entire group knew that this special moment would be in their memories for at least the next one hundred years. Everyone ordered a hamburger or fish 'n' chips. The food was incredible, and after his first bite, the president insisted that Franky join them for lunch.

Drew was probably the only one at the table without an appetite. He remained concerned about security even with the Secret Service present. There was no reason for concern, but the fact that the responsibility for Genanotech security fell under his purview wouldn't allow him to let go.

The president, secretary, and CIA director intentionally insisted on spacing themselves in the seating arrangements as to allow for group conversations. The president situated himself to be able to have direct access to Madelyn, Jake, and Lou. He was not necessarily scientifically inclined but felt such admiration for these innovators that he personally and selfishly wanted to take the opportunity to be in their company. It is a rare circumstance that the tables are turned when it comes to the president meeting new people. Conversation remained light. Jake was thinking that the president genuinely agreed with their approach to the announcement. There had always been a nagging concern that the White House would want to keep the technology proprietary to the United States; well, at least for the first few decades. When the president mentioned how inhumane it would be to keep access limited to only a portion of the world's population, Jake for the first time really believed that all their preparation was going to go according to plan.

Anna and the senator engaged in a lively discussion with the secretary. They were debating on how best to deal with seven nations the United States would directly be involved in the technology announcement. The secretary believed it would need to be a joint US-UN undertaking. The real issue was that it would have to happen very quickly. If seven nations did not have access to the technology at the same time the rest of the world did, it could result in serious chaos and possible military escalation. Getting big government to move fast—hmmm…this sounded like a larger problem than it appeared on the surface. It was generally agreed that they could not start bringing in other nations prior to announcement. How do you call an emergency meeting with the United Nations and expect agreement on an issue this complex, not to mention shocking? The leaders of the world were just human beings, and the endless ramifications of this technology were going to be very difficult for them to digest. The fact that they would be directly responsible for dealing with those ramifications would throw the biggest monkey wrench they could imagine into their daily routines of administration and government. The leaders of superpowers and small nations alike will undergo serious psychological impacts from the moment the news would be released.

The secretary shared that the president had probably only had three hours sleep since he was brought into the loop. He openly admitted that he was running on adrenaline and had not been able to compartmentalize the effect this would have on their administration. The current political climate was that the government should get out of the way of private industry. This announcement would directly affect all the governments of the world immediately after public release. This was an instance where the government would be scrambling to keep up with the private sector.

There was no way, short of not introducing the technology, to damper the initial shock waves of the announcement. Not allowing the use of this technology would be counterintuitive to human nature. They were just going to have to endure the shock! The black-market use of this technology could prove devastating, both socially and scientifically.

The closer they got to the announcement date, the scarier it was. Anna, Jim, Kathy, Ryan, the senator, Dane, and Solana had been shouldering the burden of this stress. It was good to get the White House involved if for any reason just to share some of the enormous responsibility. The team had spent almost one year preparing for the likely response from every corner of the world. The ramifications just increased in intensity with every day spent in preparation. The weeks and months to follow would undoubtedly test man's ability to cope with change.

At least Steve, Karl, and Heather were able to rely on mathematics to derive their conclusions. The public relations and government efforts are almost incomprehensible and virtually impossible to get your arms around. Most of the conclusions and facts that had been gathered to date had been spoon-fed to Steve for the forecasting database. If it were not for that, Anna was convinced she would be certifiably crazy by now.

Stan was deep in a conversation regarding global military balance with Steve when the president stood up and said he was ready for the tour. Everyone at the table immediately got up and headed to the lobby. The Secret Service agents were back in action. They had sent two men down to the facility when lunch began. A quick and orderly departure ensued, and Madelyn, Jake, Karl, Lou, and Drew joined the entourage. Everyone else stayed at the hotel.

The tour was uneventful, which Steve really appreciated, since they did tour his office. The server room was never seen.

Lou was invited to fly to Colorado with the president on Air Force One, which he enthusiastically agreed to. The Genanotech jet was sent to return Lou once the tour was finished.

37

Steve, Karl, and Heather spent the evening reassembling their lab. Steve was devising methods to incorporate Heather's insight into the "new psychology of man" into his root database. Once this was complete, he would update the memory cartridge and fly out to Tuscaloosa.

Karl received a phone call from Jim at 11:00 p.m. Jim seemed anxious and wanted Karl to commit to a boys' night the next day. Being sequestered, that meant dinner and drinks at the hotel. Jim wouldn't say what was bothering him but told Karl he would talk about it the next day. Heather thought it would be a good diversion for Karl. He had been working nonstop for six months. She didn't seem the least bit curious as to why Jim would want to get together.

They worked from 8:00 a.m. until 6:30 p.m. straight and felt they had successfully incorporated the subtle change in psychology into the root of the program. They also incorporated Genanotech as a significant power or influence.

As it turned out, both modifications had little effect on the red/green/tan dilemma. With that said, there did not seem to be any indication that World War III was going to break out either. Karl was a bit disappointed there were not more dramatic changes. The reality was that money was money and population and consumption drove the GDP of any developed nation; the higher the GDP, the more powerful the nation. All the utopian psychology in the world was not going to change that.

Discussion about spirituality and organized religion was a hot topic as they were working on the inner working of how people would think during the next ten to one hundred years. There was going to be a serious need for humans to reflect in an organized setting. Preparation for a premature death due to accident or foul play would create the same need for the devout that exists in church today.

The real change will be that people will need to spend more time thinking about how they should live their lives and how their interactions affect the lives of everyone else. The planet was about to get crowded, and they would need to do a much better job of getting along. Whole new interpretations of the ancient writings would start to pop up on Sunday morning. Worship would likely become more prevalent, and a larger percentage of the population would likely participate. The wisdom associated with considerably longer lives would grow exponentially. People over one hundred will be physically, mentally, and emotionally fit enough to maintain leadership roles.

Trying to incorporate philosophical and psychological changes that were inevitable into the math was maddening. The eventual average level of education would be exponentially increased. They were headed toward an educated society that held life precious. Mankind had not evolved nearly to the degree they would in the next fifty years.

Karl freshened up and went to the hotel to meet Jim for dinner at 7:30 p.m. Jim seemed pleased to see his buddy and immediately ordered a couple of beers. After a few minutes, Karl asked Jim, "Why so urgent that we have dinner now?"

Jim rubbed his unshaven chin and mumbled something undecipherable under his breath.

Karl said, "What?"

Jim replied, "It's Beverly; I know she knows what is going on, and it scares me that she has not let me know. Who would bring her into the loop? Certainly not Victor? He wouldn't risk losing his exclusivity on the story, would he?"

Karl asked why Jim felt this way.

Jim explained Beverly's recent behavior.

Karl interrupted and started to say that he was imagining things before Jim stopped him and continued on. By the time he finished, Karl was fairly certain he was right. They both took a long tug at their beers.

Karl said, "Let's call her right now and ask her."

Jim choked, and when he finally got control of himself, he said, "OK, right after dinner; you and I will go up to my room and get on the secure line and call her together."

Tipping his glass, he said with genuine sincerity, "You are truly my best friend."

Dinner was excellent as usual. When this was all over, it was going to be quite an adjustment not to have Franky's cooking on a regular basis. They both had what was now called the presidential hamburger and walla walla onion rings battered in a vanilla ice cream-potato chip mixture. There may have been another beer or two involved. When they got to Jim's room, they were laughing and feeling a little light-headed. The Portland microbrews that were on tap had 5 percent to 7.5 percent alcohol/vol. Jim got on the phone and dialed Drew in order to have him get a secure line in place. Drew had recently received software that allowed him to secure a nonsecure line being dialed into.

Once the line was in place, Jim made the call. Beverly answered with her new jubilant voice. Jim was scratching his head and even Karl was thinking, *Who is this person…?* Beverly was not a down person by any means. She was happy, confident, beautiful, and engaging. It was just that she was very even-keeled and rarely had any swings in her outward emotional self. This person on the other end of the phone was talking like an overexcited kid.

After the usual greetings, Jim told Beverly that he was on speaker and had Karl in the room. She said, "Hey, Karl," and then in a fun-loving way scolded Jim for not letting her know she was on speaker.

He explained that they were on a secure line. Her end had been taken care of by some new technology Drew just got. This in itself bothered her strong views on public versus private. But she had no choice in the matter.

There was some silence, and finally Karl blurted out that they were concerned that she had been brought into the loop without their knowledge.

Beverly laughed and then tried to say something but laughed again. This went on for longer than Jim and Karl could take without getting a bit agitated. Finally, with some effort, Beverly got out what she was trying to say, which simply was that she was very excited about coming on board in *17 days*, and that was it.

Jim said, "Beverly, I…we…know you better than that; you simply have not been yourself, and you have completely stopped all your inquiries about our project…this is not like you, especially seventeen days away. As we get closer to your birthday or Christmas, you get more and more aggressive to guess as to what surprise I may have for you…what's really going on?"

Beverly started to deny that anything was going on and then stopped herself. She asked again if this was a secure line.

Jim said yes.

She asked if it were secure from company personnel.

Jim said, "Hmmm…not sure; why?"

She responded with, "Well, let me put it to you this way. Someone from the company contacted me and let me know that I would be playing a critical role in the announcement of whatever it is you guys are working on and that I would definitely see a lot of face time in front of the public. There was also this little thing about some options that will be made available to me."

She went on to say, "I could care less about the money, but the thought that I could actually have the opportunity to have direct access to the public through all significant media, including TV, Internet, radio, press, and son…this is just over the top for me. I sure hope this story is as big as you guys have alluded."

Jim and Karl both relaxed and simultaneously said, "Oh, it's big."

They looked at each other, and Jim then said, "I feel better; hope you didn't give too much away. I sure wish our team would have let me know that they were talking with you. Although I can understand the reasoning behind not including me; but just the same, I don't like it. When were you contacted and by whom? Was it Anna, Solana?"

Beverly replied, "I think I have already told you too much," and started laughing again. Jim was just shaking his head. He thought he should let her enjoy having the shoe on the other foot and just left it alone.

Karl told Jim he really needed to get some shut-eye. He had a big day in front of him, and Steve was going to be out of town for a couple of days visiting some relatives.

38

Steve boarded the company plane at 9:00 a.m. His itinerary was to fly directly to the Texas outpatient facility for some routine IT maintenance work. This would not raise any flags, since as far as the government was concerned, Karl was in charge of the forecasting software. Steve would spend a couple of hours at the Texas facility and then, without any notifications, jump in a company car and head to Tuscaloosa. He would have to drive through Louisiana and Mississippi; however, the entire trip would only take about five hours. Steve hoped to be at his cousin DJ's house by suppertime. He and DJ were only a year apart and grew up together. They remained close friends, even through the twenty-one years Steve had lived on the West Coast. They would try to get together at least once a year but would usually see each more than that for one reason or another. DJ was excited to have Steve visit and spent a good part of yesterday and today preparing his famous BBQ brisket.

Tuscaloosa is typical of smaller towns in the south. With little under 100,000 residences, it is sprawling with little tentacles in the valleys of rolling forested hills. If there is anything unique about Tuscaloosa, it is that the median age is in the twenties versus the state median age of forty-two. It is close to Birmingham. The town is not overrun with the larger chain stores or industry. Many owner-operated businesses exist, and there is definitely a small-town feel. People say hi to one another in the local Piggly Wiggly or at the post office, banks and so forth. In fact, Steve's first stop was the main office of the Bank of Tuscaloosa on Jack Warner Parkway. This quick stop was on the way to his cousin DJ's home just off N. Rice Mine Road. DJ had a beautiful view of the river.

As Steve was navigating the interchange from 59 to 359 headed into town, it brought back a lot of memories. A much simpler life; same struggle but the mind-set was different. People in Tuscaloosa truly were there for one another. If you were in need, you were not alone. Seattle, though a very nice place to live, did not have the sense of community a small town in the South had. He parked in front of the bank and walked up to one of the bankers' desks, introduced himself, and cordially asked Loretta for access to his safe-deposit box.

All the bankers were different from the time Steve used to bank there, but nonetheless Loretta acted as though they were close friends and promptly verified Steve's identity and relationship with the bank and then got up from her desk and said, "Follow me, Mr. Ryan."

She escorted him through a small corridor and unlocked a large heavy door. She opened it and waived Steve in. She said she would be just outside if he needed anything and reminded him to take his time.

Steve said, "This will only take a minute."

She smiled, and he went in. Steve went to the box identified as 44b and put his key in. This was a simple switch; two old revision cartridges for the two new ones with the enhanced human-psychology programming leading to the three-government world versus the China-ruled world on the old revision.

Steve turned his key in the box, pulled it out, and set it on the small table in the center of the room. When he opened it, he gasped and almost passed out. Regaining his composure, looking at an empty safe-deposit box, his mind was spinning. He was trying to figure out not only how something like this could happen but also who took the data cartridges and when did they take them. His last visit was two months ago. Steve needed to decide whether he should leave the new revisions in the same box or take them with him and figure out a new secure place for his backups. What could have been more secure than this, though? It had to be the CIA. Steve kept thinking of Stan. If the CIA were to stumble on the long-term forecast, they would certainly stop the announcement. His stomach began to ache.

He must have been standing there for some time, because Loretta knocked on the door and asked if everything was OK.

Steve said curtly, "Yes, everything is OK; just be a minute more."

He put the drawer back empty. He was seriously considering reporting the theft to the manager and requesting an investigation when he realized his silence may serve him better. He needed to talk with the senator. He also needed to talk with Karl, whose significant one-on-one time with the government personnel could bring some insight. He felt sick to his stomach again. After taking a deep breath, he exited the room and did his best to casually thank Loretta for waiting in order to not bring attention to himself. He was not sure he was successful, as his head was in full spin as he left the bank in a hurry.

Driving to his cousin's, he called Karl. Karl was shocked. Who would have known Steve had a safety-deposit box, in Tuscaloosa of all places, and also have the ability to get access? He agreed it was either the CIA or it was...who else could it have been?

Karl involuntarily looked over his shoulder. Steve asked Karl if there was anything he could tell him about recent visits from the CIA IT personnel. Karl was racking his brain for anything he could remember from one of Max's or Viola's visits that would indicate the CIA had knowledge of the missing programming. He came up blank. There was nothing that they said or did to make him think they were behind the heist. They were obsessed with finding a way to integrate the military software to the forecasting software. This was their sole focus.

Steve asked Karl to call the senator and fill him in. He asked him to let the senator know he would be available for questions in a couple of hours on his mobile. He was in front of DJ's house, and some of the family's children were already running up to his car to greet him. DJ had seven grandchildren. It appeared they were all here, which would mean his two children and their spouses were also here to see Steve.

He could smell the brisket in the smoker from the backyard. He stepped up on the large front porch and decided to walk around the side yard to the back rather than go through the house. There were five children, aged from three to eleven, vying for his attention, and he was doing his best to give it to them. This really was a blessing in hindsight. The children truly helped him get his perspective. He was so wrapped up in the recent events that he had lost sight of what was really important.

It is common in the South for neighbors not to fence their yards, which was true in DJ's neighborhood. Homes were all on large lots, usually one to two acres minimum regardless of the price range of the property. The open neighbor-friendly atmosphere was a lifestyle not found anywhere on the West Coast. As he got closer to the back of the house, the aroma of the meat was increasingly pungent.

After all greetings had taken place, DJ asked Steve if he wanted something to drink.

Steve answered, "If you have any of that sour mash whiskey left, which we had on my last visit, I would sure appreciate it."

DJ looked sideways at him and said, "Everything OK, cuz…?"

Steve said, "Long day and a few unexpected work-related issues I have to deal with. I will actually have to field a call or two this evening. I apologize in advance."

DJ shook his head while handing over the drink to Steve, saying, "I told you the West Coast hustle and bustle isn't anyway to live. Yeah, yeah, I know enough about the move. What has it been…twenty years now?"

Steve smiled. "It's good to be loved and to be missed." He tipped his glass and took a good swig.

After a great meal, the kids and grandkids all left to go to their homes, and Steve relaxed on the front porch with DJ enjoying the warmth of the fall evening and the sounds of the crickets on a clear night filled with stars. Their stomachs were full, and they were both content just sitting in silence when Steve's phone rang. Steve went into the house and took the call from the senator.

He sat in DJ's library while he described the events of the day. The senator had no indication from any of his government contacts that there was anything at all amiss. They speculated that the CIA must not have known what was in the safe-deposit box, or they would have at least left dummy cartridges so as not to create suspicion. Why didn't they come back to put dummies in place? Maybe they had just retrieved the cartridges the previous day, and that is why nobody had a clue to their discovery yet. The whole thing was disturbing, to say the least. The senator informed Steve he wanted to have a special board meeting two days from now in order to discuss the ramifications of early announcement if it became necessary. There was also some other business that could be addressed.

Steve said, "No problem." He was scheduled to be back the next night.

Steve decided to revisit the bank before heading back to Texas and planned to put a copy of his updated storage cartridge in a new safe-deposit box, but before doing so, he would imbed a GPS tracking device in it. If the CIA was, in fact, monitoring his activity, they would likely take the new module and assume it was the latest update. If, in fact, it was the CIA, he would actually prefer that they were aware of the new analysis showing a relatively stable tri-economic power world versus the one-world government predicted on his previous module. If it was not the CIA, well...whoever it was had entirely too much information. The information itself in the wrong hands regardless of which update could cause an international event that would then completely change the outcome of the predictions. It was like a time-travel paradox. If you go back in time and change anything that had happened, the ripples were bound to affect the present. The danger of rich or powerful individuals becoming aware of the forecast contained in these cartridges was that their action from the knowledge would change the outcome of the forecast.

If the people who took the data were connected with the bank and were, in fact, monitoring his actions, they would know that Steve was aware of the data swipe because the original box was empty. The stolen data was likely more dangerous than the updated data.

After consideration, he decided not to open a new box but put the update in the original box and leave a note with it.

His note simply said, "Call me."

When Steve returned to the bank, he immediately went to Loretta's desk and asked if could access his safe-deposit box again. He decided not to let on that there was anything strange going on; just business as usual.

Once in the room, he pulled out the box and opened it. His knees buckled, and he almost tipped over. The box contained the original cartridges!

The coincidence was remarkable! The one day he shows up is the same day that someone takes the data and obviously makes a copy and then returns it? He decided to replace the cartridges with the updated version, including the GPS tracker, and not leave the note.

39

Two days went by in a blink. Steve found himself sitting in the unscheduled board meeting. Everyone seemed to be busy and preoccupied with his or her own areas of responsibility. A board meeting could take anywhere from two to ten hours. Nobody knew ahead of time how long to expect the meeting to last, but today's consensus was they wanted it to be of the shorter variety.

The senator and Dane entered the room and sat down at their designated places across from each other in the center of the long portion of the boardroom table. Regardless of how humble and pure-hearted people are, when they reach a certain level of power, they will always jockey for the power positions at a meeting table. The scientists and technology-based people will always try to tuck themselves away from the power positions. Most of them would prefer to sit in a chair up against the wall in the back of the room next to a coffee station rather than be at the table at all. Fortunately for this group that was about to embark on changing the world, there were no power struggles at all. Leaders were happy to lead, and everyone else was happy to have the freedom to engage in their area of expertise without restraint. As much as most of the team did not want to participate in the business meetings, they all knew the importance of the process and, in actuality, enjoyed getting updated on the big picture. None of them would ever admit to that.

Dane opened with, "Forty-five days to announcement, and it appears we are all on schedule to meet or beat the goals we originally set out to meet. Those goals were what we determined to be our bare minimum requirement before we let the world know what we are up to. I know all of you have been burning the candle at both ends in order to responsibly relay this incredible news to the world and smoothly execute the deployment of the technology. The fact is, no matter how prepared we are, no matter how hard we work, no matter when we make this announcement, the world is going to freak out."

After a bit of silence in order to let that sink in, he continued, "We can live in denial and have a utopian view that this will go off without a hitch and that there will be no panic, no security issues, no international disputes, no public uprisings, no violence, no heartache about those who could have been helped but were not. We can live in a world where we won't be continuously bombarded by the media and prodded and poked at by every faction of humanity imaginable. The fact of the matter is that the world is going to freak out. What does matter is that we do what we have to, to protect ourselves, our families, and our sanity. We have all worked around the clock for many months, and the real work is going to start post announcement."

There was dead silence in the room. The entire panel of board members was in a state of shock and revelation. It was as if they all just woke up from a coma. Dane was right. The board had gotten so wrapped up in the announcement that it seemed as though that was the end-all. The announcement was the beginning. Dane let his words sink in. As a businessman he knew what stress and long hours can do to a person. He also knew that there were some real threats that the government may stop the announcement and Genanotech as a whole, based on Steve's economic-forecasting data. They needed to announce and be refreshed before they could announce.

After an appropriate amount of silence, Dane continued, "The senator and I have had a discussion and would like to make a proposal. We felt a vote would be in order rather than an edict. We ask that you all take this proposal seriously:

1) "Move the announcement date to December 15, 2019
2) Take a one-week vacation in Kauai from December 1 through December 7 (all board members and any two main support staff of your choice included)
3) Make rejuvenation processes available to all board members and key staff immediately."
   Dane couldn't help but look at Jake during this part of the presentation. He then continued.
4) "Return on December 8, and make final arrangements for the announcement."

He concluded with, "If the majority agrees, we all go."

He went on to say, "On a sidenote, we will have a new member of the board joining us—Jim's wife, Beverly Mankin. As you are all aware, we were waiting to bring Beverly on board till we got close to announcement. Need to know precaution due to her relationships with the media. She is now scheduled to join us in fifteen days. As part of this proposal, we would bring her on in seven days. This would give her adequate time to get her ducks in a row to assist us with the media portion of the announcement. She will be focusing on how the news is relayed and interpreted on the net. As a further precaution, we will keep the new announcement date *top secret*; board members only—no staff, or Beverly for that matter—will be made aware of the new date until the morning of the announcement. Lunch is on the way; once we finish eating, we will vote. After we vote we will discuss some arrangements I have made to assist you post announcement."

During lunch, most of the board members couldn't fathom moving the date up and taking a vacation. They were also kind of stunned by the idea that they would actually undergo the rejuvenation process and become recipients of the very technology they were about to unleash on the world.

Madelyn was especially affected by Dane's proposal. She was concerned about the preface for the proposal in general. She had been so focused and so philanthropic in the pursuit of this technology for so many years that the very idea it could have some initial negative consequences was disturbing, to say the least. The thought of undergoing treatment was also a little unnerving. The announcement was racing toward her, and the inevitable media presence she would be obligated to and dreaded more than anything was racing toward her as well. One part of her welcomed moving the announcement up just to get it over with, and the other side of her wanted to stay in denial and pretend it was not really happening.

Overall, there were a lot of mixed emotions when it came time to vote, but in the end, it was a unanimous yes vote.

Dane stood up and, in a very relaxed fatherly way, said, "I know we have lightly touched on how things will be different post announcement for you personally. It is my opinion and based on my experience that we have not done enough to prepare you for the changes ahead. We have all been very busy, occupied, and sequestered. Once we announce, we will all come out of the closet, so to speak. We will continue to be very busy and pulled in a million different directions in the initial months that follow the announcement. We will also no longer have the need for sequestering and will be living among the general population. During this time we will not have enough time or social interface to recognize the degree of celebrity we will have, not to mention the dramatic change in wealth that will be bestowed upon us. When the company I founded took off like a rocket ship, Solana and I went through a similar experience. Our experience was a watered-down version of what each of you will be going through. Sports figures, Hollywood stars, and the like, who are catapulted into the public eye and obtain windfalls of money as a result, experience serious emotional, social, and sometimes even physical responses that are not positive. You have all heard the stories of lottery winners who made mistakes with their money and let it ruin their lives. You may not feel that this is any big deal right now, but a year from now, it will be a completely different story. We as the leadership of this company would be remiss if we did not attempt to prepare each of you for what is in store for all of us."

He went on to say in a stern voice, "People you went to school with, or who were barely acquainted with you, friend of your friends will make attempts to ask you for money or a position they are not qualified for in the company. Saying no will be difficult, but if you say yes to one, you will have a real difficult time saying no to anyone else. People you thought were your friends will turn on you because of jealousy or simply because of the change in your status. This will expose you to a completely different social circle than them."

Continuing in his parental demeanor, he said, "It is only natural for each of you to share your wealth with your immediate family and closest friends. How you do this can make a huge difference. Unearned and unexpected money can actually destroy lives, not help them. Let's say your best friend is a lawyer by profession, and they are in their third year of their own practice.

They are successful, stimulated, and fulfilled by their work. You come along and hand them enough money so that they do not need to work, and they sell their practice and retire at thirty-one years old. They end up having a difficult time coping without the excitement and struggle of running the firm on a daily basis and develop addictions to drugs and or gambling."

Dane went on, "You will meet new people who would want to be your friends, but in the back of your mind, you will wonder what their motivation is. As you can see, there are significant social issues that will arise without a doubt. We will do everything in our power to keep secret your individual compensation, but being a public company, this may prove difficult for the seriously curious. We highly recommend you do not let anyone, including your own mother, know exactly how rich you are. There is much more to consider, and there are many ways to limit negative repercussions of your fame and riches."

Solana piped in and said, "Dane and I truly care about each of you. We consider all of you family. We know the rabbit hole you are about to enter. We do not want you to take lightly what Dane has just brought to your attention, so we have set up a team of three extremely competent councillors, who will work full time for the company and be solely dedicated to the group of people in this room. At this time they do not know what our product is. This will remain confidential until we make our public announcement. They do know that we are about to release a new product that will make you all rich and famous, and they know what their role is in supporting you. This may make some of you uncomfortable, or you may think it is silly, but I assure you that it will, in a very short time, be a service that you rely on. In your e-mail is a day and time next week for you to have your initial consult. We tried to pair each of you with the councillor we felt you would best relate to. Expect your first visit to last two hours. After that we recommend a minimum thirty minutes three times a week dedicated to working with your councilor."

Again the room was completely quiet for an awkward amount of time. Dane closed by saying, "If any of you have concerns about the counseling, please see me privately. Meeting adjourned."

Steve, Karl, the senator, and Dane stayed back after the meeting. When they were finally alone, they had a short discussion regarding the confiscated data cartridge and what their immediate focus should be. Steve checked the GPS on his phone, and the new cartridge had not been moved. The old cartridge that was copied was more dangerous than the new one depending on who actually retrieved it.

Steve said, "If the Chinese took this module, we are safe. If they take the new one, it would not be good. If the CIA, as we expect, took the old data, we have problems. If the CIA takes the new data, we have less of a problem."

The senator agreed with Steve's assessment and stated, "If the government wants to shut us down, they certainly have not given us one little hint about doing so." He then went on to say, "If they do suggest a shutdown, all we have to do is show them the updated version. We can strengthen our case by reminding them that we are in control of the forecasting and thus have an ongoing advantage."

It was agreed that the focus should now be on fine-tuning the extreme short-term forecasting models in order to assist them with the initial few weeks of post announcement. This was accomplished by anticipating significant events and responses from independent nations, influential organizations, and world leaders, including celebrities. For instance, Sweden determined they would not allow their citizens to undergo the process until further tests and results were compiled…or Denzel Washington and Nicole Kidman would go public against the technology, warning the public that it was not proven or safe. Each of these events would have ripples. The ripples needed to be evaluated and incorporated into the forecasting software and countermeasures needed to be constructed.

Steve had been provided a list of all the nations and their likely initial response to the announcement. A list of all influential people and organizations had been compiled, including their relationships with one another, whether personal, financial, social, and so on, the software can almost immediately anticipate the effect on how one nation, group, or individual will affect the other nation's, group's, or individual's response. What Steve and Karl were now working on were the final and updated financial ties between large- and medium-sized corporations. Corporations hit hardest or boosted the most would have a direct bearing on their partners, subsidiaries, and vendor bases. This was all tedious work but extremely necessary to manage the first weeks post announcement.

40

Rejuvenation schedules were being set for all board members and their top two staff members of choice. Madelyn insisted on being first. She had been waiting for the green light. On many occasions she nearly went through the process without authorization but felt she owed it to the board to be a rule follower. Jake, who already went through the process without authorization, decided to come clean and tell Madelyn. He was shocked and pleasantly surprised that she was already aware of it. She had intentionally said nothing when she found out and had been waiting for months for Jake to fess up. It's not clear who was happier and more relieved, Madelyn or Jake.

Dane was not sure how the board members would respond to undergoing the procedure and was thrilled to see them all stepping all over themselves to get in line. The senator would go second, and then it was decided that the remaining board would undergo the technology based on their age, with the oldest being first. Not that it would make much difference. All personnel would be through their first rejuvenation within the next five days. Then Beverly would join the group and immediately undergo the treatment.

Madelyn finished her complete body scan, which was then downloaded into the computer for her specific analysis and nanoformula configuration. This would take approximately six hours and, once complete, another seventeen minutes to make the serum that would be injected into her blood.

During her wait she decided to go to the spa and get groomed and pampered. She never did this before, so she really did not know what to expect. By the end she couldn't understand why she hadn't made a routine in her life like most women her age. Despite the fact that she had been working, preoccupied, and completely distracted by her pursuit of the technology for the past five years, she was never really interested in improving her appearance. The fact was, she was not like most women her age. This was evident by her plain dress and simple mousy-brown straight hair usually just pulled back in a ponytail. She maintained a utilitarian perspective: comfortable clothes and hair that was not in her way when she was bent over a machine or working at her desktop. She never wore any jewelry except for the understated crucifix around her neck, which was her great-grandmother's. She didn't own any makeup, and the last time she wore any was for her first date in college, which was a complete disaster.

What was ridiculous was that in spite of her absolute absence of vanity, she was one of the most beautiful women you would have ever laid eyes on.

At the spa, she was very specific. She wanted a short haircut with bangs but with some feathering in the front and shorter in the back than on the sides.

She had a picture from a magazine she had been carrying around for seven years. She just never had the guts to get the cut. Included in the style were three colors: a couple of blond streaks in the bangs and front portion of the sides with the rest brown-and-red streaks. These were all fairly natural colors, nothing extreme.

Before her haircut, she had made an appointment for a one-hour massage and a facial. During the hair-dyeing process, she had her toes and fingernails trimmed and painted with a pale salmon color with pale translucent white tips, which was the latest rave according to the beautician.

After five hours of attention from over eight different beauty technicians, Madelyn was transformed. Afraid to look in the mirror, she just got up and left the spa. Nobody seemed to pay any attention to her as she went back into the lab until finally Lou came up to her and asked if he could help her in any way. She asked him if her analysis was complete and when she was scheduled to receive her injection. Lou just looked at her funny, flipping through his notebook, and finally said, "I am sorry, what is your name?"

Madelyn burst into laughter and said, "Come on, Lou, quit joking around."

He took another look at her and said, "*Madelyn?*" She truly was an absent-minded professor. Not much different than Jake. She then realized that she had just completely changed her appearance in the spa, and Lou really had no idea who she was. She decided she better take a look at herself. She went straight to the woman's restroom and gazed upon her new look. It was great! She probably would not have recognized herself.

She came out of the restroom, and Lou and a dozen of her colleagues were there waiting. Everyone loved her hair, and they all had a big laugh at Lou for not recognizing her. Lou then took her into the patient-processing room and asked her to undress and lie on the table. He left; she got naked and lay down. A nurse entered the room with a pack of nine different syringes. She started to explain the process that was about to occur when Madelyn asked the nurse if she knew who she was. The nurse flushed and said, "Yes, of course. I am sorry, it's just that I am so used to—"

Madelyn stopped her and said, "It's OK; just jab one of those babies in me and do your thing."

Each injection created a different tingling sensation, some quite pleasant and some slightly irritating. None were painful. After each injection, there was a computer-generated signal designed to instruct the tiny microscopic nanos of their course of action. An IV full of evacuation solution was hooked up to her hip, and a dose was administered once the technician in the other room was satisfied the nanos had completed their mission. The evacuation process was nothing more than a flushing sensation at the point of exit in her left arm just below the elbow.

Each injection and evacuation took less than two minutes. After about twenty minutes in the room, she was done. She got up and felt *fantastic*. Madelyn was now effectively twenty-five years old; amazing!

The senator went next. His process was to be experimental. Lou's team had been working on regression algorithms that could accurately enough retro-forecast the actual state of the DNA strands double the six years everyone had been comfortable with. The only hitch was that it was only thought safe for individuals over fifty. Younger DNA strands were much harder to predict beyond the six-year mark. Any alteration greater than 99.7 percent of what the strands actually were in the past would be considered a genetic alteration. All testing showed that genetic alterations did not work; in fact, they were very dangerous to the individual undergoing the treatment.

The senator felt comfortable with all the research to date regarding the super-rejuvenation process. Every "experimental" process Lou had performed had gone without a hitch. In fact, Lou did not even give the senator a warning of any kind. He just asked him if he wanted to be the first to undergo the new fifty-plus process. Because the senator was sixty-three and would be effectively reducing his age to fifty-one, he would be able to go through another process when his effective age was fifty-seven and then take another twelve years off and get to go back to an effective age of forty-five. At that point, without any new breakthroughs, he would only be able to take five years of his life every six or seven years.

The process went smoothly as expected. One modification was that the senator was tranquilized at the end of the procedure and would sleep for twelve hours prior to awakening twelve years younger.

41

Drew booked two houses adjacent to one another on Hanalei Bay in Kauai at a combined nightly rate of $9,000 a night for seven nights. The two houses comfortably accommodated twenty adults. Some large tents were set up on the property to sleep the other sixteen adults on the trip. Weather was expected to be rain-free, which was a bit unusual for the north side of this island. The setting was ideal for relaxation. The backyards of the properties gave unobscured access to the beach and a short quarter mile walk to town where there were shops, restaurants, and bars. Four large vans were reserved at the small airport in Princeville, two miles from their destination where the company jet-landed. Just a few miles north at Tunnels Beach, some of the island's best snorkeling was available, depending on the surf. Winter was approaching, so snorkeling may or may not be possible. Golfers could enjoy one of America's top one hundred golf courses at the Prince course in Princeville and a nice resort course at the Regis Makai course.

The senator woke up from his sleep fifty-one years old. Almost all his aches and pains he had become accustomed to were now miraculously gone. He felt stronger and had a lot more energy. He was in excellent shape for a sixty-three-year old, but the twelve years made an incredible difference. All the other board members and senior staff had successful rejuvenations, and spirits were high. The pending trip to Kauai was a hot topic in social conversation. Some of the staff had already signed up for zip lining and boat excursions up the Nā Pali Coast. Tee times were set for three foursomes a day at both courses. Reservations were made at the Mediterranean for a luau on the final night of their stay.

Beverly was on her flight from DC to Seattle, and the anticipation of finally getting full disclosure was weighing on her. She had been in a state of elation over the money for weeks, but now getting close to the truth of what Jim had been working for the past six months was more prominent than ever in her thoughts. Beverly was a truth seeker. She had an incredible appetite for information and investigation. The Internet was a massive archive of information and in reality gave way to the information age. The problem was that the more you know, the more you know you don't know. The other problem was that the net had a lot of misinformation. She was an advocate of free exchange of information and true transparency. The US Constitution insures this with its local, state, and federal governing bodies. She knew that much of what went on in government was not disclosed to the public. Beverly was less than satisfied. For years, the government had kept secrets. It was understandable that certain things be kept from the public. As far as Beverly was concerned, the only thing that should be kept secret was military strategy for current military involvement. Obviously, the "enemy," whoever that may be at the time, could not know what their plans were to protect their citizens. Other than that, everything else was free game. It was this strong ideal and philosophy that deeply concerned her regarding Jim's secrecy. Could it be a military operation?

Jim and Beverly had had many conversations regarding government cover-ups. Extraterrestrial contact was among one of many controversies. Jim felt that if there was a true threat, the public would not be ready to handle it, and more damage would be done than good. Beverly felt that all human beings should be made aware if contact was made regardless of the outcome. They had a right to know. The big issue here was that no high-ranking government official would come out and say that they had not had any contact. In fact, they had UFO sighting hotlines and government centers dedicated to the recording of all sightings. Could Jim be working on something to do with extraterrestrial contact? It was killing her to be in the dark. She knew whatever it was, it must be awfully important.

Jim greeted Beverly at the airport with Karl and Linda. The reunion was joyful. They quickly exited the airport, and one of Drew's staff stayed back to get Beverly's five large carry-on bags. She had to rearrange a couple of the bags to meet the maximum fifty-pound limit in order to avoid oversized luggage charges. After she did this, she realized that money was no longer an issue, and she should have just let it be. What was a couple of hundred bucks to her anymore? This new lifestyle was going to take some getting used to.

Jim was authorized to discuss the technology with Beverly once she landed. She had already signed the confidentiality agreement before leaving DC. The only tricky part was that Jim was instructed to confiscate all of her electronic devices. Drew would rummage through all of her checked baggage before she had access to them. Jim and Karl agreed that the driver, one of Drew's staff, would be the best person to pat Beverly down. Beverly was quite beautiful and strong-minded, but in spite of her strength, she was really shy, especially when it came to her body. Though Jim spent time investigating her body for the past few years, he could not find anything wrong with it at all. In fact, he thought she was the perfect female specimen. She would not be comfortable being patted down due to her shyness but more so due to her feeling that she was being violated.

Before they got into the car, Karl said to Beverly, "We need to do a complete search of you and confiscate all of your electronic devices."

She started to object, and Karl put his hand up and in a very controlled tone interjected, "Once this is done, Jim could tell you what we are working on."

She got a ridiculous smirk on her face and put her arms up in the air. Jim turned away and smiled. Karl was brilliant as usual at having his back, and he loved the guy for it.

The driver thoroughly and respectfully searched Beverly and recovered three cellular devices and two electronic notepads.

Jim explained that once they got to the lab that she would be given unlimited Internet access, including voice. She would be able to see everything out there on the net but could not send anything out without an austere security review and filter. She could use the phone, but all of her calls would be monitored.

Beverly objected and said, "You know that goes against all my principles."

Jim said, "Yes, I know, but it is only for three weeks. Once we make our public announcement, you will be given total freedom and complete access to the media." She looked thoughtful and nodded her head.

As they were approaching the freeway entrance, Jim started by letting Beverly know who the major players were and a little background of all of them. Madelyn was the young nano technology scientist and Jake the physics and engineering expert. Dane was the entrepreneur and financial backer. The senator sat on various science-related boards. Karl, of course, and Steve were with their ultra-sophisticated forecasting software. Lou was the programmer, Anna the head attorney. Solana handled public relations, and so on. This was full disclosure so that no details would be left out.

Beverly's head was spinning. She blurted, "What the heck is going on here?"

Jim finally said, "Here is the deal; we have all teamed up to responsibly introduce a technology that will allow everyone to live two hundred years or more." He then emphasized the word *everyone*. "That is, *everyone* on the planet!"

Silence; this was definitely not what Beverly had expected. Her processing was on overload. She mumbled her first thought. "Why keep it a secret?"

Jim smiled and said, "Think about it, love; we need time to be ready. We need time to provide the world with answers to the major questions. We need time to build the machines that are required for the procedure. We need enough machines built and preshipped and at ports of call in all major populated areas on the world so that any one nation or region does not have an advantage over another during the first wave of procedures. The sick and elderly will need to go first. There will undoubtedly be many people we simply cannot reach in time once the news is out. We need to minimize this. We need to make certain that big-industry leaders do not block the technology or, worse yet, take control of it. For example, let's say the pharmaceutical industry were to find out about this. They know they will be immediately put out of business. How do you think they will respond if we were not ready?"

Jim paused and looked at Beverly, whose head was now spinning more than before. He asked her how she was doing.

She said, "I don't know. It's a lot to take in. It was quite a bit for me to adjust to the idea we were going to be rich, but *rich and a life-span of two hundred years?*"

She got ahead of herself and whispered, "There was a highly likely possibility that we may live indefinitely depending on technological advances in the future." It was all too much to absorb all at once.

Jim then asked her if she noticed anything different about him.

She looked at him quizzically and finally said, "You look great. I can't put my finger on it, but you look absolutely great! For that matter, so does Karl."

Jim smiled and said, "That's because, as of last week, I and all the board members have undergone our first rejuvenation process, and I am literally years younger than I was a week ago." He went on to explain how the technology worked. "Every seven years, a unique formulation of nano machines is designed and produced based on a detailed scan of your DNA strands and then injected into you, repairing cellular damage due to aging. The result is that after the short, inexpensive, and painless procedure, you are in effect five years younger. You can do this every seven years. You do the math. Every seven years you only age two years. You are authorized to undergo the procedure whenever you are ready. It is completely safe. Over one thousand procedures have been performed without any incidence."

Beverly was speechless. The rest of the ride to her new home was relatively quiet. Beverly had a million questions but couldn't formulate any one specific question. Every time she had something to ask, she thought of something else. The ramifications were endless. Karl did a little rambling about the forecasting software and how it could predict social and economic behavior post announcement. Beverly was tuning him out and was in her own world.

When they pulled up to the hotel-cum-lab, Jim said, "Do you now see why we could not let anyone know about what we are working on? I hope you can understand why I was not allowed to discuss this with you, especially given your nature for full-information disclosure."

With great hesitation and a small gulp, Beverly just nodded in agreement.

Dane, Solana, and the senator were all waiting in the lobby to greet Beverly. They whisked her off into one of the conference suites for a debriefing and Q and A. Jim and Karl left Beverly with her new bosses.

Karl suggested that they have a beer.

Jim agreed and said, "How do you think that went?"

Karl shrugged. "It is a lot to digest for anyone. I have a new appreciation for how big this news really is and how profound it will be for the world as a whole to cope with it."

Six hours later, Beverly met up with Jim in their suite. She collapsed on the soft bed and asked him to lie next to her and hold her. They held each other without saying a word for what seemed an eternity. In actuality, only thirty minutes had passed.

She finally kissed him and said, "I need a shower, and I am starving. Is there any good food in this prison?"

Jim smiled.

Over dinner, Beverly could not stop talking. She had a gift of eating and talking without it being socially offensive. She was so excited about her role in the announcement process and the work she will be doing post announcement. She was a little nervous, understandably, about undergoing the process. Jim told her that first thing in the morning she would introduce her to Madelyn, Jake, and Lou. He assured her that once she met them and got a full tour of the process, the machines, the testing that had been done that she would feel much better about the whole thing.

Jim went on to inform her that in the first weeks and months post announcement, the only procedure performed would be aimed at healing the terminally ill, critically ill, and chronically ill. It could be months or even a year before the general population will start receiving the rejuvenation treatments.

After dinner, Jim was too exhausted for sex, and Beverly was too preoccupied to think about it. Jim fell fast asleep, and Beverly stayed awake all night.

As promised, Jim had set up a breakfast meeting with Madelyn, Jake, and Lou. Beverly still a little fuzzy from no sleep, and running on pure adrenalin was not quite her normal self. Madelyn was so down to earth and so sweet and warm that Beverly felt better after just a few minutes sitting down at the table. Food was served, and everyone had an appetite; a youthful appetite at that. Beverley commented on how good the food was, which prompted a long discussion about Franky and the president's visit.

The tour followed. Jake led most of it and was very systematic and methodical as to make it all make sense. It was as if he knew exactly what the next question Beverly would have and then answered it before she could ask it.

Five hours later she went back to her room and slept until the next morning. Jim was so happy he had her back. He had truly missed her and was genuinely worried about her being in the dark. They got through the biggest test of their relationship without discord.

42

Two days before heading to Kauai, for some much-needed relaxation, Dane called a board meeting. Beverly was invited even though her role was not as a full-fledged board member but a significant shareholder and key player in the announcement team. It was important she get to know the players. She was on a fast track and had a lot of ground to cover. She deserved a seat at the table today.

Dane opened the meeting with detailed introduction of Beverly. There was a warm applause. Beverly blushed, and Jim sat proud.

He then followed up with a big congratulations to the entire team for being at a state of ready, beating all the preset goals for announcement. He went through the numbers.

Latest report from Carlton was that 612 machine pairs had been manufactured. This was 182 machines over the latest revised goal. Approximately four hundred of these machines had been crated and shipped to various ports of call. They were all disguised as MRI, CT scanners, Automated Optical Inspection Devices, NC milling machines, and other capital equipment with similar size and weight.

Victoria and Dwaine teamed up with Solana and produced a very sophisticated program to schedule the shipment of each machine pair. Ninety-five percent of the units would be shipped by boat, and the first to be shipped were to the regions furthest away, including Madagascar, Middle East, Eastern Europe, Russia, Western India, and the east coast of Africa.

This strategy was obvious, but there are very populated parts of the world inland from any port, that is, Moscow, Russia; Ulaanbaatar, Mongolia; Sinkiang, China; Santa Cruz, Bolivia; Central African Republic, and Tombouvctou Mali. These populated spots will need some ground transport from port. The shipping platform to get all the machine pairs close to their final destination all on the same day of the announcement was quite an undertaking. Each freighter had target dates for arrival, but each also had average delay ratings. Each port had specific average hold times prior to the release of any crate. Each ground transport had different schedules and variable ETA to actual delivery. The complexities went on and on.

Nine hundred seventy-five illnesses had been cured or eliminated. Three hundred seventeen physical ailments or injuries had been repaired or reversed. Four hundred eleven rejuvenations had been performed. Zero side effects reported. All patients were accounted for.

Forecasting software had been optimized for announcement day. As things would unfold, updates would be made on the fly.

All the key leaders in all 192 sovereign nations had been identified, and current contact information was on record. Key personnel of Genanotech had been assigned to each key leader for direct interface on the first day of announcement. Top scientists in all fields were also to be contacted on day one. Direct contact with most worldwide media giants was to be made on day one. The list was really something to behold; the who's who of the who's who. If you made the day-one list, you were truly an important and influential person; the day two and three names were made up of many common household names. Notable religious leaders, relevant celebrities, and top business leaders had been identified and had Genanotech personnel assigned for direct contact within the first few days of announcement.

A second level of key political figures in the United States, England, China, Russia, Japan, France, Germany, Mexico, Canada, and Australia had been identified and Genanotech personnel assigned for week one contact. Dane apologized to Madelyn and Jake. Day one, they each had been assigned thirty individuals each. In the first week, they would each directly interface with over 120 influential people. Dane and the senator had similar workloads assigned, and the rest of the board members and key staff had about half that.

Anna was scheduled to make the first call at 6:00 a.m. EST. No other media outreach would be made until 9:00 a.m. EST. She would be calling Victor Rodchenko from the Centennial. This was per the agreement she had negotiated and contracted. Victor and the Centennial were promised exclusivity to the story. In order to guarantee an adequate period of time to syndicate the story, they were to be given the details of the announcement three hours before any other media contact. A preemptory call was to be made the afternoon before to insure Victor would pick up the phone that early.

Eight to ten hours was to be dedicated from each Genanotech representative assigned to communicate with their preidentified key individuals and media personnel on announcement day. Three to five hours would be dedicated for this purpose each day for the balance of the first week. This should keep an adequate supply of fodder for the pundits' first month post announcement.

Beverly was to spend the first month with her staff of eleven, whose sole responsibility was to track and report web and media activity.

Steve was to be exempted from any public interface. Genanotech had been successful in keeping Steve's involvement pretty private and concealed. Karl had been the front man with the government, and Steve was pulling the strings behind the scene. Steve appreciated this; he did not want or need any type of credit or recognition for his contribution. He was pretty laid-back and would likely spend the rest of his life, or at least a large portion of it, on some tropical island or sailboat, floating from one island to another.

Dane concluded, "I know many of you feel that there is still so much to do, but the fact is *we are ready*! Pack your bags for vacation, and have a great time! The following weeks will be so busy, and it is critically important that you are in top shape. Meeting adjourned."

There was an uncommon and great applause that followed. The camaraderie and individual sense of achievement was at an all-time high. It seemed after listening to Dane's speech that everyone actually for the first time realized they were ready. The enormity of the undertaking and the level of detail in the planning and execution was truly one of mankind's best efforts to date. There was a, for a lack of better words, a gasp of relief—with the one possible exception of Beverly, who was still in a frenzy and felt a little outmatched by the people in the room. She was determined to hold her own and make a contribution.

43

Three jets landed within thirty minutes of one another in Princeville, Kauai. It was 1:30 p.m. Hawaii time, two hours earlier than Washington state time. Temperature was a warm 77 degrees. Surf was still pretty flat, so snorkeling and boating both was possible options for the group. Seven large vans pulled up to pick up the travelers without their baggage, which would arrive within a couple of hours after they would be comfortably situated in their new digs.

Drew used the excuse that there would not be enough room for the passengers and their baggage, but his real intentions were security.

This trip would have been a nightmare for Drew and Dane had they not confiscated all electronic devices prior to the trip. In fact, they also confiscated all passengers' credit cards. They were not allowed to bring any cash. Virtually every restaurant, bar, and activity center on the north shore of the island near Hanalei Bay had Genanotech credit cards on file. Some of the nicer restaurants in Kapaa, Lihue, and Po'ipū also had cards on file. All the vacationers had been given a waterproof business card that would allow them to spend whatever they wanted at the designated spots. It was like an all-inclusive vacation on steroids.

Purchases of souvenir items were discouraged. None of the larger stores had business cards on file. The intent was that nobody could buy a cell phone or electronic pad and communicate with the outside world. There were three clothing stores with cards on file: one in Hanalei Bay, one in Lihue, and one in Po'ipū. Everyone was given reminders on how important it was to maintain secrecy about the technology until announcement. The upside was, they were sequestered on a beautiful tropical island with virtually unlimited funds to enjoy some of the finest food and outdoor activities the world had to offer.

Though security was crucial, critical, and important, you could not really control anyone who wanted to break the rules. Rules are like laws; they are for the abiders. What Drew was trying to accomplish was to simply reduce the ability for people to act inappropriately in hopes that they would not. If someone was intent on undermining the program, they most likely would have already done so or attempted to do so. Drew was fairly relaxed and planned on having a good time for the next seven days.

The homes were beautiful, and even the tents exuded luxury with actual colonial plantation-style beds and dressers inside each private tent. Beautiful grass area rugs were laid down in each of the tents, so you hardly felt like you were not inside an actual structure.

Mopeds, bikes, and a few vans were made available for anyone's use anytime. For the first night, Dane reserved the entire Tahiti Nui restaurant, adjacent wine bar, and party room for dinner and drinks. Though it was never said, the gathering was mandatory. After the meal, everyone was on their own for the remainder of the trip, with the exception of the last night where they would all gather for a luau at the Mediterranean. The Mediterranean probably had the best Mai Tais on the island and was just a few miles northwest of where they were staying in Hanalei Bay.

They all walked to dinner in their shorts and flip-flops looking like true tourists. They had opakapaka, an island snapper,

Kauai beef rib-eye steaks, and wild-boar tenderloins. Selections were made on the flight over. All the dishes were amazing. There was nothing buffet about the food or service. The flavors and presentation were what you would expect at a five-star restaurant. The drinks flowed, and everyone started to relax. Most people were talking about what they planned to do the next day and the day after that.

Jim, Beverly, Karl, and Heather had a tee time at the Makai course at 9:00 a.m. and decided to be the first to leave the restaurant. It was just a few minutes later, and the rest of the group left except for Anna and Solana who decided to just tie one on and sleep in the next day.

Waking up to the crowing of the wild roosters at 4:30 a.m., 5:00 a.m., 6:00 a.m., and finally 6:30 a.m., Karl and Linda finally decide to get out of bed. They took quick showers and joined about twenty of their group for coffee at sunrise on the patio. The discussion was primarily about the wild chickens on the island. Apparently, in 1992, there was a significant hurricane on the island, and most of the chickens in coops escaped. During the last few decades, they had populated the island. There were chickens in the airport, in some of the open-air grocery stores, and they pretty much roosted in all neighborhoods and resorts.

The weather was a beautiful sunny seventy-four degrees with light winds from the east; a perfect day for golf or any outdoor activity. The golfers headed out at 7:45 a.m. to check in and get some breakfast before they played. All were disappointed to find that the Regis course did not have a restaurant facility at the course. You would have to drive another mile to the hotel for prepared food. They had muffins and some more coffee instead. The course was in excellent shape, and everyone enjoyed the play. The Makai course was resort style and fairly challenging but predictable with not a lot of hazards, with the exception of the numerous sand traps situated everywhere that came into play on nearly every shot.

Heather spent most of the day in the traps. It became a bit of a joke during the later part of the round. In fact, there was one shot where she had no traps in front of her, and she made the remark that finally she had nothing but green grass in in her future. She proceeded to shank her five iron that hit a tree and then came straight back to her stance and passed her going into the trap directly behind her. Karl found this extremely funny. Heather had a hard time finding the humor in it until both Jim and Beverly doubled over cracking up. Within a few minutes, they were all on the ground laughing uncontrollably.

The next day's tee time was at the Lagoon course at the Marriott in Lihue and then a day without golf, and on day four and five, rounds were scheduled at the Prince course and the Kiahuna Plantation.

At this time of year, the surf was just starting to increase, and snorkeling was best in the early morning. Bodyboarding—or, as the locals called it, "sponging"—was great in the afternoons.

After their first round of golf in over six months, Jim and Karl both had many stories of what could have been. One thing everyone agreed on was that the ball did not fly nearly as far in the humid air. Where they were used hitting 265-yard drives, they were lucky to get 230 yards. Hitting five irons at 155 yards was difficult to get used to.

When they returned to the house, Solana and Anna were just getting up and around. They were using some very interesting expletives describing the chickens and roosters. There was discussion of going on a chicken hunt once they felt better.

Dane was on a mission to make certain the entire group was not focusing on announcement-related work or discussion. If anyone brought up work, he would quickly remind them they were on vacation or change the subject. The decompressing period would probably take the entire week, but hopefully everyone would be relaxed and energized when they got back.

The days passed, and everyone was enjoying themselves. The weather held up, and the surf was perfect. Calm in the mornings for snorkeling and decent six to eight foot swells in the afternoon for surfing and bodyboarding. The golfers were in heaven with just a light breeze during the day and perfect 77 degree temperatures. The food was amazing. Everyone was enjoying the outdoor activities, sunshine, and exercise. There was a lot of discussion regarding how youthful everyone felt due to the rejuvenation process. Coming from the sedentary office environment to getting outside and active was enough to make anyone feel great, but combined with taking five or six years off your biological self, the feeling was amplified. The future sure seemed bright!

Dane and the senator were both very pleased. Everything was going according to plan. The team was gaining perspective and building strength. They would be ready for the strenuous announcement and post-announcement times in front of them. This was true until day five.

Jim, Karl, Beverly, and Heather arrived at the main house from a great round of golf at the Prince course, which is ranked in the top one hundred golf courses in America. They entered the kitchen area, where the senator, Dane, Drew, and Lou were huddled around the table having a very serious discussion. Karl, with his bubbly personality, made some off-handed comment about the group needing to lighten up. Dane asked them to sit down in the living room; there was something he needed to discuss with them. He was very somber, and it sent chills down Karl's spine.

As the group sat down, Dane explained that there had been a boating accident off the Nā Pali Coast, and both Steve and one of the locals on board were in critical condition. Apparently they got caught in a large swell and then nose-dived into a portion of shallow reef. They were thrown off the boat. Steve suffered a broken back and internal bleeding. The local who was also thrown from the boat suffered a massive concussion and was not yet conscious. This had happened forty-five minutes ago, and they were the only Genanotech personnel to know of the incident. They were airlifted via helicopter to Wilcox Memorial Hospital in Lihue and, depending on necessity, may be moved again to Kaiser Foundation Hospital in Honolulu. Other than notifying Solana, Anna, Jake, and Madelyn, they did not plan on spreading this news until they could know more.

The foursome was deflated by the news. Karl and Heather were especially close to Steve, and this news hit them especially hard.

Dane went on to say that they had verified that the Genanotech equipment arrived two days ago via cargo ship in Honolulu.

The senator then interrupted saying that he had made contact with the governor of Hawaii in an effort to pull some strings to expeditiously gain access to the container. With the recent terrorist activity in Japan and Taiwan, all the freight entering the islands were under great scrutiny. They had already had Steve's genetic scan results from the previous week's rejuvenation sent to the concerned people via e-mail. All they needed to do was feed this data into the equipment in the container and generate two syringes of nano juice so that they could put Steve back together. Also, they preferred to do this here in Lihui rather than risking another move. "Lou and I are leaving in five minutes to fly to

Honolulu to get the medicine. We hope to be back within four hours." When they left the room, there was total silence.

Dane suggested that they split up and find the rest of the group and meet up at the hospital as soon as possible. Solana and Anna were in Po'ipū, where they were shopping and sight-seeing. Madelyn and Jake had to also be reached. They were thought to be hiking the Kalalua Trail to the Hanakoa Falls, which was a relatively difficult four-mile hike. The strict "no cell phone" policy was now looking like not such a good idea.

Drew pulled out a corporate cell phone and gave it to Karl. He said, "You four go to Po'ipū and find the girls. I have their vehicle's GPS coordinates. It is about a one-hour drive to where they are and then a thirty-minute drive from there to Wilcox Hospital. I will call you if their location changes. Dane and I will go up north and find Madelyn and Jake."

They each got into vans and sped off.

Karl and his group had no trouble finding Anna and Solana, who were eating at BUBBA's Burger. They left their food on the table and hurried to the hospital.

When Dane and Drew got up to the north tip of the main coastal road, where it dead-ended into the Nā Pali Coastline, they parked illegally next to the Life Guard station at Ke'e Beach. They immediately explained their situation to the lifeguard on duty, who complied with their wishes to remain parked there until they found Jake and Madelyn. They spotted the company van parked about three quarters of a mile down the road near the bridge. Drew being in superior physical condition suggested that Dane check out the beach and he would go up the trail in hopes to catch them.

The trail was much steeper and difficult than Drew anticipated. He did his best to move as quickly as possible but was not able to reach jogging speed until he got to the half-mile mark. He could have sworn he had hiked over a mile when he reached the marker. He was still on a narrow trail that dramatically changed elevation without warning. About a mile and a half from the parking lot, before getting to the rocky beach, he caught up with Jake and Madelyn.

After quickly explaining things, they were off to the races.

Fortunately, Dane was waiting at the van when they got back to the parking lot.

When they arrived, Karl's group, Anna, and Solana were in the lobby. They had arrived thirty minutes prior and were told that Steve was in ICU and could not be seen. They were directed to a waiting room where they could be kept informed by the attending physician. After a forty-five-minute wait, a young Japanese doctor came in and discussed Steve's condition. The broken back had caused paralysis from the waist down, and it did not appear he would ever walk again. The bigger concern was internal bleeding. He was scheduled for surgery in fifteen minutes. The hope was that they could determine exactly where the bleeding was originating from and stop it.

The doctor was very frank in saying that if they could not get the bleeding to subside, Steve only had a few hours to live. Karl was losing focus, and there was a blur of questions regarding family and so forth running through his head.

Anna said she would handle all the questions the hospital may have regarding family, money, and other matters of business. Jim and Beverly were deep in prayer and remained so through the fifty-minute surgical process.

The doctor returned with a solemn face. Shaking his head he said he was not certain he was able to completely stop the bleeding. He suggested that family be notified and left.

Dane was on the phone with the senator who informed him that Lou was in the container with a portable gas-powered electrical generator hooked up just outside. Military personnel were stationed in a perimeter to eliminate any interference from yardmen. He went on to tell Dane that Lou had been in there for about fifteen minutes, and he did not want to interrupt him for status. Dane told the senator that it would take about twenty-five minutes to generate the formulation. Dane informed the senator of Steve's condition and wished him God's speed.

The senator said that there was a helicopter waiting in the yard and that the jet was on standby, with engines running. The flight over only took eighteen minutes. They may have broken a few air speed limits, but considering the circumstances, fuel conservation was the least of anyone's concern.

The senator said, "See you guys in a few minutes, and make sure you have access to Steve when we get there."

Madelyn and Jake walked into the waiting room just when Dane was getting off the phone with the senator. They received the details of Steve's accident and current status. It was decided that Madelyn would pose as Steve's daughter in order to simplify hospital protocol for access to Steve. He was in post-op and currently unconscious. She was introduced to the orderlies as Steve's daughter. Covered in mud from the waist down from the hike, combined with the fact she was not carrying a purse or any ID, the hospital personnel did not question the relation. Anna confirmed the relation with administration as well. She went on to say that Lou, Madelyn's husband, was also on his way to the hospital. That should give them the appropriate access they would need to inject Steve with the nano formulation. They would wait to request access to Steve until the senator and Lou touched down in Lihue.

When Dane, Madelyn, and Jake rejoined the group in the waiting room, they were discussing how to get the local to Honolulu and a way to get him to the shipyard so they could save his life. He was unconscious, and his prospects did not look good. His family was in the room next to them, and Beverly and Heather had been engaged in comforting them.

Dane shut the door and quietly told the group that they would make no effort to save the local's life. They had a responsibility to the world that the announcement of this technology happen according to plan. The kidnapping of a patient in a hospital would not go unnoticed and could create serious complications. The fact that they were likely going to be responsible for a miracle in Kauai saving Steve's life and having him completely recover from a broken back and what the surgeon believed to be irreversible damage to his organs and internal bleeding was going to be challenging enough. He went on to say that what they were dealing with here was going to be commonplace around the world in just a little over one week. There would be millions of critical and terminally ill patients who would not get the lifesaving treatment in time.

This message was somber and conflicting with every noble human tendency; they had the ability to save his life but could not risk it? The logic was there, but it felt wrong.

The world was really going to be in turmoil once they introduced this technology. The mad scramble to determine who and then execute the cure for the dying was going to be one of humanities greatest efforts and most trying times in history. It would be impossible to save everyone who could be saved.

Genanotech personnel had calculated this number. Since the eradication of AIDS one hundred twenty thousand people die every day. There will be 651 nanotech systems operational on day one. A maximum of forty procedures per system per day or 26,040 could be expected best case. That is, 26,000 people who could be saved per day, and 94,000 people per day who will die because they simply would not have the capacity to save them.

Production of the systems would ramp up considerably within the first month with the anticipated massive capital influx and the ability to conduct business in the open. It was forecasted that in just ninety days, there would be enough systems built to keep up with the death toll. In the first ninety days, they anticipated losing just under five million people—that is, five million people who would die that Madelyn and her team could have saved if they had more capital. Realistically, it would take 180 days from the announcement date before there would be enough equipment in place to be ahead of the curve. Nearly seven million souls would have been lost who could have been saved. It would take years for the families of those lost to come to terms with their loss. Anger, resentment, blame, sorrow...this would be a difficult time for many.

Everyone knew this and hence the Herculean effort to introduce the technology globally and all at once. Even with everything they had been doing in preparation, there would be countless people who would not get help in time. They were just getting a taste of what was to come. It was one thing to know this and predict it in a theoretical environment, but actually seeing a dying person and not be able to get them the help they needed was different than thinking about it in an office atmosphere.

Post announcement, the world population would be growing at a rate of 351,000 per day. Within just a six-month timeframe, that number would grow to an anticipated 466,000 per *day*, which was a rate of 25 percent more than current population growth. In six months the world population would be growing at a rate of 170 million people per *year*. The ramifications were staggering.

What was interesting was that if life-span increased at a rate of eight years per generation, it would only take fourteen more generations to achieve the life-span that would be achieved by this technology now. This gradual change would be easily accepted, and humanity could cope with the change. Having the change happen all at once is where mankind is ill-equipped to cope with it. This is a true "future shock" scenario. Man's ability to cope with change will be challenged like it has never been before.

The Genanotech jet landed in Lihue at 4:17 p.m. Lou, the senator, and the serum were in route to the hospital. Steve was still alive, but his internal systems were starting to fail. Madelyn asked if she could see her father and let them know that her husband was on his way. It was only a ten-minute drive from the airport to the hospital. Dane did not have a plan on how to get Steve out of the hospital without notice. He was admitted with an ID. They knew who he was. A miracle was about to happen, and there was no way to cover it up.

44

Back in Seattle, Carlton was busy ramping up production of the nano generator systems. Significant increases in production were now possible due to the 40,000 square feet of additional warehouse space made available from the recent wave of shipments. Carlton was a genius at the technical side of operations but a horrible communicator to his superiors. He was very detailed to the point of micro management with his subordinates but often forgot to tell anyone above him what's going on. He operated autonomously as though he was the owner of the company and had nobody to report to but himself.

He had two additional lines built and operational two weeks ago that were now up and running and was working on three more to install in the new available space. He had smashed his original commitment of 590 units a week ago and to date had produced 630 units. By announcement, he believed he would have 685 units available for the world. Solana's team was completely unaware of the excess equipment and likely did not have a logistical plan for shipping it.

Carlton was complaining to his production control manager (Leigh) about the systems piling up in the space he needed for the three lines.

Leigh had a very dry sense of humor and, with a completely straight face, looked at Carlton and said, "Maybe we should stop making them; that way we would have more space to make more."

Carlton did not see the humor but did realize he should let someone in administration know he was ahead of schedule and had excess inventory that needed immediate dispatching. With the announcement only nine days away, the United States, Canada, and Mexico would be the main beneficiaries of the systems due to proximity. However, some would be sent via vessel to predetermined ports as part of the second wave of equipment distribution.

Carlton was supposed to go to Kauai, but after a compelling argument with Dane, it was decided that he stay behind. This was Carlton's wish. His value preannouncement combined with his ability to effectively delegate his role post announcement gave him the ability to vacation and rest shortly after announcement. The other team members would not have such a luxury and would be required to work very heavy schedules for months post announcement.

Carlton's passion was work, but like anyone, burnout was inevitable. He was close to being burned out, and his mind was not as clear as usual. His temper frequently flared to the point of veins popping out on his forehead. His single-mindedness and lack of sympathy for those who could not keep up made him difficult to be around. Every organization has leaders like him; these are the people who make it happen at their own sacrifice.

Solana was one of the few people who could settle him down. She was naturally a calm and peaceful person. She was also quite beautiful. Her matter-of-fact way and sarcastic sense of humor made it difficult for Carlton not to relax and gain perspective. A week without her interface had not helped his attitude. He was on a rampage; more machines, more space, work faster, work harder…after blowing a fuse at nobody in particular, he retreated to his office and sat down. He realized that when he was truly emotional, it was because he was not happy with himself and his own behavior. He sat there for a bit and put his head down in prayer, asking for guidance. When he opened his eyes, the first thing he saw was the brochure Solana had left him for a Mediterranean cruise. In one of their discussions, Carlton had expressed his interest in touring Italy, and one thing led to another, and the idea of a Mediterranean cruise came up. He immediately called his purchasing manager and asked her to book him a cruise in June. He then instructed her to book him and his wife a two-week stay in Cabo for the last two weeks in February. He would surprise his wife on Valentine's Day.

Just having some time away on his calendar was enough to make a difference in Carlton's attitude. For the first time in eight long months, he had something tangible to look forward to besides work. In his moment of clarity, he realized that he had dropped the ball and did not communicate his new production numbers to management as had planned to. Having the machines available without anyone knowing about it did no good. He was aware that lives were at stake.

He was fully aware that on "day one" of the announcement, over 100,000 people per day would not be able to be saved due to capital constraints. There simply would not be enough equipment to perform the procedures. This was why he had been so focused on increasing production at any cost, including at the expense of his own well-being. He decided to personally go to the hotel and meet with the group of individuals responsible to shipping equipment around the world. He would give them what was in stock and his new projections. The additional equipment would mean an additional 3,500 people per day worldwide will avoid death. The weight of the responsibility he had was enormous. Carlton often wondered that if someone who was not as aggressive as him was given his job, how many lives would not be saved. He would then wonder if someone superior to him in the manufacturing world had the job and built more machines than he did how many lives would be extended. He would then frown and shake it off.

Solana's team was elated to find out they had more equipment available. The timetables were set for the next forty-five days. Introducing more machines would just slip right into the existing prioritization with one exception. A management decision was made at the beginning of the shipment-scheduling process that no machines were to be in transport on announcement day. Because each destination had different freight durations, the order and priorities fluctuated with changes in the supply stream. Basically anything with a nine-day transport time or greater would get bumped. The computer did this quickly, and after the new inventory was entered into the system, a new schedule was set.

Solana was informed of the news, and she did her best not to let on that she was in a hospital worried to death about Steve living or dying. As far as any of the workers left behind knew, management was on a working retreat, not a vacation. They were all encouraged to keep any communication to a minimum because the team had full schedules. Drew intercepted most of the incoming calls and filtered out what actually needed supervisor attention. After five days only two calls actually needed the attention of one of the personnel in Kauai. The only three people allowed direct calls were Drew, Dane, and the senator. You might think that the people on top of such a giant venture would be the ones who were most apt to experience burnout. The fact was in this situation, due to the quality of personnel on the team, the top managers had it easiest. The reality was they were *energized* by their team and not overworked. They were put in a position to make a few tough decisions, but mostly the options were laid out in front of them for their picking.

Dane, Solana, and Arthur (Senator Birmingham) were along for the ride of their life. They would probably take the brunt of the media long term, which would be demanding for the first three to four months. Like any story it will subside or new stories that spawn from the changes in the world will take center stage. It will only be a matter of time before the economic shifts will settle out and the deeper subjects of energy, food, space exploration, population control, education, and so on, become the news of the day.

45

Lou and Madelyn were by his side when Steve awoke in a daze. Madelyn asked how he felt and what was the last thing he remembered.

Steve said, "I feel great. Where am I? Last I remember I was thrown off the excursion boat going head-first into the ocean…"

Lou gave him a recap of what had transpired and let him know how relieved he was to see him alive and kicking. He then asked him if he could move his legs, and Steve stood up.

Some military personnel entered the room with a gurney and asked Steve to get in. Steve, still in a bit of a daze, looked at the men defensively, and Lou nodded and pointed at the gurney. The senator had called in another favor and got the assistance from the National Guard to remove Steve from the hospital.

Steve was wheeled outside and deposited into one of the company vans without question from the hospital. Hospital administration was told that Steve was a high-ranking government official, and per the request of the director of the CIA (Stan Braxton), Steve was to be immediately transported to a government facility.

Dane was impressed by the senator's initiative and foresight. He had no plan and was really concerned that the media would be all over the unexplained full recovery of a patient in a public hospital.

When back safe and sound in the Hanalei Bay vacation home, Steve was instructed that he no longer had the privilege to leave the premises. Photographs of Steve and the local who was still hospitalized were in the local papers covering details of the accident. Steve could not be seen running down the beach or sailing in a boat or surfing or any of the things he so enjoyed doing while in Kauai.

He was totally OK with this arrangement and was just happy to be alive. What a true miracle this technology was. A complete and painless recovery in just minutes. *Absolutely amazing*, he thought.

Buried in his forecasting universe and fretting over the outcomes of global governmental changes in the next century, he had almost completely forgotten the primary purpose of the technology extension and improved physical quality of human life and, in many cases, life itself. He should by all rights be dead, or, if not dead, confined to a wheelchair for the rest of his life. Instead, he was alive and had all of God's sensory and cerebral gifts intact. He was alive!

When Steve was first introduced to the technology, there were wild discussions about how people would behave in the sports and the thrill-seeking arena. Humpty Dumpty could actually be put back together. What he just went through would be an example of the fearlessness that an individual could experience if they so chose.

Steve decided he would not make such a choice. The fear of death was still real to him. He was very scared when he was flying through the air looking at a reef just inches below the water level. Though in some sports like professional football, downhill skiing, basketball, or soccer, where the players were not facing potentially fatal injuries during the course of a game, they may choose to take some unnecessary risks to make a play. The spectators may end up being the beneficiary. The players could risk concussion, knee injuries, broken ribs, and so forth, without worry of long-term ramifications.

In the world of thrill seeking, the dangers are usually greater: paragliding, cliff diving, base jumping, trophy-truck racing, skydiving, car racing, or any other speed-related sport where the potential outcome could be immediate death. The technology will not save a person who is splattered all over the pavement. The technology should not impact the actions of the speed freak. Steve for one did not want to face death head-on (no pun intended), again especially considering the amount of productive healthy life he had to look forward to. Life to him was more precious than ever. He was happy to kick back in his chair on the wraparound deck with the sun on his back reading a novel. The home-concocted Mai Tai didn't hurt his situation either.

Some of the manager-level personnel were harassing Steve to come out and play. They had no idea that he was almost dead in a hospital the previous day. Tomorrow was the end of their vacation, and their jets were leaving Kauai at 7:00 p.m., so everyone was trying to get in their last activities. Karl, Jim, and the girls had a tee time at Kiahuna in Poʻipū at 9:30 a.m. and planned to spend the rest of the afternoon at the Salt Pond beach. Kiahuna was a nicely laid out public course with a garden feel. It was well-manicured and not overly challenging unless the wind really picked up. It was a perfect course to finish the trip with. They would all feel like their game had really improved. It should make for a very pleasant round of golf for everyone. Not anything like the Prince course, where it takes tremendous patience and self-control not to get upset with the result of your shot. Karl was feeling some kind of guilt that he should be attending to Steve's rehabilitation, but in fact there was no rehabilitation going on. Steve was as good as new. Karl thought it strange that just yesterday he was in a hospital wondering if one of his closest friends was going to die and today everything was back to normal. This new world was going to take some getting used to.

Madelyn and Jake were in their room getting ready to go out to dinner. They really were not excited about going to the luau, but as a major shareholder, there was no real way out of it. Madelyn was recalling her initial days formulating the process that had now become a reality; the days before she had funding lined up. She was dead-set focused on getting this technology introduced to the world, but she had not really understood what it would mean to the world or how it would personally affect her life.

Being relatively timid and antisocial, she was happiest when sitting in front of her computer monitor solving some ridiculously complex problem. Going to parties and board meetings and, God forbid, dealing with the media were things she did not expect to come with the job, but here she was. She thought about being recognized in the science journals and perhaps even in some history books. She saw herself giving some speeches at technical symposiums with likeminded piers. She did not fully understand the impact of what her invention would bring. The fact was that no one had comprehended the technology's full impact.

Jake seemed to just go with the flow. He never really initiated social engagement, but he always seemed to enjoy himself in social situations. He conducted himself with poise and warmth in any social setting. It didn't matter whether it was casual gathering having pizza with Steve and Karl and Heather, a large formal gathering, or dinner in a fancy restaurant with a senator and a fellow scientist he had just met. He was always very at ease and very much himself. Jake was amazing to Madelyn. She adored him and he her. They never really squabbled. They wanted to spend all their time together. There technical knowledge grew exponentially as soon as they partnered. Each was a missing link to the other. They were true soul mates.

Jake wished he could do something to alleviate Madelyn's stress and worry regarding the upcoming limelight she was about to endure. He tried discussing the issue, but that just seemed to aggravate matters. She was so cute and was such a wonderful person, and he knew the world would embrace her. She did not want praise and notoriety. If she was honest with herself, she wanted recognition from the great scientific minds in the world although she had no need for aggrandizement or attention in general. Madelyn was a bookworm at heart, and money and fame was never of interest to her. Men or romance were never a priority either, but she did find herself pretty smitten with Jake. As time passed she became emotionally dependent on their relationship and allowed herself to feel happiness and enjoyment in the romance and sex. On occasion she took time to examine her love for Jake and the growing feelings she had for him.

She had never felt she needed to experience a love relationship, nor have children of her own for that matter. Her life had been focused around science and the pursuit of perfecting nano technology for the purposes of improving physical health of human beings. What she had actually achieved was beyond her outermost dreams. At first she believed the technology could cure cancer and minor cellular disorders such as eczema and hair loss. So focused on science; she never dreamt the normal things people dream: raising a family, buying a house, taking a vacation…

Now while busy working, she would find herself daydreaming about Jake holding her at night. She was always cold and wore layers of clothing year round. Jake was warm. She thanked

God for his warmth. Recently the idea of having a family even crossed her mind. She wondered when Jake would propose marriage. These thoughts were foreign to her, and she was surprised by herself. Because Jake was charming in social situations, and people liked him; she sometimes even felt jealousy. She knew this was ridiculous, but she couldn't help herself. She really was in love.

When Jake attempted to comfort her during times where she was showing signs of stress about her public expectations, she would get grumpy and take it out on him. She felt bad about this. He was only trying to help. It actually kind of pissed her off that he looked forward to the prospects of the media attention, parties and social gatherings, and his more than fifteen minutes of fame. Somehow this made her feel distanced from him and not worthy. He could care less about it all, and Madelyn was his first priority, but with that said, he had a general attitude of happiness. Regardless of the circumstance, he was going to give it his utmost to make the best of the situation.

Dressed ridiculously in white shorts and flowered shirts, sporting new tanned and recently toned youthful bodies, they walked downstairs to meet up with everyone. When they entered the living room, Steve, Karl, Heather, Jim, and Beverly were all there looking just as ridiculous. Karl even had on some absurd necklace made of giant shiny nuts. They all looked at each other and started laughing.

The luau was, in fact, quite fun. The food was great, and the entertainment was, well…entertaining. The "Mediterranean" was located remotely at the top of the island, and their luau program was not as modern as some options tourists had in Lihue or Poʻipū. The show did not last too long, and it gave time for everyone to socialize a bit after dinner. The evening was jubilating, with everyone together all dressed up in their casual Hawaiian best. The temperature was an ideal 77 degrees, and there was a light southern breeze. Madelyn actually relaxed with the help of a few well-made premium Mai Tais. Jake was the perfect date, paying just the right amount of attention to her and still mingling with the rest of the team.

When they got home and crawled into bed, Madelyn asked Jake, "What are we going to do when this is all over?"

Spontaneously Jake said, "Get married and have children of course!" She climbed on top of him, and they made love for the next two hours.

46

Dane lifted the official ban of work discussion before everyone boarded the planes for their return flight to "work." For a small minority, it was a little depressing to leave paradise. For the majority it was invigorating and energizing to get back to process of letting the world know what they had been up to this past year.

News spread about Carlton's surplus inventory of machines, and everyone was doing calculations on how many more people would be able to undergo treatment than originally forecasted. Almost all the personnel who attended the Kauai retreat were personally scheduled to have direct communication with either world leaders or prespecified medical officials around the globe during the first week of announcement.

Lou's entire team of eighty-seven technicians would be leaving to destinations around the world in just five days to personally oversee the upstarts of the first treatment centers. Each would be scheduled to move to six different destinations within the first three days of announcement. To date, none of them knew where they would be assigned. A special team of eleven technicians would be handling video conferences from Seattle with hundreds of predetermined medical teams around the globe. This effort was coordinated by Solana's team, who had prepared technical manuals that had been published in over eighty languages. Not all dialects had been accounted for, but the announcement team had most languages covered to enable the initial first wave of equipment destinations. They were relying on meeting multilingual people who could quickly assist in disseminating the process for regions in proximity to one another.

They would never be completely ready. Dane made this clear from the initial planning phases. What was important was that the entire globe be introduced to the technology simultaneously in order to insure the people in power would not discriminate and limit its use. It was akin to what people may envision a well-planned alien invasion to look like. No corner of the earth would be left out.

It was generally understood that over 80 percent of the people in immediate life-threatening need of treatment would not be able to receive it due to simple capital capacity and geographical circumstance. It was also thought there will be many people who would on "day one" reject the technology out of religious indecision, fear, or cynicism. Karl and Steve were able to provide the team with their best scientific method to predict the initial number of people who would initially reject treatment but also stated that the math could be completely wrong. The world had never experienced what it was about to. The larger the group of people refusing treatment on "day one" will only help reduce the numbers rushing to have access to the technology. As time passed it was forecasted that well over 99 percent of the population would embrace the technology.

The expectation table was interesting to study. It was broken up into two segments; one for the terminally ill or critically injured and their immediate families, and two for the rest of the adult population.

For instance, on "day one" of the announcement, it was believed that 57 percent of the first group would reject the treatment, and within one week of announcement, that number would be radically reduced to 31 percent. One month post announcement, only 12 percent of group one would reject treatment. On day one of the announcement, 73 percent of group two would reject the treatment, and within one week, only 48 percent would reject the idea of treatment. After one month of announcement, only 19 percent of group two would reject the idea of treatment. It was estimated that it would take a full year before 99 percent of the population accepted and embraced the technology.

Dane intentionally separated the key board members of the team on the three jets returning to Seattle just in case of accident. With the help of a strong tail wind, all three planes landed safely just before midnight. A board meeting was scheduled for the following day at 3:00 p.m., allowing time enough for everyone to get up to speed in their respective areas of responsibility.

After the incident with Steve, reality set in on how limited availability of the technology will weigh on the individuals making the decisions about who gets treatment first. Anna was informed shortly before they departed that the local who was involved in the accident with Steve died. Karl, Linda, and Beverly took this the hardest. They had met with the family and knew they could have saved him. The reality was much different than the theory and the math when it came to life and death and the ability to only save a percentage of the dying.

How each region would determine the order to hand out the treatment will vary. There was a lot of discussion about this and it was ultimately decided that each treatment center develop their own system based on the local culture and belief systems. The United States was already prepared to use a lottery system. Other centers may choose chronological age with youngest first or perhaps some other random methodology. There would be panic and unrest and potential violence regarding any "order system" created. The world would just have to get through this unsettling period.

During this time there will be people in line for the treatment who will not live long enough to receive it. After six months there will be enough capital in place to handle the entire terminal population. Within eight months people will start undergoing rejuvenation treatments. It was estimated that in two years, over 90 percent of the population would have undergone rejuvenation.

Additional fallout will ensue immediately after announcement. The stock market will undergo a radical shifting of capital. Money from pharmaceuticals, hospitals, drug-store chains, medical-equipment manufacturers, and assisted-care facility conglomerates will immediately be sold off in favor of energy, housing, technology, space exploration, and food. Religious leaders will be tested immediately by their parishioners on what the churches' stance will be on the technology. Nobody will have time to digest the enormity of the long-term effect on society to have reasonable answers. Governments around the world will have to examine their infrastructures to handle the rapid population explosion that was about to happen.

Making this announcement will be like experiencing an earthquake with 192 epicenters, all located in the most densely populated places of the world. The only difference was that this catastrophic event will add to the number of humans who populate the earth rather than reduce that number.

When Steve got to his desk, he decided to check the GPS tracking device on the cartridge he left in the safe-deposit box back in Tuscaloosa. No movement was detected. He had the device installed so that he could record any movement, even if it were just the box opening. The history logs showed no movement at all. Considering the CIA's involvement with his accident, maybe they knew he was gone and did not bother to see if he had made any updates. He really thought it was odd. He thought for sure that they would have at least made an attempt to replace the cartridges by now. He couldn't believe they would just take it and bring attention to themselves in doing so...*unless the banker girl informed them of his visit?*

Madelyn and Jake were happy as clams being back in their lab working on the enhanced body-scan techniques. They were starting to believe they could bring a person's cellular level to where it was six and a half years ago versus the current technology of approximately five years. If a person could undergo a treatment every seven years and take six and a half years off their life, they would only age six months every seven years. If they started treatments at twenty-eight, they would live over eight hundred years.

The thought of this caused Madelyn to cringe. The idea of living eight hundred years was a far shot from two hundred. They both also knew that they were very close to being able to improve the genetic structure to the point of actually reversing age beyond the seven-year limit. If this was possible, then a person's life-span could be infinite, and their age could be whatever they wanted. Whenever the conversation was leading to that conclusion, one of them would divert the discussion by changing the subject or just practicing plain avoidance they wouldn't go there. Irrespectively, they plugged away working in denial toward goal that neither of them would discuss. She and Jake both decided to keep the new information under wraps. The world will have a hard enough time digesting the existing increase in life-span.

Lou had a meeting with his entire staff at noon. Some of them, being remote, were brought in via video conference. Many of the local people also opted for video conference as well because there was not a room big enough for all of them available. He wanted to insure everyone was up to speed and prepared to instruct at least one to two teams of technician per day on the process. Everyone wanted itineraries, but Lou said for security purposes that the itineraries were not going to be made available for five more days. The technicians who spoke lesser-known languages pretty much knew where they would be assigned.

Though Carlton and Beverly were minor shareholders and technically not on the board, they were invited guests in the 3:00 p.m. board meeting.

Dane opened the meeting by stating, "I hope you all had a great time in Kauai"—the group interrupted with applause—"and… are ready for the real heavy lifting."

The screen behind him simply displayed "DAY 1."

"The next and final week before announcement needs to be spent on fine-tuning the things you will be responsible for on "Day 1" of the announcement. After that, it will be by the seat of your pants. The better job we do communicating with the people designated to us on "Day 1" will have a profound impact on how smooth or how rough things will go from there. We do not want to have to backtrack. Solana has compiled a comprehensive list of people you and your staff members will be responsible to communicate with on Day 1." Being the master leader he was, Dane used an uncharacteristic almost southern drawl when he said "Day 1." *Day* was drawn out a bit, and *one* was said almost under his breath. This just drove home what his message was today. It was about "Day 1." He went on to say, "There are detailed personal profiles for each of the individuals you will be assigned. Study these…"

He paused and said again, "Study these profiles, and have your staff study the profiles. Know your audience—it will make all the difference in the world. We get one shot at this, and we have to make it count."

He went on to say, "Depending on the audience type, some of you will have to make up to sixty-five phone calls on the first day. The more technical the audience, the less calls will be assigned. Overall we will have over eighty-eight people assigned to make approximately forty-five hundred phone calls on Day 1, not to mention the Internet chatting and blog monitoring that will be going on behind the scenes. An additional fifteen hundred people around the world would get calls the following day. People need to be touched by the company that is going to throw the world into turmoil."

He reminded everyone that Victor would be notified at 6:00 a.m. EST sharp, which was the ungodly hour of 3:00 a.m. PST in Washington state on announcement day. Initial phone calls would commence three hours later per the contract with the Centennial at 9:00 a.m. EST with full Internet statement and media press release. Most people on the West Coast will still be in bed or just waking up when they get the news. The Centennial will have first and exclusive rights to publish and go online at 8:50 a.m.—no sooner. No other media will be directly contacted by any Genanotech personnel until 11:00 a.m. EST on announcement day. This will fulfill the legal agreement Anna had contracted with Victor for his quiet patience.

Karl, Linda, and Steve would be completely exempted from any outside interface. Their attention would need to be spent evaluating the forecasting data "real time" and making adjustments to the software on the fly in order to assist in decision making in the first few weeks. Madelyn was going to be limited to a handful of the top scientists in her field so that they would then be able to make commentary independent of her. She would not have to face the media until day three.

Drew had made it impossible for anyone to call in on any line associated with Genanotech, with one exception: Stan Braxton to Solana. Cellular services would be boosted by having two dedicated towers for outgoing transmissions.

Dane ended the meeting by saying, "Read your profiles, and we will meet again in five days for final preparation."

47

Karl was fine-tuning the economics model. It was highly anticipated that the FED would shut the US markets down within the first hour of announcement. The forecasted trading in various segments was horrid even during the first hour. He expressed his concern to the senator, who said he would take it under advisement. All Genanotech personnel now numbered 367. This included all the manufacturing, lab personnel, scientists, and management. All 367 signed agreements when they came on board prohibiting their ability to buy or sell any stocks anywhere in the world from the time they signed until thirty days after announcement. The agreement included purchasing currency or commodities as well. The last thing the company needed was an insider trading investigations post announcement.

The senator had no indication that the SCC or Federal Reserve Board had been tipped off and wondered if a little heads-up would not be a bad idea just before the market opened. He technically would be breaking Anna's agreement by a few minutes if he did so and decided to consult with Anna and Dane first. During their meeting it was decided to contact the SCC and Federal Reserve Bank Chair at 8:35 a.m. EST on announcement day. Because the government entities were not media per se, it was not a violation of the agreement with Victor. This would give them the opportunity to shut down the major US exchanges before they opened. The Japanese Exchange would be closed, but the European Market would still have a few hours before it closed. The senator was not quite sure what to do about that except leave it in the hands of the Fed Chair on announcement-day morning.

Karl went back to work with a model, anticipating a total shutdown of all major global markets on day one, two, and three. This would, in effect, give the world five calendar days to absorb the news before trading commenced. The most negatively affected corporations in the private sector will need some time to manage an orderly exit if that was even possible. The premarket markets will have accurately forecasted what would actually take place before it was official. Because this news will create a stock swap and likely an increase of capital influx into the stock and bond markets as a whole, there was no threat of an economic collapse. On the contrary, there was an expected bull market that would rival all previous bull markets. With population growth comes increased consumption that creates market growth. The world just needed to digest and settle down a little bit before irrational decisions were made when the markets opened.

Madelyn and Jake were busy reading the profiles of the people they would be in communication with. The list of names would be completely unfamiliar to most people, but they were some of the greatest minds alive.

Mathematics/Physics/Chemistry

Steven Weinberg
Andrew Wilds
Edward Witten
Persi Diaconis
Stephen Hawking
Roger Penrose
Charles Townes

Frederick Sanger
Alan Guth
Allan Sandage

Biology
James Watson
Richard Dawkins
Jan Goodall
Lynn Margulis
Craig Venter

Sociology/Philosophy/Psychology
Edward O. Wilson
Noam Chomsky

To most of us mortals, these people would be off our radar. To Jake and Madelyn, they were gods in their fields of expertise. To have the chance to meet any one of them for Madelyn or Jake would be like a high-school quarterback meeting John Elway. Madelyn was actually excited to speak with her list of people. This took a huge edge off the media nerves she had been feeling and dreading for months. *This may actually not be so bad,* she thought. Because Jake was more gregarious than Madelyn, he agreed to assist Solana's team with some of the world leaders and their respective military and scientific personnel.

Solana, the senator, Anna, Jim, and the rest of the team dealing with government officials met to fine-tune assignments. An initial stab at it was made by Solana, but she was not sure if she had things just right. North Korea, Iran, Syria, and Afghanistan were delegated directly to Stan Braxton and the CIA. The senator had arranged for an open line with Stan Braxton to help field incoming calls to the White House from foreign dignitaries. The president, vice-president, and secretary were aware of the arrangement. Stan and his team would sort them out, and if they ranked high enough and were on the Genanotech list, he would forward to Solana for appropriate dispatch. This was how Solana believed 75 percent of their contact would take place.

It's not like you can call President Putin's office and say, "Hi, this is Jim from Genanotech; can I speak to the president?" These dignitaries would need to be reached through channels, but after hearing the news, they would most likely be eager to accept the call.

The government leaders were still anticipating a 12-22-22 announcement date. The senator was planning on contacting Stan early evening on 14 to let him know that it had been moved up for reasons not up for discussion. This would not go over well, since Stan and the CIA's sole purpose was to know everything about everything. Information was his commodity, and the senator was going to dangle it in front of him and cut him off. This was going to be a delicate conversation because the main reason the date being moved up was to avoid the government, and Stan in particular, from shutting down the operation before the announcement could be made. Steve was convinced it was the CIA who had absconded with his partially updated forecasting module that included the stock-market predictor module interface. He and the senator still believed if the CIA could see the inevitable progression of Chinese control over the world, they may want to stop the execution of the technology. It was doubly concerning that they had not taken the updated version currently in the safe-deposit box that predicted a tri-power world government where China, Russia, and the United States are all in some state of equilibrium.

Drew was working on transforming a portion of the dining room into a "makeshift" call center. He had brought in some cubicle walls to absorb and contain sound. Per Solana's request, Jake, Anna, the senator, and herself would have a separate space in the lobby next to the dining area. They would face the large floor-to-ceiling glass panes looking into the dining area. This way, when Stan called with dignitaries on the line, she could observe the call-center activity without the distraction of hearing it. When Stan patched in incoming calls, either her, the senator, Jake, or Anna would take the call personally. Only a select few incoming calls would be sent to the call center for attention, and those would be the lower on the totem pole dignitaries. The senator did not promise to be available all day but said he would try his best to be there as much as possible. He, Drew, and Dane needed to oversee the entire operation on day 1 and be available to solve any problems that may arise.

The bulk of the calls will be outgoing from the center and start with a brief introduction. Let's say the caller was assigned Clint Eastwood. They may start with a blanket statement, saying, "I am sure you have heard the news today regarding the major scientific breakthrough. Genanotech has identified you as an influential person who may be asked by the media for an opinion about the technology. We wanted to make ourselves available to you for any questions you may have."

Then if the call would go according to plan, the caller would inform them that Genanotech had gone to great lengths in order to make this technology available to the whole world all at once. It was very inexpensive to administer, and therefore no one should be denied the treatment. They would then direct them to the official press release on the Genanotech website. A few minutes would be allowed for Q and A, and a follow-up call would be scheduled if requested. It was the mission of Genanotech to contact as many people as possible and present the company with a human touch. This will pay big dividends by reducing cynicism, skepticism, and a multitude of other ism's in the public sector.

Today less than a thousand people had ever heard of Genanotech. Next week it would be a household word. It was important the public perception was positive.

As the week progressed, everyone was becoming very familiar with their respective contacts. It was interesting to review the profiles. Solana's team did a great job to simply, comprehensively, and poignantly describing each of the people Genanotech was about to reach out to.

Each profile was broken down to five categories: (1) general demographic—gender, age, where they lived, education level, occupation, and marital status or sexual preference, (2) a comprehensive list of living family members, including commentary on anyone terminally ill in the family—a short bio on each family member, family is defined as related by blood, marriage (current and previous), and also including known close friends, (3) favorite charitable organizations, (4) religious views, and, finally (5) a detailed list of their accomplishments.

The profile information was the hot topic in the common and dining areas. Everyone enjoyed telling one another the inside scoop on their assigned contacts. There were a total of more than 5,300 profiles for individuals the company would reach out to. They believed after running through some phone trails that they could reach close to 2,000 people on day one. The goal was 2,500. Solana was certain she missed some key people. Making the list took three months. It was like deciding who to invite to your wedding. If you invite this person, then you need to invite this other person. It was maddening, to say the least. She was sure she would be offending someone.

48

The Announcement

The morning of the day before the announcement, all the sequestered patients were informed that the company was going to publicly announce the technology the following morning. They were also informed that they would have to remain sequestered for four more days and that for three of those days they would be subjected to the media for questioning. This was all part of the original contract each patient signed, but most of the patients had forgotten about that detail. There was great excitement and happiness in the entire outpatient-sequestering facilities.

Anna called Victor at 4:00 p.m. PST or 7:00 p.m. EST and let him know she would be sending him an exclusive press release via e-mail as agreed in the contract at 6:00 a.m. EST the next day, followed up with a phone call to verify receipt. She also wanted to ensure that they would both make themselves available for a quick Q and A on the phone at that time.

Victor simply said, "Thank you," and hung up.

Anna forgot how unsocial and rude this guy was. She was a bit taken aback but then realized who she was dealing with. The press release did not include a lot of technical data but rather just an overview of the technology and the means in which it will be made available to the world.

Beverly was tasked with drafting the initial release, and then it was passed on to all board members for final approval. Changes were still being made to it when Anna made her call.

Lou's personnel were all accounted for at their initial destinations around the world. Those traveling to the furthest regions like New Zealand or Madagascar were suffering from significant travel exhaustion and jet lag but should be acclimated by the next morning at nine. Only two out of the hundreds of containers shipped around the world were unaccounted for; one in Denmark and the other in Nicaragua. All the other containers carrying the equipment had been verified to be at their destinations and had or were being transported to their final destinations. The next day the crates could be opened and the equipment up and running within fifteen minutes' time. The Denmark container showed that it was received but could not be found in the yard. The container scheduled to be in Nicaragua did not show as being received but could very well be in the shipyard. At this time no foul play was suspected.

Anna had forced herself out of bed at 4:30 a.m. to help assist her in being able to go to sleep early on the eve of the announcement. She had to make her phone call at 3:00 a.m., which meant she needed to be up at 2:15 p.m. After making her call to Victor, she ate a big dinner and went to bed at 5:30 p.m. with half of a sleeping pill. She thought when taking the pill that this would be one of the very few pills still being manufactured in a year's time. Sleeping aids and painkillers would probably account for over 90 percent of the entire pharmaceutical production.

Dane asked Madelyn and Jake to have an early informal dinner with himself, Solana, and the senator. Before they gathered for dinner in Dane's suite at 5:00 a.m., the senator called Stan. The head of the CIA was not happy about the short notice but agreed to have staff ready and available for the anticipated onslaught of incoming calls from world leaders. He pressed the senator hard on why the date was moved up a week, and after repeated requests, he simply said, "It had something to do with the media, and, no, it was not Victor."

You could almost see the director of the CIA's expression through the phone. He didn't really buy it, but what was he going to say?

After he hung up, he looked at Dane and said, "Went better than I expected; hated to lie, but he forced me into a corner."

There was no indication that the CIA had any intentions of trying to quash the project or postpone the announcement. The senator thought maybe they had not figured out how to incorporate the stock-analyzer interface with the economic forecasting model. He wondered if they were still trying to meld the software with the combat simulators they had developed.

When Jake and Madelyn arrived, they all relaxed with a nice glass of white wine. Solana was in the kitchen by herself per her own request. She liked to cook independently. She set the table and then served everyone one of the most beautiful presentations of grilled salmon on a bed of mixed vegetables and lightly battered and deep fried Portobello strips and bean sprouts. A sweetened, peppered, chili, balsamic reduction was drizzled crisscrossed with a chardonnay cream reduction. A simple viola flower topped the dish. Literally it looked too good to eat.

Dane said a nice prayer, thanking God for not only the food and the company but also for the world as a whole. He asked God to guide and oversee their entire team the next day and bless the company.

After he said, "Amen," he let out a huge breath and said, "What a ride."

Solana raised her glass and toasted Madelyn. She said, "To Madelyn. We would not be here today if it were not for you. You will be a household name tomorrow and forever remembered in the history books. We hope to remain friends—if your britches don't get too big, that is." Everyone chuckled, clicked glasses, and thoroughly enjoyed their dinner.

A little dessert wine was served, and Madelyn and Jake left before 8:00 p.m.

After they left, Madelyn looked at Jake and said, "That was nice; we did not discuss business, not even once. I felt like a normal person for the first time in forever." She had a big smile, and Jake did everything in his power, not blow her bubble with a "wait till tomorrow crack." Tomorrow was going to be a big day, and they planned on being showered and dressed by 5:45 a.m.

The senator remained behind, and he and Dane went over the press release that had been edited and reedited. Currently it read thus:

> *9:00* a.m. *Friday morning Eastern Standard Time on December 15, 2022, a new independently owned company in the United States of America named "Genanotech" made a public announcement introducing a technology they have developed that will cure and reverse most known diseases, illnesses, and injuries. The treatment takes just a few hours, is very inexpensive, and is painless. Scientific details on the technology and a comprehensive report on the trial testing, complete with a list of all ailments treated, will be made available subsequent to this release. Thousands of patients have undergone treatment with a 100 percent success rate, and no side effects have been reported.*

In addition to curing or fixing existing physical problems, the technology also provides a rejuvenation process through genetic evaluation, and we can bring the human body back to where it was five years prior. This process can be done when someone turns thirty years old and can be repeated every seven years thereafter. It is estimated that the average life-span will change from today's average 78 years to over 200 years.

There are two relatively sophisticated pieces of equipment used in tandem to perform a genetic evaluation and develop a specific and custom formulation of nano machines that are then coated with a quantum star and carbon coating used to safely be exposed to the human cellular structure and communicate remotely when injected into the patient. Once injected, the nano machines get to work repairing and improving the patient at the cellular level. After completion, the nano machines are evacuated and the treatment is complete and the patient healed.

During the course of trail testing, Genanotech ramped up manufacturing and built almost seven hundred systems. All these have been disseminated around the world. Every nation on earth and all densely populated regions on earth have equipment stationed in predetermined hospitals and labs. A complete list of these locations will be made public subsequent to this release. Eighty-seven Genanotech technicians are standing by around the world to assist in training personnel on the use of the equipment. Interactive web-based training is also available from the time of this release in over eighty different languages.

Genanotech is an independent for-profit company based in the USA. Its mission is to unilaterally make their technology available to every human being on the planet regardless of color, creed, nationality, religious beliefs, or financial status. The terminal must be treated first. Each treatment center will be responsible to determine the methodology for patient order. The USA will be using a lottery system; details will be forthcoming. All governments will be required to contractually agree to some basic terms, allowing for 100 percent of their population to access the treatment, or they will not be eligible to receive additional systems.

Genanotech personnel will be reaching out to thousands of people in positions of authority and influence the day of the release to answer questions. The White House will direct calls from world leaders to Genanotech top personnel as required.

Capital production of Genanotech equipment is being ramped up, but unfortunately there is not enough equipment built to save everyone who is facing death. It will take months to equip the world to a point where all terminal patients can be treated. As a company dedicated to human life, we strongly urge the world to embrace this technology and be patient and nonviolent during the first phase of the technology's implementation.

Signed

Dane Lindsey
CEO, Genanotech

The senator and Dane gave it their final thumbs-up and e-mailed the release to Anna. They said good night and went to bed in an effort to get some sleep before the big day.

It soon turned 2:15 a.m. Anna was in a deep sleep when her alarm went off. When she finally cleared her mind, she got right out of bed and headed to the shower. Standing under the hot water, she could not believe this day was finally here. Her main responsibility for the past year had been to keep this technology a secret from the initial confidentiality agreements, the interviewing of personnel, in-depth evaluation of Beverly, and even the contract she drafted to keep Victor out of her hair. It seemed somewhat appropriate that the gatekeeper of confidentiality be the person to let the cat out of the bag.

Anna took her hair net off, slapped on some makeup, and dressed in her navy-blue suit. She got into the elevator and headed down to the makeshift announcement day headquarters in the lobby. Three seven-foot walls enclosed a space of 275 square feet in front of the glass walls looking into the dining area now outfitted like a telethon call center you would see on TV in the '90s. There were four desks and four work pads with unlimited access to the Internet. Three seventy-inch monitors were installed, one on each wall. Two would have Television News running (Fox and CNN) for the conservative and liberal views and one dedicated to MSN.com front page on the net.

It was ten minutes till 3:00 a.m. in the morning, and she was in the process of turning on the equipment when Solana walked in with Drew. This surprised Anna. She thought she would be the only one up when she made the call to Victor. Drew took over and finished getting the monitors up and running. He then did a test check on the switchboard monitor system. He said good luck to Anna and went around the corner to the dining room/ call center.

Anna sat down, took a quick look at the polished and approved press release sent to her by Dane after she was a sleep. At 3:00 a.m. PST she pushed the button and sent the formal press release to Victor at the "Centennial." She then called him, and he answered immediately, "Hello, Vic here," as if it was just any day receiving some random call at 3:00 a.m.

Anna introduced herself and said, "Good morning. Do you have the release in your e-mail?"

Silence and then, "Yes, I do; I have read it and have no questions at the moment." He hung up.

Anna was baffled! No response? She thought he must have had a whole lot of information. He must have known exactly what they were doing. You can say a lot about Victor, but there was one thing for sure: he did keep his promise and stopped investigating them. If he did know what they were really up to, it must have taken great restraint not to leak; at a minimum, just part of the story. The news must have undisputable proof that what they are writing was true. If this was the reason nothing was printed, then it said a lot about the integrity of the paper Victor worked for.

Per the agreement they were not allowed to have any direct contact with the public or other media sources until 6:00 a.m. PST or 9:00 a.m. EST. It would be interesting to see how the "Centennial" would handle the story. They had the actual paper, of course, which would likely hit the streets in ninety minutes. They also had access to television, other printer newspapers, and Internet through syndication agreements. Best guess is that they would have this story out at 4:30 PST or 7:30 EST. All Anna and her people could do now was wait and watch.

It was 4:00 a.m., and there was still no word on the news or directly from Victor. By now Dane, the senator, Lou, Jim, Karl, and Steve were all meandering around the lobby and the lobby office. Six additional monitors were installed: three in the call center/dining area and three in the lobby. This may have been overkill, but Drew felt people will wanted to know what's going on wherever they may be and he did not want everyone crowding into the lobby office.

At 4:15 a.m. PST, 7:15 a.m. EST, Madelyn and Jake joined everyone in the lobby. Coffee was flowing, and there was quite a buzz in the room. By 4:30 a.m. most of the staff members assigned to receive incoming calls were socializing in the dining area.

At 4:47 a.m. PST, 7:47 a.m. EST, on 12-15-2019, Pandora was unleashed from her box.

Simultaneous broadcast on all major broadcasting stations around the world were reporting, courtesy of exclusive from the Centennial in Washington, DC: "Seattle-based technology upstart has *cured death* and is making the cure available to the world today."

Dane was shaking his head; in all this time, he had never looked at this as a cure for death. How the media can spin things so quickly is amazing. What else is amazing is how fast news travels today.

By 5:05 a.m. PST, the European Exchange shut down. The senator thought, *Well, at least I do not have to call the FED Chair*, as he was certain the United States Wall Street would follow suit.

For the next hour, things were very uneventful. Almost so uneventful it was pushing anticlimactic. The News just kept broadcasting pictures of the release and reading through it repeatedly almost to the point of a nauseam. I guess there has not been time to get the "expert talking heads" to the news rooms yet. The entire west coast and eastern seaboard of Asia were still asleep or just waking up. The East Coast of Australia was just going to bed and it was late afternoon or early evening in most of Europe.

It was now 6:00 a.m. PST and the "Centennial" exclusivity contract had been satisfied and was formally sunset.

The first call came into Solana via Stan at 6:04 a.m. sharp. He had the prime minister of Britain on the line. This was the beginning of a very interesting day, she thought. She fielded the call and introduced herself as "Director of Foreign Affairs" for Genanotech. This was not a formal title but one she would use throughout the next weeks. The current prime minister was famous for his dry sense of humor, so she really did not know what to expect. He was actually very straightforward and serious. He initially asked if one, whether the one-page press release was true, and, two, if so, was there anything the United Kingdom could do to assist Genanotech in the upcoming months.

Solana was floored; she had prepared for months for this very moment. She had facts, figures, estimates, forecasts, and demographics memorized in order to answer any anticipated question. The question of "what can we do to help" never crossed her mind. She was starting to see how international allies worked. She simply answered with, "Yes, the release is true, and, yes, we will probably be able to use your assistance in the upcoming months." She was proud of herself; she answered without looking like a fool. She then went on to say that as of one minute ago, three important documents were being distributed to the media. The first was a thorough technical journal detailing the technology. The only piece not being disclosed immediately was equipment specs and proprietary program source code specific to each major and minor treatment available. The companies' financial future relied on selling the equipment and the treatment programs. Material cost was inconsequential, and only true cost would be equipment depreciation and technician time. By plugging the machines in that are scattered around your kingdom, you will be billed $1.8 million US per set of equipment. The machines anticipated life is one hundred thousand plus treatments or basically just under twenty dollars a treatment. It's really quite a deal, when you think about it. Forty minutes of a technician's time and twenty US dollars and you're fixed good as new. The second document being sent out as we speak is a complete list of locations where equipment has been sent around the world. The list includes contact information for the sites where Genanotech personnel are not present so they can view the web-based online instruction for equipment and process start-up. Eighty-seven Genanotech personnel are stationed around the world, prepared to start training technician on the process. They have rigorous travel schedules, putting them in two locations per day for a period of five days."

The prime minister had been intently listening but interrupted with a comment applauding the company's approach to introducing the technology. He said, "I am really quite speechless."

Solana thanked him and went on to say, "The third thing being published is a list of names and locations of the trial test patients and what they were treated for. The media will have full access to these people for three days, and then we will request that their right to privacy be reinstated."

The prime minister reiterated how impressed he was with the technology and the efforts that had been made to smoothly incorporate it worldwide. He asked if he could send a small technical team to them for training, who could then go out on mission to train and assist elsewhere in the world.

Solana said, "Yes, but give us a couple of days to incorporate them."

The call ended, and the president of Mexico, the president of Brazil, and the German Chancellor were on hold. Solana took the chancellor, Anna took the Brazilian president, and the senator took the Mexican president. This was how the morning went in the newly assembled small office in the lobby.

Most leaders offered assistance. Nobody seemed to have any kind of negativity or concern about the company's mission/agenda contractual agreements, equipment price, and so on.

It was 11:00 a.m. PST or 2:00 p.m. EST. Outreach calls were on track, and incoming calls subsided after a flurry. France was the only major player not to have called in yet. The US-French relationships had been strained over US policy in the Middle East for the past couple of decades. Not strained to the point of economic sanctions, but neither nation really wanted to go out of the way for the other.

Speculation based on the premarkets showed total annihilation of any medical-related stock.

The news was now focusing on every facet associated with the announcement. Interviews were being televised at all fourteen outpatient facilities. This message was really hitting home. Cancers cured, broken backs repaired, liver and kidney disease reversed, vascular problems eliminated, and rejuvenation before-and-after pictures. Reporters around the world were at every single treatment site. Patients were shown being wheeled in on gurneys and then walking out and facing the almost hysteretic media. Some of the top respected scientists in the world were weighing in on Madelyn and Jake's dissertation on the technology.

So far nobody tried to dispute it. There had not been any real negative press to speak of with the exception of the anticipated rush of people and chaos at the treatment centers. Reports of the US lottery system and the relatively more orderly process were injected in between news of violence and pictures of desperation in other parts of the world. There were a few problems in one of the New York City centers as well as one in New Jersey with individuals using fists to push their loved ones to a better position in line and some forgery on lottery numbers. But taking into consideration the general culture in those regions, it was not to be unexpected.

Steve, Karl, Linda, and Beverly were tucked into their cubes in the IT room. They were monitoring the news and making small adjustments as information was flowing in. Beverly was having a hard time keeping up with the postings relating to actual number of treatments being performed. Not all treatment sites were providing results, but most were. By noon PST, approximately six hours after the technology was introduced, it was estimated that seven thousand terminally ill or critically injured people had been cured or rehabilitated. That was four times the number of people treated during the trials.

The senator was popping back and forth between the lobby office and the IT room. By 1:00 p.m. most of the world leaders had had conversations with the Genanotech personnel. The White House had successfully communicated with the leaders of the nations we have poor relationships with. Representatives from these countries had had brief conversations with Solana and/or the senator. Everything was moving forward as expected. Dane was touring the facility patting everyone's back on a job well done. They had anticipated the worse scenarios and successfully averted most of them. With the exception of the turmoil at many of the actual treatment centers, the world was positive and accepting of the company's announcement. Many of the news pundits in foreign countries were applauding the company and United States of America for the incredible achievement and humanitarian effort to provide the technology to the entire world.

Most of the members of Lou's team were reporting that the training was going faster than expected. Within two to three hours, they were able to get technicians working independently. The eighty-seven trainers Lou had scattered around the world were now accelerating the travel plans. Most would be in three locations on the first day and complete their entire tour in just three days versus the original five-day itinerary. When they arrived at their second center, the treatments were already being performed. Their purpose was to insure that the equipment was performing properly and answer any technical questions. The larger reason for visiting the centers was to touch the technicians and make the company real to them. The company wanted a face with the name. It was important that there was a human being that the head of each center could call for advice and instruction. Someone they could trust. The web-based training was also a success, and similar training times were reported. Language barriers were the largest problem in some centers. Most of the treatment centers were located in densely populated areas, so there was an abundance of multilingual people available.

Madelyn and Jake started making their calls to the world's most respected living scientists. Madelyn was surprised at the level of gratitude and genuine respect and admiration she received with each call. She half expected that these people would be arrogant and possibly cynical. It was quite the opposite; they were honored to have received the call. She found it difficult to get off the phone.

She and Jake had relatively short lists so they could chat it up a bit. The reality of her accomplishment was starting to sink in. Being humble in nature, this level of accomplishment and the overwhelming acclaim she was receiving from people she had the utmost respect for was difficult for her to process. Jake was even having similar difficulty. He viewed himself as a nutty professor and did not take himself too seriously. The notoriety and respect he was receiving was a bit surrealistic.

At the end of the day, they opened their last bottle of Dom Pérignon and toasted announcement day.

DAY 3, POST ANNOUNCEMENT

Prior to the formation of Genanotech, Dane and Solana had amassed great wealth. In 2010 when Dane retired and sold off almost all of his FTLware stock, he was ranked in the top two hundred most wealthy people in the world. They were both good stewards of their money and resources. A good portion of that wealth was required to develop and provide the Genanotech technology that would forever change the world. The world could not ask for better people to launch a business that will generate more profit than any other business venture in history.

Genanotech had over $1.2 trillion in open receivables for Genanotech equipment and software the day they announced. They had only spent two hundred and twenty-five million dollars (two one-hundredths of 1 percent of top line) to date for development and manufacturing. One hundred fifty million dollars of this was tribute to Uncle Sam via an unreported grant from the chairman of the Commerce, Science, and Transportation Committee, who happened to be Senator Arthur Birmingham. The senator had no regrets in spending the taxpayers' money on this project. Not just for the fact that ends were noble but because the tax revenue the United States would receive from the sales of Genanotech equipment and software will exponentially exceed the investment.

Wires from over sixty nations had already been received and had replenished the coffers. It was estimated that after one year's operation, Genanotech will have reported over twenty-five trillion dollars in EBIT (earnings before interest and taxes). From Dane's experience in obtaining wealth from meager beginnings, he knew well what kind of challenges the key players of Genanotech will face. He planned on conducting some one-on-one counseling sessions with each of the team members in order to help them make wise decisions from the beginning. He had already had some discussions with Madelyn and Jake regarding money management. They wanted nothing to do with it and asked that Anna just take care of that for them. She agreed to manage their money for free. She would issue them each a credit card with no limit and have the billing sent to her directly. She would then set up a conservative portfolio to stash their earnings. This would include a real-estate purchasing budget that would be revised annually.

Dane instructed Carlton to immediately start interviewing for a replacement; his mission was accomplished.

Carlton asked him if he was firing him, and Dane said, "Yes! Solana will help you with the recruiting."

Madelyn's personal confidence was at an all-time high. She was not at all nervous about visiting with the media. Her first interview was with a CNN reporter she had never seen before. The interview was held in her lab, and she was standing next to a prototype of the new rejuvenation scanner. She was impressed that CNN handpicked a reporter who had a science background. It was not much different than talking on the phone, except she had to continue to remember to look up above the camera lens. This was a tip she had gotten that makes you look more sincere when on television. She was scheduled to go to Los Angeles the next day to do five in-studio interviews with the major networks. Drew ran interference for her high demand. He was booking her four days a month for the next six months on various panels and news programs. She would spend two days a month for the foreseeable future, giving lectures at a rate of one hundred fifty thousand dollars per lecture. Jake was also being scheduled at the same rate. Per their request Drew scheduled the lectures on different days so they could travel together.

Lou's mother had an agreement with the company that her identity be kept secret for a period of one year. As the first person to undergo treatment, the media would have a field day with her in the early days of the treatment being known to the public. She and Lou wanted her on record as the first human to undergo treatment for the purposes of accurate history.

By the end of the third day, over 50,000 people had been treated, who would have likely been dead today if it were not for the technology. Most centers were adopting a lottery system for order, and surprisingly the amount of violence had subsided, and people were accepting the limitations. New sets of machines were being shipped air freight to the centers with the longest lines. Lou's team had successfully trained and met with lead technicians in over 522 locations. There was nothing on the news unrelated to Genanotech.

Victor was already being touted as the next Pulitzer Prize winner for *Breaking News Reporting*. He and the "Centennial" were riding high on their exclusive press release just days ago. He and the staff from the paper were being interviewed by all the major networks. It certainly was the story of a lifetime.

ONE MONTH AFTER ANNOUNCEMENT

One million three hundred and seventy-five thousand people had been treated with the Genanotech technology. The treatment centers had expanded from 685 to 1,500 and were all operating twenty-four hours a day, seven days a week. It was estimated now with projected production numbers that within two months, the world will have enough equipment to satisfy all the people in immediate need. In four months, centers will start to be able to mix in rejuvenation patients.

Carlton's replacement, Jim O'Connor, was busy outfitting a 400,000-square facility to accommodate what seemed to be an endless demand for equipment. Carlton was staying on running operations in the original plant until his trip to Napa was scheduled in mid-February. Madelyn and Jake had almost worked out the final kinks in the new Rejuvenation Scanner technology. They were having difficulty finishing due to their many other public demands. What originally seemed like work and pressure their speaking engagements were becoming something they loved and enjoyed. They could not only talk tech to audiences who sucked it up like sponges with great enthusiasm but also looked forward to the travel. Their four days of lecture provided a one-week vacation each month to places all over the country. Some international engagements were scheduled as well but not for six months.

A week prior, Jake formally proposed to Madelyn on the ninety-fourth floor of the Columbia building in Seattle after one of her lectures scheduled in the building. It was a fairly spontaneous decision. He had purchased a ring from one of the tourist stores in the market while Madelyn was speaking. Though it was costume, it was a pretty filigree silver band. While being tourists at the viewing deck of the building looking out over the city, he got down on a knee and popped the question. She looked at him and asked if he was serious. Before he could respond, she said, "Of course I will be your wife." They embraced and kissed just a little longer than would be appropriate in a public place. A few standers-by clapped. On the way down the elevator, they kissed again, and he told her she needed to go ring shopping unless she wanted him to pick the real ring. She said they should do it together; after all, she would likely be wearing it for centuries. As they exited the elevator, Jake casually said, "Maybe we could have our ceremony on top of Sandia Peak in Albuquerque where we first met?" She got goose bumps and just smiled.

There was three trillion dollars in the Genanotech operating account. The pace was still furious for most of the board members. The initial outreach helped immensely, but many more people wanted direct interface with leaders of the company.

As expected, the news had now shifted to the subjects of population growth, energy, housing, food, education, economics, and the justice system. It seemed that every facet of society had been affected by the change in health and life-span. There were judges advocating forfeiture of rejuvenation treatments rather than imprisonment for nonviolent criminals. For example, if you were convicted of embezzlement, you would be fined for monetary damages plus a specified length of time before you could legally undergo rejuvenation. Serious criminals may have to wait twenty years for their next treatment that would, in effect, shorten their life by fifteen years.

Prior to Genanotech, there were 132,000 deaths per day. Now there were just 44,000. The world population was growing at a rate of thirty-two million people per year more than it was. Within one year's time, the planet will have over 8.5 billion people on it. At the current birth rate, the world will add a billion people every six years.

The major reshuffling of capital in the stock market had created a completely different economic landscape. Anything medical had been all but wiped out of existence. The tech industry was booming and absorbing most of the executives from the now defunct medical industry. Hospitals had been put on the real-estate market, and hotel chains were picking them up for bargain prices. Housing was booming. Venture capital was readily available for new technology development.

There was a lot of serious talk about alternative energy sources. It was likely that the people alive today would be alive when they completely ran out of petroleum-based resources if they continued to rely on it for transportation and heat. It was one thing for people to say they were concerned about their grandchildren's future when it came to their natural recourses but a completely new thing when their actions today will affect them personally tomorrow.

Karl, Jim, Heather, and Beverly had become inseparable. When they were not working, they were hanging out. Heather and Beverly had become avid golfers and dreamed of playing professionally. Jim and Karl became obsessed with the stock market now that the stock-commodity-trading curfew had been lifted per their confidentiality agreement. Though they could not trade, they had been preparing for the day they could. The girls were hoping this was just a phase and that they would get back to their normal selves sooner than later.

Last Chapter

Steve woke up on the brand-new yacht he had purchased the day before. He had dreamed of retiring on a yacht since he was in his early twenties. Living in Seattle on the Sound, he watched the beautiful luxury sailing yachts every day from his back porch. He had always planned on selling his home and purchasing a nice used yacht to live on when he retired.

With virtually unlimited funds, he could now buy the boat of his dreams. Steve was not into the fancy new designs that many of the companies today are producing. He opted for Caliber 47LRC, which has a classic look, is stout, and has very seaworthy design with a spacious cabin. Tricked out, it cost him one cool million. This yacht will never go out of style. Now that life had been extended, it was more important to Steve he not purchase something trendy.

It was June 15, 2023, exactly six months since Genanotech made their technology available. It was a sunny brisk day with 15 mph winds from the northwest.

Rejuvenations were being routinely performed around the world. Only 8,000 people were perishing per day verses the 132,000 per day six months ago. Most of these 8,000 were opting for death by choice because they rejected the treatment voluntarily for religious reasons or plain fear.

Madelyn and Jake perfected their enhanced rejuvenation process and final design of the scanning equipment. Jim O'Connor was in the process of putting together a separate manufacturing site dedicated to the scanners. After long debates in the boardroom, it was decided not to introduce this new technology until January 2025. The delayed introduction was not only pragmatic in terms of making the technology available from a capitalization standpoint but also essential to minimize future shock. The world was still reeling with the ramifications of a life-span tripling what was historically possible. The idea that people could live as long as eight hundred years or eleven times what was historically possible would be too much to handle. There would be no real humanitarian benefit to introduce this now.

Madelyn believed that people could safely undergo the new enhance rejuvenation process five years after they had had the original rejuvenation process. In essence, the new process would bring them back to the age they were when they had the original treatment. It was anticipated that only 70 percent of the world population would have had a rejuvenation treatment by January 2025 when the new treatment would become available.

The forecasting software minus the stock interface module was turned over to the federal government. They had erected a dozen highly secured facilities across the nation outfitted with Steve's systems and software. Each facility was in charge of monitoring specific trends and providing valuable guidance to address problems before they became serious. Steve, Karl, and Heather were basically retired and on retainer to assist the government with the software as needed.

There were teams of government employees with high-security clearance monitoring international economic trends, food supply, real-estate trends both residential and commercial, energy consumption and natural resources, international relations, and so forth.

Karl and Jim did get over their stock-market obsession to the delight of their wives. They were now obsessed with planning a new golf resort with a dedicated men's and women's course. The concept was unique, and Heather and Bev were totally into it.

Energy was a hot topic, and venture capital was flowing to start up alternative energy research companies. Food supply was also a hot topic, and the previously highly litigated GMO manufactures were gaining ground for a rebirth. Their rationale was that whatever harm it could potentially cause could be quickly fixed by a thirty-minute procedure. There was a lot of this kind of rationale being used today. Karl would wonder if human beings would ever truly mature.

There was a housing boom, but this time around the government placed severe restrictions on 100 percent financing. Money was flowing, and loans were being generated at record levels, but you had to have 10 percent down. People had to save and earn the right to own property. This kept the demand in check, so supply would not be so scarce that prices would remain stable and affordable. There were limits placed for investors. For at least a five-year period, people were not allowed to purchase more than four single family residences a year for the purpose of income investment. This policy was put in place so that first time home buyers could have a shot at home ownership. The serious money could continue to purchase or build high-density multifamily units. Two vacation homes could be purchased as well, but there were strict rules regarding the status. After an initial 20 percent increase in home values in the first three months after announcement, things had leveled off to a reasonable rate of 8 percent per year appreciation. The vast majority of the rest of the world followed with similar policies.

The federal and state supreme courts had full dockets on proposed changes to sentencing guidelines, rehabilitation, life imprisonment, and death penalty. Proposals at the state levels included rejuvenation-treatment limitations, complete removal of the right to any Genanotech treatment, longer sentences with treatment allowed, and so on. There was a lot to consider, and the legal community was in chaos.

Life in general was more precious now than it was prior to extended life-spans. People who were convicted of murder would definitely be banned from any rights to treatment at the very minimum. Death would become a rare and almost foreign event and will have much more profound response by society.

Violent crimes were on a significant downturn. Tensions remained in the Middle East, and the United States and Russia still were providing policing and presence in hot spots. The threat of terrorist activity was lower than recent times. There had not been one bombing or military-related incident in over sixty days. Human behavior was evolving and changing.

Twenty-seven percent of the doctors, physicians, surgeons, and nurses were taking positions in emergency response businesses or Genanotech treatment centers popping up all over the world. Traveling, ground and air, mobile Genanotech equipped units were being assembled in vast numbers. If someone had a serious accident and needed treatment immediately, it will be these first-response companies that come to the rescue. The rest of the highly trained medical community was unemployed. Genanotech had put together a grant fund available to most of the medical community for the purposes of reeducation. When the pharmaceutical firms started to ask for hand-outs, Genanotech said no. Dane had run a very successful technology company and charged a fair price and made a fair profit. He had deep resentment for the large pharmaceutical corporations' greed and ungodly high-profit margins at the expense of an ailing lower-middle-class and middle-class people.

Steve went up the deck with his freshly brewed coffee and electronic notepad. He sat down on his favorite new deck chair and kicked his feet up onto the ottoman. Anna joined him in her robe. Sipping their coffee, they went through his daily routine, Steve checking the GPS in the safe-deposit box in Tuscaloosa; Anna looked at what Steve was looking at. He turned to the front-page news on the net. Russia had been building a large military presence in Pakistan over the past week. It was now being reported that they were mobilizing and had intentions of invading India.

Steve was shocked. He thought, *It wasn't the CIA, after all.* He said out loud, "Damn that Victor."

The Beginning

Disclaimer

This book is entirely fictional. The people, science, technology, and pretty much everything in the book is from the imagination of the author. The Internet was used as a resource for technical, political, and historical information but not intended or deemed to be factual.

List of characters

Karl Franklin (Math geek)
Heather Franklin (Karl's love and pretty smart with economics)
Steve Ryan (Karl's boss and good friend)
Jim Mankin (Karl's best friend)
Beverly Mankin (Jim's wife and Heather's friend and very liberal views on information)
Madelyn Cooper (the inventor and founding member of Genanotech)
Jake Dawson (Coinventor of Genanotech and Madelyn's love)
Arthur Birmingham (Senator in Washington state—Chair of Science, Commerce, and Transportation)
Anna Kim (Lawyer, CFO, and Madelyn's biggest advocate)
Dane Lindsey (CEO and finance contributor to Genanotech)
Solana Lindsey (Dane's wife and public-relations officer)
Lou Alexander (Brilliant scientist)
Victoria Tawfeek (COO of the Lindsey Foundation).
Drew Jackson (Personal assistant administrator extraordinaire)
Carleton Thompson (Director of manufacturing)
Victor Rodchenko (Russian reporter)

Genanotech Org Chart
Dane Lindsey: CEO

Victoria Tawfeek:
Dir, bus admin
Dwaine: Science advisor
Ryan: Lobbyist

Madelyn Cooper:
COO
Jake Dawson:
CSO
Lou Alexander:
Lab director

Anna Kim:
CFO
Jim Mankin:
Liaison
Kathy:
International law

Carlton (Director of manufacturing)

Drew Jackson: Executive assistant
Solana: Director of public relations

About The Author

Allen Broderick grew up in California, where he received a degree in business management from San Jose State University, and he currently owns a successful real estate brokerage in Oregon. A veteran of twenty years of executive management in electronics manufacturing, he considers himself to be an "analytical dreamer." Mixing business and technology with medical suspense and political intrigue in *Fountain Found*, he has crafted a thriller in the mold of Stephen King, John Grisham, and Dan Brown.

Made in the USA
San Bernardino, CA
20 March 2018